A Bagful of Dragon

Inayat isn't a witch. She's a not-quite-ordinary twenty-something, screwing up her life one failed date at a time. But when she dumps the wrong magician, Inayat finds herself in a bubbling cauldron of paranoid fear.

The arrival of an unusual bag of jewellery heralds an alarming increase in frightening events, dragging Inayat and her friends into the magical web spun by her adversary. He wants something Inayat has and he's prepared to take her spirit if she resists.

Inayat has only dabbled in magic before, but now she must learn fast or lose for all eternity. She's got plenty of fight in her, but is it enough, or will she succumb to the hatred of a man who just can't lose?

Sakina Murdock lives with her dog, her partner and his two cats in bonny rural Cumbria and tries to stay out of trouble. She chats with blackbirds, rescues toads from traffic, protects deer from hunters and writes exciting, magical fiction.

Look out for more of her paranormal fantasy books coming soon at SakinaMurdock.com

G000070122

A BAGFUL OF DRAGON

by

Sakina Murdock

Cover image by EK Cover Design

www.ekcoverdesign.com

This novel is entirely a work of fiction. The names, characters and incidents portrayed in it are the work of the author's imagination. Any resemblance to actual persons, living or dead, or events, is entirely coincidental.

ABagfulofDragon.com

Sakina Murdock asserts the moral right to be identified as the author of this work.

ISBN 978-1-9993552-0-3

ACKNOWLEDGEMENTS

Heartfelt thanks to:

Sophie Reicher for kind permission to refer to her book *Spiritual Protection: A Safety Manual for Energy Workers, Healers, and Psychics*, a 101 and more besides on protection and safety in magical practice. Available to buy online at well-known retailers.

⁓

Jude Freeman for a detailed, diligent and critical sweep through story, characters and social issues.

⁓

Tina Deschamps for thoughtful discussion, story and character criticism at a crucial stage, and creative ideas that solved problems.

⁓

Rhona Lindsay for patiently sharing the magic of editing with an author who sprinkles commas like disruptive fairy dust.

⁓

Eloise J Knapp for a creative and sensitive cover that truly captures the spirit of the novel.

Kevin Beynon for continual encouragement, criticism, insistence on doing everything right, and out-and-out enthusiasm at even the darkest of times. Also for laughing at the jokes.

And for advice and time spent on early drafts, special thanks to:

    Gaynor Walker
    Susan Dorsey
    Monique Snyman.

For Shirley G.

1. Visitation

Pressure. Weight. Crushing me into the mattress. A dark, airless burden across my body, heavy like a man lying on top of me. I open my mouth, to breathe, to scream. No oxygen, no air at all. Cloying darkness fingers its way into my throat. Suffocation stoppers my thoughts, unleashes panic. I buck my body, push his weight off as I break the paralysis of sleep and claw my way into the unsympathetic night.

He plants a tiny kiss on my forehead and leaves.

⸙

Still blind in the blank darkness at the back of my room, I was smacked to full awareness by the dream's significance. I rolled off the bed onto the floor and hugged my knees.

I dropped my consciousness down to my pounding chest cavity and clicked my fingers three times. "Protect, protect, protect!"

The programmed violet light glowed inside my heart chakra and exploded through my centre, a wave of bright energy clearing away the metaphysical gunge of fear and anger left by the intrusion.

Across the dim room, a chink of morning light through the blinds gently formed familiar outlines, comforting in their stoic sameness. The desk below the window. The computer screen and the chair. Everything else a familiar jumble of possessions and clothes in my too-small room. Thanks to Indira's kindness, the guest-bedroom-cum-cloakroom of the rather posh apartment in a former stately home had become my haven after my ridiculous life sent me down yet another dead end.

The full length mirror across the room showed my defensive shape in the darkness, a shield of long brown hair across my face. I shook it back, still looking at myself and self-consciously straightened, chin raised, features yellowy in the dispersed crack of daylight.

I felt tenuously outwards for the intruder. No-one there. Not even a hint. No sense of him—whoever he was—but a genuine visitation for sure. The lingering adrenaline in my stomach, heart still knocking against my ribs—all were emotional residues, detritus rarely left by ordinary dreams. My interior being was shocked and empty. Vandalised and unclean.

Visitations, in my limited experience, normally come on the drift-off to sleep. Someone travels to you on the astral plane to tell you something important, usually unpleasant. This one was different. More real somehow, less fleeting, though I'd only become aware of him moments before I woke.

'Him'—but who?

I'd known a few witches and pagans from hanging out with Caleb, a whole 'friendship group' of hippies and activists who welcomed me in when I was flavour of his year and cut me off the moment he started fucking about. I'd seen none of them since I ran away from that life and I didn't regret it. Trust is hard to come by. Most people don't work hard enough at it and none of Caleb's mates had. I doubted anyone from back then would bother to torment me. Not even one of his witchy exes. Was there someone I knew now who hadn't disclosed their magical interests?

A light pinged on in the living room, bright through the roller blind on my glass bedroom door, startling me out of my thoughts.

"Hi, Inayat, want a cup of tea?" Indira's voice was muffled through the closed door.

"Nah, I'll get a coffee." Tea in the morning, yuck.

Jumping up, I grabbed my woollen robe, sticking my arm through the wrong hole and bumping into the door frame as I awkwardly swapped the garment around. The grog fuzzed up my head and I lurched through the door into the wide open space of the living room, dragging my hair back behind my ears in an effort to see where I was going. Indira pulled the blinds at the massive windows and a beam of sunlight hit me painfully in the eyes. It physically knocked me backwards into the doorway.

David. It was David.

I gripped the door frame at the catch, grounding myself with the cold feel of the metal corners. The knowledge had slipped into my mind like an information injection.

Of all the sorry excuses I'd been out with, surely David was least likely to be a problem. A walking embodiment of 'mild-mannered', he worked for some kind of private charity 'helping indigenous peoples live the way they want'. Nice beneficial job, lots of money, just seriously lacking charisma. He kept the name of the charity from me, elusive without seeming secretive. Come to think of it, I knew pretty much nothing about him of any value.

I've seen some seriously challenging behaviour from men before, but I'd never been assaulted in my dreams. Creeping around on the astral plane was teen witch territory. I'd done it myself when I was experimenting with lucid dreaming, but who lies on top of someone? His weight had been too real.

"What's up, hun?" Never a morning person, Indira squinted sleepily at me, her fingers wrapped around a steaming mug as she leaned against the white mantelpiece of the retired fireplace, dwarfed by its immense size. I watched the smoky tendrils spiralling upwards towards the chandelier in the high ceiling, then focused on her puzzled expression.

"Someone came to see me," I blurted. See me. In my space. My head. Lying on top of me.

"Last night?"

"In my dreams."

A heavy pause followed. Me—shell-shocked as the implications poured in—slumping against the wall because it was holding me up. The space in the room was overwhelming, weighing heavily on me. Exposure swamped me. He was only there for one reason. The same reason any man might creep secretly into a woman's bed. But why me, why me, why me? All I wanted was a normal life. Something that I could call ordinary. No out-of-control relationships and feeling like shit because I never understand why people behave the way they do to me. I was so fucking sick of not understanding.

Indira peered at me, perhaps searching for sense in my face. She placed her mug on the mantel and pulled her black hair into a loose pony tail.

"Kettle's boiled, hun."

I took a long, deep breath and busied myself with a shitty instant coffee at the breakfast bar. As I threw in four heaped teaspoons of sugar, my mind grasped at everything and came up with nothing. Was he in love with me? How could he be? He didn't know me. He'd been stood up by his internet date and I'd felt sorry for him. All I did was pretend—for his sake—to be his friend a couple of times. Probably no better than a super-cheap dial-a-date escort, paid only in free wine and dinner. I felt a bit sick. At least I hadn't slept with him.

He obviously thought I should have.

Indira said nothing, just sipped her tea and stared. For a moment I wondered how she really felt about me. I couldn't tell by looking, though I was fairly sure she cared. She lived with me for a start—we were now in our ninth month and hadn't ripped each other's heads off. We'd met at a yoga class that Leah had made me go to and Indira had bugged me to live with her from the second month I knew her. Actions always spoke louder than facial expressions, but sometimes I didn't feel like she was totally with me. Just didn't get me really.

I leaned on my elbows and sipped sugary coffee. It tasted like Marmite. "Remind me to get some proper coffee tonight. I hate this stuff."

Her black eyes examined my face. "What are you on about, hun? You going through a weird patch again?"

"I think someone did a kind of visitation on me last night."

She frowned. "What's a visitation?"

I took another gulp of coffee. "He came to see me in the ether, on the astral plane." My spiritual leanings weren't news to Indira, but she didn't always know the terms. She didn't really believe any of it, so she didn't hold it against me. She just thought I was a bit strange. Endured my superstitions on her good days, pooh-poohed them on the bad ones. Religion mostly didn't interest her.

"Hmmm." Indira sank on to a big cushion on the solid parquet floor and huddled in her robe, sipping her tea. She was settling into the drama—her natural habitat—no doubt psychoanalysing me.

"Don't you think the more you mess with that stuff, the more you kid yourself that everyone else is doing it?"

I scowled. "I haven't been messing with anything. And I didn't think he was into that stuff." He never gave even a hint. For a moment, I doubted myself. Probably shouldn't have said anything about it to him at all. He'd read my palm, as a 'joke' after I'd hinted I was into magical stuff, but never said he knew anything about magic himself. Didn't get my personality right according to my palm, if that was anything to go by. I didn't go too far with what I knew anyway. I did operate some common sense here and there. Right. Maybe the visit was him just playing about. Either way, the visitor *was* him. I'd been handed the information. All I had to do was confirm it.

And then what?

I pictured his greasy, pale face and dank, mousy hair as he quipped something mildly amusing in his Edinburgh accent. He had been desperate to impress me, but I just couldn't bring myself to take it a step beyond whatever label was appropriate for our brief friendship. A couple of platonic dates were one thing—but I didn't want to lead him on, that was the point. When he asked me out again at the end of the second I'd been straight with him. To know someone isn't interested is far better than hanging on for months, wondering.

So much for honesty.

Indira couldn't bear my silence. "You know who it was?" Her tiny elf nose wrinkled and her brown freckles seemed to pop off her face as her eyes widened with excitement. "It wasn't that guy you finished with last week, was it?"

My cup slipped in my hand and sticky beige coffee slopped on to the work surface. It spattered the car insurance papers and fuel bills spread across the counter near the wall.

"How do you do that?" I demanded as I mopped up the mess with a tea towel.

"Do what?" She swallowed some tea and folded her

legs beneath her, gaze intent on me.

"You didn't even meet him, how do you know things? I thought I was the psychic one." I picked up my cup again, holding it more carefully. "It was him. I don't know how I know, I just do. He came and lay on top of me." I took a sip. He'd been there physically, I remembered his weight upon me. It wasn't just in my head.

Indira made a puking face. "Eww. I told you not to lead him on. What do you expect if you carry on like you're going to marry them? Men don't have an off-switch you know."

Nausea rolled in my belly. "It was only a couple of dates!"

I didn't offer him sex. Didn't make myself available. Thought that was better than past performance. Did that mean I'd led him on? Of course it did. Served me fucking right once again.

During our dates his clammy fingers had scraped my hand a few times for one reason or another. Even when he'd read my palm, his touch made me shudder. Two dates was enough. I wasn't that lonely and dating without caring was a slippery slope.

"At least I didn't give the milk away for free."

She tutted. "It doesn't work unless you don't lead them on either. A single date's one thing, but two? You can't just give them hope and then tell them nope. It isn't fair."

So much for standing beside me.

"How else am I supposed to work out if they're okay?"

"Can't you tell if you fancy them before you start?"

The tears rose and I couldn't look at her. She was right. Of course I could tell. But I didn't fall in love with a body, I fell for their minds. Just sometimes the ones that seemed to have nothing might turn out to be everything. But that had never yet happened conclusively. The ones that were everything never wanted me.

Her voice softened a little. "Don't cry, for heaven's sake. All you did was dream about him."

I dared to glance at her, but couldn't say it fully. "He—came to—" The lump in my throat filled my voice box. "He lay on top of me."

The distaste was clear in her downturned mouth. "In your dream. Ugh."

"It wasn't just a dream," I snapped. "Visitations are different."

She sighed. "You're nuts, you know that, right? What're you saying? He tried to rape you spiritually? Is that even a thing?" She looked sad. "How do you think that kind of thing up?"

Bile rose from my belly and I considered a dash to the bathroom, but calmed myself again. I drew in a long, deep breath, dropped my consciousness down to my centre and into the ground and steadied my stomach. More coffee. A rush of cold shivers overtook me. He came to rape me. I hoped I woke up in time.

"Creepy bastard." It wasn't like I could just go to the police, but I wasn't without resources. "You're not supposed to do that kind of thing in magic. It's totally unethical."

Indira's tone was full-on common-sense mode. "Babe, what you did to him was pretty unethical, never mind magic. If you mess with dangerous people, they'll always bite you first. You've got to start looking after yourself better. No-one else will. Stop looking for Mr. Right. He won't be out there until you give it up." Her well-meaning lecture was everything I'd heard before and it triggered me, but I didn't need a row on top of everything else. I tuned her out a little so I could think.

What would Leah do? The thought popped into my head, unbidden. I hadn't seen her for a few weeks, but I knew what she'd do anyway. No way would she let him get away without saying something. But she'd do it on the phone. I could go one better.

"I know." I would confirm it was him, let him know I knew what he'd done. Maybe he'd stay away then. If there was one thing I was good at, it was making a fuss in public.

Indira read my face instantly with apprehension. "Oh no. What are you going to do?"

I narrowed my eyes, enjoying the conspiratorial feel of my decision. I would have a good story to tell Leah when I saw her.

⁓

"Oh hi, I—I didn't think you would call again." His soft accent, tinny over the phone, irritated the hell out of me, but I swallowed stomach acid and grinned my hardest. You can always hear a person's expression down the phone. Luckily, you can't hear them keeping vomit down.

"Well, you know, I thought it might be nice to see you one last time. We can meet up this evening if you want?" *And you can buy me dinner,* I thought.

He took the bait, a cheerful tone in his voice. "That's great. How about the Snooty Fox at seven o'clock? Do you want—?"

"—I'll meet you there, that's fab." Puke. Leeds had dozens of pubs, but the Snooty Fox was near Roundhay Park, frequented by middle-class ale aficionados. Safe enough and the scene of our previous meetings.

"I've got that white sage I wanted to give you anyway, so I'll bring that with me."

The relief at his agreement set my heart pounding. "Great. That's so kind of you." He could shove his white sage into his deepest, darkest orifice.

I put the phone down and Indira was back in her position on the floor cushion, fully dressed, her chef's whites stuffed into a holdall, the bag gaping open beside her. I realised she was up early because she must have the lunch time shift.

She sounded kinder now, less annoyed with me. "What you doing, babe? You're not getting yourself in trouble are you?"

I grinned genuinely now. "At least he'll know I know about his little journey. Might put him off doing it again to me or someone else. A bit of public humiliation."

Indira's eyes sparkled with excitement, but tried to maintain a stern expression. "Do you think it's a good idea doing it publicly?"

"Best place for it! You don't get to just walk into someone's private space and fuck them. It's not ethical. It's not right in anyone's universe. How dare he—?"

She sighed. "It isn't like he really did rape you though, is it?"

"It's just as real on the astral plane as it is in real life," I snapped. She really didn't believe in magic. And anyway, I had no idea if he did or not. I didn't even know how you could tell.

2. Confrontation

He sat across from me, insipid oily hair slicked in waves across his head, scoffing his chicken and mushroom cream sauce. A dribble of white scum ran down his chin and he wiped it with a paper napkin. I averted my eyes and tried to stay in the moment. Why the hell had I agreed to a date the first time?

I had been waiting for a taxi outside the pub one night and because I was drunk I chatted with him. His internet dating story was a little bit woeful and I always give people the benefit of the doubt. The idea that 'you never know who will be the man of your dreams' would be the death of me if I let it. Indira was right. My next self-development goal would have to be to stop looking. Surely the man of my dreams would find me, not the other way around. I had to stop responding to every man who looked my way.

Half of my judgment problem was how broke I was. Temping medical secretary wages didn't pay enough for regular steak. Turning down dates was hard because of how nice it felt to eat great food, drink wine and be the centre of someone's attention for a few hours. But if they were a loser, I was the loser.

The silence became awkward, as though he was waiting for me to speak.

"So where's this special white sage?" I blurted and took a slug of red wine as I realised how grabby that sounded. My mouth was never really connected with my brain.

He looked a little superior for a moment—it could have been the light—but his smile seemed apologetic. "I'm really sorry, it totally skipped my mind. I hope you weren't relying on it."

"Of course not." I plopped down the glass and picked up my knife and fork feeling stupid. I didn't even want the gift. Wasn't sure why I had to ask for it.

The silence continued. The chatty, super-polite man from previous dates seemed strangely absent. Maybe he suspected something.

"So tell me about your work some more," I prompted as I cut through a thick crispy rind of pearly fat. "What kind of thing does your charity do?"

He seemed so nondescript as he chewed his

chicken al fungi. I couldn't see him working any kind of magic, but people do surprise you.

He swallowed and took a swig of beer. "Some tribes on reservations want to make and sell their own produce. They weave baskets, make jewellery with silver and rocks from their own mines and rugs from the wool of their own sheep. We purchase equipment, help people get set up and find wholesalers and other buyers around the world so they can sell their products at a fair price. Help them build contacts, get them going, that kind of thing."

His answer sounded familiar, like I'd read it in a textbook with white saviour overtones. It could have been word-for-word the same as he'd described it last time I asked. While I was still at university, I'd worked part time for a shop that specialised in Navajo silver and turquoise jewellery. I knew it was a thing. The owners traded directly with the Navajo nation, so they 'did it right'. But his explanation still sounded a bit canned. Like he'd carefully researched the whole concept and said it hundreds of times before. Probably had, if it *was* his job.

"Have you ever done the whole sweat lodge thing when you visited the Navajo?"

He wheezed and coughed a bit of chicken onto his plate. God, he was gross.

"Sure, sure I have. My initiation ceremony into the

clan was the greatest experience of my life. I think I nearly died."

I took another bite of my steak, going for a casual attitude. "So, do the Navajo go in for astral travel?"

Apparently intrigued, he put down his knife and fork. "What makes you ask that? Thought you weren't really into magic."

I pulled a face. "Thought you weren't." I dared to make eye contact for one defiant second, then dropped my gaze as my mouthful took more swallowing than anticipated. I washed it down with wine and self-consciously replaced the glass in front of me. "I like to try to understand the spiritual world. It's interesting to learn how people in other cultures see things." He didn't have to know I was usually as blind as a bat on the astral plane.

He stared at me until I squirmed. "You shouldn't dabble, Inayat. Do it full time or not at all." The darkness of his pupils seemed to bleed into his watery blue eyes.

I sliced off a perfect piece of rare steak and regarded him, my wine glass perfectly centred between us, an ineffectual barrier. There were plenty of reasons why I didn't do it...much.

"Astral travel is a skill used since prehistoric times by many peoples, not just Native Americans." His toothy smile made me queasy, but he was right. Also about dabbling. I needed to get back into studying.

He paused, almost dramatically. "Had any revelations lately?"

Now there was a word. One I use quite specifically. I must have told him I got spiritual revelations sometimes.

"I'm not sure you'd call it a revelation." I gathered my thoughts. "But I realised you must be very interested in magic." He could refute my statement if he wanted.

He shrugged. "Magic has been...Let's just say, my saviour." He stopped and took a bite of his dinner. I waited. Expectantly. The air hung with pointed tension. He hurriedly swallowed. "What?"

"How interested in magic are you, David?"

He put his knife and fork down, his face clouded. "There isn't room in your belief system for my magic."

Adrenaline boomed in my centre. His arrogant reply was at odds with his harmless appearance. Yet he'd played it like he knew nothing about magic when I'd mentioned a couple of past experiences. Like he was super open minded and interested, but didn't know anything himself. Now I knew he'd been disingenuous.

I steeled myself and smiled insincerely. "Something weird happened to me this morning, wanna hear?"

His eyes narrowed as he shifted in his chair and he seemed somehow tougher, bigger and stronger. It dawned on me that I'd underestimated him, but I was here now. In for a penny, Inayat. I dove right in.

"This morning when I woke up, someone was lying on top of me, but I was totally alone." His mouth hung slightly and he was about to speak, so I panicked and rushed it. "I think it was you. You visited me."

He pushed himself back in his chair and looked at me intently. I held his gaze, but couldn't decipher his expression. Then he smiled, friendly creases at the sides of his eyes. He emanated admiration, a change so sudden that confusion touched me.

"You're so psychic," he said earnestly. "And you're *magnificent* when you're angry." His eyes shone and he leaned across the table with a wide grin. I lurched back out of his reach, openly angry now.

"You can't do things like that, it isn't ethical."

He sat back in his seat, his face frozen. "Ethical? What's ethical got to do with it?"

"Magic has to be ethical. Otherwise all you're going to do is bring hell down on your head."

He laughed unpleasantly. "Says who, Silver Ravenwolf?"

I flushed with embarrassment. The famous vampy American Wiccan might be the fluffiest kitten in witchcraft but it was her books that had first attracted me to magic as a teen. I couldn't remember telling him that. I shuddered at the thought he might have also tramped through my memories while he was fucking about in my head.

"What about the Rule of Three?" The main rule of Wicca was one to live by as far as karma was concerned. I tried to flatten the tone of triumph in my voice as I registered his scornful expression. He looked like he was about to spit at me.

He lowered his voice. "The more you learn about magic, Inayat, the less you'll believe in the dogma." His light eyes seemed to darken, flat and soulless, like shark's eyes. "Get yourself educated better."

His patronising tone wound me up, though I didn't really know what he meant by dogma. As far as I knew if you used magic to do bad things to other people, it didn't go well. Never had for me and I'd never done anything bad deliberately, but sometimes it was hard to know your own intentions. Man, that had got me into some trouble. That was why I mostly didn't bother any more beyond the odd employment spell.

"What did you think you were going to get from creeping around in my space without me knowing?" I wanted him to say he'd come to rape me. Wanted him to admit to the violation, intruding on my spirit for something as base as sex.

He laughed, first quietly, then with his head thrown back, roaring so loudly that heads turned at the tables on either side of us. Embarrassment washed over me. I'd come here to make him feel small but instead it was me.

He leaned forwards, eyes never leaving mine, mesmerising in their stare. "What do you think I got from it, Inayat?"

I opened my mouth and crossed my fingers. "You'll never get what you came for, so fuck you."

Thin tendrils of black smoke wrapped themselves around him, foggy folds barely visible, as though his hate cloaked him. His lips turned upwards again, a loathing expression across his face.

"I always get what I come for, silly little bitch."

I blinked, afraid again that he really had raped me. The vapours around him vanished, but the terror held me in place on my seat.

He tensed for a moment, staring off into the distance. For a moment I thought he'd blanked out. A blue-light siren approached the pub and passed it with the distinct pitch change. The sound faded into the distance and David's attention returned to me, speaking softly now.

"Duplicitous women, you all think yourselves so much better than you are. Not one of you alive that's as good as you think. Only takes a minute to rip your false face off you. And here I thought finally I'd found a woman worthy of my time. Fucking fool me."

The blatant misogyny triggered my adrenaline.

"You must have a really shitty relationship with your mother if that's the way you think about women," I shot back, a stab in the dark that shook me, but he blinked—a flinch—so fleeting I might have imagined it. A direct hit, no less.

"My mother," he breathed. "My fucking mother." He wrinkled his nose like a scornful pig and looked down at the table for the briefest of moments, breaking the connection. Next moment, his eyes were glued to mine, a strange internal glow within.

"Think you can humiliate me?" He shook his head as though I was foolish beyond belief. "You want another visit? You want me to come to you every fucking night? I'll chase you down in your dreams you little bitch and you'll fuck me like you want it. You got nothing you can do about it."

I stared at him, fear threatening to overcome my brain while I sorted through the possibilities. I didn't know if he was really a vindictive person or if it was just talk. Didn't know him well enough to tell. There was no way out of this situation that could be peaceful. I'd driven it to this. Driven him to hating me even more. Passed the point of bringing it down to lighten it. He braced his hand on the table to stand. I had seconds to do something. Anything. I might as well deserve the persecution. Give him a solid humiliation to hate me for.

"Fuck you, man." I picked up his uneaten dinner and

dumped the plate upside down in his lap. It slipped onto the floor with a bang. A few thick lumps of chicken clung to his trousers on their way to the floor, leaving trails of creamy greyish sauce. Not a good look for any man in a public place.

He shoved his chair backwards so hard the rear legs caught on the stone flag floor and tipped him over. His head cracked on the balustrade behind, but he up-righted himself awkwardly.

I grabbed my jacket from the back of the dining chair and shrugged it on.

"Stay away from me, David," I warned him. "Or I will call the police."

Rage filled, he kicked his empty plate across the floor with a clatter and pushed past me too closely, too aggressive, too near. He glowered at me with an evil that ignited another explosion in my belly and I tried to keep the fear out of my eyes as it burned me from the inside out.

He stamped to the gents and I grabbed my handbag, stalking to the bar with as much dignity as I could muster to order a glass of wine, hands shaking as I fumbled cash from my purse. An abandoned *Evening Post* on the bar scrunched under my hands I scrambled onto the stool. Its headline blared at me: *Paediatrician Vanished Near Canal*. I plonked my bag on top of it, a woman's beautiful smile sticking out from underneath it. I pushed it out of the way.

"Are you okay?" the bar girl asked. "We saw what happened."

"I'm sorry," I said, close to tears as adrenaline pumped the blood round my head. Thank God I was away from him. "I'm so sorry for making such a mess. He scared me." I handed her a tenner and she gently grasped my hand as well as the money. The firm, supportive touch brought a sting of tears to my eyes and I blinked them back.

She shook her head and popped open the cash register. "As long as you're okay. Do you want a taxi? I can call one."

Tears threatened to well up again. She was being too nice. I needed to snap out of it, not blub myself into an expensive and unnecessary taxi.

"No, it's okay. Do you mind if I just sit at the bar for a while?" I didn't have enough in the bank for random taxi rides and home was only fifteen minutes walk around the edge of Roundhay Park.

"Sure."

She handed me my change and we both looked around as the door to the men's toilet swung shut with a bang. David walked across the floor to the vacated table and called for the bill to a nearby waiter. The front of his trousers and shirt were stained light. My heart thumped with a rush of adrenaline and I turned back to the bar reflexively. I nervously sipped my no-strings wine.

Through the mirror on the opposite wall of the bar, I watched him leave with no glance back. My heart steadied towards its normal rate. Someone sat in the stool next to me and ordered two mojito cocktails.

"Hello," said a friendly female voice to my right. A pair of merry brown eyes looked down at me, framed by a shock of brown curls and a smiling face.

I couldn't help but smile. "Hi. How are you doing?" A skinny lady, possibly in her late forties, with a three-quarter-length winter coat and a large floral handbag on her lap.

She nodded. "Would you like a little drink with me? Can't let a girl drink on her own." She passed me a mojito without waiting for an answer. Not that I was given to turning down free drinks.

"My name's Molly Blue and yours is something pretty unusual, isn't it?"

That got me. Today had been weird enough.

"Inayat Tate. How do you know me, please?" I took a sip of sweet minty cocktail.

She shook her head and drank some mojito through a straw.

"I don't know you, but I've been brought to find you and it's important you listen to me."

I blinked. She didn't sound bossy, but she was firm. Her features turned serious. "That man you were seeing, he's not very nice, is he?"

I stilled the panic and went with the moment. Everything happens for a reason. I shook my head and picked up my straw from the bar.

"He basically tried to assault me. Secretly, if you know what I mean?" I imbibed delicious mojito, its green freshness waking up my mouth.

"I know what you mean." Our gaze held. She conveyed a message of knowing more than what the words had exchanged. "He isn't going to let it lie, you know. You'll have to be careful."

"How do you know?"

She smiled and dropped her eyes. "Let's just say I know, okay?" They flickered back up to me and then she gazed over my shoulder distantly. "You're going to have to listen to me," she repeated. I noticed the kindness of her eyes against her stern expression.

"I've been heavily pressed by at least a couple of your ancestors to get myself up to this pub and get you out safely." She lowered her voice. "I'm in my PJs under my coat!" She shifted her long winter coat to one side, revealing a leg swathed in white fabric with a Cath Kidston pattern. "There's a man wearing a turban and he's got an army of soldiers, all in turbans and white skirts and they've all got scimitars. That's your grandfather, right? Angry guy, but not with me, wants me to help."

I pushed the confusion out of the way. "My great-grandfather, maybe. Not my grandfather." I didn't know my family much anyway, my heritage hadn't been a big part of my upbringing. Whoever the hell this woman was, she seemed to know more than me.

She shook her head tiredly. "He won't leave me alone, just stands in front of me every way I turn, his army crammed into my house and all around the outside. When I went out with the dog, they filled the street! And there's a woman in a pinny with a rolling pin. Been hanging around for days, but tonight they made me get a bloody expensive taxi all the way over here from Seacroft. I've never seen owt like it."

I drank my mojito all the way down to the noisy ice and thoughtfully sucked up the dregs. Was she making it up? How could a stranger know about my ancestry? She seemed genuine, but could be off her head. Looking closer, she didn't seem like someone on drugs. Possibly ill? She stared at me till I sheepishly stopped with the ice-sucking racket.

"What's going on?" I wasn't sure I wanted to know.

"We're going to get a taxi back to yours. My bet is he's going to try and get you as you cross the park, so we'll drive back instead. All I've got to do is see you home safe."

There were plenty of dark shadows around Gledhow Hall. Places for someone bad to hide and spy.

Molly twinkled. "I do know how bonkers this sounds. I

suppose the question might be—do you feel safe with me?"

I smiled. Surprisingly, I did.

"Let's get going, then." She zipped up her handbag and got off the stool.

We left the pub and, as if by magic, a taxi rolled up.

Molly winked. "Just when you need it. But if you're waiting for a bus in the pissing rain...nothing, every time."

We got in the back, told the driver where to take us and five minutes later, pulled up to the gate.

"Can you drive right up to the door please?" I asked.

The driver grumbled. "It's awkward round the back there in the dark, no room to turn. You've only got to walk fifty yards." His dismissive tone was impenetrable.

I shut up—too annoyed to speak—and shot Molly a glance. She paid him and we got out each side of the cab and let him drive away.

Molly looked distracted. "He's here. Let's go!"

I dug in my handbag for my keys as we ran up the drive to the large Yorkshire stone porch. Molly dropped behind quite quickly but my panic kept me going. I couldn't remember if Indira was working or not and the light was out in the porch, which was odd.

I entered the porch still at a run, stuck the key in the lock and—

"Hi Inayat."

My shock reflex yanked the key back out of the lock and I dropped the bunch on the floor. I turned slowly towards the familiar voice. David stepped out of the shadows and advanced on the porch steps. I was trapped.

He smiled. "I wanted to say I'm sorry I visited you. I didn't realise how you'd take it."

He didn't *look* scary, but given the level of hate he'd just shown me, no way did this feel safe.

"I took it just fine, thanks, David." I furtively eyed the keys a little distance to my right. "You need to leave now."

He was on the step, still smiling crookedly, moving slowly towards me. I backed up a little. Where was Molly? She can't have been far behind. I resisted the urge to look for her, didn't want him to know she was there yet.

He scowled now, his face impossibly mobile, as though he was made of plasticine. He seemed to morph into a cartoon version of himself. I blinked, but he didn't come back into focus properly. The black smoke was around him again, thicker now.

He kicked the dust. "I'm sorry, okay? It was wrong. I'm not a bad person, you know? Just get a bit carried away sometimes."

Here was my chance to make peace. Play nice to stop him hounding me in my sleep. I held my breath for a long moment until the blood pounded in my ears.

"Okay, well, I'm sorry that I wasn't what you thought I was. I just wanted to get to know you." I floundered, searching for the right words as they evaded me. "I didn't think I was being duplicitous." He narrowed his eyes. Using his words was the wrong move. I needed to finish the conversation and get away from him. "I just don't know how to get to know someone if I'm not spending time with them."

I crouched down for the keys, but as I came back up, he grabbed me hard around the waist and threw his weight into me. I landed heavily on my hands and knees.

The door opened in front of us illuminating the ground in the hall light and someone screamed. A yelp behind me heralded a thud and David's body landed next to me, his head stoved in with a rockery stone that bounced on the porch to lie beside him.

3. The Police

Molly and I stared at each other in horror as I clambered to my feet. Indira stepped out of the doorway, a tiny figure with her hand over her mouth.

"Is he dead?" she whispered.

I knelt and put the back of my hand to his open mouth. His head wasn't completely smashed in, but the nasty gash on the crown had done its job. He had broken some teeth as he went down, a few crumbled white pieces lay around his face and I was careful not to touch him. A shallow, moist breath touched my hand and my stomach turned. I leapt to my feet.

"He's alive, what are we going to do?"

Molly closed her eyes for a long moment. "Call an ambulance."

"Oh my God, babe, how did it get to this?" Indira turned towards Molly. "Who are you?"

"Call an ambulance," Molly said. "Can you call nine-nine-nine? Have you got a phone?"

Indira stopped short and stared at her, eyes wide. "Yeah, inside, I'll call them." She turned and dashed into the house.

"What are you doing?" I whispered to Molly. "What are we going to do?" Faced with a grim police officer, I didn't have much hope for my brain to connect with my mouth. I was the shittest liar I knew. I couldn't coordinate my tongue with what passed for considered thought at the best of times. I didn't have it in me, not feeling like this.

Molly must have seen the terror in my face.

"We need the police as well," she told me in a normal voice. She was very straightforward, down to earth. "We're fine. Just tell them everything. The visitation, everything. Tell them you're into witchcraft and pagan stuff. They won't section you. You've got witnesses in the pub for your story."

I had a sense I was falling. "Me? But you hit him. You can't put that on me." She was a complete stranger and she'd nearly killed the guy and now she was dumping it all on me.

She smiled, but her eyes filled. "I'd never do anything to you like that." She sniffed and blinked, dashing away the two tears that ran down her face. "You tell them the truth and

I'll tell them the truth and because it's the truth, we'll be fine."

I was scared. "They're going to say it was my fault. I shouldn't have gone out with him when I wasn't going to sleep with him. I don't want them to say it was me, it's going to be us in court, not him."

She stepped forward and rubbed my shoulder. "It's going to be okay, don't worry about it." She smiled encouragingly, didn't seem worried at all. I looked into her eyes for a long moment, but she had nothing but reassurance for me. I couldn't believe her. My foolish actions surrounded me, acting out my flirtatious laugh and the way I thought up new things to entertain him. And all the time I had no intention of sleeping with him.

Indira came out of the flat, talking on the phone.

"I don't know, he's unconscious, I've no idea who he is." She advanced on me, making meaningful faces at me as she spoke. "Hold on, I'll give you to someone who knows what's going on." She covered the receiver with her hand. "It's the ambulance people, they asked if you want the police."

I took the phone and stepped past David's prone body, wandering down the drive a little way away from the lit scene outside the porch. The tears were coming, like an overwhelming tidal wave of fear and shock, but I had to do this call.

I steadied myself. "Hi, what do you need to know?"

"What's your name?" The operator's voice was calm, almost disinterested.

"Inayat Tate."

"What happened, Inayat?"

My stomach spasmed as I remembered the feeling as he grabbed me. I couldn't speak, too busy holding down the freak-out. I took a long, slow breath, gradually let the oxygen back into my body.

"A man tried to attack me and we've knocked him out with a rock."

The voice at the other end exuded common sense. "There's an ambulance on the way right now. Do you know the name of the man?"

"David."

"Do you know his surname?"

I couldn't remember. Something weird.

"Okay, we're going to patch you to Police Headquarters. I'm going to put you on hold, okay?"

I waited through the beeps, looking towards the entrance of the drive. Some kind of fabric billowed in the wind behind one of the stone gateposts. I squinted, but couldn't make it out. A police operator interrupted me on the line. "We have your address, there's a patrol car on its way. Just sit tight and wait for them."

I ended the call and walked slowly back up the drive to

the porch, the rippling fabric forgotten.

Indira leaned against the porch door, chatting to Molly. They both seemed oblivious to the body on the ground. I hoped he hadn't died. That might complicate things. I didn't dare look. I went indoors to get a blanket to put over him and when I came back the ambulance had arrived.

Sergeant O'Brien led me around the side of the house, notebook out and pen poised. He didn't seem the overly sympathetic type, but I had in my mind the things to say. Stick to the truth, just not all of it.

The blue lights on the ambulance lit unusual parts of the rockery and drive, backlighting the policeman who towered over me in silhouette. He guided me to sit on the stone windowsill of our living room, the dim light within casting a tiny glimmer on his face compared to the flashing blues. I stayed silent. My ability to incriminate myself was far greater with a flapping mouth.

"So, do you know the injured party?" he asked, scrutinising my face. I stared back, but tried to look glum not defiant.

"He took me out for dinner tonight." I tried not to think about the other two times.

"Didn't go well?" he guessed.

"It went like shit. I didn't want to go out with him again. He threatened me, said he was going to follow me until I did." My whole body shook as I lied. It sounded flaky as fuck.

"Follow you. Like stalk you?" His voice was cynical, as thought he didn't believe me. It panicked me because already I wasn't using the right words. I hated lying. Never thought I'd ever try it with the police. I reminded myself that it technically wasn't a lie. But it was. I sensed all chance for a normal life disappearing into the distance as thoughts of prison loomed in the darkness. I could get done for perverting the course of justice.

"I dumped his dinner in his lap when he said that."

"So you escalated the situation?" He didn't quite roll his eyes, but his tone said it anyway.

I squirmed but said nothing. Obviously I knew at the time that chucking food over him was going to anger him even more, but the policeman pointing this out wasn't helpful. I was right not to mention the previous dates.

"So he threatened to stalk you, you threw his dinner over him, and then he turned up at your home when you got back?"

I nodded wanly and picked the skin on my thumb till it bled.

"With your friend? Did you meet your friend in the pub with him?"

I shook my head, wondering suddenly how to explain Molly's mysterious appearance, given her talk about my ancestors. "I don't know her. She was just there already, think she saw everything that happened. She offered to come home with me to make sure I was safe."

I glanced around for Molly and could see her talking animatedly to the other police officer. His face was totally stoic as though he was made of rock. The living room light went on in the flat behind me. Indira must have been sent back inside already.

O'Brien looked up from his notes with a frown. "Interesting. You weren't safe. Do you think she knows him?"

I shook my head. "She didn't say she did."

He made another note. "So what happened after the pub exactly?"

Now his tone sounded flatter, more cynical, as though the fact I didn't really know Molly played into the implication that I hadn't told him everything. Which I hadn't, but he couldn't know that. I was reading too much into everything.

I took a calming breath and tried to curb the panic. "We got a taxi back here and he was waiting for me. He gave me a fright and I dropped my keys. He apologised for the things he said, but when I picked up my keys he grabbed me from behind and threw me onto the ground. Molly hit him with a rock and he fell next to me."

O'Brien made more notes. "How was Molly able to come on him like that?"

"I was scared when we arrived. I ran up the drive when I got out of the car but she didn't run."

"You were scared but she wasn't?"

"I don't know."

"And he'd already grabbed you when she hit him?"

I nodded wordlessly. She'd saved my life. And asked me to tell the truth. And I hadn't. The lump in my throat choked me.

"Got any injuries?"

My knees felt sore. I bent down and rolled up my left jeans leg. A scrape and a developing bruise on my knee was the only evidence. He made a note.

"Any other witnesses?"

I looked at him in shock. David's word against mine and all I had were friends as witnesses.

His face was unreadable. Not disinterested, but maybe disbelieving. "Your flatmate? Anyone at all?"

I didn't know what Indira had seen. She'd opened the door when I was still on my knees. Maybe she'd just seen David on the ground with his head bashed in.

I slumped and shook my head, tears washing my face. "You'll have to ask Indira. I don't know what she saw."

O'Brien closed his notebook with a snap. "Stay there."

The order rooted me to the spot. He walked back to the doorway and had a quiet word with the other officer. I saw him nod and he returned quickly.

"You're in luck," he said sourly. "Your flatmate says she opened the door to see him throw you to the ground and that's when your new friend hit him over the head. Convenient."

I glanced up at him but his face was still closed to me. It *was* too convenient. Sounded like we'd concocted it all.

"We'll see what the—man—says." He shot a look at me, as though he could see right through me. "But given the only witnesses are all known to each other to some degree, you're not significantly hurt and it's his word against yours, Crown Prosecution likely won't bother pressing charges."

If they knew I'd led him on they might.

"He jumped on me as I picked up my keys and threatened me in the pub," I repeated. "There was a dark-haired woman behind the bar, she saw everything."

O'Brien was unmoved. "There's a lot worse going on in the city lately. I'll be talking to the staff at the pub if he wants to press charges, but not until then."

I was struggling to get the information into my head. "So you're not going to arrest Molly?"

He sighed and closed his pocket book. "Not sure how this works, are you? Look, CPS only like cases they can win, but if there isn't the evidence, they won't bother a judge. After I've interviewed your would-be assailant, we'll be able to take a clearer view on the situation, but there's enough to do around here at the moment. We're not about to add to the load by dragging your friend into the station until we've got a full picture." He looked across to the porch area, bored already. "If he wants to press charges, we'll see about witnesses at the Fox regarding your altercation. If their story matches up with yours, CPS will throw it out."

The only altercation anyone had seen was me reacting aggressively towards him. I didn't even know why I'd encouraged him to talk to the bar staff.

"What happens if their story doesn't match up?" I just wanted to hide and never see anyone ever again.

His stare pierced my skull this time, gave me a headache. "Why wouldn't it match up?"

"It was a private conversation, they might not know what was said."

He sighed. "Wait for us to let you know what we establish. You and your friend will be hearing from us if it looks as though you're going to be charged with assault. I can't see it happening. Even if he does, from what the witnesses have said so far, defence of another will probably ride."

The ambulance left with a crunch of tyres on the drive and the blue lights with it. Left in darkness with only the living room illuminating us, O'Brien closed his pocket book with a snap. "If you've got nothing else to add, we can head back over there." Around the corner of the house, Molly and the ambulance had vanished and O'Brien's partner was examining the porch light with his torch.

"Probably smashed it with a rock," he told us, gesturing with two plastic bags. "Your pal's inside." He bent down and collected the rockery stone. "Surprising how strong someone can be in stressful situations. She made a big mess of him."

He handed it to O'Brien who turned it over in his hands, weighing it. "We'll talk to the gentleman as soon as he's in a fit state," he said. "You ladies try not to skip town, okay?"

As they drove away, I paused in the quiet darkness of the porch. Gledhow Hall had been around since the 1760s. Its history was full of important people and a lot of splendour, as well as being a hospital during World War One. It felt like ghosts, but I never saw one. I never saw anything on the astral plane, no ghosts, no spirits, no nothing, no matter how many hours of meditation I put away. The house walls hadn't been sandblasted, so its industrial black coating of two hundred years of pollution gave it a brooding atmosphere.

Outside was dark and damp. Winter was endless and unrelenting in the city. You never got to see real greenery.

From the side of my eyes, I caught something light tucked behind the drainpipe at its base. I walked over to it and pulled it out. A set of keys and a wallet. I flicked through the wallet. David's face stared out from his driving license, his eyes watching me. I slammed it shut and dashed through the hall into the flat.

"Look what I found."

"Where'd you find those?" Molly was instantly suspicious. Unusually for me, I could read her face like I knew her well.

"Outside, behind the drain."

She frowned "On the floor?"

I shook my head. "Tucked behind the downpipe."

She scowled so hard I thought she was mad with me. I thought of what she'd said about telling the truth, but kept it to myself for now.

I handed her the wallet and she opened it up, peering at his image on his license. "It's not like he just dropped it, is it?"

It wasn't. He'd deliberately tucked it away behind the pipe. He'd planned all along to attack me.

"Get it handed in, love, best if the police have it." She narrowed her eyes as she turned it over. "Don't want any kind of connection left with him, nothing—" She broke off and looked up brightly as she passed it back over. "Do you want my telephone number? We should meet for a coffee in a day or two."

I knew I should admit to her that I didn't tell the truth. I owed it to her if nothing else. But I didn't know how to say it. It might be best if I never saw her again. She waited expectantly.

I looked over at Indira. "Have you got a pen?" She waved her iPhone at me. "I'll text it you."

I never knew where the bloody thing was, could never find it when I wanted it and usually discovered it was out of battery long before I thought to charge it. I heard no beep as she texted me, so it probably wasn't in the room.

The taxi arrived for Molly and we said goodbye at the porch. Indira turned and went straight back in, but I paused in the doorway. The darkness was powerful, but as ever I felt blind, hemmed in by city walls and the night. Only a breeze stirred a few leaves. Even out here in the suburbs, in the grounds of a stately home that had gradually suffered the encroachment of residential estates, it wasn't enough. I shut the heavy door securely and returned to the flat.

"Nice policeman. Lucky you're white or you'd both have been arrested. You should have seen the way the other one looked at me until I said I lived here. Drink your tea." Indira pushed a mug of steaming liquid towards me. "I've got the early shift in the morning, I'm going to be knackered. What are you going to do now?"

I looked at the clock. Half-past midnight. "Bed. I'll take

the wallet and keys to the police station in my lunch break." I left them right in the middle of the breakfast bar so I couldn't miss them in the morning. I certainly didn't want to have anything that belonged to him. Way too much of a link, given his apparent magical abilities.

I drank my tea and attempted to sleep.

4. Enter Caleb

I woke with my alarm, but lay in the darkness with my eyes open. Who knew what David had tried to do to me two nights ago? Hopefully he wouldn't remember anything about last night. A crack on the head like that was enough to finish anyone's short-term memory.

I wanted to phone Molly today, needed to understand what had happened to us, but would leave it until I got home from work. I toyed with the fear of admitting to her that I lied, but figured it was better to tell her anyway. The priority was to get his belongings out of my possession. I didn't want anything of his in my home. Apart from anything else, I didn't know what other magical stuff he was capable of when he recovered from the life-threatening injuries. I had the impression that the Navajo sweat lodge wasn't his only magic-related endeavour, though who knew where I'd got that from.

There was so much more to him than he had shown me. None of it good, from what I could tell.

Leah popped into my head again. Man, I missed her regular company. Some sensible go-getting advice was what I needed right now, but we hadn't been out together for a while. I figured she'd call when she was ready. Sometimes I didn't know if it was okay to chase for her company or not. Friends could be confusing sometimes and I didn't like to push myself on people. We usually went through phases anyway. A brief pang of loneliness stung me but I pushed it away. We hadn't fallen out, so there was that.

I dropped back to sleep.

It wasn't until I sat on the bus—chest heaving at the effort to get to it in time—that I realised I'd left the bloody keys and wallet at home. As the bus chugged and heaved away from the roadside, I thought about how David had taken the items out of his pocket and hidden them behind the drain.

His 'apology' was a way of getting close enough to grab me.

A tiny, paranoid part of me wondered—like Molly—if the wallet and keys were some kind of ruse— a trick to leave a connection between us—but logical me wouldn't let the idea pervade. A gift, like the promised sage, perhaps. His ID and house keys? Not so likely.

I would check through his wallet a little more carefully when I got home. Missing something obvious when it was in my unsupervised possession would be unforgivable. No coincidences. If I was 'supposed' to hold on to it a bit longer, the reason would pop up eventually.

Indira made spaghetti bolognese for dinner and true to her usual style, heaved a mountain of food on my plate.

"Aw, you don't have to put so much on my plate, you always make loads!"

She shoved the meal across to me, pushing David's belongings to the side of the counter out of the way.

"You've got to eat properly babe." She smiled as she looked into the massive cooking pot. "You could be right though. I'll stick the rest in the freezer, or we'll be eating bolognese for the next fortnight."

She was a feeder for sure, a bistro chef at work, making intricate delicious morsels for death-defying prices, but a comfort food addict at home and I was a greedy sod. I couldn't leave anything on my plate.

I could see another pot simmering gently on the stove. "What's in there? Another meal?" I carried my meal over to the dining table.

She smiled in a self-satisfied way. "It's chicken stock,

babe. Can't waste anything, you know that." We'd had roast chicken a couple of days before.

I shook my head inwardly at her food obsession. She was worse than me by a long way. Had made a career of it.

Mind you, she was the sensible 'normal' one. She didn't care about relationships, all she wanted was to run her own kitchen.

As I munched through slick spaghetti and rich meaty sauce, I tuned out Indira's chatting. I didn't know how safe I felt any more.

My phone buzzed in my bag and I got it out. I never knew if it would have enough battery for me to see the message in time.

Gona catch up w/ you soon.

My breath caught in the back of my throat and scraped across my vocal chords. I didn't recognise the number. I noticed a missed call and swiped the screen. A private number. Fear melted into my belly acid.

Indira stopped in mid-flow, her voice tight with suspension. "What does it say?"

The doorbell rang.

I swallowed. "Are you expecting someone?" It rang again.

She shook her head, eyes terrified and excited all at once. "Do you think it's the police come to save you a journey with the keys and stuff? What did the message say?"

The bell went off again, repeatedly, like it was now stuck.

"It says someone's going to catch up with me."

"Who?" Indira's voice cracked with strain.

I wished we didn't live in the flat right next to the front door of the building. It was too easy to see when we were in or out.

"I don't know the number." The doorbell stuttered and stopped for a moment. Sergeant O'Brien could be checking up on us. Or come to arrest me. I put my fork down and got up, reluctantly walking towards the flat entrance. Footsteps rattled past, leaving the front porch and ran up the stairs. Maggie lived above us, an artist who exhibited in London and Paris. She'd shown us around her flat one time, sculptures and installations that I didn't understand at all. I hoped the visitor was for her. The massive iron-studded door closed with a thick clunk. I listened, but heard only my own breath.

I slid the chain off as quietly as possible and unlocked the catch. The click was deafening to my ears. I opened the door a crack and then a little wider. The murky hallway was empt—

—*Shit!* My view was blocked by a familiar and unwelcome figure, who stepped into the space and shoved his foot against the door.

"Caleb, what are you doing here?" His customary studded jacket had gone. Now he wore a long overcoat, but nothing else had changed. His tousled dark hair had receded a little, but his skin was as pasty as ever.

He twisted his face up in a miserable expression. "She's left me, hasn't she? Why did she leave me? Why did she do that to me?"

"You aren't serious. Why would I care?" My scorn leaked through my teeth like tallow from an old-style candle.

He stared at me, piercing blue eyes through dark eyelashes, swaying gently on his feet.

All the wasted time rolled in on me. Months and months of stupidity—almost a year—and two years of picking myself up and falling down again. Of trying to live straight—to be normal—and continually getting it wrong. People aren't so easy to judge when you don't trust your own judgment on anything and sometimes life feels like a series of lessons. Like, right now. If he thought he was coming round here to get sympathy from me, he was crazy.

The pain of wanting him had gone, but betrayal lingers far longer.

"I know you understand, Inayat, thought you'd help me." His broad Yorkshire drawl was as lazy as ever.

I tried to shut the door, but his foot didn't budge an inch. I glowered at him. "You don't fucking think, do you?"

I had met Caleb a week after I'd created my first ever love spell. Again, not exactly a coincidence. I asked for my soul mate, but I suspect that little phrase doesn't mean what I used to think. I didn't know it would bind me to an unknown man of chaotic tendencies and dubious intentions. I know now. I've never cast another love spell since.

And now he stood there lazily, looking at me like some kind of quiet blast from the past. Someone I knew intimately, whose mind I knew even better. Whose soul I was apparently irrevocably attached to. Whom I had to live without because he didn't actually want to be with me.

At my current stage of understanding, the spirit isn't the same as the soul. Your soul is maybe a thousand times bigger than you, a larger unit that encompasses lots of spirits. Your soul mate is another spirit from the same soul. Possibly. My view on the universe is a little cluttered and I viewed soul mates differently back then. I used to think they were the person with whom you are destined to spend precious time in each incarnation.

Turned out it didn't matter what my understanding was, the Universe's interpretation is final.

My main takeaway was that you can't guarantee meeting your soul mate will be the best experience. Over two years later, here he is, weeping about how someone else left him.

"She took my ring. My gran's," he moaned.

I gave up in exasperation. He wasn't going away, probably wanted something. I couldn't do anything about his foot in the door.

"For God's sake, come in, you're making the place look shabby."

He entered the flat and brightened a little as his calculating look around the room revealed the gorgeous Indira.

"Witty woo, how do you do." She'd left her dinner on the table and stood questioningly in the middle of the spacious living room. He grabbed her hand and pressed it to his lips.

She tugged it back, giving me a hard-Indira look. She smiled at him, but it didn't reach her eyes.

"Who are you?"

"Indira, this is Caleb. He's probably just leaving."

"Shuddup, Scary." He winked at Indira and cunning crossed her face, replaced instantly with wide-eyed openness.

Her tone was matter of fact. "I don't believe I've ever heard about you, Caleb." She smiled wickedly. "I tell you what, let's have a coffee and a piece of cake and then you should probably leave." She busied herself with the kettle.

"So where in Inayat's life have you come from?"

Damn it, she was a nosy bugger. I hadn't known Indira yet when I was in the throes of love and heartache for this fool and I just hadn't talked to her about it. Too much pain and humiliation to reintroduce into my life. And now the dickhead was here in person.

"I'm a warlock," he confided, untruthfully, as far as I knew. "Little witch can't get enough of me."

"Caleb, shut the fuck up." I marched across the room to the dining table as my phone's screen lit up with another message from the mysterious number. I picked it up. "We've had enough of stupid men this week and the last one ended up half dead, so you won't stand much of a chance."

I held my breath and opened the text.

Ima get my shit together, feel bad I
haven't seen you.

That seemed more friendly. Could be Leah on a new number. I texted back.

Who's you?

I headed back to the kitchen bar, phone in hand and dropped it into my open handbag near the wall.

Caleb coughed like he had the plague and pulled up a seat at the bar. "What happened?" He wiped his eyes and took the proffered coffee and cake while we told him the story.

"The wanker left his wallet behind, so I've got to traipse all the way down to the police station with it," I complained and immediately realised my mistake. Caleb's eyebrows shot into his hairline.

"This wallet?" His never still fingers hefted the wallet straight away, fingering its pockets looking for money.

"And his keys," blurted Indira, to my horror. I scowled meaningfully at her, but it was too late. Caleb didn't seem to pick up on it, though.

"Is that right?" He spoke absently as he peered at the guy's driving license. "Looks like a twat."

I watched him closely, sliding my hand towards the bunch of keys as slowly as I could, the better to do it without him noticing. Just as my fingers almost touched the keys, he shoved the wallet and license into my stuck out hand.

He hooked up the keys and examined each one in the light. I tried not to look as desperate as I felt, but kept my eyes on his hands at all times. His ability to lift something right in front of the owner was legendary. Everything I knew about sleight of hand I'd learned from him.

To my surprise, he threw them back down on the counter with no discernable trick—which wasn't to say he hadn't. Still worried he might be more interested in them if I made a fuss, I didn't make a move towards them yet.

Indira, apparently unaware of my stress, slid out of her seat. "Back in a minute." She headed into her bedroom, presumably to use the bathroom.

"Are you leaving yet, Caleb?" I asked as she crossed the floor. No point in pretending I was comfortable in his presence. He knew I wasn't and I still didn't really know why he was here. "What did you really come here for?" Indira's bedroom door closed with a click.

I felt weird—heady—as though I was under attack. So much time had passed since all that hoo-ha. My need for his love had taken over my brain for so long that when I forced myself to move on, everything normal felt unfamiliar. And now, here he was, large as life, toxic and unwelcome in my life and home and still here after half an hour. I'd already had my space invaded twice in the past two days—and now Caleb? The pattern, if it was one, bothered me.

"Olivia left me." He looked forlorn again.

I narrowed my eyes. He was pretending. "And she took your Gran's ring." Some vintage Art Deco monstrosity. I tried not to smile. I hoped she'd sold it already. "It was a gift, Caleb. You gave her a gift, so you don't get it back." It was easier to be twatty than to empathise.

No-one empathised with me when Caleb regularly turned up at my home all hours, raised my hopes they would split, then dodged me for six months after a massive fall out while I obsessed and thought about him nightly, locked in my flat with a spliff and my diary. I cringed. That six months had ended with a visit from Olivia herself, the only girlfriend he'd ever had who wasn't into witchcraft, as far as I knew. Her spell was apparently stronger than anyone else's.

He stood up and went to the sink to wash out his cup. I grabbed the keys while his back was turned and dropped them into my handbag with a clink.

"How did you track me down?" I didn't know anyone from those days any more.

"Just asked around. Does it matter?"

"It matters. *Why* did you track me down, Caleb? Not just to moan about Olivia, surely?" I was surprised she'd only just ditched him, given the trauma he'd put her through.

He returned to the counter but didn't sit down, just leant on it, as large and charismatic as ever.

"I want my ring back. You can get it back."

The bloody ring. He was the worst of his star sign, a Leo, like Indira. But not at all like Indira. What's his was his, even if he'd previously gifted it, I always knew that. It was understandable to an extent. Cash and his few possessions were the only security he'd ever had.

I stared at him for a long moment, wondering what he had in mind. "How the hell am I going to do that?"

No way would I face Olivia for him. I thought of her standing on my doorstep shrieking at me, her eyes, nose, and mouth red and blotchy from crying. I remembered being surprised when she ripped at her own hair, I hadn't known people really did that. She deflected all her wrath that she'd saved for Caleb on to me, even if I did indirectly deserve some of it. Everything in their lives had started to drop apart. All a direct result of Caleb's drug-fuelled, jacked-up behaviour, but my big mouth and his raving about magical attack had convinced her I was more terrifying than Satan. I'd never seen her since. The thought of even passing her in the street shot me full of fight-or-flight.

The stock pot on the hob behind him bubbled louder. I peered around him just in time to see it boil over, a steaming, sizzling mess all over the cooker.

"Shit!" I ran right around the breakfast bar to the hob, pushing him out of the way as he turned to look. He moved towards the wall to give me space as I turned off the ring and grabbed a couple of tea towels. Stock and bits of crap everywhere. All I did was slop it around the surface. Viscous fluid and herbs coated the front of the cupboard below, splattering onto my shoes.

"For fuck's sake, Indira!" I yelled.

Indira came out of her bedroom at a trot.

"What happened? What a mess!" She grabbed a towel and cleaned up more expertly than me. "Can't even leave you long enough to go to the loo," she chided.

Excitement over, I wished that Caleb would just leave. I turned to him to tell him that, but he tilted his head on one side, cajoling me to play his game, leaning against the wall as laconic as ever.

"You're a good witch, Indus girl. Just get it for me, Inayat. Pretty please." His blue eyes glinted through his exaggerated squint. I couldn't find the words and for one treacherous moment didn't know whether to be pleased he thought that, or angry he continued to use me.

Angry. Indus girl. He used to call me that when we were together, as though we'd spent a life together in the Indus Valley civilisation. Screw him.

"Get the fuck out, Caleb. I don't think I'm going to do you a favour any time soon, do you?" I didn't even know if I could magically retrieve his ring for him. I'd never tried. These days I normally just called up an angel to help me out when I remembered to ask.

I stamped to the hallway and switched on the light. He didn't move from his position at the breakfast bar. "Go."

He advanced on me slowly, but pushed past without shoving, looking at the pictures on the wall as he went. He kept glancing back, smirking. When he got to the door, he turned and nodded at me. Then he was gone. A moment later, the flat door slammed and finally a heavier slide-and-clunk as he exited the building.

Indira and I looked at each other. She shook her head disapprovingly. "What a bloody mess. I don't know why the pot boiled over," she said. I didn't know either.

I sat back down to my now cold meal and picked up

my fork. My eye fell on my handbag at the other end of the breakfast bar. No longer snug against the wall, it stuck out at an angle as if it had been moved.

Or rifled through.

Adrenaline boomed in my centre. I almost tipped the stool over as I scrambled to get to it. To my relief, I pulled out the bunch of keys. He hadn't taken them. I didn't know how many were on the fob in the first place but they seemed intact.

Indira followed my actions but said nothing. She handed me a plastic sack and I scooped up the wallet and popped it inside with the keys. Everything went back in my handbag.

No forgetting anything in the morning.

Indira and I finished up our cooled but still tasty meals and relaxed into our evening in front of the television. Or at least, she relaxed. My whole system had been shaken, emotionally rocked to the core as though some kind of magic just happened. My mind kept auto-replaying the stock pot boiling over and the handbag's new position. I'd missed something. The mysterious texter bothered me too. They hadn't replied, so I presumed it wasn't Leah.

I don't believe in Fate, but I do believe in intersections. We're all on our own life tracks, within our personal spheres. When our paths cross, the events that spin off from these are life changing. Working magic has the same effect, but often more intense—one reason why I don't do it much.

Caleb's appearance felt like a portent. Either that, or I'd been caught in an intersection.

5. Mysterious Loot

Waiting for the bus, my phone rang. The mysterious text messaging number.

I picked it up. "Hello?"

Leah's casual tones crackled through the bad connection. "How are you doing, babes?"

Relief surged through me hearing her sensible voice. "It *was* you!"

"What was me?"

"The messages the other night!"

"Who else did you think it was?"

I groaned. "You wouldn't believe what's been happening."

She laughed. "Been busy?"

"You could say that. Fancy a trip to the police station

with me"

"Me? No way thanks. Why'd you need a visit there?"

"That guy I was messing around with tried to jump me. Left some things at my house, so I've gotta take them back."

She was silent. "To the police station?"

I tried to lighten it with a laugh. "Yeah, there's a lot I'm not telling you. Stood in the bus stop." I lowered my voice. "Bit close for comfort."

"Okay, you want me to tell you about black people and police?"

Embarrassed, I blurted, "I'm not in trouble."

"No, *you* won't be. But by the time we get out of there, *I* probably will be. Gotta a career to consider, sorry hun."

"Fuck's sake, I'm sorry, I didn't think about that."

"Yeah." Her tone told me that I didn't *need* to think about it. White people white peopling as usual.

I gave up and changed the subject. "So what gives?"

"Got that interview tomorrow!"

Excitement rushed through me. "Team Leader Leah! You'll crush it!"

"I know that!" She sounded smug. "Can't guarantee anything, so I'm swotting up on it now." She'd been tipped for the job anyway, but I knew she was up against it. Pump engineering was a white man's world. Complacency would do her no good.

"What time is it at? Want to celebrate afterwards?"

"We'll see, I might go out with Jez if he bothers to get finished early."

I could almost taste my disappointment. My instincts were right, she didn't want to spend time with me right now. I could never gauge it because I didn't really understand why. We didn't have issues between us, but I never knew if I was really accepted by my friends or if they just tolerated me to be nice. Or if I just expected more of them than was normal for friends.

"Let me know," I said brightly. "It's still buy-two-glasses-get-the-bottle-free at The Crypt."

She laughed and promised me she would call if her boyfriend didn't sort himself out. They'd been together years, ever since I'd known her. He hadn't started out as the reliable type—youth had got the better of him for a while—but somehow they stuck together through everything. I didn't know how anyone managed that. The prospect of finding a partner to trust my life with was distant at the best of times and right now, I couldn't see it ever happening.

As I got off the bus in the direction of the police station, I couldn't decide whether to ask for Sergeant O'Brien, or otherwise what to say to the person on the desk. Police stations give me the creeps—they're so cold and bleak, windows like blank eyes watching everyone. The recently constructed building loomed overhead and the traffic whipped past me, stopping impatiently only to allow crossing at the lights.

I yanked my tights up and my skirt hem down, said a little prayer to my angels and buzzed on the intercom.

"Can we help you?" The voice was crackly, though the equipment was new.

"I was involved in an assault. I've got some items I found after the police left."

They buzzed the door open and I stepped in and up to the too-high counter with its glass partition. I glanced around nervously. The foyer was empty, its walls busy with missing and wanted posters. A pretty woman who looked faintly familiar was missing. I stared at the poster but couldn't place her. A complicated poster showing CCTV images from a recent demonstration demanded that the public give up anyone they knew to the police.

The desk sergeant's voice made me jump. "What have you got?"

I snapped my head around to face him. He rubbed the top of his balding head and replaced his glasses on his nose as he peered at me.

I pulled out the keys and wallet. "A guy tried to assault me on Sunday night, but my friend knocked him out and put him in hospital." I pushed the items into the teller tray under the glass hatch. "I found this stuff hidden round the side of my house, looks like they belong to the man."

The sergeant turned the wallet over and expertly removed the driver's license. He knocked his glasses wonky again as he scratched his nose.

"I heard what happened. Good, thanks, I'll pass it on to Sergeant O'Brien."

He lifted the keys close to his face and flipped through each one carefully. I turned to go, relieved I had fulfilled my decent duty.

The door to the side of the waiting room buzzed and swung open.

"Just a minute, Miss Tate." O'Brien stepped through into the space. "Can I have a word?" He looked deathly serious, like a school teacher with a naughty kid.

I stared at him, mouth numbed with shock.

"Come this way please." He held the door open. I was about to be arrested. Heart pounding and my body shaking, I felt sick, I walked through into a corridor. He led me down the way to a door and entered, switching on the light.

"Take a seat." He nodded to the Formica table in the middle of the room. I realised we were in an interview room.

"Am—am I in trouble? I just brought the guy's stuff back, he left it behind the gutter."

O'Brien frowned as he sat down opposite me. "Behind the gutter? What stuff?"

I nodded. "His keys and wallet were tucked between the downpipe and the wall."

His eyebrows shot into his hairline. "Keeping them safe, was he?"

I shrugged. I couldn't work out if he was on my side or not. The interview room was claustrophobic and creepy with its strip fluorescent lighting and shadowy corners. The flickering lights irritated me, but I kept what cool I had left.

O'Brien sighed and pulled out his pocketbook. He flipped the pages and made a note.

"Right. I've got a few things I want to ask you about. Some information that doesn't add up to what you told me. Are you ready?"

I just stared at him.

"Do you need a drink of water?" His tone was ice cold.

"Am I in trouble?" My voice came out in a cracked squeak.

"I've had a chat with the individual who attempted to assault you." He flipped some notebook pages over. "It seems you dated him a couple of times before Sunday night. That true?"

The horror of my lie washed over me. I nodded in a fug, unable to even articulate the word 'yes'.

"So, why didn't you mention that before?"

I could only stare at him. All words had vanished from my mouth.

"Miss Tate? Why didn't you tell me you knew him for longer?"

I took a breath, trying to force words of some kind into my brain. Nothing came. Another breath. Still nothing.

"Miss Tate." He didn't seem angry. More curious than anything. "Miss Tate, I can see you're in shock, but you're going to have to tell me the things you didn't tell me on Sunday."

All I could think was that now he knew, he would also know I was a total fraud. That I deserved everything shitty that ever happened to me.

I pushed air through my lips. "I'm not a slag."

He frowned a little. "No-one's saying you are. Tell me what you know about the guy."

"I went out with him a couple of times." Indecision rolled around my brain. I didn't know whether to just tell him everything. The visitation, the dates, the threats, everything. Panic washed over me repeatedly, like a tide of adrenaline coming into shore. The walls and the door changed perspective repeatedly, closer one moment, far away the next. I felt like an ant on an iceberg, no grip, no solid context.

"So why didn't you mention this on Sunday?"

Lying by omission is still lying in the eyes of the law.

"I'm not a slag." I cursed my inept mouth. Couldn't keep my brain steady long enough to make sense. My hands were shaking uncontrollably. I moved the visible one under the table away from his eagle-eyed sight.

He sat back, intent on my face. "So you're not a slag. You didn't sleep with him."

I shook my head. "He took me out a couple of times and one time I went to his house but I didn't sleep with him." The fact that he'd enunciated the words gave me a verbal straw to grab hold of.

"Do you think," he began slowly but stopped. "Did he attempt to assault you because you didn't sleep with him?"

Misery swallowed me. Only the truth wanted to come out. I had nothing else inside me. I couldn't believe I'd managed not to tell him everything the first time.

"Mr Catcheside was quite clear he'd been out with you a couple of times. Said you'd invited him back to your house and then someone hit him over the head when he got to the door. Does that help?"

I stared at him. I didn't think he would believe the visitation. No way. I was going to be carted off to the men in white coats if I started telling a police officer all about that. The silence got longer and more awkward.

"Funny that he didn't mention his missing wallet,"

mused the police officer. "You'd think that would be the first thing on his mind. Makes the assault look premeditated."

He could have accused me of stealing David's wallet. I was confused. Why didn't he? I could have done. It would have looked real. Tease lures him back to her house and coshes him so she could steal his bank cards and house keys.

"He was a creep. I told him I didn't want to go out with him again, but he—" I faltered. I couldn't tell him about the dream. "—I knew he liked me. I went out with him again, but this time he wanted to sleep with me." I sounded like a way bigger dickhead now.

O'Brien narrowed his eyes. His police sense was probably screaming at him.

"But you didn't invite him home?"

I scowled at the thought. "Didn't you talk to the bar girl at the Snooty Fox?" At least she would confirm I didn't leave with him.

He shook his head. "Not yet. So no cosy invitation to your house?"

"No way, I don't know how he knew where I lived." Yes I did. Gledhow Hall was easy to find on a map and I was bound to have told him where I lived. I was a fool.

"A couple of meals and bottles of wine and he thinks he owns your body, right?"

His words registered slowly. He wasn't being horrible

to me. "Something like that."

He sighed again. Did a good line in sighs, I noted.

"Look, let me give you some advice. I'd tell my own girls the same thing if they got themselves into a mess like this. You go out with someone and you don't like them, it's simple. Don't see them again. You don't have to see them again and you don't need to pay someone in sex for a date."

The tears washed through me now. "I led him on."

"This isn't the Stone Age. He doesn't get to club you over the head and drag you back to his cave."

That wasn't how anyone else saw it. Indira. David. Probably Molly if she knew. I made some kind of mumbling sound.

O'Brien made some notes in his booklet. "So it's fair to say he lied to me?"

I nodded slowly, guilt on the tip of my tongue.

He stared across the table, but not directly at me. I realised he was looking at my quivering hands that once again rested on the table top. I attempted to steady them.

"I still feel like there's something missing here. Some information I'm supposed to know. You wouldn't know about that, would you?"

I dashed the tears away and shook my head, trying not to think about the visitation and David's threat. The police couldn't help there anyway. Not much point in trying to police the astral plane.

"Instinct's telling me to suggest you press charges against him, but I'm still not convinced CPS will pick it up, even with the wallet behind the drainpipe. Six of one and half a dozen of another. He attempted to assault you, was assaulted in the process. Technically twice if you include the dinner."

Numbness. Maybe David would leave me alone if I didn't go further. Maybe he wouldn't.

I tried to shake the thoughts out of my brain. "Has he said he's going to press charges on Molly?"

"He has not and I would discourage it if he did, wasting police time by the looks of things."

"What should I do?" I asked dully.

O'Brien stood up abruptly. "Get yourself away," he instructed. "I'll be in touch. Thanks for bringing in the items. Don't go anywhere." He opened the door of the interview room and I stood up.

As we walked into the waiting area, he nodded at me. He didn't seem angry, just a bit forbidding.

"If you remember anything else important, give me a call please." He handed me a business card.

I took a step towards the exit.

"Just a moment," said the desk sergeant.

My heart tripped and I turned back, dread crushing my chest. O'Brien remained in the corridor doorway.

The desk guy shook the keys. "Any idea which one is the house key?"

I frowned to mask my terror.

"No idea. I only went to his house once in the time I knew him." It was a massive stone pile near Street Lane in Roundhay. I couldn't remember what kind of lock the door had.

The sergeant nodded at me and raised an eyebrow at O'Brien. "Thanks for your help." He opened a zip-lock plastic bag and popped the items inside.

As I left, uncertainty scuffed up guilt, like dust in the wind, heart pounding unnecessarily, a vicious circle of fear. I didn't know Caleb had nicked anything. I shook myself internally and applied logic to my thoughts. The bunch of keys seemed the same. As far as I knew, they were exactly what David had left behind. I focused on somehow 'knowing' that the keys were intact and nothing was wrong. Tried to feel how I would if Caleb hadn't appeared.

Still my brain played tricks on me, round and round on a single track. Sergeant O'Brien knew I was still holding back. He knew there were things he didn't know. This was going to bite me so hard if I didn't spit it out, but I couldn't see any way to tell the story so that they didn't throw me into a straitjacket. And I didn't know why O'Brien was being nice to me when I hadn't told him the truth.

Indira was half dressed-up to go out when I got home. I figured I'd see her out the door and make the most of having the flat to myself. Candles, music, TV of my choice. Bliss.

"I thought you must have gone out for a drink," she mumbled through her toothbrush.

"Why did you put your lipstick on before you brushed your teeth?" Even frothing at the mouth, she was ridiculously glamorous.

She spat froth into the sink.

"I didn't. I got ready, but ate some licorice torpedoes. Needed the sugar. I'm so tired." She was on her feet all day, never stopped until the end of her shift. I hated kitchen work, the relentlessness ended me. I wouldn't have the energy to go out afterwards, but Indira was a powerhouse most of the time. The rest of the time, she slept. I guessed that was her secret. She took care of herself pretty well and I was sure a lot of that was because she never let anyone walk all over her—not without a fight, anyway.

"Is it the vending machine guy?" I'd forgotten his name already. Something English and nondescript. As long as he treated her well, it didn't matter what he was called.

She stared at me, then laughed. "I haven't seen him for ages! Not my type, too—boring. Cute, but boring. Off to see

Goldfrapp with the gang tonight. Jimmy got tickets for everyone six months ago."

I grinned. Jimmy and Indira had birthdays on the same day. They both loved beautiful things, great food and electronica.

"When are you going to marry Jimmy?" I knew she never would, they were just good friends, part of a wider group whose dramas kept them them all busy enough without all having relationships together too, but it was a running tease.

"Life isn't about meeting The One and settling down, babe. If you don't know that by now, I can't help you."

I shook my head with a smile. "Don't take drugs. Don't drink too much. Don't lose your purse. Don't get your toes trapped under a door this time." The marble doors of a club's ladies' loos had almost broken her foot the last time she went out in strappy sandals.

She scowled. "Don't stay up too late," she retorted. "You need your beauty sleep more than me."

Cheeky bitch. "No need for that."

"You know I never buy drugs," she pointed out tetchily as she tightened the straps on her high heels.

"I know that babe." I gritted my teeth. Sure, she never *bought* drugs. Jimmy was generous with most material joys. I kept my mouth shut. Least said, soonest mended. None of my business anyway, people in glass houses and all that. "Just be safe and make sure you have a good time."

She pulled on her top and straightened everything in front of the mirror.

"There's curry in the fridge, hun. Help yourself." Her obsession with keeping us in great food was a measure of her kindnesses too. She kept my household costs down and mostly refused the help, said she earned more than me and was more concerned that I paid my council tax than contributed to the food bill. I got the impression she was glad to have someone to live with, though I could never figure why none of her close friends had ever moved in. Maybe they all had their own lives and families to live with. I didn't know any of them well enough to know. She kept us pretty separate. Probably because she thought I was weird.

I saw her off, a tiny figure tottering down the cavernous hallway in spiky boots and a flowing scarf. We didn't always understand each other, but she stuck with me, regardless of my dickhead situations I got us both into. That was worth putting up with a few judgey comments here and there.

I stepped back inside, grabbed a fork and sat down with the stew and mash Indira had plated up, let myself get used to the feeling of being alone at home.

The room was immense, a kitchenette in one corner,

my bedroom built like a false box into another and a huge blank fireplace with a marble hearthstone.

I loved that a place where unbelievably rich people once lived and partied was somewhere I could call home, despite just scraping by on the meagre wages of a temp secretary. Even William Gladstone had visited Gledhow Hall during one of his tenures as Prime Minister back in the eighteen hundreds.

Appreciating the irony meant enjoying its grandeur in my own way, so after dinner I lit tea lights and incense sticks on surfaces around the room and knocked off the big light. The shadowy atmosphere was far more comfortable.

I ran a hot bath and added drops of lavender and tea tree oil, inhaled the heady fumes as they hit me. A stream of sea salt crystals poured into my hand was the earthy cleansing for my spirit. I opened my crown chakra and imagined white light streaming through it, filling me up. I drew energy up from the earth through my feet with each deep inhalation. When tingles lit up the centre of my body, I directed it as blue-white light down my right arm into the salt.

I scattered the faintly glowing salt into the steamy bath and added some cold, stirring the water to dissolve the mineral. Sitting on gravel wasn't the best experience.

I undressed and inspected my hair in the mirror. Split ends told me I needed a cut, but that wasn't likely, given my current finances. A few greys were starting to come through. Probably stress. I tied it up, but just as I stepped into the bath, I heard a bang in the hallway and a series of heavy knocks at the flat door. Adrenaline exploded in my centre and I froze. My bathroom was the communal one for the flat, so it was built into the entrance hallway. I was locked into a darkened room with no windows in a dim, candlelit flat and surely no-one in the driveway could tell anyone was home.

What about Indira?

Something might have happened to her. Stuff was always happening to Indira. Usually other people. The guy she was with wouldn't know how to get hold of me. She would never let me live it down if I pretended I wasn't home. She knew I wouldn't have gone anywhere.

The knocks reverberated through the walls. I clambered out of the bath, wrapped myself in a towel and unlocked the bathroom door. I waited with it still closed. Another loud bang. I tiptoed out of the room. The hall light was off. Whoever it was couldn't tell I was in through the spyglass. I crept up to the door and peered through the spyhole into the house entrance hall. The wood panelling of the staircase opposite the flat was illuminated, but no-one stood before me.

I waited. A sound came from outside the door, someone's foot scuffing the tile flooring. I looked again and leapt back in fright as the person knocked loudly and shouted. The voice was muffled and echoey, indistinct, but I recognised it at once.

I unlocked the door and opened it less than the chain's length. "Go away, Caleb, I don't know what you want."

He slid round the edge of the door frame. I hadn't seen him through the spyglass because he had stood against the wall to the side of the door and knocked from there.

"Let me in! I've got a present for you." He grinned and stuck his tongue out at me.

"I wish you'd just go away. Why won't you leave me alone?" He tired me, bored me. Frustrated and vexed me. He had betrayed me when I loved him and now I was over him, was apparently squirming back into my life. However innocuous it seemed, it was outside of normal, a Trojan horse to my well being.

His face changed to annoyance. "Don't be sulky. Let me in, I've got a deal for you." He lifted a heavy plastic bag up to my face. "You can have this."

I slammed the door shut in his face and breathed for a long moment. He knew me too well but I didn't have to fall for it. Curiosity was the lesson I never learned but Caleb was a failed exam that would come round again if I wasn't careful. A familiar demon whose dancing I knew wasn't beneficial to my life. You think you're in control for a while, when all of a sudden, *pow.*

I wondered if whatever he had might be saleable. I couldn't do this any more. But I needed money so badly. I couldn't do Caleb any more, I knew that. My mental health wasn't up to it. But money. That affected my mind too, or the lack of it. Part of the problem was that I wasn't money orientated. I didn't strive for jobs where I might have earned more, mostly because those jobs wouldn't have me. Indira would have pulled him through the door in a flash—well she would if it was jewellery. Fuck knew what it was. It depended what the contents of the bag were.

I wouldn't know if I didn't let him in.

I didn't want to know.

I wasn't that good. I was down to my last fifty quid if that.

"What's in the bag?" I asked loudly through the door.

"You'll never know if you don't let me in."

The bastard. He knew how to lure me.

I was so tired of being broke. He probably wanted me to sell it for him. If that was the case, it would be stolen. No fucking way. I wasn't going to prison for this fool. I'd run that risk for him before.

I drew my thoughts together and made a pact with myself. He could come in, show me the bag and if he wanted me to sell it, he could leave. If it was crap, he could leave.

Right.

Maybe I could get one over on him just this once. Or just get something out of it for once.

Pigs might fly. My thinking wasn't joined up enough. Decision making was tough at the best of times. Under pressure, it was almost incoherent.

Fuck it.

I steeled myself and undid the chain.

He swaggered in with a bulging Morrison's bag-for-life, carrying it straight into the living room to dump on the kitchen counter. It tipped over, pouring out silk fabric pouches that rattled as they landed. I picked one up, clinging to my towel with the other hand.

"Feels like stones." I worked the bag's closure undone. The smell hit me. "Smells like incense." The bag opened up to reveal rune stones.

"Smells like shit to me." Caleb mocked.

A candle rolled onto the counter, then another. Pillars, yellow and green. Good quality wax. He shook the bag again. Boxes of incense sticks. A good brand, too.

I felt in the bag past the herbs, reminded of the lucky dip game at church fêtes when I was a kid. Stones and jewellery and something large, solid and very hard snuggled right at the bottom. As I pulled it out, the pit of my stomach jerked. The fist-sized amethyst geode glittered with energy.

"Caleb, where the hell did this stuff come from? What did you do, rob a crystal shop?"

He rolled a thin cigarette and popped it in his mouth.

"I'll do you a deal, Inayat. This is yours. You don't even have to agree to the deal. You're kind of—owed it. It was—surplus to requirements." He sparked a match with a dirty thumbnail and lit his fag. "Must be about four-hundred quid's worth of gear in there."

I slowly tipped the rest of the bag's contents on to the surface. He did owe me plenty of money. I found two handfuls of large crystals and thumb-stones, an odd assortment of jewellery and a lifetime's supply of incense.

"You don't know how much is here. That geode could be worth hundreds by itself."

A silver ring with a dark red stone beckoned to me. I picked it up, examining it. "Is this a garnet?" The stone had a special energy all of its own. It pulsed in my fingers, even reverberated up my wrist, a living crystal.

Caleb shrugged. "Dunno, do I? You gonna sell it all?"

I searched his face, looking for some clue as to how he'd come by all this stuff. It was almost certainly robbed. His sharp blue eyes teased me. He knew something I didn't and it was written all over him.

He smirked again and stood up straight, but when he spoke it was in a wheedling tone. "Go on, Inayat, find my ring."

He fluttered his ridiculously long black eyelashes, a parody of a child begging for sweets. "You'd have liked my gran. She was a witch like you. It's a protection vessel. I shouldn't have given it away."

I stared at him. He really thought I could get his ring for him.

"Please." He seemed desperate and—genuine, not a quality I associated with Caleb as a rule.

He leaned into my space, lowering his voice. "Witches never really die, Inayat. Her shade won't leave me alone. Says I should have kept it. Keeps telling me I'm gonna need it." His eyes flickered past me as if someone stood behind me, his paranoia evident once again.

I turned and briefly caught a shimmer of a woman like a heat mirage in the kitchen light behind me. His gran. She'd been the only parent figure he trusted when he was a kid.

A vulnerable ache in my midriff was a danger signal. I opened my mouth to refuse, but changed my mind as I spoke. It might be a useful thing to try. He wasn't forcing the issue, just bribing me.

"I'll give it some thought, okay? No promises."

His whole demeanour changed. The desperation left him immediately.

"Enjoy, nice to see you, take care." He took a step

towards the door.

"Just a minute, give me your number." It felt wrong asking for that. I wasn't interested in him. God knows I didn't want *that* after everything I had done to myself over him. That was for masochists. But letting him go with no way of getting in touch might not be smart. I prayed I wasn't kidding myself, secretly hoping for something more with the dickhead.

"How can I give you the ring if I don't know how to get hold of you?"

He was shifty, told me I couldn't call him, but I got the phone number. I couldn't test it because who knew where my mobile was, but a scribbled number was as good as I could do in my undressed state.

He escaped and I went back to the bag of booty. I picked up the ring again and gazed into its red hue. I was uneasy—unsure of the stone's provenance and intrigued and attracted to the ring. I threw it and the whole lot back in the bag, herbs and all, tucked it closed and shoved it in the back of my wardrobe under my towels. If they were stolen from somewhere it would be better to split the sack up and use some of the items. No-one could prove a thing then.

God! What was I thinking? Just like when I was his girlfriend, colluding on stupid pranks and preoccupations. I hated my mind sometimes.

I went back to the bathroom, locked the door and sat

in the tub, considering events. Considering Caleb. A 'good witch'. The stupid, warm feeling I got from that pissed me off. Why did his opinion of me still matter? I wasn't any kind of witch, not really. Wasn't sure I ever had been. I wondered if his dead gran had told him to find me and hoped she wouldn't now chase me to get the ring back.

My unintentionally devastating contribution to the confusion of our strife had been to tell him at the height of our fall out that I'd cursed him and Olivia. Cue the disintegration of their lives—but nothing to do with me, despite my big mouth. I had no intention of wickedness, no idea how to cast a hex—I only knew about Wicca in those days, with its rules around what you could and couldn't do to others. But my righteous anger had let me justify using his natural paranoia to terrify him. Even though he'd ghosted me, I had known he would live in fear, psychology over magic for once.

When I'd first met him, he believed he was on the run from the Freemasons, hounded every night in his dreams. By the time he dumped me, I knew he went through phases of feeling persecuted. My angry claim sent him back over the edge into a downwards spiral and eventually terrified the daylights out of Olivia, hence her appearance on my doorstep threatening to call the police.

And now here he was, wanting me to find his ring as if he'd never accused me of trying to destroy his life. Needing my help so much he'd possibly nicked a load of magical supplies and jewellery and brought them to entice me. And I'd almost fallen for it.

I didn't have to do a thing.

I relaxed.

6. Debrief

I awoke in the middle of the night at the witching hour, the glistening moon through my window. The Goddess didn't show up until well after midnight on my side of the house and she had begun to dip towards the top of the wall. I wasn't sleepy at all. Wide awake but peaceful. Nothing to show for why I was conscious, unless it was the moonlight. Entirely feasible, given the illumination in my room.

I relaxed myself back down into sleep mode, keeping out the draughts under the covers. As I stared up at the ceiling, I heard a rustle. And another. The tiniest of noises, almost less than a mouse might make. Paper on paper, or plastic bag on paper. I listened hard, ready to locate the sound when it came.

Nothing. No hint of any creature moving about in the room.

I held my breath till my heart pounded too loudly to hear anything external to my head. I softly expelled the air, ears still straining, but the old house was silent and strong around me. It had seen many things and there was nothing to see right now.

The moonlight fell on my face as I turned over and settled under my duvet again. Just as I was dropping off, the rustle came again. It reminded me of a friend's pet tarantula I once looked after. She had liked the waste paper bin.

I grounded and felt outwards, searching for some kind of presence in the room. A tarantula would be a real surprise but there might be a spider of some kind. My spider sense was pretty good, usually.

Something lurked. Not the spiky impression of a spider, but large. Gigantic, even. It had a deep vibrational hum, not a sound—a vibration.

Everything—real world and ether—has its own hum. I don't know why, or how it works, just that it does. Something to do with beings—whether living or dead—vibrating at different frequencies. This one felt so large. As if it surrounded the whole room, ceiling and walls. A presence of massive proportions. Heavy, but not exactly oppressive. I couldn't pinpoint more than its deep-pitched metaphysical hum.

I lifted my head to look into the room again and a tiny midgie screamed past my ear. The gnat flew so close I started and flailed my free arm around to discourage it. I sank back into my bed and wrapped my duvet around me.

I fell asleep before my heart slowed to resting pace.

I rang Molly at eight in the morning, half-wondering if she would act like she didn't know what I was talking about. She could have sleepwalked her way to the pub, rescued me, spoken to the police and gone home again without waking up. Right. Or maybe she woke up but just winged it. Either of those would explain the PJs.

"Hello my lovely, how are you doing?" Her chirpy voice immediately allayed my worries.

"I thought it might be nice to meet up for coffee."

"Got something to tell me?" she asked, still upbeat. I thought she must be smiling at the other end.

"I don't think so." I didn't exactly know why I was ringing her. Needed to get my conscience clear and tell her what I'd told the police. "A debrief though, I could do with that. I'm not honestly sure what happened the other night." Chatting about what happened in the cold light of a different day might help make sense of the bizarre events.

"Of course you do," she said sympathetically. "Anyone would. Why don't we get a cappuccino at BigBean when you finish work today?"

Seemed legit. "Sounds great." It was something to look forward to and having someone else to ruminate with about the situation would be fun.

"It's my treat," she said warmly.

⁓

As I left for work, I noticed Indira's handbag on the breakfast bar. Home but not up for work. Maybe she'd changed shifts now. I hoped she was okay and located my dead phone at the bottom of my own bag. I grabbed Caleb's number scrap and tucked it into my purse to input later.

I'd almost closed the flat door when a thought occurred to me. I stepped back inside our hallway and felt outwards again. Nothing. I went to the living room and tried it there. I could sense Indira faintly in the next room. I went back to my bedroom, stood in the doorway and did the same thing.

There it was. The presence was still there, centred on my room. Wrapped around it. I wished I wasn't so blind on the astral plane. Some energies I could almost see, like the earth's energies I poured into the protective salt in my bath and occasionally my own aura, but when it came to entities, I had no clue what I was looking at. Like feeling in the dark.

I headed for my bus at a run. There weren't enough hours in the day to be spiritual *and* physical.

I ran up the steps and into BigBean, where Molly waved from her post near the door.

"Thought I'd better keep an eye out for you, in case you got away." She winked and her pretty beaded earrings jiggled.

"Who are you, the police?" I asked, uneasy, my joke awkward. For a panicked second, this meeting felt like yet another internet date.

"That's me, Detective Blue." She grinned. "What are you having?" Her upbeat ease dispelled my fears and I dodged a couple of people with take-outs and took my place at the end of the queue.

BigBean was heaving with people who had beetled out of work for a blessed Wednesday evening bunk-off. Normally it was dead mid-week. I wondered if there was some event I had missed. I wasn't keen on crowds anyway.

We loaded up on cappuccinos, fudge cake and weird caramel mug-melt wafers and headed for a tiny table between two sofas. Squeezed in there, we were shielded from the noise of the bustling crowd. Remarkably shielded. It was eerie how the 'walls' of the sofas and the back wall of the café muffled everything.

Molly pushed a huge slice of cake towards me and offered me a spoon.

"Where do you want to start, love?" she asked. "It's up to you."

She felt knowledgeable to me. She knew things I didn't, that much was certain. I cleared my throat. "So, how did you know I was in trouble?" Might as well start with the hard stuff.

Molly picked up her own spoon and smiled sagely. "Your granddad, what was he, some kind of Indian prince?"

"I don't know a lot about my family." It did sound more like my great-grandfather. My grandfather had lived in England and wore a hat. Sometimes he wore a fez.

She nodded. "Well I've seen him around on and off for a few months now. I haven't been listening to him. You can't listen to them all. But on Sunday night he stood in front of me from about seven o'clock." She took a sip of her coffee. "Ridiculous! Couldn't get a thing done."

I had a vision of her opening a cupboard under her sink and my illustrious great-grandfather leering out from the darkness.

"How do you see him?"

"He's just there," she said easily, tucking into her cake. "Like you or me, love."

"What, like that old TV series, Randall and Hopkins?"

"Randall and Hopkirk, Deceased," she corrected me. "Yes, but it's not just one, there's loads of them."

I processed that slowly. Molly had the sight I wished I had.

"How did you know what to do?"

She paused and gave me a slight frown. "He told me. When I listen, I can hear them. Don't want to hear them all the time, though, there's all kinds of screams and racket." She carried on eating. "Never get anything done listening to that lot."

"So you're a medium?"

She shook her head. "It's not something I do, I'm just me." She poked the cake with her spoon. "And them. I'm a Reiki master, but honestly it's not worth the hassle most of the time." She looked right at me. "Reiki changes your life, chucks everything into the air. I just can't face it sometimes."

I finished my cake and washed it down with coffee, considering everything. There was me this morning, wishing I could see the presence I sensed in my room and here was a lady in the afternoon, telling me she can probably see it.

"What else can you see, is it just ghosts?" I didn't have a full understanding of how the spirit world worked, to be honest. Didn't have a lot of contact with astral beings, beyond my unidentified guides who influenced my thoughts occasionally but never appeared. I suspected the problem was mine, not theirs.

Molly sat back in her seat and wiped her mouth on her

napkin.

"There are more things in heaven and earth, Horatio." Her eyes twinkled at me again and I smiled as I recognised the line. Molly didn't seem a likely Shakespearian scholar, but Hamlet was appropriate.

"All kinds of weirdness out there?" I hazarded.

She dug about in her purse and pulled out a torn and folded piece of paper.

"It's not just all the nasties that are out there on the astral plane. Look what I found in the *MetroPolis* of all places today."

Woman Fed Dead Skin to her Room-mates

A woman is accused of scraping dead skin, presumably from her feet, and adding it to hot chocolate, which she then provided to her room-mates.

Arrested by police, Jenny Squalz of Albion, Indiana, was charged with the weird crime which constitutes second-degree assault on her friends, Kathryn Sabbot and Janey Davies Hunter.

The 27-year-old Squalz attempted to console Sabbot, who had just broken up with her boyfriend, with hot chocolate, according to the Albion Gazette Online. Sabbot gave her drink to Hunter who then choked on the beverage, bringing up shreds of what appeared to be human skin.

Sabbot then tasted the drink and court papers say she vomited into a sink as a result.

Police were told Squalz had an obsession with folk remedies and was only trying to help Sabbot who was one of her only friends.

An official report by Albion's Sheriff Deputy Anton Jamieson states: 'Sarah P. Squalz, 27, was jailed Wednesday in lieu of 10 percent of $15,000 (£7,250) bond due to food contamination and committing a second-degree assault on Janey Davies Hunter and Kathryn Sabbot at their residence on Ten Mile Road during the incident Friday.'

I gagged. There was no other natural reaction.

"What is that? Ugh. Why would someone do that?" My undigested cake waved hello from the pit of my stomach.

Molly's grin was wicked. "Magic, that's what that was meant to be. That's what she was doing. Scraping bits of her feet into someone's food, disgusting, but some idea she'll have picked up from the Internet. Probably did it wrong." She pulled her coffee towards her as I tried not to retch. "Ordinary people in all walks of life use magic. They get it off the internet. You've got to keep a lookout."

I suddenly remembered why we were here.

"So did you know what was going to happen before it did?"

"Well I didn't expect to hit someone with a rock!" She laughed out loud and took another swig. "It's just funny how things turn out sometimes." She looked secretive. "Just think. If he'd walked over to your house instead of driving over, we'd have arrived first and none of that would have happened. I got to the pub in time to see him leave, so we couldn't have made it home quicker."

That tickled me. "Isn't that victim blaming? He drove so he deserved it?"

She shrugged. "He was a nasty piece of work. He attacked you. He deserved what he got. Probably would have smashed his way in if we'd beaten him there."

That chilled me. Indira would have been terrified and angry. She would have been alone. Might have done something brave and stupid.

Molly sipped her coffee and pulled a face at its bitterness.

"How long had you known him?" She reached for the sugar.

"About two seconds! He took me out a couple of times and then hit me with the visitation on Saturday night while I was asleep." She'd already known about that on the night.

She nodded. "You didn't tell that policeman any of that though, did you?"

I flushed, actually felt my face go hot. That was rare. "I didn't think he'd understand."

"I knew you didn't. Don't worry kid, it'll all come out in the wash. You'll wish you'd told him everything by the time it's all done and dusted. Would have been easier to do it from the start."

I fiddled with my cup for a while, feeling sheepish. "Why do you think that?"

"Just a feeling I've got. People surprise you."

"The sergeant figured me out anyway. He interviewed the guy who told him he'd taken me out a couple of times and I'd invited him back and bashed him on the head."

She added a brown sugar cube to her coffee and stirred it in. "He's a liar and a sneak. Disgusting. Very bad behaviour. Shouldn't be allowed. Can't rely on the law though."

"Do you think he—?" I didn't want to say it. "Did something to me?"

I'd been invaded a few times. Waking up from a drunken stupor and feeling sore. Waking up while it was happening, not knowing what was going on. High on drugs and not knowing how to say no without causing a horrific fight. Not being able to throw the guy out because he just wouldn't leave and the police wouldn't care. I knew how it could feel in real life, but the ether was a whole different concept I was only beginning to get my head around.

She shook her head confidently, brown curls bobbing.

"Didn't have time. Don't worry about that. Though I don't see much protection round you. You want to think about raising a couple of shields to hide you."

"Can I use violet light?" As a spiritual resource, violet light has the highest vibrational frequency. My hair was this colour for years.

She nodded thoughtfully. "Don't forget, your protection has to be stronger than the force that comes against you. Bubbles of light won't cut it if someone really wants to hammer you."

"Not even if I blast them with it?"

She smiled. "Are you talking about a bubble of light, or some kind of laser beam?"

I shrugged. "I pull up the energy from the earth and draw a violet beam down from the sky through my crown. I gather it in my centre and then direct it to where I need it to go."

"So if you blow it outwards from your centre, you can create a shield?"

I nodded. I did that when I went to the supermarket and when I felt uneasy walking somewhere.

"What else do you use it for?"

I dodged her eye contact, like I had been using the light for nefarious means.

"Sometimes I fire it at people who are behaving really badly."

To my relief, she grinned. "Like a weapon? *Pow-pow!*"

"No!" She made me laugh but that wasn't the idea at all. "It's supposed to convert darkness into light. Negative nasty crap is driven out by it. You can add different vibrations to it, like silver for healing or diamond for demons or addiction, that kind of thing." Whether or not my manifestation of the light was up to fighting magic on a major scale was entirely down to me.

Serious again, she nodded. "Use it, by all means, but just remember, when you shine a bright light, you attract everything. All the moths and little creatures of darkness, everything comes to the light. If you don't protect yourself with a few different layers, you'll pick up all kinds of horrid." She finished her coffee. "Not to mention that nasty piece of work when he comes out of hospital."

I sincerely hoped he would stay in hospital as long as it took. Something else was bugging me, but I wasn't sure how to articulate it. I puzzled over it as I drank the dregs of my coffee.

"Why did you really help me?"

She looked quizzical. "How do you mean?"

"Even if my ancestors were bothering you, how come you're so nice to me?"

It wasn't that people weren't nice to me. They often were, although sometimes it was a tough-love kind of nice. Indira was a case in point. But mostly no-one offered anything without expecting something in return.

She smiled serenely. "You'd be surprised what the spirits say about you, dear. Hang on in there, we'll get you sorted."

I didn't know how to answer that.

We stood up to go and I noticed the cafe had become properly crowded. A swathe of people talking in the middle of the room appeared to be the queue for the counter.

A group pushed past, just as I heard a familiar peal of laughter. I snapped around to see the back of a black girl with brightly beaded braiding.

"Leah!"

She turned and I could see she was on her phone. She immediately waved her Minku clutch bag at me and finished her call. With a smile she pushed through the throng for the briefest of hugs and blew a kiss over my shoulder.

"Smashed the interview! Don't know if I got it though. They're gonna let me know tomorrow," she announced. "Typical small company shit. If they give the job to some posh white boy, I'm going to quit. I'm not working with that shit."

"You out with Jez?" I was still hopeful she had time to spend with me.

"Joker decided to work late. Like it's every day." She turned away and surveyed the crowd behind. "Said he'd try and meet me here, but there's no chance. Time to head home, I'm way too hungry to wait. You going to the bus stop?"

"Give me five minutes, I just need to finish up here." I realised I was being rude. "This is Molly," I dragged back her attention to my new friend.

Leah peered at Molly and went straight into mega-polite mode.

"How do you do, Molly." They shook as daintily as two full-size humans could.

Leah looked across the cafe and stepped away, but leaned back towards me. "Can I just have a quick word?"

I stepped into the fray, buffeted by people moving past and blasted by the roar of the crowd as everyone talked over each other. The difference between that and our quiet haven behind the chairs was immeasurable.

Concern shone in Leah's eyes. "You sure she's good people?" she asked.

"She saved my life," I said, defensive on Molly's behalf. Leah didn't know her at all.

"Oh jeez, I don't think I want to know." She shrugged, "I thought I saw a kind of—shadow—around her." She examined my face. "Go on then, I do want to know. What did she save your life from?"

"Just don't even ask," I conceded. "I didn't know you saw things."

"Yes you did." Actually, she was right. She didn't see stuff all the time like Molly, but she did sense weirdness. I hadn't realised she saw things right then and there though.

I turned back to Molly who had sat back down, waiting

for me. She handed me my coat from behind her chair.

"So what's next for you, chicken?" She was bright and friendly and I felt like I'd known her my whole life. I wished Leah hadn't seen something strange. I liked Molly a lot. I would reserve judgment until something she did troubled me.

"Home, work tomorrow and hopefully get life back to normal," I said. "I had an unwanted visitor the last two nights, too, an ex."

She looked concerned. "Another visitation?"

I fiddled with the zip on my bag and tried not to say too much.

"A real life pain in the arse." That plastic bag of goodies troubled me. Caleb never gave me anything with no strings attached, no matter what he said. "I'll let you know how it goes."

"Same time next week?" she asked.

I felt pleased. It was so nice to meet a new friend, especially one I could talk weird shit with. Indira did her best most of the time and sometimes used stories about Islam she remembered from childhood to make connections with the spiritual stuff I said, but spiritual development was one thing, magical practice another. That, she didn't like. Leah knew about magic, but she wasn't at all keen on it. Her gran was a rootworker and had put the fear into her grandchildren about using magic, so Leah definitely didn't like to encourage me.

Molly was a fun new experience. It just went to show, something or someone new was always around the corner.

I waved goodbye to Molly and waited for Leah who was on the phone again, earbuds firmly jammed in. She finished her call and followed me through the bedlam and down the steps into the weather. The rain whipped around our faces and blew our words away.

"He's such a joker, he never does anything I want him to."

I said nothing to that. She would only defend him if I agreed, I'd learned that with most people through experience.

"So how did it really go?" The interview was everything she'd been hoping for during months of being torn about boredom, wanting to leave, but needing something better to work up to.

"No fucking idea. Could be playing me. They know the way I work. They know they can trust me. I don't know if they're dumb enough to put their trust in someone they don't know, or to push through and develop me the way they know I can go."

"Why wouldn't they?"

We stood at the crossing at the top of The Headrow and waited for the lights.

"Well put it this way, every white male manager available was on the panel. Dunno what they did with Ms

Human Resources, just one of her lackeys instead. Everyone always hires people like them."

"Racism but not provable?"

"Fact of life, babe. Racism, sexism, it's all interconnected. They'll kid themselves that the other guy was better qualified or had more experience, or that the team won't work well for a recently qualified, young engineer, but there's no excuses. They don't hire me for this, I'm gone. It's up to them." She could work anywhere for anyone. I'd never known her out of work the whole time we'd been friends.

"What was your selling point?"

She grinned. "Pulled a fast one on them. They had to write it down. Asked me what my management style was." She pulled open the door to The Light shopping centre and let me into the foyer. "Told them I'm a conduit. I open the right channels and let the energies flow the way I need them to. People like to work for me like liquids like to flow for me."

Her flash of inspiration was surely the best thing I'd heard all day. I wished—not for the first time—that I had control of my mouth the way she did. "You fucking smoothie."

She flashed a smile, nothing more, and we strode through the mall, dodging school kids queuing at the Vue Cinema for the latest Marvel film and exited the other side, a little less wet for the detour.

As we hit the street on the other side and waited in the

crowd at the crossing, she nudged me. "So how did your trip to the police station go? Didn't get arrested?"

"Oh god, I nearly did."

"No way, what did you do?"

"That guy I was seeing, he tried to attack me on Sunday night, but Molly bashed his head in with a rock."

Incredulity poured out of her. "Not that dude with the charity? I thought you got shot of him."

I groaned inwardly. I was in for a lecture. She was as bad as Indira. "He came to me in my sleep, tried to assault me."

"In your sleep?"

"Like a visitation. He lay on top of me and it was only because I woke up just then that I knew what he'd done."

"Like for real or in a dream?"

We pushed through the people on the other side of the road, avoiding eye-defying brollies and walked down Merrion Street.

"Like a dream, but for real." The wind blew my hair across my face as we walked past the churchyard.

"Magic?" She grabbed my arm and looked at me intently.

I nodded, glumly. I knew what was coming next.

"I wish you'd stay away from that shit, Inayat. You're going to end up dead or separated from your body or something."

I let the defensiveness rise a little, but it wouldn't do me any good.

"It wasn't me doing it. He was lying on top of me and then I woke up and pushed him away and he wasn't there. I didn't do anything." Why did everyone always blame me?

"Did he know you were into that kind of thing?"

We turned the corner towards the bus stops on New Briggate, finally shielded from the rain a little by the buildings and she pulled me to the side out of the way of two men pushing a huge trolley filled with rapidly soggy cardboard boxes.

"I might have said I was interested in it."

"If you tell them and they're into it, they're always going to try it on you. You're a challenge."

"I didn't know he was into it."

"That's because not everyone's got a massive mouth like you. Why do you have to tell people? Even I know you're supposed to keep it a secret."

I hated myself again. I knew the rules, but I still opened my gob. Constantly looking for a way in to people, I supposed. She was right and she knew it. To be fair, her gran operated a pretty tight ship and Leah knew plenty of things about magic that made her stay away from it.

Her bus was already there. We waited in the queue,

filing forwards one step at a time, quiet now, while I worried about how I hadn't told her about Caleb yet. That was going to be a much longer conversation.

She nudged me. "We gonna get together for a night out?"

I wanted that so bad, but I couldn't realistically see it happening for a while. "No money, none at all for a few weeks. Every bloody penny is going on bills at the moment." If it wasn't for Indira I'd be going hungry, given my payments back to the bank at the present time on my meagre weekly wage.

"I'm off for the rest of the week. Lunch on Monday? If I'm still in a job!" She grinned. "You can manage a sandwich in City Square!" Her work HQ was on the edge of the city centre and Monday was admin day.

She got on to the bus and showed her ticket to the driver. As she went up the stairs, I gave her the thumbs up for Monday, glad to be back around her. She energised me, even as she bollocked me for fucking about with magic. It wasn't fair, though. Everyone said it was all my fault. Well, everyone except Molly. It was my fault, for letting on more than I should, but I hadn't been dabbling in anything. Hadn't touched magic proper for months. Longer. Not that anyone believed me.

7. Unexpected Shackles

The rain got the best of me between the bus and the house. Gledhow Wood Road was a stinker of a hill, especially with ice rain whipped into the eyes. I lost a layer of epidermis from my face by the time I made it to the front door. The weather blew me into the porch and I trudged through the hallways straight into the living room trailing waterlogged footprints behind me. Indira glanced up from serving dinner.

"Hold on, hun, don't move! I'll get you a towel." She dropped the slice of chicken on the plate and dashed round the counter towards my bedroom. She wouldn't be able to find it. My room was way beyond her threshold of mess.

Her muffled voice drifted from inside my closet-sized room.

"Erm...I can't even see a towel in here." Out popped her

head. "Is there one in the bathroom?"

"They're folded up at the bottom of the wardrobe." My room was the size of a packing box, so I had to be canny in some ways. The overall impression was that I'd been burgled, but I knew where the essential things were.

Surprised noises emerged as she dug around in the bottom of the wardrobe and I remembered too late what else was in there.

"Ooh," she said, as she emerged with towels and a large plastic bag. "What's this?"

My inner self shook its head with regret. Indira could sense jewellery from a hundred paces, my little Leo. She loved it, even though she didn't wear it on a daily basis—cheffing always came first. True to her star sign in all its positive ways—unlike Caleb—she had a great eye for it, so sometimes bought it on occasional visits to Dhaka and sold it on when she came home.

She threw me the towel and sat down on the sofa, my half-plated dinner cooling on the side. "Do you mind if I have a little look?"

I dried my hair and took all my clothes off where I stood. I was wet through to my knickers. "Why don't we look on the table while we eat?"

She put the bag on the table and flashed me a dazzling-but-meaningful smile. "We can look afterwards."

I wiggled my eyebrows mysteriously at her and headed for my bedroom to change. "I'll tell you all about them over dinner."

—✍—

"Where do you think he got them from?" Indira's eyes were as wide as they could get. "He's not a burglar, is he?"

I cast my mind back to the time when Caleb had borrowed a pair of washing-up gloves and crept around outside the home of a man who we believed had robbed us. And another time when he turned up on the doorstep at seven a.m. clutching a computer and software acquired from the home of a man who owed me money for a job. Funnily enough, I never got to keep the gear.

"I'm sure he's just done some deal with someone, that's all." I forced a reassuring smile. "He hangs with the types of people who own witchy shops. I'm sure it's probably someone with a magic shop who's done a deal with him."

I was labouring the point too much. If I truly thought that, why did I still feel anxious about the gift? How many times did I need to say "I'm sure" before I convinced myself?

Indira held her concerned look for a moment. Then she brightened.

"Can I try a couple of pieces on?" Her enthusiasm couldn't be squashed even by dodgy provenance.

I acquiesced and sat back in my chair. She bubbled over with enthusiasm, touching a few pieces with sounds of appreciation. The garnet ring appeared in her fingers and she held it up to the light.

"Nice colour and no flaw in it. Is it a garnet?" It flashed as she glanced at me. I nodded, though I didn't know. "Nice silver work too." She wriggled her finger into the shank and slipped the ring over the main joint. "Ooh, weird." She frowned as she fiddled with the ring. "It's like it tightened."

"What?" Rings didn't tighten. "That sounds like a bad line from a customer in a jewellers. Can you take it off?"

"I'm not joking, babe." She twisted the ring on her finger but it didn't come off. "It's not coming off."

Her finger looked the same as the other one. Seeds of doubt sprung up in my heart, but she reached out and gave me her hand, so I fiddled with the ring myself. She was as genuine as ever. It turned stiffly, too much friction. Dangerously tight.

"Has it cut off your blood supply? How did you get it stuck on your forefinger?" All my rings fell off my forefinger. I didn't wear them on that one any more.

Indira shot me a furious glance. "That finger was closest to the ring size. It was *too big*. My finger must have swelled. Maybe I'm allergic. Is it really silver?"

I didn't know. Looked like silver.

Panicked, she went to the kitchen sink and dribbled

dish-washing liquid on the ring. It twisted round her finger but would not slide. She compared it with her other hand. The be-ringed finger looked a little more pudgy, but only because the ring constricted the flesh.

"I did wallop this hand yesterday at work," she said critically. "That finger joint looks a bit thicker than the other one. I'll give you some money for it, hun." I inwardly rolled my eyes. She didn't hold back from generosities, but she never spent more money than she had to.

"I hope you don't bump into the owner," I blurted. I didn't know why I said that. Frightening her wouldn't help.

She flinched. "Thought you said it didn't have an owner."

I picked up my phone which was unusually alive. The charger at work had sorted me out.

"Let me check Google, I don't know what garnets are worth."

"Is it definitely a garnet, hun?" Indira reached for her purse.

"That's what he said," I lied. I wasn't selling anything on for less than the best worth possible. Indira wouldn't, even to me. My eyes fell on a couple of listings similar to the one imprisoning Indira's finger. "You're talking about forty quid." She wouldn't want to pay that. Not for a ring she hadn't planned on buying. "Why don't you wear it for a day or two? It might come off when you wake up in the morning.

Indira was clearly relieved. "Aren't our bodies less swelled up in the morning than the evening?"

I hoped so for both our sakes. Rings that tightened by themselves were definitely not normal. Indira might have still been rationalising, but my mind was already running over the alternative possibilities.

We sorted through a few other items, but Indira didn't ask to try any more on, though she fiddled with the garnet ring continually. A filigree-style wire cuff shone invitingly amongst a few pendants made of transfixing crystals. And a pair of mesmerising amber earrings winked at me. Their twisted wire drew my eyes to follow it round and round until I had to force myself to look away.

I pushed all the pieces together in a pile.

"I wish I was sure about where it's all come from. The only places I've seen jewellery and magical supplies together like this is in witchy shops." I popped them one at a time back into the plastic bag in silence. "I don't need anyone coming after me."

Indira swayed slightly. "How will they do that?" She twisted the ring more urgently, examining every smooth surface. She said in a small voice, "Are you talking about weird shit again?"

I didn't know, but she looked scared. I couldn't give

her an attempt at a magical explanation, that would only make it worse, especially as I didn't have a clue what had actually occurred. "We'll go to a jeweller's and get it cut off if it doesn't come off in a day or so."

Her eyes were so huge they made the rest of her look tiny. "They can't do the scary stuff if you don't believe it, right?"

To my surprise, I realised she *did* believe it and anyway, yes they could.

"I've never heard of a magical ring in real life. Don't worry about it, you'll be fine." I dusted off her fears with a matter-of-fact tone. "Just get the bloody thing off if you can."

I couldn't let her get any more upset. It wasn't responsible. I didn't even know how to find out about a magical ring. Who would know about something like this?

Caleb.

I was trapped in a god-damn fairy tale. An old one, with monsters, not the sanitised kind.

I went to meet Caleb after work the next day. As I sat on the benches in Millennium Square near my office in Leeds General Infirmary, I watched the pigeons as they fought over an upside-down carton of chips. Two of them openly fought over one miserable, road scuffed potato chip, jabbing alternately at the food and each other. Right next to them a scrawny bird stood on top of the pile of chips and polystyrene, pecking away to his heart's content.

Caleb skulked up to my bench and sat at the other end, hunched away from me. His behaviour stung me. "I'm not talking to your back, Caleb."

He turned around, still hunched over. "We can't meet here," he muttered. "Give me a thirty-second start."

Head down, he strode off across the square in a straight line, kicking the pigeons' chips out of his path. The birds scattered but settled nearby, keeping an eye on the food as I set off at more of a meander.

He crossed Great George Street and took a left along the pavement, disappearing down the steps into The Crypt pub. Dark and dingy, a good place for vampires to hide during the day. Also for me and Leah on a better day. Speaking of whom, she was going to kill me if she saw me with Caleb. I hoped we wouldn't bump into her.

The door was still swinging when I got to it. I pushed through into the bar and saw Caleb's boots disappear into a booth.

I slid in on the opposite side from him. "Did you get a drink?"

He smiled sleazily and cocked his head from side to side. "Guinness, Guinness, good for the heart, the more you drink, the more you sh—"

I left for the bar. God, he annoyed me. Forced his way into my life again, only to mess me about so I didn't know what was going on. The pattern was perfectly clear. I could see this coming. I thought back to my therapy sessions. I could avoid the strife by remembering that he didn't give a shit about me. I had nothing to prove and certainly not that I was a nice person. My first glass of wine went down too easily while I waited for the Guinness to settle, so I bought another and walked the glasses back to the booth where Caleb examined the menu.

I put the pint in front of him with a thud. "I'm not buying you dinner as well."

He didn't even look at me, running his finger slowly down the menu.

"Want a burger? My call." He carried on, engrossed. "Might have a burger."

"Where've *you* got money from?" I bit my tongue too late. What I wanted to know, he didn't want to tell me. I would have to be more cunning than a brick through a window.

"Shut up," he said comfortably. "I have money."

"Never your own. Where's this money come from?"

He got up to go to the bar and smirked. "It magically appeared in my hands. Do you want a burger?"

I stared at him. Bright blue glinted at me through dark lashes, laconic but crafty as ever. I nodded. A free burger was a free burger, even if it was bought with blood money. As I watched him amble to the bar, I pushed my second thoughts away.

I sat back in my seat and drank semi-cold Pinot Grigio, but drifted back to Caleb in the flat, the stock pot boiling over. My hackles rose. No joke, the stock pot was my clue. He'd turned the heat up. I was such a fool.

My idiocy loomed in, darkly oppressive and nausea swished around my belly. The maybe-missing house key. No 'maybe' about it. Tears pricked my eyes as panic threatened to overwhelm me and I blinked them away as Caleb turned around to come back.

He slid into the booth and stared at me under his eyelashes. "What's the matter now?"

My eyes were so wide I thought my eyelids would stick. I couldn't hide from my fears and he knew me too well anyway. Fuck it. I pushed anger in front of fear and leaned past my wine glass.

"Did you take a key from my attacker's bunch the other night?" I scoured every part of his face, looking for a flicker of muscle, a hint that he was hiding something.

"You what?" His eyes, to his credit, were completely blank. "Why do you keep making out like I'm a thief, Inayat?"

"Because you are one. I know what you're like. Are you sure you didn't do it?" I had to play angry ex-girlfriend. I didn't have any other mode for Caleb.

His eyes maintained their blankness as he shrugged. "If that's what you think, that's pretty sad. We had some okay times."

"No we didn't. It was all totally crap." Our burgers arrived with bright yellow chips and onion rings on the side. I tucked into mine immediately, still not convinced.

Psychic information can be hard to weigh up. It often comes to you bit by bit and you're led to what you need, not told, so being able to tell the difference between a useful download and your own thoughts isn't as clear as you might think for beginners. Knowing how lower and higher vibrations feel to you is the most useful thing you can learn.

I lacked conviction on every level. Maybe this information was my imagination. I was still bitter about Caleb and me, he had been such a waste of time. Nothing changed. I put down my burger.

"Caleb, where did you get the bag of loot?"

"I told you, it doesn't matter."

"There's a magical ring in the bag." The words blurted out by themselves and tears pricked my eyes again.

He stopped eating and his eyes flickered around my face. "What kind of magical?"

"The kind where someone puts the ring on and it tightens so they can't get it off."

He smiled as he checked out my hands with their absence of jewellery.

"Pretty little Indira," he guessed. "Is it the only one?"

"A lot of the jewellery pieces felt enchanted. Really...mesmerising."

He took another bite. "No-one told me about that."

"When?" It was the first time he'd mentioned someone else with regards to the bag. If that was the truth, it would have already come up.

"I bought them, didn't I? Knock off. Might have been pricier if they'd known they were magical."

For one agonising moment, I doubted myself, but his smile quickly became a smirk, as icy as ever. He wasn't telling the truth. He needed something to replace the idea he'd nicked the gear.

I leaned in. "What the fuck am I going to do about it? Indira's got her finger trapped and I've got a sack of scary jewellery."

He laughed. "No point asking me. Sell 'em, silly bitch. You know that's all I'll say. Give 'em away. I don't care what you do."

"You never fucking did."

He snapped, "I don't care, Inayat," but stopped and looked at me directly, now solemn. "I can ask my lass if she wants one. She's in a little coven in town. Maybe she'll get some orders."

My face rushed with heat and the ground fell away a little.

"I'll be fine," I said stiffly. "We'll cut the ring off if we have to."

I piped down and focused on my burger. I didn't know how to process the information that he was with someone. Hadn't realised it still mattered, because the possibility hadn't even occurred to me for a moment.

We managed the rest of the meal without a fight and finished our drinks. David's key pestered me and as I put my coat on, I dove straight back in.

"Caleb, you promise you didn't rob David's house, right?" I had less to lose than before our conversation.

He didn't flicker, his stare dead straight as though he thought that would convince me he told the truth. "No."

He was so hard to follow, exhaustion overcame me. "No what?"

"No, I didn't rob his house. I bought the fucking things."

His hurt expression begged for sympathy but I didn't fall for it. The only advantage Caleb had in life was his gift for sculpture, but his chaotic behaviour dispensed with any privilege his art might have given him. He didn't need sympathy. He needed a leg up in life and took every opportunity to achieve that.

"Who from?"

Now he was defensive. His eyes flashed once and his lids lowered again, hiding something. "You don't need to know. You just don't, okay?"

I shrugged anyway. "Okay, I believe you." I didn't.

He sarcastically semi-bowed at me and whisked his way up the steps and into the darkness of the outside streets.

I put my gloves on and wrapped up warm, thinking.

He was a cunning bastard. Trickery was his game, no matter what the situation. Turning up the stock pot and creating a distraction was child's play. He must have easily had time to remove the key from the ring in my handbag.

As I ran up the stone steps, a large carrion crow landed on the railings. It turned and gave me a lazy caw as I passed through the gate. I stopped and acknowledged its presence, but it took to the pavement with a single flap of its wings and ignored me.

～✦～

When I got home, Indira was still out. I lit the flat up with every lamp and light and put the TV on low. As I poured boiling water into a pot of tea, I heard a key in the flat door. Someone came in and shut the door. I heard sniffing and gentle whimpering. My heart dropped into free-fall.

"Indira?"

She took a deep intake of breath.

"Oh my god, Inayat, I was attacked." She sounded like a little girl, breathy and high pitched.

I threw the kettle back into its stand and ran towards the hallway. Indira appeared in the door, bedraggled and filthy. I took her by the arm and led her in. "Babe, what happened to you?"

Indira wept great big tears. "I was so frightened, I thought I was going to die."

8. Indira's Story

Indira got off the bus at the bottom of Gledhow Wood Road. Two scruffy white men in grey overalls got off ahead of her. One of them had a bicycle. They headed up Roundhay Road in the opposite direction and she thought nothing else of them.

She worried about how to get the ring off her finger. It seemed to have got tighter even since yesterday and unless she held her finger straight, the discomfort made it numb. Prepping veg had been a dangerous job all day.

She crossed the road and glanced back at the bus stop. To her surprise, the two men had changed direction and were about to cross to her side.

"Don't be silly, Indira, they're just going into Harehills instead," she said to herself. She remembered a story she'd read in the *Evening Post* about a woman who was raped last week in Roundhay Park. A bit close for comfort. She walked to the first junction that led off the hill to a housing estate and looked behind as she crossed. The men were walking quickly up the hill towards her.

She set off at a run and when she reached the shadow of a bulging rhododendron bush, she spun around. To her horror, one of the men was on her heels, reaching out at her.

She swung her bag of work clothes around at face height and he dodged it.

"Who are you?" she screamed. "I don't know you, who are you? Leave me alone!"

His friend arrived and threw his bike down on the pavement.

"Shut up, bitch, gimme your handbag."

"Fuck off," she yelled, stamping at them. "Help! I don't know you! Go away! Leave me alone!"

The men simultaneously leaned in and got hold of her shoulders. Indira's left arm swung upwards as though it had a life of its own and a red beam of light exploded in her palm. A rush of wind swooped through her body, out of her mouth. She heard herself roar like a djinn, a deep vibration filling her lungs, widening her throat until she felt it would burst open. A bright light passed through her lips and shot into the sky as it knocked her head back, the force as strong as a hundred-mile-an-hour wind. Gasping now for oxygen, breathless and unable to breathe in, she thought she would suffocate, but the tail end of the gust whipped out and she flew ten feet into the gutter instead.

As she wobbily raised herself to her feet, she could see a white branch on the pavement near by. She blinked. An arm, not a branch. A curled-up hand at one end signalled the terrible truth. She dry heaved while someone else sobbed.

One man staggered towards her in a serpentine across the pavement, his shoulder clutched with his remaining hand. The other lay unconscious, his head at an unnatural angle. Indira's stomach retched repeatedly and she took a step towards the walking victim, but his face twisted into a silent scream and he ran away back down the hill without his arm.

Indira stumbled and sobbed in the opposite direction, towards home.

I gently helped Indira get out of her clothes and into her nightie and dressing gown. A cup of tea healed nothing but it felt normal. As she settled under her duvet on the sofa, I put the kettle on, thinking. Her description of what happened baffled me. No bomb or firework would go off without a bang.

"Was it a fire cracker?" I mused out loud. "Did one of them set it off when they were up close to you?"

"There was no bang. It blew right through me, came

out of my mouth. All I could hear was the wind and then nothing." She sipped her tea and nibbled cheap bourbon biscuits. She welled up every few minutes, dabbed her eyes with Kleenex and pretended again she was fine. This, on repeat. She was so strong and resilient and damaged, she didn't deserve to be frightened or thrown about. I hated seeing her like this.

"Did it definitely come from you?" I asked. "Maybe it was your guardian angel."

She finished her biscuit. "I'm Muslim, hun. We don't have guardian angels."

"Aw, everyone has a guardian angel. You don't have to believe in them."

"I don't believe in any of that shit, Inayat. Don't you get a silent hot wind with a bomb sometimes?"

"Do you mean the blast, like a shock wave?"

She had a strange look on her face. "I must have passed out when they attacked me. Hallucinated that stuff. That happens to people when they're scared sometimes doesn't it?" She blew her nose loudly. "Do you think someone came and saved me but ran off before I woke up?"

I didn't think anything of the sort, but I wasn't going there. I encouraged her to bed and once she'd gone, I put out most of the lights and lit a candle. I sat in the semi-darkness, feeling the warmth of the flame on my face as I meditated. For the first time, I felt the presence in my bedroom was now around the whole flat, but it didn't feel as strong.

Indira's incident was completely unexplainable.

"Let me ask my guides, what happened to Indira this evening? What blasted those men?"

Pressure struck me right in the third eye, pulling at my forehead. In my peripheral vision, the light reflected off water at the edge of the breakfast bar, pouring off the corner in a steady, sparkling stream. I turned my head to look, but the bar was just the same as usual, dark green, clean and dry. I looked away again, expecting to still see the water, but the darkness remained. No answers presented themselves.

I closed my eyes and tried to stay as present as possible, but drifted off a little, thinking about the ring. I imagined putting it on my own finger. I wanted that ring back. It had something I needed.

Next morning I got up to find Indira already about and reading a newspaper.

"How are you feeling?" I asked her as I popped two slices of bread into the toaster.

She took a long moment to answer as she munched on toast, scanning the headlines and turning the pages of the paper quickly. When she spoke, her voice was cold. Almost unfriendly.

"Surprisingly well-rested. I'm not going into work today. I rang and told them I was mugged."

I'd never known her miss work for anything. I looked at her hard, but her face was devoid of expression.

She paused in her page turning. "Do you think we'll hear about the men in the news?"

"Not in yesterday's newspaper," I said, recognising my *Evening Post*. The battered face of a local woman looked out from page seven. Her swollen, half-shut eyes seemed to watch me. The upside down headline read *Would-be Rapist's Special Tattoo*. I remembered the story. I'd admired her for making her ordeal public. The tattoo had been in the guy's groin area. The drawing was hard to decipher—some kind of weird star—but the woman had done her best.

"Oh." She closed it and pushed the paper away.

"Are you all right?" I gently prompted her. "It's not every day that weird shit happens to you. It's okay to be upset, you know." Indira was tough, I knew that. But she seemed angry. I wondered uncomfortably if she blamed the mugging on me for some reason.

She didn't look at me. "And that's the problem isn't it?"

I girded my loins. The storm was coming and I had a feeling I deserved it. "Tell me."

She looked at me for the first time. "You really believe the weird shit, don't you?"

Her face was impossible to read. I could tell she was angry, but she wasn't doing the angry face yet. "I've seen it work."

"Worked because you made it work?"

"Worked because either I made it work or I know someone else did something."

"And why do you do it?"

"Do what?"

"The weird shit?"

"Do you mean magic?"

She shot me a filthy look, her fury simmering behind the reasonable tone. "Whatever."

I drew a long, quiet breath and steadied my juddering diaphragm.

"I know you don't believe me, but I haven't done anything proper for ages. Literally years. Not since I was with Caleb. All I ever do is ask an angel for assistance and talk to my spirit guides sometimes."

"But when you do it, why do you do it?"

"When I ask my angels for help?" I dropped her piercing gaze and stared at the counter top. "It's because I feel powerless to sort out the problem in any other way."

"Isn't that just lazy?"

Her words cut me with a knife. I'd asked myself that a million times. But no, it wasn't.

"Magic is for the powerless to have power. It isn't lazy, it's literally when there's no other way. If there's no way at all, the magic doesn't work anyway."

"Right, whatever," she cut me off. "So why don't you just ask God instead?"

The toast popped up and one of the pieces flew onto the counter surface. I picked it up and plopped them both on to the board.

"I don't believe in God." I sounded petulant, even to me. "Well I do, but not the way you mean."

She sat up straighter in her seat. "See, you know I'm not really religious, but there's a story that keeps coming back to me from when I was a kid. It's from one of the Surahs in the Qur'an." She paused and fiddled with the ring still on her finger. "It's called The Spider." She looked at me again and I stared right back at her, though her eyes hurt my head. She dropped her gaze and continued.

"When you put your trust in something other than God or Allah, you're building it on a flimsy basis. Like a spider's web. Magic is a pile of shit and when you meddle with it, you're building some kind of idea of salvation on a pile of stinking crap." She shoved the butter towards me and handed me her knife. I placed it on the counter top. "But I just realised the bit they didn't tell us at Mosque. The worst thing about it is that just like a sticky spider's web, when it falls apart, you take everyone else around you down with you into the shit."

Her words punched me in the stomach with their condemnation. I had no air for a reply, but she continued anyway.

"I don't even believe in it, babe, but I know when something's a bad idea. You're the one messing with this shit and then all of a sudden you're attacked by someone and then more weird shit happens and and now I've been mugged and some kind of monster came out of me and might have killed someone. Sense a pattern at all?" She enunciated every word so crisply, it sounded like a clock ticking. "You're attracting the shit and taking me down with you."

I could have howled with frustration. I wasn't even 'messing with this shit', but on some level, I felt she was right. I'd read that even the smallest amount of magic makes a person into a beacon on the astral plane. Not knowing how to handle the problems that emerge, that was the issue, not whether or not I should use it at all. I took a long breath to ballast myself.

"What kind of monster do you think it was?"

"The fuck I know! It feels like a horrible dream. Oh!" She stopped, mid-sentence, and stared into the distance. "I just remembered my dream. Oh no. Oh, that's not good."

"Tell me," I repeated.

She focused back on me. "I was riding something,

miles high in the sky. I looked down and I'm on a massive snake creature with wings, like a dragon." She filled up with tears. "I was so safe and happy."

She didn't look safe and happy now.

"Why are you upset about that?"

"Dragons aren't exactly good news in Islam, babe." Her tone was so sharp, it bit me. "They're what Allah uses to punish unbelievers after death. I'm not an unbeliever. Why have I been sent a dragon?"

Panicked tears welled again and dripped down her cheeks.

"Do you think it was a dragon that came out of me? I don't want to be tortured by dragons." She grabbed her tissue again.

I tried to think quickly. Dragons weren't necessarily bad. Hell, nothing was automatically bad in magic. Good or bad depended on the person controlling it.

Telling her *that* wasn't going to work. Nothing was going to work. She was starting with a spiritual crisis, saying she didn't believe in it and then asking me if it really happened. I stalled for time.

"What colour was it?"

"Colour?"

"What colour was it in your dream?" I begged my spirit guides to give me the words to reassure her or

146

resolve our problems right now, but I was rapidly losing all faith in my ability to get through this and still have a friend and somewhere to live.

She refocused through the tears. "Like a kind of orange with gold scales and a red jagged spine thing down its back like a steg—a stegosaurus. Copper. Not orange."

The understanding hit me from nowhere. "We need to get that ring off you."

It was my fault after all. Not my involvement with magic, but because I hadn't dealt with Caleb properly, I was now hurting my friends and people I cared about. I didn't know *how* to deal with him. I'd tried to make him go away, but he wouldn't leave me alone. I should have taken the whole lot back to him, never mind asking him where he got it all from. Did I want him to keep coming around? My rational mind didn't want that, but who knew what the hell was going on in my subconscious. I didn't even know any more. I'd been gutted when I realised he was seeing someone. That should have been a sign, maybe.

"The ring?"

The knowledge poured into my mind and I kicked myself for not getting it sooner.

"The ring's the source of the dragon. You haven't been sent a dragon, you're not being punished by God. It's the ring."

"How can it be?"

"It's a magical ring, you need to get rid of it. Get it off."

She started to cry again. I'd never seen her like this. Never thought I'd ever see her weeping from fear. "How do you know?"

"How do I know it's magical? I don't! I never heard of this outside a story! But it tightened on your finger and it's the only thing that's changed for you in the past two days. You wore it, you got mugged, you roared like a monster, you said so yourself and now you're dreaming of dragons. Get it off."

She was quiet for a long moment, patting her eyes with the tissue, her weeping arrested. She fingered the ring thoughtfully.

"Do you think it protected me?"

I suppressed an urge to bash my head against the kitchen counter.

"Yes, it probably did, but it's frightening you. Get it off, you'll feel less connected to everything. Maybe things will stop happening if we just get rid of everything." We could only hope. I dreaded to think what would happen if we got rid of things that could actually protect us. We still had David to worry about, never mind Caleb.

"I'm starting to get used to it. It's quite comfortable." She spoke too quickly. Almost desperately.

My heart sank to my feet. Her finger was bloodless, for heaven's sake.

"No, honestly, I think we should. Please," I pleaded. She didn't seem to hear herself. One moment she was quoting the Qur'an at me and the next she was telling me she wanted to keep the bloody thing.

"I don't know if I want to." Her voice was small and guilty-sounding.

"I just don't think it's going to end well if you keep on wearing it."

"You were the one who brought it into the flat!" Indignation laced her tone.

I kept my voice calm and low, looking her solemnly in the face, every bit of strength in my being keeping my words coming out in a coherent order.

"Indira, you can't keep the ring. I don't think it belongs to either of us and until we know who its owner is, I think we need to be careful. You need to try and take it off." Her face relaxed a little out of its scowl and I went for my final warning. "I would be so sad if something happened to you, especially if it was because of me." I hated that this was my fault, but it was. I should never have let Caleb leave the bag. Nor let Indira try anything on.

I shoved the cold toast out of the way and grabbed the butter, squeezing it in my hands under its paper.

She fiddled with the ring, avoiding my eyes, crying softly with no move to stop the constant flow of tears now.

"I'm sorry, babe. I don't know why I wanted it so badly."

I handed her the softened butter. "Try this, it might be better than the washing up liquid."

She took a hunk of the butter and mashed it over the ring and her finger, working away at the ring. Minutes passed as she slowly persuaded it over the joint of her finger.

"I've got to be quick and keep moving it or it tightens where it is," she grunted.

Five more minutes later, she made it over the hump of her now thoroughly swollen joint. She held tightly on and quickly slid it right off her hand, placing it on the counter surface with a clatter.

Her eyes met mine with undisguised horror. "It tightened back on even near the tip of my finger."

I nodded and got a small plastic baggie for the ring. The less we touched it, the better.

"I'm going to sort this out once and for all," I promised her. Her face told me I needed to. Fast.

As I rode the bus to work, I messaged Molly.

What time you available for a catch
up?!

All roads led back to Molly, it seemed. I hadn't told her

about Caleb last time because I didn't know her that well. Caleb's story was a long one. But if anyone knew what to do with a magical ring, it would be her. Me gibbering at non-magical people wouldn't do any good.

Her message popped back straight away.

I can get off at 3:30, if you want. How about 4pm at BigBean?

I could escape an hour early if I told work first thing.

See you there.

I let myself relax. Molly would know what to do. She had such a confident way about her, she must know what was going on.

9. Geraldine and Alon

Molly and I sat down at the same little table we found last time. It was like a secret sanctuary that no-one else knew about. As soon as I stepped between the sofas, the muffled soft hubbub of the café became nothing more than a gentle backdrop instead of the clashing scrapes of chairs and endless chatter.

She placed two hot chocolates—molten with marshmallows and topped with cream—on the table and sat down, looking at me expectantly. Probably already knew what I wanted to say.

I took my coat off and handed it to her, squeezing into the tiny space.

"How come it's so quiet in this little spot? It's like walking through a curtain."

She smiled warmly. "Makes it easier to have a proper chat, doesn't it?" She winked at me as I looked up at her, made me feel safe.

"I'm impressed. I wouldn't know how to do that."

"Focused visualisation," she said, laying two plates out. "Are you keeping all the cake?" Carefully, I split the slice of rocky road and the beautiful buttery Eccles cake, sharing them equally on the two plates.

Molly beamed as she ate cake. "So what's going on? Sounds like something's been happening."

I felt inside my handbag. "What do you make of this?" My fingers fumbled around the lining and I found the baggie with the ring tucked in a fold at the bottom. I handed it across the table.

Molly turned it over, viewing it closely from every angle. She put the bag down on the table in front of her, but still held it.

"Where did you get this?"

"My ex-boyfriend brought it to me in a batch of other jewellery and incense and stuff."

She frowned at me. "Funny present."

"Magical supplies," I added. "It was a massive bagful. I thought he might have robbed a crystal shop."

She nodded. "Like Crystal Nirvana on Central Road off Vicar Lane? They were broken into a couple of weeks ago. I was talking to the owner."

I shrugged. "He's totally off his head and a first-class liar. I couldn't even guess." I couldn't tell her my suspicions. I needed her to confirm it without being prompted, in case I'd got it wrong and she was influenced by me." I sipped at the cream on top of my hot chocolate and let it melt soothingly on my tongue.

Molly spooned melted marshmallow into her mouth looking thoughtful.

"Do you mind if I take it out of the bag?"

"That's fine, just don't put it on," I said quickly. We didn't need more drama.

As she opened the bag, Molly's demeanour changed. She stared at me, looking more and more shocked, as though she was listening to something. I didn't think she could see me.

She focused on me properly. "You've got something special here, but I don't think it wants to be here."

I couldn't tear my eyes off her. "What do you mean?"

"There's something attached to the ring." She scowled. "I don't think it wants to be here. It's complaining." She tilted her head as if listening. "He. *He's* complaining. Did your ex trap it in the ring?" She emanated sternness from the other side of her hot chocolate.

Speechless, I shook my head. "What?"

"It's a—*he's*, sorry, a dragon, bound to the stone and he can't escape." She smiled. "His name's Alan."

"Alan?" She must be joking. "There's a dragon and he's called Alan."

Molly laughed at me. "Don't get your knickers in a twist, it might not be Alan exactly, but that's what it sounds like to me—what?" She looked away distantly. "Ah-lon. Ah-lon. Okay, okay, I've got it." She smiled. "Maybe Alon." She popped the ring back in its bag, but left it open.

"Wait." She rolled her eyes upwards again, listening. Frowned. "It's angry. *He.* He's compelled to protect his keeper and bring good luck, all that shite. Says he wasn't put in this Universe to look after humans."

"Like a kind of genie?" We'd been hijacked by fairy tales again.

"Wait." Molly looked pained as she listened. "Someone powerful has bound it to the jewellery. And now it's—*he's* been taken from his keeper. I think he's hoping to escape. I didn't know people did this kind of thing. It's horrible." Her eyes shone and she blinked hard.

I needed to be properly present. I dropped my awareness down into my ground, breathed in deeply and brought some of the earth's energy into me for a couple of inhalations.

"Do you know who its keeper was?"

She 'listened' again with rising horror. "Oh no, no, no."
She shook her head hard. "It had to be, didn't it?"

I stared at her. I'd known it. I'd known it all along.
"David?"

So all the jewellery and crystals belonged to David, not just the ring.

"Is he still in hospital?"

"I don't even know. He was a mess." He could have been killed. It might have been better if he was.

Guilt stung my cheeks for letting myself think such horrible thoughts, but Molly didn't notice.

"Did you know he was into that kind of thing? Spirit entities and jewellery?"

I sipped my hot chocolate, dodging its thick skin of marshmallow.

"He was so dull and ordinary. Didn't want to talk about his job."

"What does he do?"

"Something to do with Native Americans and indigenous peoples. A charity." It was all I had—ridiculous that I knew so bloody little about him.

"Well dragons aren't a thing in Native magic as far as I know. Is he into magic generally?"

"He was initiated into a sweat lodge, said it changed his life." I slurped up the marshmallow. "Maybe he's been into magic since then."

Molly nodded slowly. "I'm not getting anything about him at all, zip. He could be unconscious. Or shielded, if he's some kind of adept. Might get more from a photo."

A magician, not just a randomer playing with magic. I couldn't see it. He had absolutely zero charisma. I thought magicians needed that for their workings. But what was he doing with enchanted jewellery if he wasn't part of that world? I put my empty cup down on the table, worrying, but Molly broke my stupor.

"He's going to come out of there pretty soon. We'll have to get our skates on. Just because I'm picking up on nothing doesn't mean he's gone away. He might even know you have the ring and his gear."

She finished up her drink and shrugged her coat on. "Let's go and see if Crystal Nirvana is still open. You're going to need a few things."

"Wait." I remained sitting. "How could he know I have his stuff? Wasn't me who robbed him." My voice sounded petulant, even to me.

"Two things. First, he left his keys at your house, so even if you didn't burgle his house, you could have done." Molly stepped out into the café and put her handbag on her shoulder. "Secondly, he may be able to track his belongings psychically, especially if there's a particularly nice crystal in there that he's very fond of. Crystals have strong links with their keepers." She waited, expectant, but patient.

I thought back to the massive amethyst geode. That would be anyone's favourite. Its gorgeous dark-to-light-purple quartz would be like a TV aerial to the guy's senses. I wondered if I should tell her about the way the rest of the jewellery buzzed, but decided to save it for the time being.

I dragged on my coat and followed her out.

When we arrived at Crystal Nirvana, a brisk walk across town, its lights were out. Molly pressed her nose up to the door and banged on the glass. "I'm sure I can see someone there."

A movement stirred at the back of the shop and a woman came to the door and peered through the window. She smiled in recognition and unlocked the door.

"Hi Molly, nice to see you, what's up?" She glanced at me as she spoke. She was an attractive forty-something, with reddish curls that bobbed round her cheeks as she spoke.

"Geraldine, this is my friend, Inayat, she's got a small problem. Can we have a chat?"

I hadn't expected Molly to tell someone else, wasn't ready to deal with that. I felt it best to check people out before sharing magical insights and in most cases this worked for me. A tiny part of me did hope Geraldine knew how to handle 'small problems' like this. I said nothing.

"Come in, ladies." Geraldine opened the door fully and we walked in.

We stood in semi-darkness while she locked up again and followed her through the shop and behind the counter to a room hidden only by a bead curtain.

A circle of chairs was lit by fat pillar candles dotted around the room, creepy but atmospheric.

"Mind you don't trip over anything. We're having a meeting this evening." Geraldine walked to the back of the surprisingly large room and picked up a kettle. "Nettle tea okay?"

"Sure," I said for both of us as Molly made a tiny gagging sound.

I watched the woman as she filled the kettle and plugged its lead back in. A meeting had to mean something witchy. The ring of seats didn't scream yoga, that was for sure. And she wasn't some frumpy middle-aged sky-clad witch out of the pages of the Farrars' *Witches Bible*. She exuded adjectives like solid, strong, and powerful. I didn't know how much I wanted her to know.

Geraldine busied herself with the tea. "So how can I help you ladies?"

I glanced surreptitiously at Molly, who nodded

reassuringly at me as she spoke. "Geraldine, what do you know about spirit entities bound to jewellery?"

I was relieved. We weren't just going to get the ring out and tell the woman everything. Molly had a degree of subtlety after all. She was always so direct with me, I hadn't expected tact.

Geraldine turned around slowly. "What did you say?"

Molly seemed to be having trouble facing her directly. "Jewellery with spirit entities attached, like they're bound or something." She carefully examined her hands for no apparent reason.

"Oh goodness, Molly, have you got one? You haven't been doing that, have you?"

Molly looked right at me. "Inayat, show her the ring."

I stared at her in horror. So much for tact and subtlety. I didn't want to show the ring. I wanted to run away out of the shop, but that wouldn't be subtle either. I hazarded a glance at Geraldine, but her face was carefully arranged in an interested expression, a line between curious and nosy, the sort of look someone nice might show. I could be wrong about her.

"Inayat?" Molly was puzzled and I didn't blame her. I was asking for the woman's help. She couldn't help me if I didn't tell her what was going on.

I fumbled the ring out of my pocket in its plastic baggie but held on to it.

"I think we need to talk about it," I cautioned, as diplomatically as I could muster. "I don't feel good bringing it out all the time."

Overwhelmed with the certainty that she shouldn't look at it, my hand twitched independently, wrapped around the ring.

Geraldine saw the tiny shake and looked at me intently.

"It's okay. You hold the bag open and I'll just touch the ring through the opening with my finger."

I slowly passed her my hand with the ring held tightly in my fist. I loosened my fingers a little and allowed her to touch the ring through the mouth of the baggie. She squinted into the distance and raised her eyebrows, refocusing on me as she stepped back.

"Wow. I never experienced that before. He's an angry, angry boy, isn't he?"

Her eyes were clear brown and they held my gaze for a moment longer than was comfortable. Molly's disappointment was clear on her face. She'd really thought Geraldine could help.

"So do you know anything about it at all?" I pressed her.

Geraldine shook her head. "Almost nothing. I know they're out there on the web and all. If you can think of it, you can buy it, right? It's not my scene at all." She stopped. "One of the lasses here tonight, if she gets here early, she might know more. She's had...experience in this kind of thing, of a sort."

A little trickle of fear started in my centre. Too many people were already finding out about it. The sense of being exposed to god knows what became almost overwhelming. A one-legged rabbit with a juggernaut bearing down on it had a better chance of escape, but at least I hadn't mentioned the other pieces of jewellery.

My growing discomfort must have shown on my face and Geraldine stepped forward. "Don't worry sweetheart, we're all friends here." She offered me my tea.

As I took the hot glass mug, it dawned on me that honesty is usually the best policy.

"Geraldine, can I level with you?" I coyly watched the steam rise.

She waited and I began. I told a brief truth of how I had come by the ring and then what had happened when Indira tried the ring on and the attack the following evening that I suspected was due to the ring's power. I missed a lot of details.

Geraldine nodded. "I'm surprised she didn't feel like she was on fire, but the dragon's flight gives him air qualities as well." She sipped at her drink. "Wind is so fitting. Nice touch, really."

My ears pricked. She did know about it. Knew more than me, anyway. I glanced at her face, but the lines of her features and the softness of her skin made her look mature and trustworthy. She seemed genuine enough, but I don't find faces a good reflection of people.

"So, what do you want to do?" Geraldine turned to include Molly who nodded at me encouragingly.

"Go on, love, you decide," she urged.

"I'm scared to do anything," I muttered. "This bloke tried to psychically rape me. God knows what he's capable of if he's into all this shit. I'd rather just give it all back to him, to be honest, so he didn't know it had gone. We don't even know when he's coming out of hospital."

Both women just looked at me. I hadn't mentioned the first attack and Geraldine hadn't asked what our involvement was with David prior to the burglary.

Molly broke the silence. "Do we know what the options are? Can't decide anything if you don't know what the choices are."

I could work with that.

Geraldine grabbed a pad of paper off the side and sat down in a chair, leaning on a rickety side table. "What have we got?"

Molly nodded emphatically. "One, hold on to the ring and wear it."

Geraldine wrote something down. "Two, hold on to the ring and hide it." She noted that. "Three, return the ring and all the other items to their rightful owner before he notices." She looked up, poised for the next point. "What else is there?"

I thought about it. "Could take them to the police and grass up Caleb." I'd often dreamed of that a few years ago. Offloading everything onto the police didn't feel like a good idea when I hadn't told them everything already. Explaining my relationship with Caleb and following it up with the reasons why I suspected they'd been stolen would be more complicated than I was prepared to go.

Geraldine started to write it down.

"No, don't bother." I stopped her. "There's no need, no way am I going through that."

Geraldine smiled smoothly. "Don't think I would either." She put the pen down, but looked thoughtful. "Can I ask you a question?"

I waited.

"If you could release the dragon from the ring, would you do it?"

I stared at her but she calmly smiled at me. I hated the thought of captivity, wouldn't stand for it for an animal or a person. I didn't even visit zoos. Before today I hadn't known a spirit could be captured. Thought it the stuff of fairy tales. I imagined the suffering of the spirit entity as it eternally fought against its bonds. Even though I hadn't seen the dragon, I didn't want it to suffer. Both women regarded me over their tea cups.

"Of course I would."

Geraldine nodded sagely. "Leave the ring with me. I'll have a chat with my ladies tonight and maybe we can break the bindings. He doesn't seem like a troublesome spirit, just annoyed."

Molly and I walked briskly up the pedestrianised zone and out onto Briggate.

"My bus stand's outside Tiger, Tiger," she said. "I'll wait with you at your stop. They arrested that lovely doctor's boyfriend, but he didn't do it."

"Do what?"

"They had to let him go. The children's doctor who disappeared walking her dog along the canal. God knows what monster's prowling the streets. You need to be careful."

I vaguely remembered seeing a headline somewhere. People were always disappearing.

We walked the few yards to the bus stop on New Briggate.

"Are you going to take the stuff back? Be better if you

can get it back in place before he knows its gone."

"If I can figure out how."

"Wait to hear from me before you make any moves, I'll give you a call when Geraldine rings me."

"I need to know where his house is," I said. If I had to put it back so that he didn't know it had been stolen, I'd have to get *into* his house, never mind just knowing where it was.

"I thought you'd been there." Molly picked up a second-hand *MetroPolis* from a bus stop seat and flicked to page five. She fished out her glasses and perched them on her nose.

"I could get lost on a postage stamp," I said gloomily. I noticed the headline on the front. Witches 'interfering' with US politics. "What does it say?"

"Apparently a bunch of pretty witches in Brooklyn, New York City, are against the favourite presidential candidate, so they're casting spells to make him lose his hair."

That made me smile. "Do you think they'll manage it?"

Molly grinned conspiratorially. "Every spell I've ever cast has worked."

"And how many's that?" I flicked a glance sideways at her. Her brown eyes were teasing but direct as ever.

She grinned. "A few. But they all worked."

As the bus pulled up, I hoped she would always be on my side.

10. Recce

All the lights were ablaze when I arrived home at Gledhow Hall. The porch light was mended, the tiled hallway lit up and when I opened the flat door, the interior hall light was also bright.

I could hear voices in the kitchenette and as I rounded the corner into the living room, a male shout of pain rang out. Caleb took a step back from the sink area, grabbing at his crotch. Indira was uncomfortably backed up against the sink and her relief at my entry was obvious. Actually, she looked furious, eyes black as black and face set in stone.

I grabbed the heavy glass vase from the console table.

"What's going on, Caleb?"

"Nuffin'," he mumbled turning as if to leave the kitchen zone.

"Fucking wanker. Get the hell out of my house." Indira gave me an angry scowl behind his back.

"Wait!" I didn't want him to leave, we couldn't lose the moment.

Indira stared at me with increasing fury, but I kept a tight grip on my vase and widened my eyes at her meaningfully.

"Caleb, I know you stole that stuff from David."

He frowned. "I haven't done anything, Inayat." He glanced at Indira and smirked. "I was here when it happened. You'd vouch for me, wouldn't you, little pretty?" She was staring at me across the room, her chin set, then she grabbed the kettle and filled it as he leered at her. He leaned across the counter top with horrible laughing eyes.

I smacked my handbag down on the counter. "Caleb, I don't care that you did it. But now I have to sort it out before it lands *me* in the fucking shit."

He turned around sullenly. I lowered my voice a little.

"You have to show me the house where you got this stuff. Please?"

He scowled. "I'm not taking it back."

He might walk right now. I braced myself, let the vase ground me and kept a level tone.

"I don't want you to do that. I just need to know which house."

"Are you taking it back?"

I shrugged, staying cagey. The less he knew, the less bullshit I would have to endure. That was the usual pattern.

"I don't know what I'm doing with it. Caleb, there's at least one entity attached to that jewellery and I'm sure the rest of it is bewitched." The thought had occurred to me more than once. Those earrings were fatefully mesmerising, like they would take hold before you had a chance to escape.

His face was passive. "What kind of entity?"

"A fucking dragon, Caleb!" I'd almost had enough of him. "You gave me a fucking dragon that nearly killed Indira, *did* kill someone and ripped off someone else's arm." My voice reverberated around the room.

He was furious. "What would I know about a dragon, Inayat? Fucking spirit entities, what kind of magic do you think I'm into? That crap's for crazy bastards."

"You're both off your heads," snapped Indira. The kettle came to a boil and she poured herself a cup of tea. Slopping it as she walked, she stamped to her room and slammed the door loudly. I couldn't blame her. I wanted him out too, but I couldn't let this moment slip past.

I lowered my voice back to normal. "You didn't know about it at all?" I needed him to stop his flake act, just for once to do the right thing by me.

He turned his hands palm upwards. "I used to go out

with a girl who had them things. You can get demons if you've got a bit of spare cash. I stay away from that shit."

I shuddered. In comparison, a dragon didn't seem too bad.

He looked directly at me for a long moment. I held his gaze, furious, head held high and proud. He was going to help us if it was the last thing he did. I shifted the vase to my other hand.

He grunted. "I can take you there now if you want, it's a bit of a walk," he said grudgingly.

I knocked on her bedroom door and stuck my head around it when she spoke.

"I'm going to see the house."

"Come in," she said urgently. I entered the room and closed the door behind me, mindful that Caleb was probably going to nick something.

"What are you thinking? He just tried to jump me and now you're going off with him?"

"I'm going to sort this out once and for all. I'll take the bag of stuff back to the guy's house before he gets out of hospital."

"And it's the same guy that attacked you?"

"Caleb stole the fucking key to his house." I should have told her already.

"Fuck, Inayat, just fuck." She sipped her tea, watchful

and wild eyed.

I could only agree.

"I'm going to call Jimmy, he'll have some Valium I can have."

"Hey, go steady," I didn't want her taking crap like that just to deal with being around me. "Don't be taking drugs because of me."

"Jimmy's easier than going to a doctor. I'm not like you, babe, I don't overdo everything. I wasn't brought up that way."

I processed that. She was still angry with me, but hiding it. I pushed on without further comment.

"I need you to time how long it takes me to go to the house and come back. Might need to know when I take the bag."

"Why don't you take it back tonight since you're there anyway?"

Sheepishness made me fall over my words. "I can't, I've got to—wait for the ring to come back."

"Where is it?" Her hand slipped on the cup and spilled tea on the duvet. "What do you mean?"

This was going downhill fast. "I've given it to someone to release the dragon."

"What?" Dumbstruck with horror, her mouth opened but nothing else came out.

"I had to get help, there's no way I could handle this stuff by myself. I went to see Molly and she's helping me."

"Molly's got the ring?" She seemed to relax slightly.

"Not exactly," I admitted.

Indira fumbled for her phone. "Just go, sort it out, come back in one piece for heaven's sake. I'm calling Jimmy."

As I re-entered the living room, Caleb was waiting impatiently at the doorway.

"C'mon, I've got stuff to do."

"What did you come around here for anyway?"

"Fancied a chat with Indira," he said ruefully and rubbed his crotch regretfully.

"Dickhead." He had a fucking girlfriend, why did he need to come and hassle Indira? She'd had enough of me as it was. I hoped she'd kicked him good.

We set off walking in silence. He was never much of a talker anyway. He walked too fast and I trotted to keep up, but I didn't bother complaining. The sooner this was over, the better. At least it wasn't raining. I lifted my face to the breeze and smelled the air's damp diesel character, reminded of doing the same thing on a hill at home and smelling wood smoke that time. We strode along the suburbs that ran behind Street Lane for what felt like twenty minutes. Tree-lined avenues with cars parked in front of the houses.

We finally turned a corner and Caleb stopped dead.

"That's the one."

Now I remembered. It was the street almost opposite the Deer Park pub. I didn't know how I'd forgotten. The night I went to David's home, some of the men smoking outside the pub had jeered at us as we'd passed. I searched for a street sign. Shaftesbury Avenue.

We walked along the road, past the mini arcade of shops. I stared down the rows of houses, but couldn't see anything familiar. Just dozens of three-storey town houses, one semi-detached after another.

The very next house stood on the end of a row, facing into the avenue opposite. The others were red-brick homes, built in the 1940s to accommodate the population boom, but this one was older and built from stone. Even the porch was sandstone. It wasn't as big or grand as Gledhow Hall, but loomed impressively in the darkness.

We stood in silence for a moment. I wanted the key. Otherwise I'd have to break in and the litany of crimes the guy could charge me with would grow. Also I wasn't sure I could even break in successfully.

"Caleb, I need the key."

He grunted some kind of dissent at me.

"Caleb, you have to give me the key, otherwise how am I going to get in there?"

He dug around inside his jacket and pulled out a silver

chain. A key dangled on the end of it.

"What will you give me for it?"

I quelled the angry retort. "Caleb, just give me the bloody thing."

"You have to get me my gran's ring, Inayat. Fucking bitch is dead and she's still giving me shit. Says I'm going to die if I don't get the ring back. If I give you the key, that's a solid deal." His piercing look told me he knew I wouldn't do the job for a bagful of dragon.

I met his gaze. "How about a bit of fucking loyalty?" He'd never looked after me, never protected me and now he'd put me in even more danger stealing this shit from someone who was already out to get me. "Some payback would be nice."

A wide smirk spread across his face. "Make the deal, Inayat." He spun the key in his fingers and dropped it to his chest. He was on the verge of leaving and I would never get the gear replaced in the house.

"Okay, okay, I'll find your ring, no guarantees, but I'll try." I took a deep breath. I could do some candle magic, that would be easy enough. If it didn't work, so be it.

In answer, he ripped the chain from his neck and threw it to me. I caught one end and the key slid onto the ground. I picked it up quickly.

He stood for a second or two, then abruptly turned with a swish of his long coat and was gone, striding down the street too quickly to chase.

I was reminded of the fabric I'd seen the night David attacked me. Something billowing behind the gate stoop as I talked on the phone with the police. Caleb in the wind, spying on me.

I turned and headed home again.

⌁

I sat up late with a sneaky spliff. Indira was long abed and the quiet of the flat was peaceful. No hint of the drama at all.

I got the jewellery out one more time and separated the pieces from the crystals. I left the geode in the bag. The more blind that was, the better. The silver blinked in the candle light and I gazed at the little pile of treasure, wished it wasn't magical and that I could be sure I wasn't crazy.

I contemplated my decision to return stolen items to the home of a man I was afraid could magically blow me apart. Who had threatened me with physical violence and meant it. My choice couldn't be rationalised at all. The less crazy-sounding version was that someone I knew had burgled a home and given me some items and I wanted to return them. I was pretty sure that was breaking the law. Probably aiding and abetting or harbouring, or handling stolen goods.

If I was going to do this, I really didn't want to get caught.

I had been trapped in an intersection of life tracks after Caleb's first visit to the flat. He'd taken the key then, right under my nose. All events after that were ripples, aftershocks stemming from the first. The bastard had already taught me the futility of love spells. Now he was back to teach me something else.

11. Dragon Release

I had two blissful days without drama of any kind. Indira and I watched a crap TV movie on Saturday night—a rare night off for her, but her manager was taking it easy with her since her mugging and she was happy enough to take advantage of that. We drank some wine and slept in the following day.

Molly phoned me on the Monday afternoon. "We're on. She reckons they can do it."

I was in the office, smack in the sights of the watchful Christine, so I kept my voice down. "When?" I was supposed to be typing hearing aid assessment letters, with a backlog of more than fifty files, though I was mostly worrying about taking the bag of jewellery back and discreetly looking up invisibility spells on the internet. Beyond an ancient one from sixteenth century Paris that involved beheading a cat and inserting seven broad beans in its orifices whilst incanting to some minor devil, there wasn't much on offer and I didn't fancy that one. Anything that harmed a living creature was firmly filed under P for psychopathic.

"Bring the ring to the shop on Wednesday evening after work. I'll meet you outside the HiFi Club at five-thirty, just wait for me there."

The nightclub was on the opposite side of the road to the crystal shop, below a department store.

"What are they going to do?"

Christine glanced up at me with a short-sighted scowl and I tabbed my screen back to my letters. I didn't want to be a cautionary tale for temping secretaries at the hospital for years to come.

"There's a way to break the bindings, but they've got to send the dragon away or it might take revenge on whoever's available." Molly was muffled, obviously keeping her own voice down.

"Jesus, Moll, am I going to be in on the rit— ceremony?" I caught Christine's foreboding eye, magnified through her thick bifocals. She never missed a trick.

"I dunno, kid, see what you think before you arrive. They might not want anyone else there. Witches can be funny."

She hung up and I went back to my work without

attempting an explanation to Christine. Silence thundered distantly in the office for the rest of the afternoon.

～✐～

As I arrived home, in the hallway I could hear sobbing from the living room. I rounded the doorway and Indira met me in tears, waving a newspaper.

"Those men, they're in the *Evening Post*." She put a Kleenex up to her nose and handed me the paper so she could blow it.

I read the headline at the top of a tiny article with a huge picture of the decomposing arm being placed into a police evidence bag.

Man Found Dead With An Extra Arm

A man's body and a detached male arm have been found on Gledhow Wood Road overnight. The body appears to have been dead for at least five days, leading to speculation that the corpse and the extra arm were dumped on Saturday or Sunday night.

The police are making enquiries at A&Es in the immediate area and request anyone with any information to step forward.

Neither the man or the arm have been identified and no missing persons reports match the description of the dead man.

With the recent disappearance of a junior doctor and the attack on a woman in Roundhay Park, some local councillors have suggested the men may have been the victims of a vigilante and may even have been the perpetrators for those two crimes, neither of which have been solved as yet. However, police urge caution in speculation.

One possibility is that the owner of the arm managed to get home but may have died before getting help. Readers are urged to report any mysterious smells emanating from homes or garden sheds.

"Do you think they'll work out there was someone else there?" Indira's voice was wobbly.

I wondered if part of the dragon's magic had been to conceal the effects of its counter-attack for a few days.

Indira took the paper back and laid it on the counter, poring over the images.

"It really happened, hun. I started to think it was all a dream, but there it is." She wiped her eyes again, mascara-streaked cheeks crossing her freckles in a dot-to-dot. "I didn't kill the guy did I?"

She was still so unsure about what had happened. My heart broke for her forlorn need for reassurance. If she didn't kill the guy, the dragon did. And she didn't really want to know that either.

I gave her a hug. "The ring protected you. Lucky you had a dragon on you, or it might have been a lot worse." The mugging was independent of the magic. She would have been mugged anyway, the dragon ring was happy timing. I hoped.

She gave me a look but said nothing more and got her phone from the counter, ratching through her handbag.

"Let's have curry tonight. I'll get a delivery. I can't be bothered to cook." She pulled out a small clear bag with some round blue pills and fumbled one out.

I took my coat off, eyeing the pills but trying not to stare. Looked like Jimmy had made good on her request. "I can cook, you know."

She ran half a glass of water and took the pill in one. "You don't have to do that, I feel like lamb chops and some chana chat and a na'an bread. Do you want some rice as well?"

I headed for my bedroom and left her arguing in a mixture of Urdu and English with a bloke on the end of the phone who apparently couldn't understand her in either language. She didn't believe him.

As I swung the door open to my room, I stopped. Something didn't seem right. I glanced over each and every item spread around the room, but nothing was obviously out of place. My third eye pounded in the centre of my forehead and I dropped my consciousness into my ground, felt outwards into the room. A deep hum, in and out, like a radio signal.

Indira came off the phone and I turned around to her in the doorway. "Has someone been here today?"

She frowned slightly. "Been here like how, hun?"

"No workmen, no Caleb, no nothing at all?"

She slowly shook her head, mouth turned downwards.

"Have you been in my bedroom for something?"

She was indignant. "What for, babe? Why all the questions?"

I smiled at her. "Just had a feeling someone's been in my room. Don't worry about it, I might just be paranoid."

She pulled her shawl over her head. "Hopefully the curry'll be nice. Dunno what it'll be though. The guy on the phone was so rude."

The weather was back to its usual tricks by Wednesday night and I trudged towards the crystal shop through river-lined streets under a brolly. The ring was tucked safely into the inside pocket of my jacket but I felt for it every time I passed someone. I thought for a moment it would be more sensible to put it on but dashed the treacherous idea from my head immediately. Its influences were strong. That thought had popped up many times in the two days I had waited.

I saw no sign of Molly when I arrived on the steps of the closed-up nightclub over the road, so I tucked myself under its folded up canopy and waited, out of the downpour. The door of Crystal Nirvana was easily in sight from my standpoint, so I amused myself watching customers enter the shop. No-one seemed to come out again and after playing with the idea they were all being murdered one by one, I realised they were probably part of the coven that was going to perform the ceremony. They just looked like ordinary people.

A cool shiver shimmied up my spine. I didn't know what was going to happen but I felt as though I should ask to be in there. Suspicion bugged me. I couldn't trust they would do what they said but even if I was present, I didn't have any way to tell if they hadn't. I never saw anything astral and I wasn't exactly familiar with ceremonial magic. Or Wiccan coven rituals. I didn't know anything about the coven. I guessed Wicca, but you never know what people get up to behind closed doors. They weren't going to let me watch, but I probably should still try. It might be pretty hard to get the ring back if I didn't keep it in sight.

I was so torn I didn't notice Molly until she tapped me on the elbow.

"Penny for 'em?" She was as bright and excited as ever. Her energy buzzed me.

"I don't know whether or not I want to be in on the ceremony. Do you think they'll ask me?"

"No idea. Like I say, witches can be funny buggers. That'll be why people always think they're up to wicked stuff. Wait and see what she says."

We walked down towards the shop and Molly put her hand on the door. "Take a deep breath," she advised. I took one.

Geraldine stood behind the counter in a long black velvety number, writing something down in a large book. As we came through the door she quickly shut the book and leaned on it to greet us.

"Lovely to see you ladies, thank you for coming. I'm honoured."

She walked round the counter and met us in the middle of the aisle.

"I wanted to thank you for doing this. The Universe needs more people who are prepared to help others. We felt it was unfair to leave a being of any kind trapped in a solid earthly vessel."

I smiled at her as I handed over the plastic baggie with its precious cargo. Her face took on an unexpected tenderness. She held it in the light, all her attention on it now, ignoring us completely. Molly scuffed her shoe against the floor and Geraldine snapped her focus back to us.

"I'll call you when the ring's ready to pick up. Should be tomorrow night."

We were dismissed. She hadn't asked me to stay, but suddenly that was all I wanted. I shot Molly a look. She left no clue on her face as to what I could do. Geraldine was impassive, but I tried anyway.

"Can I stay and watch the ceremony, please?" The please made it a request, not just a question that could be brushed off.

Geraldine's eyes burned a hole in my soul. They were dark orange fires here and there. She smiled, but it stayed at her mouth, incongruent with her hard gaze.

"Sorry, love, we've got a rule, no visitors during workings. The energies have to be totally under control."

Mutiny formed inside me, but it was only common sense. If someone was there with a different intention, a spell could get complicated. Or it could fail. If I was there and everything went wrong, they might not say it but they were bound to think it was my fault.

By Thursday afternoon, I jumped every time my mobile beeped. The office phone gave me palpitations. No call or text came from Molly.

In the end I rang her as I walked to get my bus.

She sounded as baffled as me. "I haven't heard a thing, petal, not a whistle. Shall I text Geraldine? See if she answers?"

I thought about it for a moment. "Actually, do you think she would mind if I texted her?"

"I think that would be absolutely fine," she said

without hesitation. "Try and be tactful about it, though, don't just tell her to give you the ring back.

It was like she knew me well. Tactful wasn't the easiest performance for me. She gave me the number and as I sat on the top deck of the bus, I tried out a few variations of the same thing. The end result was:

> Hi Geraldine, sorry to bother you, but
> is there any news on the ring please?
> Cheers, Inayat.

I psyched myself up to hit send, but instead the phone rang with a private number. My Maroon 5 *Payphone* ringtone filled the deck quickly and curiosity killed me so I grabbed the call.

"Inayat, it's Police Sergeant O'Brien."

I forced a smile, afraid of the sombre tone in his voice.

"Hi Sergeant, how can I help you?" I glanced around but no-one sat close enough to hear.

"I wanted to let you know, they're discharging David Catcheside from hospital in the next few days. Thought you should know, in case you get a visit from him again. Bit of prior warning." He paused for a moment. I looked out of the window to see where I was. The bus passed the roundabout at Harehills, the Asian supermarket brightly lit through the windows of the bus. My stop was soon.

He continued. "If you do hear from him, make sure

you call it in as harassment. Don't encourage him, please."

I groaned. "I just want to be left alone." The bus lurched to a halt, one stop before mine.

"Feels like this one might be a nuisance. If he calls you, turns up, or otherwise makes his presence felt, call one-oh-one and let us know, okay?"

"When is he due out? David Catcheside." I tried out his name. I'd forgotten his surname.

"The memo says 'towards the end of this week', dated Monday." He sounded glum. "Apologies, Inayat, I didn't pick up the email until today, our system's been down at the station."

The bus was nearing my stop. "I have to go, Sergeant."

"Inayat, promise me you'll call the police if you hear—" I cut him off accidentally as I grabbed hold of the rail to get up. The thirty seconds it takes to get off the bus is all you've got before it sets off.

As I descended from the top deck on the still-moving bus I accidentally sent the text message. The thud of horror when I realised sent a tsunami of adrenaline coursing through my veins. Ridiculous reaction, the message was fine. I checked I hadn't added something inadvertently and relieved, popped the phone in my pocket for the trek up the hill.

When I got home, Indira was showering in her en-suite. I got out of my coat and found a jumper to wear on the top of my bed. My mouth was dry and sour, so I boiled the kettle, but a distant beep reminded me of my phone and the message I had sent.

It was Geraldine.

We're doing a long-form cleansing
action. Won't be long now. Maybe
another day. Don't worry.

That didn't sound good, given O'Brien's message. I had to get the bag back into David's house before he was discharged from hospital. It annoyed me she assumed I was worried. She'd told me it would be this evening and now I was asking how things were going. I might as well not have bothered wording my message tactfully.

I forwarded her message to Molly with the caption: 'What do you think?'

Don't worry, you'll get the ring back.

Everyone thought I was worried.

I was worried!

The knowledge David was going to be home by the end of the week made my decision for me. I would return the items to his house but it had to be tomorrow. Surely he wouldn't be discharged on a Saturday. So he would be out either sometime tomorrow or Monday if they missed the window to see the consultant.

Indira wandered out of her bedroom across to the

kitchen counter, wrapped in her robe with a towel in a beehive on her head. She graciously accepted a cup of tea.

"What's new, hun?" She seemed strangely serene.

I dug a packet of chocolate digestives out from the back of the bread bin and offered it to her.

"David's coming out of hospital and will probably be home by tomorrow night."

She blinked at me then dug at the side of the biscuit wrapping with her gilt-edged nails and edged out the top two. She took a bite, still thoughtful.

"Have you taken his stuff back?"

I shook my head slowly, eyes never leaving hers. "I still haven't got the ring back from the witch woman."

Indira washed her biscuit down with a slug of tea.

"Do we need to put the rest of his stuff back tonight? Maybe he won't notice the ring for a day or so."

I noted the 'we' with confusion and shook my head again.

"I feel like I should wait before I panic. Molly says it'll be okay." Putting my trust into someone I'd only known two weeks sounded crazy but I did trust her. She'd proven herself when she clouted David. "I'm mad because nothing ever goes smoothly when you involve other people."

Indira nodded sympathetically.

I wondered how much Valium she'd had. There hadn't

been that many pills in the bag, but she didn't seem herself somehow.

"How long are you going to wait?"

Her relaxed interrogation helped me think.

"I can't go until after work so I can wait till then. If he's home that'll be it, but if I beat him there I'll win."

"If he's at home he'll be in bed. He can't be fully recovered already." Indira's hint was strong. I could hardly believe what I was hearing, though. Normally she was the sensible one. I wondered again about the Valium.

"I'm not sneaking into his house when he's there." My sense of direction sucked. I could get lost anywhere and that included inside complicated big houses.

"You might have to. At least he won't be looking for his stuff if he's in bed recovering from a head injury."

I couldn't imagine a more terrifying scenario.

12. Taking Risks

Friday morning loomed miserable and grey, with rain coming straight down in stair-rods. The weather in Leeds is always a little bit shittier than it has to be. Even if it's sunny, it's windy. I took my brolly, but nothing saved me from wet feet the entire day.

Just after eleven my phone beeped with a message. Geraldine.

Come and get the ring.

I nipped out at lunch time and headed for Central Road. With three clicks of my fingers I invoked violet light protection and entered the shop. Geraldine was behind the counter, all smiles.

"Hi darling, well done, we did it." She warmly held out a tiny box.

My fingers closed around the box. They tingled at the tips as I took it. I smiled at her. "What did you do exactly?"

She glanced at her watch but stayed smiley.

"Certain spells are used to bind the creature to the item. We reversed the exact spells and sent the dragon through the tunnel of light to the Fifth Dimension."

The tunnel of light and the Fifth Dimension didn't sound very Wiccan, more New Age spiritualism, but if it worked, it worked.

"So it's gone?" I opened the box. Inside lay two rings—the original and a new solid silver ring. "What's this?" Suspicion stirred wakefully at the back of my mind, leaking around the edges of my smile, but Geraldine beamed at me.

"Nothing but a gift. Do with it as you will. After we transferred the dragon, we wove a spell around a new ring to give you peace and happiness. It's just a gentle charm, but since you're returning the garnet, we wanted you to have something nice."

I slipped the box deep into my coat pocket and wandered back to work via a sandwich shop, wondering if it was wise to accept a magical gift from someone I wasn't sure about. Geraldine unsettled me and I didn't know on which level, psychic or normal. This whole spirit-guide thing was still too new to me and I was sure I was missing a lot of messages. I missed the obvious at the best of times.

I escaped work at 4:07 PM, thanks to the formidable Christine taking an afternoon off at three for a funeral, and made a beeline across the city centre, slightly ahead of the crowds.

I reached home before five, ahead of Indira. I'd expected her to be in, was sure she had the lunch time shift only today. Maybe it was just as well. She would only worry while I was out. Mind you, worry was better than being dead...or captive in a house with a crazy guy. That was only basic lone worker policy. Someone had to be home to know I wasn't home yet. Now I wished she was here already, but I didn't want to wait. I had the gumption to do it right now, but it wasn't going to last.

I stripped off my grey office gear and dragged on my jeans and a t-shirt, followed by a purple sweater. Around me I wrapped my long black dress coat and as I pulled on my hat, Indira clattered through the flat door.

"You weren't going without telling me were you? Who's gonna call the police when you don't come back?"

"Oh God, don't make it worse, this is the most terrifying thing I've ever done in my life."

"It's the most ridiculous thing you've ever done." She took her coat off and hung it up with emphasis.

"I can't see there's any better way to do it."

"For God's sake don't break into the house. Just leave

the bag in front of the door and get out." That was more like the Indira I knew. However, what she didn't know didn't hurt her. I had already made up my mind. Leaving the items on the doorstep would only alert him to the theft and he was bound to jump to the conclusion that it was me who had stolen the items in the first place.

"Yeah, yeah, I will, don't worry." I felt like a teenager going off on a sneaky night out, telling my parents I was out to see a film but headed for a pub crawl

She uncrumpled my collar for me and straightened my coat with a tug.

"Even if the door's broken don't even think about slipping the bag inside, just leave it outside." The no nonsense tone of voice belied her concern, but the way she was fussing over me, I could tell. "And don't forget to leave the key."

"Don't worry." There was no way I was leaving any connection to him in my possession. I assessed myself in the hall mirror. A slightly glamorous burglar looked back with huge kohl-rimmed eyes, a black beanie hat and leather gloves emphasising the situation. "It's going to look bad if I'm seen."

"Are you going to be all right? Should I report you missing if you don't come back in a couple of hours?" She was genuine and serious.

"It'll take me twenty minutes to walk up there, a couple to leave the bag and another twenty back, I shouldn't be any longer than an hour." I hoped she would stay off the Valium for the duration.

"I'll give it another hour before I call the police in case you've just been held up."

I turned to hug her. "Just give it thirty minutes, I won't be held up by anything unless it's him."

I spun on my foot to go, but stopped and turned back.

"Thanks, doll, you're so thoughtful. I didn't even think of safety stuff like that." I had, and she was unknowingly part of my improvised lone burglar plan, but she was so stressed out, she needed to feel good about herself. Besides, I was lucky she'd come home when she did or I'd really be going it alone.

She didn't fall for it. "Just come back in one piece," she said as I left the flat.

Dusk made shadows along the edges of the roads and street lamps flickered on as I walked, but despite my dark clothing I felt so conspicuous I dropped off the main road and onto a residential street that ran parallel behind the shops. As I walked, I could see the target house directly ahead, a sentinel on the T-junction with its outsize stone porch.

I stood behind a tree on the pavement, my back to the house, breathing in deeply to calm myself. It was now or never. I turned to survey the target. No window was lit and the door was closed. All seemed good, but I didn't know what to do. Queen of Not Planning Properly strikes again. I'd gone over the chance he could catch me so many times, I'd forgotten I needed a plan for getting in.

The fear gnawed into me. I couldn't defend myself on any level, magical or otherwise, feeling like this. If his magic was what bound the dragon to the ring, he was a powerful practitioner and the sort of person I avoided at all costs. My ability to accidentally piss people off is too risky.

I wondered if he'd already started on me. The anxiety could be a fast result. Then I remembered the stories of what can happen under magical attack and quashed that. If the results of an attack were just a bit of anxiety, my luck was strong. Highly unlikely.

Sheepish realisation dawned on me so clearly. I smiled and thanked my guardians. I could go through the front door and no-one would be any the wiser for it. That was what the key was for. No onlooker other than David himself would be able to tell the difference between me and the government-contracted social carers that might be sent to look after him while he convalesced.

I marched right up to the front door, key in hand, a deceptively confident stride.

The key slid into the lock with a smooth series of clicks. Heart in my mouth, I turned it as quietly as I could. The Yale latch on the inside slid across and the door swung open into darkness. All pretence of being a social carer now out the window, blood pounding through my ears, I leaned forward to listen through the gap. The house felt empty. As I stepped into the hallway, the door knocked against something above my head. I looked up. A bird skull dangled from above the frame with some kind of beading hanging from it. A shiver ran through me.

As my eyes got used to the gloom, I dropped into my ground and felt outwards to check the house. No presence. David wasn't home.

I pulled the key from the latch and shut the door behind me. At the very end of the hallway through a room that looked like a kitchen, I could see the back door. A street light glistened through its window. When I'd come here before, he'd taken me straight to his kitchen. To my right, the stairs led to the next floor, but directly ahead, the hall offered me at least a couple of doors to try. I prayed his store of magical supplies was on the ground floor. No way was I going upstairs. A vision of me having to leap from an upstairs window in a panic compounded that decision.

I crept forwards. Even knowing he wasn't in the house, I dared not make a sound, not even a scuff with my feet. The first room seemed unlikely to be the one I looked for. The windows were sat directly in view of the street. I accidentally tapped my foot noisily on the tiled floor. Admonished by the rush of adrenaline, I crept more quietly onwards. The loudest sound in the house was my heart beat.

Another door on the left loomed out of the murk, a room at the back of the house. Focused on its wooden form, something brushed against my face and I stifled a scream. A feathered Indian headdress displayed on the hallway wall. How I'd missed that, I couldn't know. I kept going. Another two steps and I realised I had two doors to choose from. The one on the left and directly opposite, one on the right, built into the stairs, a wooden panelled affair with a series of bones hung across it, small to large, like a xylophone. A xylobone. I smiled despite myself. I took another step so I was level with them both and the left hand door swung quietly open as though I'd triggered something.

Sick with fear, I had to still my panicked legs as they jerked me around. I wanted to run straight out the front door. What the hell was I thinking to be in someone's house, never mind someone who had it in for me? I should have just left the bag on the step. I just wanted to make it less obvious what had happened, but it would be so fucking clear if he caught me in there.

Almost expecting booby traps Indiana Jones-style, I peered into its depths. Lit badly by another street light, the walls were some dark colour, almost blood red in the dim orange glow, hung with dozens of items all the way along. Bones, feathers, pouches and strange frames in unfamiliar shapes. I could see something white, a weird shape, on the back wall.

My nausea rose in my belly but determined, I stepped into the room, pushing the door wider. The handle felt warm to my touch as though someone had been holding it for a while. The white thing took shape. An animal skull with dark horns that I hadn't been able to see from the doorway. Maybe a goat or a sheep. I didn't know. It seemed too large to be either. The horns curled downwards and the eye sockets—they had a presence, as though they were watching me.

Rationally, I wondered if my imagination was taking over. Screw that, my imagination had probably taken over two weeks ago.

Curious, I peered at the contraption below the skull. A complicated series of shelves and a table, each shelf contained one type of item only. A sheathed knife. Three pillar candles. A bowl of salt. A cathedral-style censer with an abalone shell laid next to it, a half-burned smudge stick nestled within its bowl. A huge crystal obelisk on the table, with feathers scattered before it. I wondered if they had been thrown down for some kind of prediction, a soothsaying style similar to i-ching or rune stones.

This was the room. I stared in wonder at the bone mobiles hanging from the ceiling, the African masks on the walls. I hadn't seen so many magical artefacts outside of a museum. The room felt crowded with presences. Not just the skull, a whole population of weirdness. I got the sense that everything had its place. It was tidy, despite the chaos. Shelving on each wall and between the windows showed nothing but the most organised arrangements of magical artefacts. Crystals on one shelving unit. Books on another.

I brought myself back to the present. I was here to deliver the bag of stolen items and get the hell out. The table in front of one of the windows presented itself. Littered with tiny boxes and items that I couldn't make out fully, it seemed out of place with the rest of the room. No order at all, only disarray. As I stepped right up to it, I knew this was where Caleb had been. Jewellery, crystals and tiny figurines populated the surface, scattered around as if they'd just been thrown there and tipped out of their boxes.

Touch nothing, Inayat. He would know if I did. With an earth-shattering thud, my heart dropped through my stomach. He would know. Anyone with a room full of magical items like this would know that someone had been here. Would know it was me.

He would know it was me.

I tried to rationalise. I was returning the items, not stealing them.

He wasn't going to be rational about it. I'd made the situation far worse than it was ever going to be if I'd just dumped the bag on the step and run away.

A tiny noise, like a scuttling across the floorboards, alerted me to the far end of the room. I snapped my head around, but saw nothing. The feeling that I wasn't alone grew with every second. I had to get out of there. A shadow moved in the corner of my eye and my panic rose over my head. The room spun and I gripped the table to steady myself. It wobbled crazily. I let go, took deep breaths. Fainting in his house would be a good way to die a million times.

I planted my feet firmly on the floor and dropped through my ground into the earth below. The energies felt uncertain, as though I wasn't grounded at all. I looked down. Then around my feet at the wooden floor. Daubed on the boards, a complicated pentacle with unfamiliar characters. I had placed my feet perfectly in the centre. A shot of adrenaline burst in my stomach and I skipped out of the seal onto a clear area. I was done with this place.

The bag unrolled, I tipped out the contents amongst the mess already left by Caleb and threw the key on top of the pile. Maybe the energies would be messed up by the thief's energetic footprints. Once David had looked through everything on the table, he'd realise he had everything anyway. Maybe it wouldn't matter that someone random had been in his house. Maybe pigs would fly.

He was going to know it was me, no two ways about it.

A light flashed past outside and car pulled up. My breath caught in my throat. A door slammed. My heart tried to leap through my mouth. *David.* Another door slammed, a heavier one, like a boot lid.

I chucked the empty bag under the table and ran the few steps to the doorway. Held my breath. Footsteps coming up the steps outside confirmed my worst fear.

I looked down the hall to the front door. His figure was silhouetted in the frosted glass. He was fiddling with the door. I fingered the key in my pocket. I had seconds. The door under the stairs directly across from me cast an invitation. I hoped it wasn't a cloakroom and stepped one stride across the hall and through. As I closed it quickly behind me, I nearly fell down the stairs. The smell was damp and musty, like a cellar. No coats. I could hear the xylobones on the outside swinging gently, scraping the wood. I willed them to stop.

I listened. A series of taps and bangs began, presumably the front doo—

—*crash.*

My body shook with the strength of a heroin addict on a comedown. He'd broken into his own house. I heard slow footsteps on the tiled floor of the hall. One. Two. Pause. I held my breath. I couldn't hear the bones sliding on the cellar door any more.

He took another two steps closer and I prayed to my

spirits that he wouldn't check this door. The whole frame of the room creaked, the door, the stairs, everything groaned. And again. The stairs, he was on the stairs, heavy footed and slow, like someone truly tired. Agonisingly slow, he moved to the next step and the next. I counted thirteen, the wood straining around me till he stood directly above my head. He stopped. A creak of a wooden banister, or perhaps a floorboard, then nothing. Nothing. Nothing. He was listening. Not falling asleep, listening. Suspicion leaked through the cracks in the stairs, dribbling down the walls in the space between him and me.

I couldn't breathe. Couldn't let myself draw the same air he was breathing above my head. The longest moments stretched out and I wondered if this was it. Was he looking at me directly through a spyhole in the ceiling?

He took another step. And another. And ano—his foot slipped on the stairs with a bang. Another step and his weight moved to a different part of the stairs, upwards beyond the cellar ceiling. He shuffled across the floor and I realised he'd made it to the upstairs hall.

A door handle rattled distantly and a loud click confirmed he was entering a bedroom. The door slammed. Two more steps and I heard a loud dull thud, as if he'd sunk into the comfort of his bed. I waited. Counted to thirty. No more movement above my head.

Praying for quiet, I pulled the cellar door open as gently as possible so that the bones weren't disturbed. I didn't bother closing it, just left it ajar. He would know someone had been in anyway.

The hallway seemed longer in this direction. Further to go. I tiptoed across the tiles, thankful no floorboards could creak and give my game away. As I reached the front door, I found it ajar, the whole Yale lock bust off the frame, splintered wood decorating the ground. I didn't remember if the door squeaked, just knew I had to get the hell through it and away. I swung it open carefully, but it hit the bird skull above my head with a clatter. Shocked, I leapt through the frame without closing the door. As the glorious night hit me, I ran down the steps and path and on to the pavement at full pelt, crossing the road and sprinting straight down the street in front of his house.

My coat banged against me as I ran and I pushed my hand into the pocket to see what was there. To my horror my fingers closed around a small box. My chest tightened with panic. How could I have forgotten to return the ring? The black night closed in on me.

I turned on reflex to go back and chuck it in the bag, but someone was standing in his upstairs window. I dove behind the nearest tree and peeped around.

I couldn't go back. I hadn't counted on him realising

so soon that I'd been in there. It was too late.

I stayed behind the tree for what felt like an age, but I didn't dare look around its trunk to check. I peeled my ears to listen for the sound of the front door, for steps that indicated he was coming after me. He'd seemed so slow moving up the stairs, I never imagined he'd get up again, never mind come after me, but maybe he'd known all along I was in the house.

Minutes passed. I thought I should go home but I didn't want to set off straight away. As I acknowledged my hesitance, heaviness in my bones pulled me back to rest against the tree for a moment. Tiredness spread across my body and I propped myself up, sagging against the ash trunk. I weakened and the ground invited me lovingly but I made myself stand. Fear told me he was coming for me, but I was more afraid to keep moving.

After a while, I felt a little lighter. I stood up straight and poked my head round the ash tree for one last look at the house. Through the upstairs window a doorway opened briefly into the lit hall and he passed through it from the room into the hallway. The door closed and the room was in darkness again.

Relief flooded in. My spirits had held me there, made me stay a few minutes longer and he missed seeing me walking away. I thanked my angels and guides and goddess for giving me respite from another confrontation.

I gave it another minute then strode off homewards, down the avenue. All the way home I fiddled with the box but I didn't open it fully.

Indira met me at the door.

"Are you okay? Have you been? You were ages," she scolded. "I nearly called the police. How did it go?"

I couldn't see her sympathising at the fact I still had the ring but I wouldn't let myself get away without telling her.

"I gave the bag back but he nearly caught me."

"Why, what happened?" Indira's eyes were as huge as they could go.

"I'm an idiot, that's what happened." I took my coat off, leaving the ring box in the pocket, and entered the living room, Indira right behind me, dying to know more.

A cup of tea and a piece of cake later, I relayed the tale and steeled myself for the bollocking.

She was aghast. Almost speechless, for her.

"Oh my God, babe. I can't even..." She stopped. "He saw you? Is he going to start coming round here? Do you think he'll break in here, like tit for tat?"

I hoped not. Maybe it wasn't his style. I thought about him jumping me at the front door. I hadn't expected that to be his style either.

"I can't believe you went in there." She took a slurp of her tea, still processing my story. "And the ring. So we've still got the dragon?"

I nodded dolefully. "Might come in handy if he starts on me."

"So you do think he's going to come after you?" She was more than alert, eyes flickering across my face, like she was thinking a million things at the same time.

"I just don't know. Maybe he didn't know it was me." My answer was the lamest of lame.

"I even told you to leave the key," she groaned. "I didn't think I had to mention the ring. I thought you were going to sort this once and for all."

I'd let us both down. She was going to ask me to leave, I could feel it coming. I felt like crying. I just wanted the whole thing over with right now. I wished David was dead.

"Do you think anything else is going to happen? What are you going to do?" she asked.

I shrugged, head hanging low, tea getting cold. "I'll ask Molly."

In the morning, Molly was more sympathetic than I expected. She was also extremely businesslike.

"Hide the ring—somewhere you can throw it out of the window in an emergency. You'll have to do your protection properly. Violet light won't cut it."

"What like?" Violet light generally shielded me from other people's negative thoughts. I didn't know how powerful it would be if it was just me fighting someone who knew what he was doing with magic, but the guy who had initiated me into its use seemed pretty certain it was good for everything.

At its core the violet vibration transmutes darkness into light so it doesn't just burn off the esoteric gunge our souls acquire through living, it changes its very essence. This has always been my experience of it, but I might just have to work harder at it now.

"I'll get a book sent to you, it's one I picked up last year and it's got some pretty good tricks in it."

"I'll probably be okay with the violet, you don't have to do that." I had already used it for protection and healing for all kinds of tiny situations.

"Nope, I'll do it as soon as I get off the phone, you'll need it. There's all sorts in it. She properly knows what she's doing, the woman who wrote it, you'll see. No argument."

Bloody Yorkshire people, you can never stop them from giving you things. I gave in for an easy life.

"You think he definitely saw me?"

"I think you're asking for trouble if you don't batten down your hatches. He'll probably know you were in there, even if he didn't recognise you running away." She wouldn't commit to the worst scenario, but her firm tone was impossible to ignore. "Did it not occur to you to just dump the stuff on the doorstep? When you said you were going to take it back I never thought for a second you'd literally break into his house."

"I'm a literal person. I usually mean exactly what I say," I said sulkily. "I thought it was better if he didn't know it had gone."

"He's a magician," she said flatly. "If you blow your nose on his hanky, he's going to know."

My naiveties blew me away, gave me a sense of floating through nothingness. Waking up now to the possibilities was the slowest thing I've ever done. But I needed all the friends I could get right now and I had a feeling Indira and I were on shaky ground in that respect at the moment.

"Are you mad with me?" I asked in a small voice.

She sighed. "Not mad with you, but I almost can't believe what you did. You're either very brave or very stupid."

"Think I've been a bit naive," I admitted. She might as well know.

"I'll say. I know it's hard to understand when someone is out to get you, but you've got to wake up, kid. It's not like you're new to magic."

I tried to put the terror to one side for the moment. We still hadn't a chance to sit down and chat about everyday life.

"Do you mind me asking what you do for work, Molly?"

"I work for a security firm, love, at Airewater Place, you know the big skyscraper on the way out of town towards the motorway? I'm in there."

"Wow, nice place to work."

"You mean apart from the dead pigeons hitting the windows on the 15th floor and the dead people in half the rooms downstairs?"

"Dead people?"

"Used to be a bus station, a popular place to die."

She sounded like she was grinning mischievously.

"You're having me on, right?"

She took on a bus tour operator's tone. "So, welcome to Airewater Place. As you walk across the foyer, mind you don't accidentally walk through the homeless trio." She tutted dramatically. "They like to stand smack in the middle between the door and the desk so when someone new first comes in, they almost always walk through them." She paused. "Then you've got Mamie in the lift. She's a little girl who was crushed by roofing sheeting coming in on a windy day. The lift just happens to be in that spot so that's where she is. Up and down all day. Bit pale and unhealthy looking. Next, along the corridor—do you want me to go on?"

"Are they really ghosts?" I'd had conversations many

times with different people about what they thought ghosts and spirits to be. My spirit guides were distinctly there but still invisible to me. I'd never seen a ghost, but I'd felt a lot of weird shit.

"I don't know what they're made of, but all spirits are spirits. Those ones I just told you about are stuck where they are. They don't talk to me and it's like they're in their own worlds. Other ones like the boy in one of the conference rooms..."

"What?"

She gave it a good long pause with plenty of dramatic effect. "I was doing a final sweep of the building one night, ground floor, could hear a football smacking a wall. I opened the door I thought it was coming from and there's a sixteen-year-old boy playing kick-about. He came over when he saw me, confused, but I could see the light behind him, he was being called in. He didn't know he was dead. He was run over by a bus at Gate Twenty-three, thirty years ago. I just said to him, 'You're dead, go into the light', and he looked at me weirdly and picked up his ball, like he wasn't going anywhere without that."

Her clarity of sight staggered me.

"Hell, Molly, did he go? Did you save him?"

She sounded pleased. "He went. But he was reachable. The others are beyond where I can reach them. And I think the homeless trio suck a bit of energy out of people every time they walk through them."

Bile rose inside me at the revolting thought.

"All the residents have complained for months they think Airewater Place has sick building syndrome. Everyone feels more and more fed up after they enter the building. You wouldn't believe the sickness absence rate. It's literally a ghost building some days. Just me and the ghosts."

"Can't you do something about the homeless ones?" She could have said she had superpowers and I would have believed it.

"They won't talk to me, probably having too much of a good time and there isn't the light behind them like the boy. There's exorcisms and suchlike, but I'd rather just stick to my Reiki for now and I don't even do that unless I'm up to it. Interfering doesn't get you anywhere good unless it's truly necessary."

We were silent together for a moment. Interfering was a different way of seeing help. I wondered which one had Geraldine done for us. Her gift of the additional ring felt off, like something wasn't congruent, didn't match up with my expectations.

"Show me a picture of this bloke," Molly said unexpectedly. "I can't remember what he looks like. Is he on your Facebook?"

"No, I didn't even know his surname until yesterday."

"What's his name? I've got the laptop open."

"David Catcheside." I could hear her typing at the other end.

"Oh, we found him. Something's coming through," she said, breathing fast. "Oh, shit, it's coming through. It's nasty, whatever it is, it's nasty. He's using it to get to you. Oh. Oh, shit."

"What's going on?" I realised she was crying.

"Oh god, it's horrible. Where the hell was this thing when he was right in front of me? I smacked him over the head and didn't even see it." She sounded gutted, empty even. She moaned a little. "His eyes, he's not a nice person at all." She gasped. "I'm getting—ugh—deep water. Don't go near—Don't know where it is. Stay away from deep water. Dirty water."

"Eh?" Apart from the occasional puddle, I didn't have much to do with deep water.

"There's junk in the water. A car. Metal things." She breathed in hoarsely. "Drowni—Have you got salt? Get a bag of salt, sea salt if you can and go round your hou—can you walk right round your house?"

"You can the house, but not round our flat by itself." My heart was pounding out of my chest. "It'll take a tonne of salt to do round the whole house."

"Cooking salt, anything you've got." She was breathing more easily now. "I'll get that book to you on express delivery. You'll need every bit of help you can get."

"So, you just want me to stick the ring somewhere?"

"Just chuck it to one side. It doesn't matter any more, does it?" Her dismissiveness surprised me.

"They gave me another ring, too."

That caught her attention. "Why'd they do that?"

I fingered the box and opened it up again.

"I don't know. She said it was a gift from them to me. They put a blessing spell on it." I took the solid silver ring out of the box and turned it over.

"You going to wear that?"

"I don't know if I buy it."

"What do you mean?"

I weighed things up in my mind as I followed the lines of the ring. Molly was someone new to me, but I trusted her—so far. She'd proved herself. Geraldine was someone Molly knew, but that didn't mean she was okay.

"If Geraldine wasn't a good person, you would know, right?"

I could hear her smile.

"It doesn't really work like that, love. I don't know her, I just chatted with her for a while when I bought some sage a few weeks ago. How about I take a look at it for you

Wednesday? Might not be able to tell a thing. Don't wear it, or the other one. And don't go near water *at all*."

That sounded sensible and she hadn't defended Geraldine at all. Relief crept in. I snapped the box shut over the garnet and tucked the silver ring in my purse.

"Don't forget that book's coming," Molly continued. "Do everything in it. In fact, go get yourself some large glass bottles and start picking hawthorn and blackthorn twigs."

"What for?"

"You'll see."

13. Salt and Afflictions

I walked down to the nearby Tesco to buy four kilos of cheap cooking salt. I didn't have the kind of wage that would fund sea salt at that quantity. The witchery I had done here and there hadn't used it for protection, other than to mark out my circle, but it had been effective as a catalyst for an employment spell a few times. Salt is effective for all its magical uses, whatever its quality, the everyday table version as efficacious as the fancy stuff in most cases.

The supermarket was busy, a line of customers at every live till. I didn't bother grabbing any other items, just stood with my salt, sandwiched in a queue for fifteen minutes.

The light outside dimmed towards dusk and a splatter of rain scudded across the windows with extra murk. A small knot of customers at the main entrance cleared and the sliding doors opened. A whoosh of cold air entered the building with what almost sounded like a growl, a noise that jerked a few heads around, not just mine.

I paid for the salt, split it between two bags for balance and set out into the darkening wilderness. Wind howled down Gledhow Wood Road as I trudged up the hill, head down, eyes half-closed. Splatters of rain began in fits and starts and as soon as I turned the corner at the top, I sped up my legs to an almost run.

With my head well down, I pounded the pavement only looking ahead. I was aware of a massive puddle on the road to my left, but as I came level with it, a car passed and drove straight through the flood, drenching me from my hat to my shoes.

I stood for a long moment to see if they were going to come back and rescue me but the car drove on, apparently oblivious to just rendering someone's day from pretty bad to sucking donkey balls.

In the increasing rain, I sensed an odd subconscious hum. A sort of presence. Something low level and distinctly sinister, like a minor note, very deep. Even two consecutive notes together in a clash. Something large, an obvious vibe, now I'd noticed it. I felt silly and paranoid, but took off at a half run again, sopping feet slapping the wet tarmac. Nearly home.

As I reached the gate to our drive I looked back. I saw no-one but when I sensed outwards, whatever stalked me was still there. The paranoia made me queasy. I didn't know what was real and what was just me playing tricks on myself.

When I got home Indira was busy in the kitchen.

"I just felt like cake and you never have your phone and I couldn't be arsed to go to Tesco." She poked at the batter. "I definitely should have done it with a recipe. Seems a bit stiff."

She turned to look at my dripping form in the doorway and dropped the spoon into the bowl.

"Why does this keep happening to you?" She marched into my room to find a towel.

I stripped and wrapped the proffered bath sheet around my shivering, clammy body. "Why does this never happen to anyone else?"

"Is it raining that hard?"

"It was a twat in a car and a puddle at the top of the hill."

Indira snorted and grinned. "You got splashed by a car?"

She handed me my PJs but I didn't put them on. I'd be going out in a few minutes.

"It's the second time in my life this has happened." No-one could deny me my crown. "How many people can say they've been half-drowned by a car-puddle situation twice in their lives?" I pulled a face at her and smiled. Best to laugh at yourself first before everyone else got there. "How's the cake?"

She frowned and picked up the wooden spoon to poke the offending batter. "It just doesn't seem right. Can't bear heavy cake."

Hands down, I was a better baker than she was. "What does the recipe say?"

She smiled. "Not following one, I thought I knew how to make cake."

I'd never known her make cake in the whole time we'd lived together.

"How many eggs did you put in?"

"Two."

"How much butter and flour?"

"I did four-four-four-two, babe."

"Those eggs are only tiny, I'd chuck another one in there." I stood for a moment, wondering if my time at her flat was coming to an end. She didn't seem any different from usual, despite the conversation the night before.

"Indira."

She glanced up as she beat the batter. "What's up?"

She was too distracted and focused on the cake. I

faltered. "Never mind."

I left the cake-making and headed for my room. I texted Molly.

> *Drowned in a puddle on the way*
> *home from Tesco! Hope it's not an*
> *omen. All I have to do is get the salt*
> *around the house? How thick the line?*

She came back immediately. Always did.

> *As thick as you can manage in this*
> *weather.*

She was right. The night was atrocious and squally, so wet and windy I'd be lucky to get it down as any kind of barrier. I had to put some serious intention behind it.

In my bedroom I changed into a new set of clothes and a dry coat and steadied my nerves. I dropped my attention down to my heart area and felt the calm earth below.

I nipped back into the kitchenette, grabbed the scissors and headed into the hall with the packs of salt still in their carrier bags.

"I'm just going out to—for a walk," I said quickly. More witchy stuff might send her over the edge. I hadn't detected any Valium since Thursday, but that didn't mean she didn't have any.

She looked at me sharply. "In this weather? Did you not get wet enough already?"

I closed my eyes for a long moment, but knew I'd have to come clean. I couldn't think quick enough to lie.

"I'm putting some protection stuff down. Just in case he really did see me, okay?" I was ready for a fight, but she shrugged, stony faced and beat her batter harder. Any more of this and I was for the high jump.

"I'll be back in about half an hour." I hoped it would be sooner, but who knew. I didn't even know how long it took to walk round the hall at a normal pace, never mind clumsily fighting the elements while I made an esoteric barrier with grains of salt. I hoped it wasn't the witchy equivalent of pissing into the wind.

As I stepped outside the front door, I didn't initially detect the hum presence. I tore a wide corner off the first pack of salt, slipped my left arm into the handles of the shopping bags and made myself fully present. I centred, grounded, and focused on feeling safe, despite the storm. As I took my first step into the weather, the wind whipped my shoulders around and I staggered, dragged down by the weight of the salt. Straightening, I leant into the gale and readied my mind.

My hackles rose with a shiver up my spine. The presence was still there. Deep, powerful and—threatening. Near.

I faced the wind, ready to go clockwise around the building. I would follow the shape of the house, right at its base, rather than making a perfect circle.

Close up to the wall the wind didn't blow the salt around so much, so I carefully poured it out in a thin solid line, going back over bits I noticed had blown a gap.

The rose bushes at a gable end of the house gave me a bit of trouble, their stabby, scratchy stems poking into my face and neck, so I went around them and carried on close to the base of the building until I was almost all the way round. I hoped the start of the salt line was obvious because I couldn't remember properly where I'd begun.

As I turned the corner of the house for the final straight, the creepy hum presence washed all around me like I'd walked right through it. It dissipated a little so I held my nerve and poured the salt—on my fourth bag by now—as quickly and neatly as I could. The thick line was luminescent even without moonlight.

I got to the base of the porch and joined the line to its tail, thick with all the salt left in the pack. As I ran up the steps to enter the house an almighty crack filled the air. As I leapt for the entrance, a massive branch from the ash tree opposite crashed to a rest right across the porch steps, its twisted tops almost touching my heels.

I dashed into the hallway and slammed the massive door closed. Its iron studs were a reference to another age when metaphysical properties coincided with common sense.

The studs didn't just strengthen the wood. They were also a guarantee against certain types of magic. I hoped this storm fell into the right category.

Indira came into the hallway from the flat, tying her robe tightly. "The tree's gone down. We were lucky not to get smashed windows."

"I was lucky not to be killed," I said, gasping. I leant against the wall and rubbed my face. That had been a bit close to handle and the presence was more than just my imagination. I still didn't rule out the possibility I was just a bit paranoid, but my instincts had begun to be eerily close to right. I didn't want this fear to be real in any form but I could miss the signs if I was too rational.

Indira gave me a hug, but she wanted to take a look at the tree.

Footsteps from upstairs rattled downwards. Maggie stood on the first landing above us.

"What happened? That was an almighty bang."

"The tree came down just opposite the door. We nearly lost our windows," called up Indira. "I'm just going out there now."

"Not in your nighty," I said to put her off. "The weather's way too horrible to go out in, just stay put till tomorrow, no-one can sort it till then. The drive's like a wind tunnel, you could get hit by something."

"Don't go out now," Maggie backed me up. "You don't know what else will be flying around. Just call the office in the morning."

She was such a caring person and her voice had just the right level of sensible in its tone. I was relieved, Indira wasn't noted for doing things I suggested. Besides, there was no point ringing the potentially expensive call-out line for the landlord when it could all be handled for free in just over twelve hours. Indira gave in to the pressure from both of us and came back inside with me into the flat.

As I hung my coat up, I smelled burning.

"What's that smell?"

Indira stared at me in horror. "It can't be, I only just put it in twenty minutes ago!" She dashed into the kitchen and I heard a clatter as she dumped the offending article on the counter. As I rounded the doorway, I could see it, a smouldering mass of burnt cake in a tin.

She turned to me with fury. "What happened to it? It's like the oven was on four-thousand degrees!" She looked at the clock. "Literally twenty minutes." She shoved it angrily towards the wall on the counter and came back to take off her own coat.

A burnt cake was probably the least of our troubles, but I worried again that Indira would make connections. She had surely already had enough of me. I couldn't live with not knowing, not being able to prepare for the worst. I took a deep breath and faced her as she hung up her jacket.

"Indira."

"Uh oh." She looked at me curiously, cake anger gone. "That sounds like you half an hour ago."

I sighed and avoided her eyes. "Do you want me to leave?"

"What? Why?" She walked into the living room and I followed her.

"Find somewhere else to live?"

I glanced at her. She flopped onto the sofa and looked at me questioningly, so I pushed through my fears. Better to know one way or another.

"I'm scared everything's going to get weirder."

"You worried that guy's going to come round? Shall I get Jimmy and Dale to stay over for a couple of days?"

Those two would certainly be fun to have around, but that wasn't what I meant. I stuck to being honest. "I'm just worried. The tree was seriously close. I was nearly killed just then."

"That was the wind, hun, the guy doesn't control the weather does he?"

I thought about that for a long moment. Magic could control the weather, but the storm wasn't localised to Gledhow Hall and this weather wasn't unusual at this time of year.

Problem was, magic tapped into available opportunity.

"He doesn't, does he?" she prompted me, her eyes wider now. She didn't want to believe in any of it, but she'd already seen enough to chip her cynicism.

I opted for the safer option, but felt as though I was tricking her now. "He doesn't control the weather exactly, but he might have taken advantage of it."

"So the tree fell down in the wind because he made it happen? What about my cake?"

"I just don't know. But I want you to be safe."

She picked up the remote and switched on the TV.

"Sounds like the ramblings of a madwoman," she dismissed me, flicking through the channels. "The tree fell down because it was windy and the tree was old."

Hope flickered inside me.

She selected a channel and shot me a sideways look. "If you move out, I'm up shit creek. Don't forget you pay half my rent. I'll never find someone else at short notice."

"Might be better paying it yourself than having some unimaginable accident." Harsh, perhaps, but she had to understand the possibilities. Magical practitioners could be a bit more inventive than your average serial killer.

"Until I own my restaurant, I'll take my chances, babe. No-one's going to want to live in that tiny room of yours and I don't want to move."

I still felt guilty. She wasn't fully aware of the possibilities. Neither was I, but I wasn't in denial. "If you want to start looking for a new flatmate, just do it."

She didn't even reply, engrossed in her programme. The conversation was over as far as she was concerned.

I lay on my bed for a long while, more than a couple of hours. I drifted in and out of sleep, not trying to nap but practising being present. The more 'in the moment' you are, the more effective you'll be. It's the key to magic of any kind. Presence makes the intent clearer. However, knowing this doesn't mean you do it. So practice.

My dreams were distant and lonely, jogging around a canal, running furiously over a bridge. Chased. A person in a full-length, hooded black cloak, standing in the trees, or over the bridge, watching with burning eyes. Someone grabbed me from behind, countless times, and once they threw me into deep water. I woke myself up, spluttering and gasping, my heart racing. Falling asleep, I was running again, sprinting for my life, the person in the distance, still there, eyes still glowing like the embers of a fire.

I looked up at the ceiling. The spot directly above my pillow seemed to be larger than usual. I stood up and felt it with my finger, aware of an intense heaviness in my limbs. The tip of my finger was blood red.

I lifted it to my nose to sniff and the bed turned into a

whirlpool and sucked me down into—

I clawed my way out of sleep and sat up on the side of the bed, reaching for my phone.

> *Hi Moll, did the salt, nearly got killed*
> *in the process. Coincidence?*

Back she came, fast as ever.

> *No such thing as coincidence. Are you*
> *safe now?*

I sincerely hoped so.

> *What else do I need to do?*

She always had an answer for everything. I liked that in a person.

> *Start collecting red thread, a black*
> *candle, 9 iron nails, blackthorn,*
> *hawthorn, cayenne pepper...can't*
> *remember the rest but you'll get that*
> *book tomorrow. Some big glass bottles*
> *you can seal shut. At least one.*

I had no idea what the glass bottles were for, but I had an inkling about some of the items. Iron again, with tangled red thread to confuse the devil. Thorn bushes have protective qualities and cayenne pepper would sting the eyes and cause breathing problems.

Molly texted again.

> *Are we still up for Wednesday?*

I was counting on it if I was still alive.

⁂

Monday morning dawned as miserable as the night before, if a little less windy. Indira and I inspected the damage to the tree but it was too heavy for us to even rock. The porch steps and balustrade weren't damaged, only blocked by the tree. I searched for my line of salt but only remnants remained around the front of the house. I wondered uncomfortably if I should replenish it and spent a good part of my journey to work imagining coming home to a smouldering shell of a house.

The worry developed into a churning belly and the noises emanating from its anxious knot got me concerned glances from Christine who looked like she'd never heard someone's stomach churn.

"Are you ill?" she asked, delicately.

I shook my head. "I don't think so. No pain and I'm not hungry, my stomach's just making stupid noises." I was looking forward to seeing Leah at lunchtime, no overactive belly would get in the way of that.

By eleven o'clock, I was in pain. Just a low grumble, but more painful with every move. I tried not to let Christine see how much discomfort I was in. I couldn't afford to be off work. Lunch with Leah didn't seem like such a great idea now.

At midday Leah's laugh as she spoke to the receptionist around the corner from my office was the signal for me to go. I stood up abruptly, swung my bag over my shoulder and took a step away from my desk. The ground came up to meet me and everything disappeared. I awoke to confusion, Christine trying to roll me over as vomit welled up through my gullet. As I barfed a miserable slick of bile and phlegm onto the floor, she shoved me away and someone shoved a cardboard tray under my face. My stomach heaved the rest of its contents—mostly coffee—while I lay helpless, shattered as abdominal spasms wracked my body.

I could hear Christine in the distance.

"Probably food poisoning. She went downhill since eight-thirty. I've been watching her all morning."

Leah's voice was in the background talking fast, but I couldn't hear her properly. Her voice was muffled as though she was in a different room.

My diaphragm heaved again but nothing was left. It couldn't be food poisoning, I only ate at home. I retched yet again but my body let go of the spasm a little sooner and I let myself lie there with my face in my own vomit, so weak I couldn't even lift my own head. Someone stroked my hair and pulled it back away from the mess on my face. A damp sponge drawn over the back of my head cooled me down a little and I was aware of Leah's voice again.

"It's okay babe, they're here, you're gonna be sorted." Louder. "Can I get some help down here please?"

The ambulance crew were kind and quick to clean me up. They asked me if I could walk and when we tried, I could, so we headed for the ambulance, Leah's hands on my waist, the paramedics' arms supporting mine.

Just as we reached the ambulance I was wracked with a rippling cramp that split my entire body. I stumbled, but the ambulance men had a strong hold under my arms and directed my staggering legs to a gurney in the back of the van. As I lay down the pain moved lower into my abdomen, as though it had purpose.

As they slammed the doors closed, Leah called something out to me. The only word I made out was "hospital".

I vacantly watched a mark on the van ceiling as it wiggled its way across the roof. The ambulance men were dead spirits without substance, who flitted in and out of my vision. No-one spoke to me and I wondered if I was dead too.

When I properly awoke, we were in a hospital corridor waiting. Initially, all I knew of was the presence, a heavy, dark weight. An anchor, dragging at my left-hand-side attention, a mini black hole in my consciousness. I tried to turn my head to look but my body was too tired to move. The pain was firmly lodged low down in my abdomen and spiked me with every gurgle of my belly.

Someone far away mentioned acute appendicitis. Someone else said it had come on too quickly. A man in a white coat came up and bent over me.

"Can you understand me?" he asked. His breath smelled like sour apples.

I nodded.

"Can she understand me?" he asked someone else.

I nodded harder and blinked my eyes frenziedly. My head barely moved, but a paramedic noticed my eyes.

"Hello, Inayat, are you having trouble moving?" he asked me at face level, staring into my eyes.

I blinked hard a few times.

"Try twice for yes and once for no," he instructed.

I blinked twice.

"I'm going to touch you to see what you can feel." He held my hand. "Can you feel that?"

I could. He went to my foot. "How about now?"

No problem, I just couldn't move. My body couldn't be bothered.

"There's hopefully no paralysis and no broken bones. Do you feel very weak?"

I blinked twice. And then again to be sure.

"On a scale of one to ten, how bad is your pain?" The man in the white coat was back.

"Blink the number," said the paramedic.

I blinked eight times. As if in response, the cramps in my belly shot an especially nasty strike but my body no longer spasmed. It'd had enough. I sagged into the pillow and my eyelids dropped unbidden. I forced them open with difficulty.

"I'm going to give you some morphine," said the man. "But first you get something to stop you vomiting."

I wished they'd given me that sooner. I drifted off to a happier world with the morphine injection and waited for my operation the following day.

14. Spiritual Protection

On Wednesday afternoon, Leah came to see me. I heard her laughing and joking with someone from down the corridor long before I saw her. She always had something to say to everyone she met.

She stopped in the doorway and scanned the ward, smiling when she saw me.

"Oh my God what a mess you were." She dumped her handbag on the side table, pushing the jug of water to one side and assessed the state of me now. "Look a lot better without that sexy pool of sick!"

I pulled myself to a sitting position, grateful to see her. Hospital without visitors is the most depressing place in the world.

"It was appendicitis. Came on really quick. They didn't

know what it was for ages."

She frowned. "Didn't know you got sick with appendicitis. My cousin had it, really bad pains in her belly."

I shook my head. "You don't normally. Took them ages to figure it out." I remembered her news. "Did you get the job?"

She looked deathly serious and I felt gutted. Then her face lit up with a grin.

"Yep! I start as team leader in a month!"

"Yay! Better money?"

She nodded. "Not great considering it's one of those jobs that gets everything to do, but I'll give it six months and if it's shit there'll be something better out there. Might go work for BP, long term. Gotta keep moving!" She pulled a water bottle out of her bag and took a swig. "Want some water from your jug?"

I didn't. "It's got amoebas in it." I hated water that had been sitting around.

She did a double take at me and pulled a face. "Nice, Inayat. So, did you get your other problem sorted out?"

I slid down in the bed a little and looked away. "It may have got worse."

"What did you do?"

"I didn't tell you Caleb came round, did I?"

She pursed her lips and shook her head slowly. "Wonder why, huh?"

"I was going to tell you on Monday."

"Uh huh. Sure you were. What did that weasel want?"

"He wants me to get his engagement ring back from Olivia."

"That bitch? Tell me you told him to get fucked."

"He kept coming over, brought me a bag of stuff. I didn't know it was bad."

"Wait, why'd you even let him in? I presume he wasn't doing all this on the doorstep?" She was just getting warmed up. In a way, I was glad. When she stopped getting mad—that was when she didn't care any more.

"He forced his way in."

"Broke the door down, right?" Her cynicism hurt, but the little dead part of me on the inside left by Caleb all those years ago, it knew she was right to be that way.

I whispered the rest. "He stole the stuff from the crazy guy who attacked me."

"How did—seriously? How did he do that?" Her eyes flicked across my face. "Did you ask him to help you?"

I shook my head. "He stole the guy's house key from me when he came around the first time."

"'The first time'—how many times did he come over?"

I couldn't look at her, thinking about how I'd been to see him about the ring too. She wasn't going to like this. "Four times, I guess."

She sat up straight, head back and looked at at the ceiling for strength.

"Jesus Christ, no-one can help you. You're what's known as 'beyond help'."

I knew that. I had to cut to the chase before she got pissed off. I whispered again, "Long story short, I took the stuff back, broke into his house and returned the bag of stuff."

"Oh. My. God." Her lips just formed the words without sound. She closed her eyes and rested her head in her hand. "What happened then?"

I didn't know. "I think he might be after me."

She sat up again, shaking her head. "Oh no, we're not going down this road again, I'm not dealing with this shit again."

"Not Caleb, the other guy."

"Inayat, I don't want to know. We're not doing this again. Fixations, magic, paranoid android, just no. No, no, no."

She got up and replaced her water bottle in her handbag.

"You're not well and you're obviously not in your right mind. I'm going to come over and see you at home when you're a bit better. When are you home?"

"Dunno when they're going to discharge me."

"Sunday. I'll come over Sunday. You'll be out by then,

they don't keep you longer than a working week unless you're dying." She backed away, still talking. "Get yourself well, but don't be thinking like this. The paranoia that comes with all this shit isn't going to help you heal."

I felt like the stuffing had been knocked out of me. "I'm not being paranoid."

"We both know this road, babe." She tucked her clutch under her arm. "I'll see you Sunday. Get yourself well and just focus on nice stuff. I'll bring wine. We can talk it all over then—bet you'll be feeling more like your proper self by then. I know you got it in you, do it for yourself, okay?"

She waved and turned on her heel, heading off through the double doors of the ward as fast as her legs could take her. I couldn't blame her. I couldn't expect my friends to just keep giving me everything I needed to continue being a fool. My fixation on Caleb had been one of the hardest times for our friendship. She gave me sensible advice that I repeatedly ignored but when I needed picking up off the floor, she was the person I called to make things right again. Actually, I didn't much know how we were still friends.

As reality left the room, magic walked straight back in. The ward's double doors swung hard with Leah's exit and regurgitated a short skinny lady with brown hair and a large handbag.

Molly. I stifled my tears and smiled at her. Two visitors

on one day was definitely a good day, even if it wasn't going too well so far.

My phone had died almost as soon as I'd gone into hospital but she'd heard on the grapevine somehow, arriving with chocolate, mint tea, ginger beer, flowers, a card and a book.

"What's with the face?" she asked brightly.

"Nothing." I didn't want to tell her about Leah. My friends generally didn't like each other much anyway and it wasn't Leah's fault, it was mine.

"You won't have been at home when the book arrived," she said, arranging the flowers in the amoeba-ridden water jug. "So that's my copy while you're in hospital and you can give it me back when you get home."

I looked at the cover. Entitled *Spiritual Protection*, it depicted a pair of hands on the cover, clasped together in supplication. I hoped it wasn't Christian exorcism rituals.

Molly saw my face. "What's up with you?" she chided. "There's a lot you probably need to learn and that book's got everything useful." She opened the book to a particular page and pointed at a paragraph about witch bottles.

"It takes time to get those together, but once you've done it, it's a shield for a long time."

That was what the bottles and thorns were for. I flipped the book over and read the blurb. The author's no-

nonsense style shone through and was just what I needed right now. At first glance, her magical practice was an acceptable number of light years from Christian exorcism rituals.

I lay my head back on the pillow. "I think I'll use everything in it, thanks. Thank you, you didn't have to." It was always nice to be bought a book, never mind at times of direst need.

"Yes, I did. We didn't get there soon enough and look what happened to you." Molly was pretty gruff but I could tell she cared. She pulled a bottle of ginger beer from her bag, unscrewed it and popped a straw in the neck. That bag was like a magical sack. Every time she put her hand in, she pulled out something else.

I wondered how she stayed so thin, but noticed she didn't get one out for herself. Maybe that was how it worked.

We operated the bed so I could sit almost upright and I drank the sticky biting fizz. It was better than anything served in the hospital.

"When do you think they'll let you out?" Molly looked around the ward. "I can't see them letting you do the things in that book while you're still here. I'll keep you hidden until then."

"They're talking about Friday but I'm going to see if they'll let me out tomorrow. Every time someone comes to the ward door I expect it to be David. My nerves can't take much more of this."

"He won't come himself. I wouldn't like to guess what he'll send, but trust me, he won't find you."

I lay my head on the pillow and looked at her from the side. Golden light wafted around her head like a heat mirage. She was hiding me somehow and I was glad of it.

She looked at me hard. "How's the pain?"

"Just wind." We both laughed and she dug in her bag and threw a box of mint tea at me.

"You'll need that, then. Can't stand the stuff myself, but it's good for windy pops!"

I popped it into the top cupboard of my bedside cabinet.

Her smile dropped. "Anything unusual about your operation?"

I thought back. "They said my appendix was gangrenous, I could have got peritonitis. Also they said normally it starts grumbling for a couple of days before it gets bad. That's why they weren't sure what it was to start with. Mine happened in a morning and I threw up everywhere. There was nothing wrong with me at all before I got to work."

"You're still 'at' work, aren't you?" said Molly thoughtfully. She felt inside her handbag again. "I made this little talisman for you. Hang it around your neck on a chain or put it in your pocket." It was a tiny black velvet drawstring bag, filled with salt, an amethyst and a sprig of hawthorn.

I had neither chain nor pocket, so she tucked it under my pillow.

"Get yourself better," she said, leaving. "I don't think this is going to be all he does."

Molly woke in the middle of the night in a hot sweat. She endured it for a second and glanced at the clock. Three a.m. She tried to roll over to get out of bed but her body didn't respond. She couldn't move. Something's weight pressed down on her middle and anchored her to the mattress. She tried not to panic but she couldn't shift it. She got angry and patted the bed to her left side, feeling for Harry, her husband. He wasn't there. She couldn't see the creature, exactly, but negative matter whirled above her, a figure within the chaos.

It briefly released her but before she could roll over it materialised with more conviction and sat on her chest. Now she saw it clearly, stared in horror over its foul stomach at a huge red devil with twisted horns, aborted babies crawling around its neck like snakes, dragging their bloody umbilical cords behind them. Its mobile mask undulated into many different tortured faces. She thrashed around on the bed with her arms and legs but it held her down tightly, its face near hers, flicking flames from its tongue across her face. The warmth licked her cheek and mouth suggestively and the babies reached out for her breasts, their open mouths as wide as their faces. One of them could have been her child. Her lost one. The one that never made it.

A terrible grief welled up inside her, all the loss and the pain that she'd locked away inside. *God was supposed to look after the little children.*

The demonic screamed with a thousand tones. Molly jerked herself present. She was falling down a rabbit hole. She gathered herself, crushed beneath this denizen of someone's imagination and willed up the love from the bottom of her heart chakra. All the love for her lost child, every drop squeezed out and given as a gift to this monster.

"You can't get me," she told it, levelly. "I've got nothing for you but love."

It threw its head back, still changing up the faces and laughed with evil abandon. Its bass tone was split by throaty growls.

"Not you, where is she?" It grasped her shoulders and shook her till she rattled. "Where? Find her."

It pulled her to a sitting position and hurled her back to the bed, pulling her up again, down-up-down-up, till she didn't know how she was still conscious, but she mustered a breath as he let go.

Reaching towards her neck, fingers like talons, it came in to finish her.

"In the name of Jesus Christ and the Almighty God, our Heavenly Father, I command you to leave me alone right now," she shouted and sent love. An ethereal mist of pink materialised around them. She focused on her baby, how much she'd wanted that child. How much she loved it, even though they'd never stood a chance together.

It laughed all the harder, closed impossibly powerful fingers around her throat.

She drew her last breath.

"In the name of Jesus Christ and the Almighty God, our Heavenly Father, I command you to leave me alone right now!"

It pulled her neck upwards and as she choked into darkness, she knew it would tear her head off.

Hours later she awoke. No demon, no darkness, just morning light through the curtains and Harry in the shower.

He came to the door of the bedroom, drying himself.

"You were out for the count this morning."

Molly rubbed her head, remembering.

"Feel like I was up all night." She got up to look in the mirror and stuck out her tongue. It was yellow, going black towards the back. "Think I'm coming down with something nasty."

This didn't look good. That hadn't been the same demon she'd seen when she looked at the social media profile picture of David Catcheside. Maybe there was one that controlled him and one he controlled.

Molly took two paracetamol just before leaving for work and stuffed the box in her handbag. She had a feeling she would need it.

I awoke just before the witching hour in darkness, only the muttering of the new patient in the bed next to me to break the monotony of night. I listened to her mumbling for a few minutes, trying to make out words in the muffled sounds, but gave up. The softness of my pillow bundled around my ears until I could only hear my own heart beat. Sleep had been elusive that night and the ward was unsettled. At about one o'clock, my bed and all my belongings had been moved to make room for the newcomer, but a quick shot of oral morphine from the staff nurse had kept my whimpering to a minimum. I'd slept and the drugs helped, so now I wondered what had awoken me.

The clock on the opposite side of the room clicked to exactly three o'clock.

The woman's noises became chattering, louder, but just as impossible to discern. She shouted the odd articulation and the tinge of fear in her tone lifted my head to look. To my shock, astride her bed was a gigantic creature that might have been bipedal, except that its seething tentacles were easy to mistake for more legs or arms. Its monstrous ever-shifting face leered close to hers and it lifted her torso and smashed her against the head of the bed repeatedly.

I screamed, realised I wasn't dreaming and hid under my bedclothes, shaking, panicked and sure I was about to die. Clutching at any kind of normal, I wondered if it was some kind of manifestation of her illness, but I wasn't about to pop my head out and take another look. I wasn't clairvoyant anyway, seeing a demon of someone's illness was bloody unusual for me. The thought occurred to me that I might have been the target.

That had been my bed space until I was moved.

My heart pumped so loudly, the demon could have heard it in the next bed. The air under my bedsheets became hot and humid with the smell of my own unhealthy breath, but no way could I move now. My twitching ears could hear only bumps and distant voices in the room. I dared not move though my wound began to sting like it was exposed. Something pressed against the bed cover across my shoulder and again, nearer my head. It scrabbled closer at the opening above my head and I threw the covers off myself with a shout.

A nurse leapt back into the cabinet, knocking the jug

of water over the edge. The plastic hit the floor and its lid burst open, water everywhere. She began mopping it up with some blue roll, talking to me from the floor.

"I just wanted to see if you were okay. You alerted us that something was wrong."

The demonic was gone. The muttering woman was quiet, her bed surrounded by staff. Her body hung half out of her bed and they heaved her back on top. A nurse moved out of the way and I realised her head seemed teardrop shaped. As I focused on what I saw, my stomach nearly went again and I closed my eyes as someone drew the cubicle curtain between us.

I was so stunned, I couldn't even cry—usually my stock response to anything. All morning, I lay next to a crime scene, with a police detective, an undertaker, the Coroner, a crime scene investigation officer and two police constables who spent varying amounts of time inside the lady's curtains. They took her away quite soon, in the company of the morgue manager, and the Coroner left a little later.

A constable came to speak to me. He got straight down to business.

"You were the person who alerted the ward to the problem. What did you see?"

I took a long moment. I had to stick to my guns and tell the truth now, no matter how bizarre, but I knew I'd feel a total fool if someone called me out on it.

"You saw something." He made it a statement, not a question.

"It could have been a bad dream," I said.

"Doesn't look much like a dream to me," he said disapprovingly. "More like a nightmare on Elm Street."

I ignored the reference. Dreams materialising in the real world were the last thing I needed.

"I woke up at just before three o'clock and heard the woman talking to herself. She started getting loud and I took a look." I hazarded a glance at the police officer's face. He seemed interested enough.

"A massive demon with tentacles and a constantly changing face was stood over her beating her up."

The policeman's mouth hung open slightly, but he recovered himself quickly. "A demon." He looked down at his notepad as if he didn't know what to write.

He started slightly. "Are you on medication, Miss Tate?"

I nodded. "I was given Oramorph at about one a.m."

He noted that down in his book, wrote the word 'demon' in capital letters and circled it thoughtfully for a few moments before returning to the present.

"Do you think you might have seen something a bit more—explainable—while you were asleep and your mind changed what you saw?"

I couldn't argue with the rationalisation but I definitely didn't think that's what I saw.

"It's impossible to say what's real and what isn't in a multidimensional universe," I said vaguely and hoped he would leave me alone.

"You still high, miss?" He sounded wary.

I forced my eyelids to rise. "I just see the world a bit differently from other people, that's all."

He gave it a long moment but I closed my eyes to help him on his way. I wasn't culpable, I was a witness. I'd told him what I'd seen and if he didn't believe me he certainly wouldn't find out who murdered that poor woman.

Indira picked me up in the afternoon, full of questions about the murder in the bed next to mine. Every step pained me and every bump in the road all the way back in the car made an indelible print in my soul. The ward staff had wanted everyone out and a number of patients had already escaped before a doctor's round decided to discharge me. I was glad to go, but hell, my stomach was tender.

"Did you see anything?"

I had dreaded that question. "I saw everything, Indira." I looked out of the window pointedly but she ignored my subtle messages.

"Like how?"

"With my eyes."

She frowned, never one to hide her frustrations. "Why won't you tell me?"

"It was a great big fuck-off demon, that's why. And no-one will believe me and that's fine." I didn't want to be a crack-pot witness in a court being reported on by local newspapers.

"Oh no, we're not still going through this shit are we?" She glanced at me as we pulled out of the end of a road. "I'm really worried about you, babe. It's like you're hallucinating all the time."

"You weren't hallucinating when you saw the dragon."

Her face was set as she concentrated on driving. "Maybe I was."

"I've got some protection stuff I've got to put in place."

"Wouldn't it have attacked you if it was real? Why did it attack someone else?"

Demons could be other people's attachments. Maybe the Oramorph had given me wings and for a brief time I had been able to see through the veil.

I pictured the woman's smashed body. Yeah, right. Maybe the magic missed me somehow.

"Can we talk about something else? I don't really want to think about it any more," I pleaded. I lied. I couldn't think of anything else, but I didn't want to talk about it.

Once home, we made me comfy on the sofa under my duvet with appropriate medication. My wound ached dully but only stung if I moved around. Indira tucked me in with a hot chocolate and a box of tissues and we settled to watch movies for the rest of the evening.

"This is better than having some man lounging around," she said as the opening credits began.

High on tramadol, I slumped into my movie watching pose, comfortable in the sofa's depths. I let the drugs settle my mind, so I didn't keep whirring around last night's events.

As the credits rolled on the second film of the night, Indira turned to me.

"Sorry, babe, I can't stop thinking about that poor woman. What really happened to her?"

I slid my eyes towards her. "I only know what I saw."

"Don't you think you were high? There must be a rational explanation for it."

That was another problem with magic. Like the tree that fell during the storm, there often is a rational explanation, but it doesn't mean the cause wasn't something magical.

I tried to straighten my brain. Indira was back on the cynicism and in a way that was a good thing. I didn't want her thinking she could be attacked like some kind of collateral damage.

"The thing I keep thinking is that there's one way of thinking that suggests all illness and disease has a spiritual origin. So some Christians or spiritualists see demons as being at the root of dementia or heart disease or epilepsy and especially mental illness." She was beginning to look cross. I knew her sister suffered from depression a lot, so I moved on quickly. "I don't know about that, but I swear this was an actual creature. Not a metaphor at all."

Indira looked nonplussed. "So what does that mean, babe?"

"Let me ask my guides," I said, hoping they would be loud and clear. Maybe they'd been trying to contact me, but under the influence of drugs and hospital environment, I would have been impossible to reach.

I made myself as present as I could—not easy, given the tramadol—and asked my question silently. *Please show me in a way that is clear and easy to understand, why the demon killed the woman in the bed next to mine.*

My phone rang. Molly was businesslike again.

"How you doing? We're going to need some strong protection. I had a visit last night. Not very nice."

"Last night? What time?"

"I don't know. I wasn't looking at the clock."

She relayed her tale, with the demon sitting on her stomach and laughing at her. Then she told the rest. The violence staggered me.

"He pulled your neck?"

"Like a chicken. I passed out before I 'died'. I think that saved me."

I thought about the dead woman on the ward. "Would that have broken your neck?"

Molly let out a low whistle. "You bet it would."

I told her what happened.

"Whoah, girl, stop right there." Molly's voice was stunned. "That's not what the creature I saw looked like, but that's exactly what it did to me. Kept punching me against the bed. Kept asking me where 'she' was."

"Who?"

"You, I presume. My shields are good!"

I glanced at Indira and lowered my voice to a whisper, hoping the TV was loud enough for her to mishear me. "Did they try to get me and miss? My bed was moved in the middle of the night and the woman was put where I was."

"That's not how magic works, love."

"How do you explain it killed someone else?"

Molly was silent for a moment.

"I think they didn't know where you were and came to me to find out. I knew you'd been in that bed, but I didn't know you'd been moved. The demon only knew what I knew, because they couldn't find you on any plane. Probably the drugs you've been given."

I contemplated that bombshell for a long moment. I wondered if the tramadol gave me an invisible edge. Invisibility really was the spell I needed right now if that bastard was looking for me in this way.

"So they literally got the wrong person?" My mouth was sticky and I had nothing left in my head except that I was on a magician's hit list.

Molly was quiet for a moment. She cleared her throat.

"I'm not getting anything through, but I'll keep the channels open, see if something comes up."

It was hard enough living in a reality-based world with one foot in a magical one and the biggest pitfall was the urge to ascribe everything to magic. The woman may have had an epileptic fit—there could be any other explanation beyond 'it was a magical attack'. But she clearly had a broken neck and a smashed-up head, both acquired on the same night Molly had her nasty visitation. I knew what I'd seen and I'm not keen on coincidence as an explanation.

Molly promised to call on me on Saturday and we ended our conversation.

Indira didn't take her eyes off the TV. "There are demons in Islam as well," she said in a conversational tone.

I nodded. "They're real to me."

"We call them djinn. Just metaphors for really big

problems." She turned to the TV and flicked the channels idly. "Like good and evil and plague and pestilence."

I pushed away the frustration. She was only trying to help.

"They could be a metaphor, if you blocked yourself off completely from the possibilities, like a *God Delusion*-type atheist, but then they're more likely to cause those things, the way I see it." I leaned my head back against the sofa and silently thanked my guides for their assistance. Molly's call had been more than timely.

"You don't think your friend Molly is a bit nuts, do you?"

I closed my eyes. "It sounds nuts, but it isn't to me."

"All she's doing is encouraging your paranoia." She stopped the channel on a reality show about fashion make overs.

"I'm not paranoid."

"She's made you think it was a real demon and it's after you. That's not normal, hun."

"We don't know." Nothing I did was 'normal'. Normal was slipping out of my grasp every day at the moment, a desire that got more distant the harder I tried to reach for it.

"If you always think everything is because of magic, you'll never find normal." Sometimes she seemed to read my mind in ways I could never manage.

I tried to sound sensible. "It isn't always magic, not deliberate. Magic is just energy manipulation. A lot of the time it's just the nasty things people think about you. They send it your way, or it just finds you and you get covered in their slime." Indira pulled a face, but I pushed on. "Even if it is magic, not everyone who uses it knows what they're doing. Desperation makes them do it. They go for love spells, money spells and mind control type stuff."

"Does it work better when you know what you're doing?"

"I guess if you know what you're doing everything you do *should* have more potency. I'm not sure it always matters. It's more about how present and powerful you are right at the moment when you cast it and whether you really know what you want."

"Do you know what you're doing?"

"I have no fucking idea. I'm going to pull together some protection spells from a book that Molly gave me and see if the weirdness stops." I sighed, right from the bottom of my tramadol-fuelled belly. "I just want it to stop."

"Can you magic yourself so that you don't think about this stuff any more?"

"It's not going to make it go away. If Molly's right, that guy's going to be unstoppable."

Indira swished the last of her tea from the bottom of

her cup.

"There's so much pain and suffering caused when people can't let go."

I knew more about that than I wanted to and I had a feeling we were a long way from safety.

15. Green's Ironmongers

I awoke at the sensible time of nine o'clock and listened to the birds and traffic outside. In my head I played through the couple of protection techniques I could remember from the *Spiritual Protection* book Molly had given me and fished it out from under my bed to re-read a few more.

Regardless of what Indira thought, I was sure we were under attack but I didn't know if every negative manifestation was a result of that. Every action I took from now would add to the situation with a dozen ways to play out.

Was the attacker David? Although the answer seemed obvious, perhaps it was too glaring. Surely the guy had head injuries. What about his concentration? Would he even be able to think clearly? I imagined him with his head bandaged, dancing around a fire circle in a long black cloak, and shuddered. Thinking about him at all was bad. Picturing him in my mind felt like I was dangling over Hell's precipice on a piece of elastic, tempting the Devil with thoughts.

I carefully swung my legs over the edge of the bed and sat up. My wound twinged to remind me not to be too active, so I rested for a moment. As I grounded and felt outwards a sense of seething anger and chaotic pain consumed me. Mesmerised, I struggled to drop the connection. With difficulty, I closed my third eye down as far as I could, made myself as present as possible.

I shook myself awake properly and stood up before it drew me back in. I wouldn't let it take over like that, so I headed for the kitchen for scrambled egg with buttered toast and a powerful coffee.

I flicked through the book and wrote a list while I ate.

> *Preserve jar*
> *Black candle or wax*
> *Thorn twigs*
> *Iron nails!*

I circled the last item. Where was I going to find iron nails?

I wasn't supposed to be traipsing about anyway. My wounds were definitely not messing about and Indira was on a long day shift, so I didn't have the car. I couldn't send Molly on a treasure hunt for me—if she'd wanted to do that for me, she would have already offered. I had to search for the items myself, put something of me into the spell.

I raided the kitchen drawer and cupboards for anything useful. A set of kids' crayons with a black one turned up, so I threw it on the side to keep. I could melt it down to seal the bottle. No nails and no jars, though I was sure Indira had bought some canning jars a while back.

I crept into her room and stood in the corner to see if I could identify a suitable jar. I didn't want to go through her stuff but if there was something obvious on the side I didn't think she'd mind. I'd weather her reaction, however she took it.

I spotted it on the corner of her dressing table, filled with Christmas lights. I followed the cable back to the plug and remembered I'd seen it switched on quite recently.

I flipped the top open, about to pull the mass of tiny lights out of the jar, when I remembered it was a gift from her beloved niece.

I couldn't undo what someone had made for her out of love.

I gave up and sat dejectedly on the sofa in the living room. Cabin fever had already set in and my wound ached continually. I wasn't going to get anywhere sitting in the flat and I didn't have any safe way of getting out and about.

I leaned back in the sofa, resting my eyes, let my mind

wander to the ring box. I imagined opening it, putting on the silver ring. What harm could there be if Geraldine had told the truth? Why did I not give her the benefit of the doubt?

I resisted for another couple of minutes, drawing myself back to the present, but one more image presented itself, the silver ring, fat and solid on my finger. I opened my eyes.

I opened the box on the kitchen counter, aghast when I saw the garnet ring alone, then remembered I'd placed the silver one—the 'gift'—in my purse. Laid out under the spotlights, the garnet flashed at me, but the plain silver ring was somehow mine, even with my misgivings. I wanted it.

I got it out of the purse and turned it in the light. It glinted, beckoning, so I slipped it on. An overwhelming rush of energy blasted me off my feet with a devastating intermittent roar, as though someone placed and removed their hands over my ears repeatedly.

I rolled over on my front, my wound poking me, struggling to my knees against the force as I tried to work the ring off my finger, panicked by the noise. The wind shoved me from every direction, no blast longer than a couple of seconds, no pause more than one. I worked hard, resolutely twisting the ring towards my fingertip. It finally slipped and I flipped it over the end of my finger. Everything stopped. I sank to the floor, out of breath.

That wasn't a 'luck and good fortune' blessing. I struggled to regain my breath, a deadening exhaustion ready to overcome me. I picked up the ring with a fork handle and fiddled it into the ring box.

The garnet ring stood fine and proud in the box. It wanted to be worn. It might tell me what had happened. I might not understand the message anyway.

I gritted my teeth and sat down on the sofa with the ring box in my lap. I could have sworn the garnet watched me. I picked it up and turned it in my fingers for a moment. What if it got stuck like it did on Indira?

I pushed back on the nagging doubts and slipped the ring on my middle finger. It tightened comfortably and the wind rushed around me, no longer through me but this time it was constant, circling me at a dizzying speed.

A hissing noise filled my ears over the roaring wind. It split and whistled and whispered words. They shimmered in the hurly-burly, swept away in a breath, but a few phrases came clear through the gale.

"Put the other ring on too. Foul witches, their greed tortures me, their gift is poison in the throats of their young. Put on the other ring." The voice was louder and insistent, forceful in parts. Its owner had come closer. I fought against the gusts and clutched hold of the silver ring.

"Put it on."

I slipped the ring on. Everything stopped. Silence reigned.

"Um," I said. "Are—are you there?"

A breath of air as something flicked past my cheek. "Like I have a choice! Choice is only for the fully free." Its bronzed, orange face was right up in mine, breathing hot air at me. "Corporeal body or captivity!"

I blinked, shocked at the sight, an otherworldly creature I'd only read about in fairy tales, not quite solid in appearance, but irrefutably right in front of my eyes. The dragon's scales clashed together as it zigzagged its neck with a jabbing head movement.

"The witches were supposed to release you! What holds you here?" I kept my questions short, if only to get a word in edgewise.

The creature laughed maniacally and pushed off from me. I sprawled across the sofa, righted myself, but stayed sitting. Not so far to fall. His shove was very real.

"What do you want?" I thought of the dead woman in the hospital ward. I didn't even know spirits could cause death like that before then. It didn't comfort me in the face of being shoved around by an angry, lunatic dragon spirit.

"Get me out of here," it screamed and dove low over my head.

"Why don't you just fly away?" I yelled, waving my

arms high.

It flashed into nothing but reformed immediately and alighted on the sofa armrest, massive claws gripping the leather tightly. Indira would be furious.

I lay back and viewed it through half-closed eyes, a long, sleek head that tapered to a horned nose, ten feet above the sofa. Its great wings grazed the ceiling. They fluttered lightly to keep its balance and the breeze stroked my cheek. Calm descended upon the room.

"I'm bound to the rings," it said, in the tone of one talking to a five year old. "I can't just leave. Someone needs to release me."

"Don't I just become your keeper?" I asked. I didn't have a clue how these things worked, no more than what I'd picked up from Molly and Geraldine.

It hissed lightly and its forked tongue flickered out, with a puff of smoke.

"I didn't think you were the type," it said dolefully. "Thought you said you believed in freedom for all creatures."

I felt ridiculously embarrassed. Of course I did.

"Sorry, I just thought if you're bound to the ring no matter what, I don't mind looking after you." That sounded wrong.

"So if someone gave you a person as a slave and said it was the law they should be a slave, you'd just take the person as your slave instead of giving them release?" All the 's' words were lovely slippery hisses and I felt dreadful. So much for spiritual justice.

"How can I release you?" The only polite thing to say.

"Look into my bindings. The magic is strong. He uses dead things. Someone comes."

It vanished. Sort of. A wisp of—not smoke—mirage, twiddled its way upwards on the end of the sofa and I was left feeling not entirely alone. As though it lay dormant, wrapped round our space. The same presence I'd sensed since the night the bag had been brought into the flat.

The doorbell rang.

I sat stock still in case the person looked through the blinds, but it rang again which meant they were still in the porch. I couldn't answer the door. What if it was David?

The bell sang out again and I shrank myself into the sofa hoping there was no outwards sign of anyone home. That was normal on a working day.

My phone rang from the kitchen counter. I got up gingerly and moved across the room as quickly as my wound allowed. I got the call on the third ring. It was Caleb.

"I know you're home, let me in."

"What do you want? I can't be bothered, Caleb."

"Let me in." He cut the call.

I let him in, but stood in his way in the hallway,

preventing access to the rest of the flat.

"What do you want, Caleb?"

"Did you sort that guy out?"

I tried to stand as tall as possible and fixed him with a glare. "Yes, I replaced the items you stole from him, thanks."

"Did you give him the ring back?"

"Yes," I lied.

"Did you keep the other ring?"

My eyes widened. "How do you know about that?"

He smirked. "Let's just say I know things."

"Fuck off, how do you know?"

"I know people," he said. "Cup of tea?"

I was wild. "I'm not making you a cup of tea. Who've you been talking to that knows that?"

"Cup of tea or I won't tell you."

I hated him.

I boiled the kettle and made tea.

"You know the coven at Crystal Nirvana?" He was suddenly clearer. "My lass is one of them."

"What, Geraldine?" I was surprised. She didn't seem his type, but if that was what he wanted, I wasn't going to get upset again. I didn't feel the same upsetting pull I did the last time he mentioned his 'lass'.

He smiled and cocked his head on one side. "One of the other girls. You won't know her because you didn't meet them."

I couldn't argue with that, so I waited for what was coming.

"You and your mate asked them to release the dragon from the ring, but they didn't want to waste the—opportunity." He took a swig of tea and reached for the packet of biscuits I hadn't offered him. I slapped his hand away.

He continued. "They tried to transfer the dragon to a different vessel, but their release spell was shit and it was too hard for them to re-bind it on the other ring. Sucked donkey balls, according to Susanna."

I regarded him for a long moment, ignoring the name.

"So what was the result?" It would be better not to tell him everything, especially if he was consorting with one of the coven.

He glanced at me shiftily. "Those rings have got a twisted, tortured dragon spirit split between them. He could be unstable like that. They found him dangerous. The bindings on the second ring aren't safe and the ones on the original may have weakened. Did you send both rings back together?"

I picked up my mug pointedly with my bedecked fingers on display. He clocked both rings straight away with a grunt.

"I kept them both by accident. They were in my pocket,

not in the bag, because that's where I'd put them when I met with Geraldine."

He sniggered. "That bitch. My lass's thinking about getting out. This kinda thing isn't for nice people. She wanted you to know if you still have the rings, she'll probably be able to handle the dragon."

My ears pricked up and a cold breeze flowed over my body. Everyone wanted some kind of ownership on the dragon.

"They wanted me to keep the silver ring but not the garnet. Why do you think they did that?"

He leered at me. "Makes the dragon useless. With the two rings, at least you've got access to the whole dragon. Won't be in a good temper though."

I shrugged and opted to change the subject. "Caleb, have you got a car?"

He smiled. "I only drive pretty chicks."

"Fuck off, I need you to take me to an ironmongers and somewhere I can get a black candle."

He squinted at me. "You doing some candle magic for me?"

"Why don't you ask your 'lass' to get your ring?" I asked cattily.

He shook his head. "Reasons, Inayat, reasons." Maybe he didn't trust her. Or she didn't know what his ring looked like.

"No. I'm making a witch bottle," I told him flatly. "I've done your spell." The lie would have to do for now.

He nodded. "Get your stuff. I'll get the car."

Caleb returned in a beaten up old Ford Mondeo, a metallic pastel blue monstrosity, pumping black smoke with every gear change. The back of the car was filled with human skulls. I stopped and peered into the rear window. Human skulls, but most of them were weird colours.

He leaned over and opened the passenger door for me. "I'm selling them on the markets," he said.

He was a skilled and talented sculptor. No-one could take that away from him, no matter how numerous his vices. I reached in the back, pulled out a skull and a different shaped candle from the avalanche in the rear seats. The alternate candle was a detailed dragon, curled round an obelisk, every scale and curl of its tail perfectly rendered in wax. The skull was smooth and hard and life size.

Caleb revved the engine. "Get in. We'll go to Green's in Hyde Park, I know the guy."

I laid the candles back in the rear seat and got into the car. The seat was fixed down with only one bolt at the back so I held the hand rail on the ceiling all the way, every bump swinging the chair and twisting my wound. It would have been more comfortable on the bus.

He pulled up outside the shop. "Get out and wait for me. I'll find somewhere to park." Leeds traffic wardens are everywhere and apparently proud of their jobs.

As I waited, I gazed into the shop window. A man stood behind the till, talking to a customer. Someone walked past the window in a blue coverall and then the man at the counter looked directly at me and smiled. I could see the colour of his sky blue eyes even from that distance.

I half-smiled back but I didn't know if it was me he was smiling at, or just his customer. Caleb joined me and we entered the shop.

The served customer brushed past me as he left and the man behind the counter looked our way. His eyebrows rose as he saw Caleb. I didn't know where to look. His eyes fascinated me with their bright colour, but I didn't want him to look at me directly, didn't think I could stand the eye contact. Reddish hair fell over his forehead in a way that made me want to brush it aside. With my face. My heart rate quickened. I self-consciously stared around the shop instead.

"How you doing, cock?" He pushed a large tree of Chupa Chup lollies out of the way and lifted the hatch on the old-style counter. "You know we've got CCTV in every corner, right?"

Caleb stopped. "No need to be like that."

The guy leant against the counter with folded arms

and I tried not to look at his biceps pushing against his shirt sleeves. "Too many people around to get away with it anyway."

I could have sworn that sounded like a challenge. Caleb was an inveterate thief, compulsive, skilled, and not limited to burglary. I glanced around. Two or three staff members in blue overalls and only a couple of customers.

"Inayat, get your stuff," Caleb said out of the side of his mouth.

"I need a couple of Mason jars and a black candle." I had a sense of being a crook's accomplice, playing a distraction game. "I'll find them," I said hurriedly. I didn't need the shop guy to have to leave Caleb.

"We only do packs of candles. They're at the end of the barbecue aisle, after the Doodle scented candles." He pointed towards the back of the shop, still looking at Caleb.

I headed for the back of the shop noting the location of jam and preserve jars as I passed them. A heady floral smell grew stronger as I neared the Doodle candle display. The table candles I wanted lay in coloured packs. I pulled out the black ones, stung by the high price. Branded candles were far too expensive but this was my only chance. I headed back to the jar display and pulled out a one litre flask with a metal clasp and rubber seal. A cold shiver ran up my spine and I somehow knew I would need two. I could have done without the extra expense. I stepped away from the shelf and the shiver came again. Irritated, I grabbed a second jar.

The two men stood in silence as I approached the counter. Neither was looking at the other by now.

"Have you got iron nails? Rusty ones would be fine."

"Rusty nails? What are you making, artwork?"

I nodded. A witch bottle was a step too hard to explain. No way was I going down that route with a stranger.

"She's making a witch bottle, dickhead," growled Caleb. I stared at him, horrified.

"Don't tell people, Caleb!" I couldn't believe he'd said that, but I'd heard it with my own ears.

I hazarded a look at the bloke. His attention was on me now.

Caleb spat on the floor. "I've known him my whole life." Then to the shop guy. "Get her helped, she's good people, in deep shit. I'm helping her out. Do her a favour, a few rusty nails won't kill you, Arkwright."

To my surprise, the man nodded and offered me his hand. "Jed Green."

"Inayat." I looked into his hard blue eyes with a jolt, expecting another Caleb, but saw no callousness or mockery in them. His hand was smooth and cool. My heart dropped through my stomach and I retrieved my hand from his grasp too quickly.

He stepped back through the hatch. As he turned his

back to the bank of tiny drawers on the shop wall, Caleb leaned over the end of the counter and pulled out a Swiss army knife from underneath. The display cupboard must have been open. It disappeared up his sleeve as he stood up.

Jed turned around with a handful of suitably rusty nails. "I've given you ten in case you lose one." He popped them into a paper bag and rolled the opening closed. "All of them on the house."

I couldn't bear it. I'd spent long enough being associated with Caleb's deviant behaviour. If I did nothing, when Jed discovered the theft he would have good cause to think I was in on it. I still needed a lift home, though.

As I took the bag of nails from him and handed him the jars and candles, I pointedly rolled my eyes in Caleb's direction. Jed caught my look with a slight frown. I slid my eyes round again, then widened my eyes suddenly at him.

He swung his gaze to Caleb.

"Hey, Caleb. Wanna bring the knife back now? Save you a journey."

Caleb cocked his head. "What knife?"

"The knife from under the counter."

"Dunno what you're on about. Have you paid, Inayat?"

"Man, don't be so fucking stupid." Jed looked almost sad. "I know where you live, innit?"

Caleb shrugged. "So?"

"Don't think anyone'll thank you for bringing the police into the squat." Jed fished out his mobile phone. Caleb spat again and pulled out the multifunctional knife, stepped forward and slid it onto the counter from the end, plenty of distance between him and Jed.

Jed picked up the knife and shook his head slowly. "Fuck off, man, just fuck off."

He put the jars and the candles into a plastic bag and handed it to me with a smile that rocked my core.

"On the house," he said warmly.

He held his gaze steady on me so long I thought I might be sick with the pulses of electricity firing from his eyes, but the doorbell rang as Caleb left the shop. A flash of euphoria filled me and I smiled back, scurried away without another word.

I ran after Caleb as he walked up the pavement.

"Stay here."

"I'm coming with you."

"Jed freaked you out?"

"Not at all."

We reached the car, parked round the corner on a pay-and-display site.

We got into the rickety vehicle and I poked in my bag for my compact. My face was pale, I had huge bags under my eyes and I hadn't worn make up today.

Caleb didn't start the car. "Just be careful, Inayat, he's got a few girlfriends, a few secrets, too."

"Right." He had to pop my balloon. "A cute guy just did something nice for me for no reason and now 'he's got a few girlfriends'. Not jealous, are you, Caleb?" Maybe he wasn't but he didn't have to say anything. I also knew Jed was just saying thanks.

"I know you ratted on me," he said and lazily grinned. He put his hand in his pocket and pulled out a handful of Chupa Chup lollies. "Want a lolly?"

I stared at him. "When did you nick those?"

He grinned proudly. "While he was staring at you."

I couldn't help my own smile and shook my head in a failed attempt at disapproval. I took a rhubarb and custard lolly and a peaches and cream one for Indira.

"Stay away from him, Inayat." He started the car and unwrapped his lolly. "You're a big girl, make your own choices, you'll see. People are different in private."

"Don't I know it," I retorted and jammed my lolly inside my cheek.

Caleb drove me home and dropped me off outside the flat.

Indira was home. As I walked into the house hallway, she was talking to Maggie from upstairs. They both turned to me. Indira's nose was red and her cheeks lined with black streaks.

"What happened?" My heart was again in my mouth.

Maggie squeezed Indira's shoulder gently and looked over at me.

"Bad luck is contagious, isn't it? You girls need to take special care of each other at the moment."

Indira gulped and a tear rolled down her face. "My cousin. Died giving birth to her second baby and they couldn't save the babba either."

For a freaky moment, I wondered wildly if this was a continuation of the magic, but I knew the paranoia was taking hold. I had to let it go.

I ferreted for the right thing to say.

"I'm so sorry. That's horrible. Poor girl. You going to be okay driving over there?" Her family was mostly in Manchester, down the busy M62 motorway.

She dismissed my concern, her mind already ticking over her plans. "I'll stay over at mum and dad's tomorrow night after the funeral and come back on Sunday, hun. I'm working Monday. You'll be okay by yourself. There's a tonne of food in the fridge and meals in the freezer. Don't eat the dates, I've been stocking up. Ramadan starts on Sunday."

She took care of me far better than I deserved.

We spent the evening with a big pasta bake, salad and a deep red bottle of Shiraz, a bit of lazy girl time before she left the next day.

16. Witch Bottle

As soon as Indira left for the funeral I began the witch bottle construction, *Spiritual Protection* by my side. I needed a wee but hung on, knowing what was coming. The iron nails I'd gotten from Jed tinkled as they landed, a tumble of pick-up sticks in the bottom of the jar. I dropped in some nasty bent pins, scraped a heap of dust from the corner of the hallway and smashed a glass on the floor in a bin bag. Everything went in. Indira had volunteered some rusted razors and I added a tablespoon of the most potent chilli powder in the kitchen, along with sprig of hawthorn from the driveway up to the house.

When I ran out of items to add, it was time to pee in the bottle. The instructions said 'piss on your enemies', so that was the plan. I hadn't mentioned that part to Indira. She probably wouldn't be keen.

I took the jar to the bathroom, dropped my pants and wedged it between my legs. My bladder was so desperate to go it immediately took me past the point of no return. I couldn't stop if I'd wanted.

I was a tit. I could have done the deed into a jug and poured it safely into the bottle. Maybe the magic would be more powerful because of the personal edge. Right.

The urine showed no signs of dissipating and I panicked as the liquid level got nearer and nearer the top. I knew I was close to finishing but not if it would be in time.

Hot pee slopped over the top of the jar and I dribbled to a close. Giggling at my idiocy, I lowered the bottle and held it over the toilet to inspect. It was completely full and warm, light iridescent yellow in the overhead strip light. I lowered the toilet lid and placed it carefully on top, then I pulled up my jeans and sealed the top of the jar with the metal clip.

The heavy jar clonked against the sink as I washed it with tea tree soap. I held it tightly and more carefully. The last thing I needed was smashed glass, piss and pins everywhere. I wiped down every surface in sight, regardless of whether or not it looked wet.

I returned to the kitchen, stood the jar on some thick newspaper on the worktop and dug out a lighter. As I tipped the black candle out of the Green's Ironmongers bag, a strip of paper slipped onto the counter. A telephone number. I picked up the paper and turned it over. *Call me sometime*, a message on the back. I turned it back over. I didn't recognise the number and the clear handwriting in block capitals definitely wasn't Caleb's scrawl. Jed Green. A shiver ran up my spine, as though my spirit guides were warning me.

I sat for a long moment, considering the possibilities. Someone like him wouldn't want someone like me. Mind you, I couldn't have towed a bigger advert for weird than Caleb. And if he grew up with that fool, Jed probably wasn't normal in the usual sense. Also he knew about witch bottles. The familiar stirring of fixation began to swim around my head, but I had an open jar of urine to deal with and a witch bottle to complete. The last thing I needed was another man to fuck up my life. I stuffed the number into the kitchen bin and forced myself to refocus.

The black candle lit easily though I dripped wax over nearly everything except the jar to begin with. If I was lucky some of the drops hit the seal of the bottle. Fifteen agonising minutes later, blobby thick wax covered every part of the join between the jar and the seal.

I hadn't decided where to bury it yet but had figured it would be best in the rockery somewhere. While the wax was hardening, I searched out a suitable old spoon in the cutlery drawer and headed outside for a recce.

Every gap in the rocks was filled with plants and in the end I dug one up, intending to bury the bottle beneath it. The tiny recess of mud it left behind was disappointing. I'd forgotten rockeries are made of rock with a tiny bit of soil. I put the plant back and apologised to it, hoped it would get a lift from some rain after such an ordeal at my hands.

I returned to the flat, annoyed I hadn't thought this through properly. To place the jar down the drive or in the rose beds round the side of the house would make the effort redundant because neither was near our flat.

The bottle looked completely wrong on the kitchen counter for so many reasons and I could just imagine Indira's reaction if she knew so I shifted it into my bedroom on the newspaper and sat looking at it.

"Let me ask my guides. Please show me the possible places I can put my witch bottle for the best effects."

My eye fell on the gas meter cupboard at the far side of the room near the window. I didn't know if there would be space but crawled forwards, shoving some storage boxes to one side and yanked the door open. A moth flew out, crazed in the light. I squashed the fright and brushed the velvet fluttery creature away, then felt round the edges of the cupboard with my hand. It was half as deep as it was high.

The witch bottle fitted in the space as though it was meant to be. I tucked it in. There was no sign of it from the meter in front. I could just see the shadow of it in the darkness behind. A large spider scuttled round the other side of the meter.

"Protect that bottle, spider," I said. He knew what I meant. Hopefully.

I quietly thanked my guides and ancestors for guiding my steps.

Molly arrived in style, as ever, bearing a slab of rocky road, a bunch of flowers and a bottle of red. A purveyor once more of wonderful things to eat and drink, I wondered again how she stayed so trim. I'd never eaten so much cake.

"If you can't get out and about too much, you might as well enjoy it," she said, opening and closing cupboards in the kitchen. "Save the wine for yourself, drink it later." She found a suitable cake tin, cut two generous slices of rocky road and switched the kettle on.

I tiredly sat on the sofa and watched her whirl around the kitchen finding mugs and plates. My wound ached and it was nice to feel I didn't need to do anything. I decided to save the wine for when Indira returned, a good way to remind her I appreciated everything *she* did too.

Molly drew out the big tray, piled it high with tea and cake and settled herself on the sofa beside me. She regarded me with a long look and took a breath.

"So how are you?"

I attempted a smile. "I think my surgeon is waving dead

chickens over my file because I've been disobedient and done too much."

She frowned and a little furrow appeared between her brows.

"You've got to look after yourself. You're the number one person in your life. Stay home, in bed, till nothing hurts any more." She paused and the furrow disappeared. "It really hurts, doesn't it?"

I nodded and tears welled up a little. I stared at a mark on the floor till a big fat tear splashed my cheek.

"Oh, pull yourself together," she snapped. "Stop feeling sorry for yourself. This isn't you, all this self-pity. You know what to do."

"What do I do?" I blubbed. She handed me a paper handkerchief.

"Call your surgeon's office and get a follow up appointment on Monday. You might have an infection. You'll be okay, but you have to get along there."

Seemed obvious. I didn't know why I hadn't considered that already. I worked in a hospital as a medical secretary for fuck's sake. If anyone knew how the system worked, it was me. Pain does funny things to a person's brain.

"So what are your plans for work?" she asked as she poured a second cup of tea.

I inwardly groaned. Trying not to think about it was top

of the list today.

"Two weeks off work will mean two months of catching up with the backlog. Might as well stay off work till I'm well."

She smiled. "Fair enough, don't blame you." She looked around, taking in the posh surroundings. "Where's your mate? Out on a hot date?"

I laughed. "She's gorgeous, isn't she? Runs in the family." I reached over and passed her the picture of Indira and her sister.

I caught a flicker of a frown on Molly's face as she looked at the photograph. She smiled and handed it back. "Beautiful."

As I took the picture back she noticed my rings. "Ah ha, I thought you would end up wearing them. Is the dragon still there?"

Alon stirred but I sent him feelings of calm. "He's here and as long as the rings are touching each other, he feels okay."

"So they tried to pinch him, not release him?" Molly was definitely a quicker thinker than me.

"He says they were greedy. Caleb's girlfriend offered to take the rings off my hands. She's a witch in Geraldine's coven apparently. What a load of bullshit they are." Bitterness loaded my distrust. "The dragon got it right, people are full of greed."

"If you think about it, having power makes people think they can have more. And power means they can just take anything they want." She cleared the plates back on to the tray and took everything to the kitchen. "Power's like money. People with money always want more and they think they can just take other people's stuff."

I thought about that as she noisily ran a sink of bubbly water. I didn't feel powerful but obviously I never had any money. I only ever concentrated on having enough, not having more. Maybe I was doing it wrong. Or the universe would kick my arse if I tried that shit.

Molly let the pots drain on the side and sat back down with me.

"Well, chuck, you'd better batten your hatches and get some proper protection going right now. Do you know the Lesser Banishing Pentagram?"

"I've got directions for it." The book, of course.

"Go get them, let's do it. And then you've got to do it every day."

I checked through the instructions and wrote the words down on a piece of paper. "Don't forget there's no 'b' sound in Hebrew," said Molly. "You say them like a vee sound."

That sounded weird. "What about 'Gabriel'?"

"Well no, that's got a 'b' in it." She frowned for a moment, but it passed. "I don't make the rules, do I? Just use 've gevurah"

She sat on the sofa with the book and I took my position in the centre of the room.

"Face East," she instructed. I turned forty-five degrees to face the windows, standing tall and proud, like the priestess of an ancient mysterious sect. I pictured a powerful ray of golden light from the ceiling that stopped above my head. I held my hand into the light and drew down a golden rod through the crown of my head to my third eye.

I tapped my forehead and shouted *"Atah!"* A glance at my crib sheet and I brought my forefinger down the centre of my face and touched my breastbone. *"Malkuth!"* The power plunged into the earth and I held my attention there for a long moment, chasing the energy's descent into the deep.

I poked my right forefinger in my right shoulder to send the energy in. *"Ve-geburah,"* and acknowledged its warm power as it entered my heart. I poked my left shoulder, *"Ve-gedulah,"* giving an exit to the power line. In my mind's eye the energy shot out of my left shoulder and I followed it with my arms stretched out to my sides in a cross shape. *"Le olahm."* I held there a moment, imagining a cross of gold energy meeting at my centre then folded my hands as if in prayer, left over right, pulled to my chest. *"Amen."*

I drew a circle joined with electric-blue pentacles in the four directions and placed the four archangels around me in their allocated positions—Raphael, Gabriel, Michael and Uriel. The air built up increased density.

The pentacles hung in the air in my mind's eye and as I placed the six-pointed star above and below me I felt as though I stood on a pinnacle of rock above a huge precipice surrounded only by the piercing blue pentagrams, the infinite firmament above me. I completed the ritual, following the whole routine backwards, returning to the sofa unnaturally exhausted but with a greater feeling of safety.

Molly pulled the blanket from the back of the sofa and tucked me in. "My bus is due in twenty minutes at Tesco." She shrugged on her coat and did up the buttons. "Promise me you'll do the LBP every morning after you've had your coffee."

I nodded. "Can't you get a taxi? There's been a few attacks lately, not just to do with me."

"I'll be fine. *Promise* me," she said forcefully.

"Of course I will, I promise."

She was serious. "I'm so sorry, love. Things could get seriously tough. You're in for a really hard time. I'm here for you, okay?"

"I'll be okay. I'll call the surgeon on Monday as soon as I get up." I had to sort out this appendix wound.

Whether my eyes were closed or open in the darkness, all I saw were twisted faces, women and children in pain and suffering. I wondered if it was a side effect from the medication I'd had last week but I wasn't even asleep. As the images became more frenzied they turned into demons ripping at the flesh of animals and babies.

I opened my eyes but the darkness was so deep the images remained—a dog writhing in front of me, its guts hanging from the gaping wound the length of its belly—so I turned on my bedside lamp and drove the images away. In the dark, even with my eyes open, my brain replaced the lack of stimuli with whatever I was accidentally visualising. At least with the light I was protected from that.

I sat on top of the bed covers and leaned against the wall, sensing outwards. I felt things in the ether. The whirling chaos, the ominous presence and now an ethereal green light in the periphery of my consciousness. A neon green shield rose from the far side of the room and disappeared into the ceiling. I touched it with the fingers of my mind and found it stretched over the flat completely. Just the flat. Its greenness ran across the ceiling in my mind's eye and I realised where it came from. The witch bottle was committed to its job.

I walked across the room to the window and pulled up the blind. The light behind me in the room shone on the glass and reflected my face. I tried to look beyond it into the darkness and pressed my nose up to the glass.

With a crash, an ugly twisted face slammed up against the window directly on the other side from mine, its mask a writhing snout, its lower fangs glistening needles tapping at the glass as it leered into the room. I screamed and leapt back as the blind clattered down the window. I shot across the room and sat on my bed, heart pounding the blood through my veins so fast it made me shake. I listened for any further sound but the wind buffeted the windows and nothing more. Maybe I was in a dream. Too real for a dream. Some kind of visitation? Was I saved by my witch bottle?

I made myself as present as I could and slowed my heart rate a little. My ears twitched. Then I heard it. Scritch-scratch. Scritch-scratch. Scritch...scratch. Like claws—or teeth—at the window. I pressed myself into the corner of my bed, praying I was in the shadows against the wall, stared at the blinds over the windows. No light, no silhouettes but I was a sitting duck right here, invisible yet totally exposed. I had to get out of the bedroom.

I crept through the door into the living room, round the edge of the wall to the side of the massive bay window. I twitched the velvet curtain and the full horror hit me, a solid line of demonic militia, armoured monsters looming out of the darkness. They stamped, shook their weapons and fists, pushed and shoved each other. The crowd bulged near the porch as a fight broke out and a massive creature in a helmet crowned with a horse tail pulled two apart and threw them both to its side as though they were plastic toys. I heard nothing but the sound of my own beating heart in my ears but their mouths opened in silent roars as lightning struck overhead.

A scream pierced my trance.

17. Live Things

I pulled the blind further from the window and searched for the source of the scream, my eyes ticking across the crowd of demonic minions. They stood many deep, not just a single line of evil. Another cry sounded and a wall of roars and yells hit my ears with force like a percussion bomb as if the shriek had cracked the glass. A bulge rippled through the crowd and it spewed two wiry creatures dragging a small struggling human with long black hair. They tossed her slight form to the ground on her hands and knees.

In shock I saw Indira clearly, tunnel vision to her terrified face as she looked around. She began to scramble to her feet but the entity behind placed its foot in her back and forced her lengthways onto the ground. Fire licked around its foot and left a sooty imprint in her back, grey smoke curling into the night.

The monster kicked her now still body and began to dance swinging its axe around its head as though it taunted her. Fire licked around it and its dark red skin bubbled like lava across its muscles. The force of the upwards axe swing popped plates of armour from its arms. A moment passed, as long as eternity and he brought down the axe on my beautiful friend.

I dove to the floor, away from the window as fast as I could. I scrabbled along the parquet floor to the rug and hauled myself into a crouch.

I couldn't save her. If I'd run outside they'd have killed us both. It was a trick. It couldn't be her. She was fine. She'd gone to a funeral.

I sat on the rug in the middle of the floor, knees up under my chin, arms around my shins. I didn't want to close my eyes but couldn't bear to see anything else either. I should have been asleep but I was awake, seeing things that belonged in nightmares. But awake.

Curled up and exhausted I fell asleep.

In the early morning, Indira came to me. She looked different. Brighter, with a light in her dark eyes, a gossamer veil over her hair. She led me to bed and as I lay down cupped her hand over my appendix wound for a moment. Her bright black eyes twinkled at me and she stroked my cheek just once.

"Babe, don't worry, I'll be back soon. Don't leave my room a mess," she whispered.

⁓

I opened my eyes and still felt her touch. I couldn't remember what she'd said but grim panic gathered in the pit of my stomach. I got up and plugged in my phone, switched it on. No messages.

I texted Indira. No reply. I checked the time. Ten o'clock. She would probably set off soon. I texted her again and checked Facebook. She hadn't been on it for fifteen hours.

I made coffee and paced the parquet floor. My footsteps were silent, padding across the solid wood in my bare feet.

A siren screamed in the distance, closer and closer. It stopped and a moment later a heavy vehicle drew to a halt outside, blue lights winking through the Venetians. I rushed to the window to spy. An ambulance waited outside and two paramedics strode into the porch, laden with equipment. I jumped when the flat bell rang, galvanised into usefulness.

I dashed out of the flat to the front door.

"Who are you here for?"

"Maggie Crowther. Upstairs flat," said the paramedic in front. I stood back silently and he passed carrying a spinal board and a heavy holdall.

The second man nodded at me. "Thanks for your help."

They shot upstairs and I loitered, wandering slowly back into the flat. Maggie kept herself private, but she was always lovely to both of us. I didn't want another disaster that could be attributed to me.

Twenty minutes later their footsteps descended the stairs more slowly. I opened the door and peered out. They carried Maggie down the stairs on a gurney and set it down on its wheels in the hallway to negotiate the heavy front door.

"What happened?" I asked, transfixed by her twisted shape beneath the ambulance service blanket. "Maggie, what happened to you?"

"Maggie's had a nasty fall. You take good care of yourself," said one ambulance man as he guided the gurney through the door. I followed them out and laid my hand on Maggie's to comfort her as they opened the rear ambulance doors. She opened her eyes wide, muttered something to me.

I leaned in.

"Something's here," she breathed. Cold dread stirred my gut. I stared at her and saw only fear reflected back. I stepped to the side, shaken, as the men lifted Maggie down the steps and into the back of the ambulance. I closed the front door on the flashing blue light and stood in the dim light. I was alone in our wing.

Something tapped across the floor upstairs in

Maggie's flat. Seven slow knocks that moved from one part of the ceiling to another and stopped. Footsteps but not feet. I choked my breath in my throat and listened, paralysed. My heartbeat pounded in my ears, louder than a train, adrenaline rushing through me, waves of panic.

I waited.

And waited.

No other sounds came. Slowly, I gathered my energies, dropped my consciousness into my ground and felt outwards, cautiously feeling up the stairs into the flat above.

Nothing. No presence.

I breathed again and returned to the flat feeling grim. I locked the door and left the key in the lock in case I had to get out in a hurry.

'Something's here' gave me shivers, never mind some mysterious footsteps when I knew Maggie lived alone, her partner in Europe. Everything was worse with the unease at Indira's lack of communication. It wasn't just me in danger, everyone around me had been dragged in too. I didn't even know Maggie. My head spun. I sank into the sofa and drew one deep breath after another.

By lunchtime, panic consumed me. I rang Indira's phone three times and listened to the dialling tone before it switched out, but the fourth and fifth times, the line went straight to 'unobtainable'. She'd turned it off because she was driving. Of course she had.

I couldn't eat. I hadn't used any energy. I knew I should have already done the Lesser Banishing Pentagram but my brain was over-occupied with Indira and worst-case worries. I slumped on the sofa catastrophising, unable to help myself. Thought of Molly. She'd be mad I hadn't done the LBP yet. That did it. I couldn't even ring her till I'd performed the ritual.

I had to calm my mind. I picked up my LBP notes from the night before and considered my problem. The answer stared back at me from the page.

I stood in the centre of the room, arms relaxed at my sides, deep inhalations to steady me. I dropped my consciousness down to my centre and exhaled, feeling nothing but my breath in my lungs. I kept my breathing smooth and focused on being present—in the now—dragging my thoughts back from Indira's whereabouts.

As I touched the pinnacle of being present, my breathing found its sweet spot, the right depth and speed. I relaxed in my space, my place in the universe. My body and spirit were part of Source, not separated by thoughts and stories inside my head. Instead my centre contained every bit of my being. I took my time—around five minutes—breathing at the steady rate set by my own vibrations.

When I felt just right I exhaled hard until I ran out of

breath. As I did so, I plunged my two grounding cords deeper into the ground, one for incoming, the other for downwards energies. I visualised them growing into the earth like a mass of intricate roots and inhaled again. Every outwards breath fuelled an increase in growth which strengthened my grounded state and I built a base of calm and peace within me. Even my spine straightened gently as the muscles relaxed.

I started the ritual right where I stood. My crib sheet was near but the words had been surprisingly easy to learn despite the unfamiliar Hebrew. I drew the pentacles in the air as tall as I could go, blue light alive in my mind's eye. I wished I could see the archangels as I called their names but figured my vision would come with time and practice. Their presence around me imposed an aura of tranquil solidarity. Indira was fine. She'd made the trip back to Manchester a million times. She would walk into the flat in a few minutes and I would feel really stupid. Stupid and happy.

I slept on the sofa for a couple of hours, listless and not properly asleep. My brain made patterns behind my eyes and half asleep I followed their swirls, mesmerised.

My phone rang and I scrabbled in my bag to retrieve it. As I picked it up I noticed I'd had two missed calls from a mobile number I didn't recognise.

I slid the call open.

"Sergeant O'Brien, sorry to bother you, I'm catching

up on paperwork tonight." His voice was calm and unhurried. "How are you, Miss Tate?"

Caught unawares, I nodded. "I'm fine." I waited.

"Do you mind me asking again, are you planning to press charges against David Catcheside? It would be handy to know, because if not, I'll complete the write-up of the incident tonight."

I deflated. "Sergeant O'Brien, my flat mate hasn't come home tonight yet and she was due at lunchtime." Maybe he saw me as a silly hysterical woman. Surely the first place to try would be her parents. I didn't have their number and I should have.

"Is that Indira?" He swished a couple of papers, possibly looking at her name. "Where was she coming from?"

"She went home to Manchester for a funeral, staying with her parents."

"Did she set off to come home?"

I didn't know. "Sorry, I shouldn't be wasting your time. I haven't got her parents' phone number and I don't know where they live."

"What's her surname?"

"Khan. K-H-A-N." Hope lifted its head inside me as I heard the squiggle of a pencil at the other end.

"Why don't you try to relax this evening and if anything comes up I'll let you know?"

His suggestion sounded calm and a little unlikely. She would probably come home tomorrow. Either way I would just have to wait.

The doorbell rang. I shot into a sitting position and my wound stabbed deep inside my abdomen.

"I have to go, but thanks for helping me," I said, suppressing a yelp. I doubled over and the bell sounded again.

"Don't forget to make a decision on—."

I firmly ended the call, realised too late he was still talking. He would get over it. The pain made me indecisive, more cautious than ever. It could be anyone at the door. It could be David come to finish me off. That wouldn't take much.

Silence lingered longer than before. Perhaps the person had gone away. Holding my middle protectively I crept to the side of the bay window and looked out through the Venetians, careful not to nudge them. A figure in a long coat leaned against the porch wall. He stepped backwards into the evening sunlight and I realised it was Caleb.

He shook his head and then his whole torso, flinging his arms around as though he was fighting off a cloud of flies. He stopped dead, bent down to the stone balustrade and rolled his head against the rough surface. He stood up, his face bloody in the light and I hammered on the window.

"Caleb! Stop that! Get in here!"

I ran to the flat door and down the hall to the main entrance. As I opened the door he staggered through the gap, his hands writhing around his head, grabbing his hair, his ears, his face.

"Worms," he uttered. His mouth twisted into an agonising grimace and he dropped to his knees. For a moment he relaxed. He tried to get up but made it only as far as his hands and knees before another spasm took hold of his arms and he tried to crush his head into the floor.

"What are you doing?"

I grabbed his shoulder and dragged at him, a desperate attempt to lift him to his feet but he grasped blindly at his head again, thumping me in my neck. As I landed on the hard tiled floor something tore in my navel and a sharp pain shot through my abdomen. I got up slowly, away from Caleb, leaning on the wall for support. Nausea threatened to heave foulness from my gullet and I breathed deeply and slowly to discourage it.

I looked over at Caleb. He climbed to his feet like an old man, both hands gripping the stair bannister. He frightened me, a shadow of the driven person I knew. He slowly turned, looking for me.

"They put worms in my brain." He spoke in a monotone, as though he had given up all hope.

"Who put worms in your brain, Caleb?" My fury

rushed in on the back of my fear. "What have you taken *this* time?"

Drugs aside, his paranoias were often centred around the mysterious 'they'—usually Freemasons or Illuminati, whoever he had in mind at the time. He came with paranoia installed. The drugs didn't make him crazy, they just made him worse.

"I know what I saw, Inayat."

"What have you taken?" I almost spat the words out. He was his own worst enemy. He never looked after himself. He lied about everything and I never knew what was true. And I *still* fucking cared about his lying, cheating carcass.

"Fuck's sake, I'm not high," he spat.

Holding my stomach, still feeling like death, I realised we were both in a bad way.

"Come inside. Just come." I walked him into the flat. As I shut the door behind him, he grabbed at his head again and slid down the wall.

I always knew he wasn't as tough as he made out, but he'd seemed invulnerable at times. He survived two attempts on his life while I knew him and was a boundary pusher when it came to illegal substances. If it wasn't drugs, what the hell was it?

His body relaxed again and his hands slipped to his sides.

"Caleb, look at me."

He slowly raised his head. His eyes were bleak, pale and glassy with misery.

"What happened?"

He spoke thickly, feeling his way around the words. "Got in trouble in the pub yesterday."

I frowned. "What sort of 'trouble'?"

"Some dickhead glassed his girlfriend in the face so I punched the dickhead good."

His face gnarled up in a silent scream and he cupped the sides of his head in his hands. He keeled over to his side, agony wracking his body.

Unexpectedly, he relaxed quickly and sat up.

"Is it getting quicker each time?"

"Hurts more." He gave his head a couple of dazed shakes, but no worms fell out of his ears.

I crouched in front of him. "Do you think it was the guy you hit?"

He flicked his head in irritation and winced. "Little hairs in my drink, swallowed some of them before I realised."

"What drink?" It dawned. "The guy who held your pint while you punched the glasser?" I'd always had to be psychic to understand him fully. "Are you sure there were hairs?" I couldn't see him drinking something that had hairs in it. He was a picky eater at the best of times.

He clutched at his head in answer and went down gasping. "Fucking worms in my brain." Sprawled along the skirting board he left clean patches in the dust.

I needed Molly. Even if it wasn't magical, she'd know what to do. I stood up with purpose but stopped. I knew her first question would be.

I bent over Caleb again. "What did the guy look like?"

Caleb shrugged and grabbed his head again. This time he stayed sat against the wall as he squeezed out the words through clenched teeth. "A greasy-looking dick next to me at the bar. Scottish accent. Manky hair." He let out a groan and curled up again, head between his knees.

David.

I got up and went in search of my phone, leaving him where he lay.

The doorbell rang and I heard Caleb groan in the hallway. The bell rang again and with a sinking heart I knew it was for me. We didn't need any complications.

I trudged to the door as the person pushed the button again but I didn't call out. As I pulled on the brass handle, a welcome but angry sight emerged.

A furious Leah tucked her purse back into her handbag and pushed back a square black satchel that hung across her body.

"That Uber bastard. Lucky you were home. I asked him

to wait and he drives off anyway. Why do people go out of their way to vex me?"

She grabbed my shoulders and gave me a quick hug and an air kiss. As she drew away her face became troubled.

"Are you all righ—ew. Oh no. You're not okay at all." She dropped her voice to a whisper. "Did someone die?"

I realised I looked like death. "Not yet. But oh fucking God your timing is unbelievable."

She looked wary. "Uh oh, that doesn't sound good."

"Seriously, come in." I stepped back to allow her through. "Babe, I have a problem, a huge one. You might be the only person who knows what to do."

She smiled, a little smug, but eyed me with narrow-eyed uncertainty. "I'm not feeling any better about it. What's going on?" She stepped into the hall.

We walked to the flat door but dallied outside. "Remember Caleb?" I shot her a flicker of a smile.

She backed up towards the front door shaking her head. "Oh no, no, no, no, no, no, no."

"Wait, I don't know what to do."

"Tell him to get fucked. He in there?"

Holding back pointless tears, I nodded. "He thinks someone put a hex on him."

She swapped the bag that held the wine to her other hand. "Someone's always put a hex on him, according to him.

Shouldn't spend so much time doing shit things to other people. Where's Indira?"

She was worried, I could see that, not just angry.

"That's the worst thing. She hasn't come home."

"Hasn't come home from where?"

"Her cousin died, she's in Manchester at the funeral."

"She not just staying over a couple of nights?" Scepticism reigned.

"She should have been home by this afternoon. She's working tomorrow." Even Leah knew Indira would never miss work unless something was really wrong.

"So Indira's vanished and now Caleb's turned up with some kind of hex?"

I nodded miserably.

She drew herself up tall. "You know what this sounds like?"

I looked at her with hope.

"A shitshow. No fucking way. You are on your own." She pulled out her mobile phone and checked the time. "Damn."

"What?"

"Half an hour before Jez finishes. Don't stress yourself with me. I'll wait for him here."

"Please, Leah."

She turned her head away. She was shutting down,

closing me out, and I wasn't going to win this. She began to text on her phone, presumably to Jez.

"Leah."

"Don't push me, Inayat, or I'll walk home, I don't need to wait." Her voice was deathly calm.

"I can't do this by myself."

"You get into it by yourself." She still didn't look at me. "Sometimes I think we're only friends because you can't solve anything for yourself."

"I do stuff!"

She couldn't help the irritated eye roll and her voice was fake nice. "You just keep putting Caleb ahead of us, that's fine. No more than I'd expect."

"It isn't even about that!"

She looked at me directly. "Inayat. It's exactly about that. I'm not even talking to you about it." She turned away again and her mobile phone screen lit up. She bent her head to text back.

I took a breath and stepped back. She didn't turn towards me. I had to go back and face whatever was lying on the floor of my flat before I lost everything.

I opened the door cautiously. Caleb sat dejected and unresponsive in the entrance hall, staring at the floor on the opposite side of the room.

I let the door swing closed. It didn't click shut fully,

never did.

"What do you want me to do about it?" I asked him. My voice sounded echoey in the room, as though no one else was in there. I had nothing. No way of handling something like this, not even for myself and definitely not for him.

On cue Caleb grabbed his head with a screamless howl, his breath scraping against his throat like a dead man's final grasp on life. He panted for a time and spasms twisted his body. His face ran with rivulets of sweat. He seemed even worse than he'd been when he arrived.

"Worms," he groaned.

I remembered I'd been about to call Molly. I headed for the kitchen to find my phone.

The call rang out but she didn't pick up. For the first time in the short time I'd known her, she wasn't at the other end of the phone. Panic ripped through me. Something had happened to everyone I knew.

A blood-curdling squeal ripped through the very fabric of the building. I slipped and fell over my feet as I tried to rush back into the hall. The floor came up to meet me and I only just put my hands out in time to save my face. My phone slid to the door and I followed it on my hands and knees, picking myself up at the door.

Caleb was sprawled across the floor, hands clutching his head, noises like an animal in pain filling the space.

As I scrambled towards him, the door opened slowly and Leah's curious, horrified face appeared around its edge.

"You okay?" she breathed at me.

I shrugged and lifted Caleb's head from the floor. His eyes were open but glazed. I couldn't tell if he was conscious or not. He didn't focus on me, didn't move at all.

Leah slipped through the door into the room with us. "What the fuck was that?"

"He says someone put hairs in his drink, gave him worms in his brain."

"Worms?" She knelt down on the other side of his body. "How'd you get from hairs to worms?"

Caleb howled, yanking his head out of my grasp and threw himself backwards into the wall.

Leah backed up against the door with a thud, her eyes wide. She felt for the door handle.

I mouthed the word 'please' at her as he quietened down again.

Leah stared at him, still talking to me. "You want me to call an ambulance? I'm an engineer, not the bleeding Light Fantastic."

"I think it's hoodoo." I drew breath for my next sentence, but stopped myself.

She read me anyway. Light and understanding dawned across her face, but just as quickly she shut it down again.

"My gran won't even talk to me about it. Even if I dared to ask her."

For the first time in our friendship, it hit me that fighting her would make no difference to the outcome. I'd played stupid white woman too many times already. Even if Leah was a soft touch with me, her gran wouldn't be. I stopped and sank to the floor. Caleb howled again, his hands ripping his head from side to side as though tearing his head off would end the torment. He stopped abruptly, the breath lost in his throat, hands dropped to the floor. Eyes closed, he hung his head like a rag doll, a marionette that had lost its controller.

I raised my eyes to hers. "It's bye bye Caleb, isn't it?" My voice almost disappeared into the quiet left by Caleb's cries.

She stared at me, biting her bottom lip. "Oh for fuck's sake. She'll never speak to me again." She fished her phone out of her pocket.

18. Urine Trouble

I sat in the hall for the next few minutes and glumly watched Caleb as he alternately curled up on the floor in pain, screaming quietly, and sat up in between, uncommunicative. Leah's voice filtered through the living room door. She laughed and hopefulness touched me again.

The quiet brought the pain in my midriff back to my attention. I pulled up my top to check my wound. A smudge of dark red blood seeped from the tiny incision. I lowered my shirt and pressed it gently against the bleeding spot and wondered where Indira was.

Caleb stared at me now but his eyes seemed dull, unfocused, as if he didn't see me.

His face twisted into an unrecognisable mask.

"What am I going to do, Inayat, what the fuck?" Tears

streamed down his cheeks now and his pain pulled at my heart strings. The tragedy rose in my chest, but I pushed it away. He got himself into this mess, as with every drama he created, like the fight he interfered with in the pub, typical Caleb only ever had himself to blame. But when it all goes wrong, whose doorstep does he turn up at? Why me? It was always me.

"Leah's going to do something..." I trailed off, uselessly.

He held his hands out to me, desperate, a drowning man reaching out.

"They're eating my brain." He laughed, mirthlessly. "You always called me shit for brains. Eat shit you bastards!" He whacked the side of his head against the wall with a thud, then another and another.

I leapt towards him. "No! We'll sort you out." I grabbed his shoulder and swung him around. He cracked the back of his head on the wall.

"Stop! Caleb!" I dragged him forwards across his knees, but he was so much stronger than me. He swung his head back again and I scrambled to get between him and the wall. I tripped over his flailing arm and fell over him, legs akimbo, crushing his head against the inside of my thigh. He struggled to get loose from me, tipping me backwards against the wall.

Leah stepped through the doorway. She stared at our

crumpled bodies, Caleb trying to shake me off and clutching at his head once more, grunting at the effort of keeping it all in. Me feeling like I'd taken part in a rodeo and possibly looking as though I'd just sat on his face.

"Guys, guys, get a room. Seriously. No-one needs to see this."

"Tell him that smashing his head against the wall isn't going to cure anything," I retorted, trying to recapture a vestige of dignity.

She waited patiently for us to straighten up though I saw her look at her phone once. Caleb sagged as the pain passed again.

"I've tracked her down. She's at her friend's house. I'm gonna need a few minutes," said Leah.

The hope inside me plummeted towards the ground again. It hadn't occurred to me that her gran wouldn't have a mobile phone.

She took a deep breath. "Can you guys just keep it down while I'm talking?"

I nodded and kicked Caleb's leg. She could have all the help she needed.

She slid her phone from her pocket, plugging her earbuds in and dialled the number as she stepped back into the living room.

Caleb sat against the wall, his head resting in the dent

he'd made in the plaster. He turned his attention on me. A shadow scuttled away from him into the corner between the wall and the floor, but when I looked properly there was nothing.

"She know what she's doing?"

I cast him a withering look to imply he wasn't worth saving. "If she can help it'll be a long shot." I couldn't even let him have hope. I was angrier with him than I'd ever admitted to myself. Torn, because something in me wanted to save him, even though part of me hated him.

Leah pushed the living room door to as she started talking. I could pick out a few words, but read more into her tone of voice. She was stoic to begin with and calm, but defensiveness crept in when she began answering questions. She stopped and popped her head through the doorway, hand over the microphone on the earbud cable.

"It was a white guy, right?"

I nodded.

"And you're only feeling that in your brain, Caleb, nowhere else?"

He nodded forlornly, but groaned and grabbed his head again, straining until he was red in the face.

"He gave his pint to someone to hold. Said there were hairs in it when he drank it." I wondered again if there were really hairs, or if Caleb had created the 'memory' in his panic.

She nodded a thank you to me and disappeared into the room again, leaving the door slightly open. She paced towards the bay window.

Her voice became more animated and I caught some words of what I thought were Patois as she explained our crappy situation to her gran, then she stopped. She tried to interrupt a few times, but fell silent for a time. She stepped back through the door, nodding only. She seemed sad.

She covered the microphone again. "Sorry, did you actually rob the guy?"

Caleb was silent, staring daggers at me, so I replied, never taking my eyes off him. "He did."

Leah turned back to her call and moved further into the living room away from us again. Her tone was now glum and her answers quite short.

Caleb threw a mocking look towards me. "You've always been a bitch to me, Inayat. Can't even be nice to me on my death day."

I drew breath to tell him to go fuck himself, but Leah went completely quiet in the living room. I listened, but she said nothing more. After a couple of minutes, she re-entered the hall, earbuds around her neck. Her face was expressionless, as though she was trying to show nothing. Fear sat within me, deep in the pit of my stomach, a roiling mass of empty loss. The worst was upon us.

She spoke to Caleb. "You need to urinate into a jar." She looked at me. "You got something he can piss into?"

I remembered the bad feeling I'd had when I picked up the second jar for the witch bottle. I dashed into the living room, grabbed it off the side and handed it over. Leah opened the bathroom door and waited. Caleb knelt for a moment then pushed himself standing, using the wall as a prop. He walked gingerly towards the bathroom as though he expected to be struck down any moment. He wasn't. He reached the door and stumbled. Leah gave him a long look.

"Just wee into the jar and bring it back out, okay?"

He took the vessel and entered the bathroom, swinging the door closed as he went.

She checked it was closed and moved away from the door. "He's fucked."

A chasm seemed to open up in the floor beneath me. "You said he had to pee in a jar."

She looked at me steadily and I held myself together. "He doesn't need to hear this. Just listen, let me get it out." She took a deep breath, one eye on the bathroom door and whispered quickly. "There isn't an antidote. Not one we can get. Only American or African roots work on live things in you. He's a dead man."

I looked at her in wonderment. "Not even on the web?"

"For fuck's sake, you think I haven't thought of that?"

Chastised, I shut up.

"They're a kind of parasite. You've got maybe forty-eight hours to get them out. Ebay takes time. Hoodoo is magic, not miracles."

That was true about any magic. If something wasn't possible, it just wasn't possible.

She pursed her lips together sourly. "Stupid white man gets fucked over for being a bastard and I'm asking my gran to help an oppressor using the magic of our ancestors? It's not even appropriate. I'm embarrassed." She stared me down, daring me to disagree. "He's a parasite himself on every level. Deserves everything he gets."

I nodded numbly. It wasn't reverse racism, not even *schadenfreude*. Caleb probably wouldn't piss on her if she was on fire, so why should she help?

A moan came from inside the bathroom. His suffering pained me, but I didn't know why and I couldn't understand why I wanted to help him either.

She leaned against the wall and sighed. "I begged her. I fucking begged her to help. This has cost me." She looked so sad, as though she'd lost something she could never get back. As her gaze met mine, she brightened. "Apparently most of the antidotes work by the person vomiting it out. Nice, huh?" She smiled grimly. "She told me to make him throw up. Drink his own piss with salt in it, something like that."

"She thinks that'll work?"

"I don't think she gives a fuck. But it got me thinking. How much of magical remedies are real?" she demanded.

I couldn't think how to answer that. "Most of them?"

"Most of them are cons. It's put a lizard in your sock and in the morning your rash'll be gone. Believe it hard enough, you'll get shot of it."

I realised where she was going. "Caleb will believe anything." Belief had never been a problem for Caleb. His paranoias were based in it and I never did know if they were imaginary or true.

She looked knowing. "Especially now he's on death's doorstep."

"Better say a prayer over it then."

"You're doing it."

I shook my head. "If he's going to believe it's an antidote, it'll have to be you."

"Make it good, Inayat." Her chin was set. This was as far as she was going to play along. She'd done enough. More than enough. I owed it to both of us to pull this off. She didn't look at me. I leaned over and tugged her sleeve. She glanced up suddenly and I nodded.

She scowled. "What goes around comes around. Do what you can, you can't do more. She said if it didn't work it's because God decided not to save him."

God helps those who help themselves. The bleak and astute statement crept into my mind, one that summed up my grasp of Christianity and its inherent attitude to charity. Caleb never helped himself except to other people's belonging.

The bathroom door handle turned and the jar of urine preceded Caleb through the doorway.

"Quick," he rasped, "Take it before it hits me again."

Leah pulled a face. "No way am I touching that without rubber gloves."

"Quick! I can feel it com—"

I grabbed the jar of piss from him just as his body stiffened, his face a mask of blank terror and pain. The urine didn't slop and the glass wasn't wet around the sides. I thanked the gods.

The muscles in his neck stood up in ridges, Adam's apple working furiously as he fought against the torment to remain standing. It passed and I took his arm.

"Come sit on the sofa." He complied. As he sunk into the cushions, he grabbed his head again and fell against the side arm, his face twisted into a fucked-up Pierrot clown mask. He keened like an injured animal.

My heart pounding once again, I placed the jar on the breakfast bar and tried to breathe slowly, relax a little.

"What do I need?" I could never see what needed to be done.

"Table salt and a tablespoon." She sat on one of the stools at the end of the counter. I brought the items over and placed on the work surface. She checked the spoon. "That an actual tablespoon?"

I nodded. It was one of the antique ones I'd had since I left home. Leah placed the items side by side before me, straightening the creases in the bag and opening its mouth.

"You ready?" She looked at me hard. "Add the salt, say the prayer I gave you," she winked, "and let's get him sorted."

I stared at her. She hadn't given me a prayer. She widened her eyes meaningfully at me and I realised she was playing it as though she'd given me instructions.

I took a deep breath. I hadn't even thought who to say the prayer to. Or what prayer.

"Wait," Caleb tried to stand up but struggled to get out of the sofa, staring at Leah. "Why aren't *you* doing it?"

Leah turned to him with all the dignity of a priestess. "It won't have the same power unless someone who loves you does it."

I scowled at the side of her head but straightened my face as he looked at me over her shoulder.

"Sit down and shut up." I hated him. He was the living embodiment of every mistake I'd ever made with my life. But she was right. Only someone who loved him could save him. I loved and hated him. I would have to do.

I dropped my consciousness down through my chakras and into my ground below. As I breathed in, I drew in stillness and calm. The darkness and confusion of the situation seemed to lift. Clarity beckoned, but I couldn't quite see it, didn't understand my feelings.

I turned to Leah. "Can you take a few steps back? I need a bit of personal space."

She walked around the counter to stand next to the sofa. Caleb sat silently now, watching my every move.

I prayed in my head for inspiration. Then I remembered. Medea. A goddess of witches, poisoner and a being who understands all the complexities of love, including murder. But no time to write her something thoughtful.

Almost under my breath so the other two couldn't hear me, I brought the words out of my mind and laid them in front of the goddess for her inspection. "Mighty Medea, I call on thee, with this salt, I petition thee." I added a single spoonful of salt to the jar and laid the spoon back down. "Purge the monsters from this fool's body and soul, release him from his torment. Soothe his pain, restore his brain and bestow upon him peace in life, so mote it be."

A heavy presence stirred in the room as though the ether filled up the space like syrup. I collected the energies from my aura and brought them into an electric mass in my centre, pushing them out through my arms into the jar of urine. Silently, I thanked the goddess. In some deeper, hidden part of my brain, I hoped there would be no comeuppance for asking for assistance in such a haphazard way and pushed the feeling of being a fraud away. I preferred to prepare for workings, develop the spell so it rhymed and said everything in the right way. But worrying would do it no good.

Caleb flipped backwards again, this time onto the back of the sofa and roared in pain. I ignored him and picked up the jar to gently swish the urine around, dissolving the iridescent salt. I fought to stay calm and smiled softly as I placed the vessel back on the counter and looked across at him.

As Caleb sat up again, I saw he was shaking like an addict with withdrawal. Leah nodded at him. "Are you ready to help yourself, Caleb?" she asked, her eyes black in the low light. "All you have to do is drink the piss. All of it in one. No sipping, no messing about, just get it straight down."

"And it'll get the worms out?" He didn't want to drink piss for no reason. I didn't blame him.

"It'll either kill you or it'll get the worms out," she said lightly. "Don't really think it's gonna kill you."

To my surprise he nodded, no argument to present. He took the jar and looked inside.

"Not in here," said Leah quickly. "You'll need to do it over the toilet, it'll make you sick."

Understanding dawned in his eyes and he quickly took the jar into the bathroom and closed the door. We turned to each other solemnly.

"What do you think his chances are?" I couldn't help it. I didn't mean to pressure her, but despite myself, I wanted so badly for him to be okay.

She shrugged her shoulders theatrically. "You're the one who made the spell. Looked good. Very realistic." She sat back down on the sofa and frowned. "Thing is, what's it all about? Why would a white magician use black people's magic to attack another white person?"

I frowned. "How do you mean? It's white people appropriating other cultures, isn't it? See something they like, use it."

She dismissed the obvious with an eye roll. "Judging from my gran's reaction, live things is a bit hardcore just to be something he got off the internet." She looked at me expectantly. "Someone's taught him it."

I thought about all the bones and framed feathers hanging in David's magic room. The xylobones on the door. He wasn't so much a dabbler as a practitioner. Or a collector. Maybe he'd been trained in it. Collecting knowledge.

"He seems to know his stuff. The charity job he does, he gets access to all kinds of cultures. Was invited into a sweat lodge with a Navajo tribe." I formed the words slowly, as if they came from afar. "Loads of charity stuff just seems to benefit the people providing the charity. What if he does it so that he gets access to knowledge for his own ends?"

Her eyes were shadowed. "What kind of ends?"

I thought of Molly's warning. "Don't think he likes it when people say no."

"You think he's hurt someone before this way?"

"I think he'll stop at nothing to get what he wants."

A crash from the bathroom. Leah and I locked eyes.

A series of thuds and another crash resounded through the door. A muffled tinkle followed. We looked at each other.

I didn't want to face a frantic Caleb. "I don't want to know."

"I hope that wasn't the mirror. He's had enough bad luck for one person," observed Leah.

Another crash. We both jumped back on reflex. It had to be the mirror.

19. Mirror Signals

I steeled myself, took a deep breath and burst through the door into the brightly lit bathroom, Leah just behind. Caleb stood half naked in the centre of the room surrounded by scattered toiletries and cleaning products. He was bent over, pushing something into his belly.

My brain couldn't make sense of the scene before me. He sparkled like a glitter ball with every movement. The wall over the sink was coloured a weird brown square with an uneven mirrored top edge, the main of the glass gone from its setting, the top quarter still clinging to the wall. We skidded to a halt as he turned towards us, arms raised high. Even his biceps had smaller shards of mirror forced into them. Out of his stomach poked the largest. He glinted as he turned towards us.

But no blood. I could hear Leah gulping weirdly, like she was about to be sick.

He gurned at us, his jaw working mechanically, no sound coming out. His eyes were the most desperate I'd ever seen.

"Help me, Inayat," he whispered, his face fighting him as though his mouth refused to speak the words.

He took hold of a small shard of mirror in his cheek and plucked it out. A rivulet of blood ran down his face, but he pulled another and another from his neck, his ear, his jaw, flicking the pieces of glass towards us as he went. They clinked as they hit the floor at my feet and I jumped backwards, knocking into Leah.

"Stop! What are you doing?" I yelled.

He grimaced wildly at me, fingers reaching for more mirror sharps across his chest.

I looked around the bathroom for the jar of piss. "Did he drink the wee?"

She didn't take her eyes off Caleb. "If he drank the wee he'd have his head down the loo."

A piece of mirror glanced off my shoulder and I danced backwards. "Why won't he stop if he wants help?"

"He can't." Her eyes narrowed as if she was looking at something around him. "I think he's not in control."

My heart dropped into my stomach and the adrenaline

boomed in my centre. I couldn't help him unless I stopped him. I bounded three steps focused on grabbing his wrist but he swung awkwardly away easily dodging me.

He pulled the huge piece out of his stomach like a sword from a scabbard and held it at arm's length. I flailed for his arm but he dropped the shard directly in front of him. It must have been more than nine inches long. He staggered. The wound poured with blood and he retched. Leaning over from the waist, he threw up onto the floor. I danced backwards, avoiding the spatter.

"What the hell can we do?" Leah screamed in my ear. "He's going to bleed to death."

"Call an ambulance."

She left the room straight away. I turned back to Caleb who was still on his feet, though he swayed widely.

He looked at me imploringly but not with the longing I had dreamt of when I was desperate for his love. Worse than that. As a man who saw only death in his future he reached for someone he trusted. Caleb trusted me. The realisation filled me with sorrow from the base of my being and took my breath away. After everything we'd done to each other, he came to me. And I couldn't do a damn thing.

His fingers caressed a vicious-looking splinter of glass on the left side of his chest. I reached for his arm again but he stepped back despite his instability. He was so much bigger than me, I couldn't hold him if he didn't let me. I had no options at all, no way to help him.

He saw that too. His face streamed with tears and now he was scared. So lost. He looked down and tugged gently at the glass lodged in his chest. He wasn't going to survive that one. I could see him being trapped in the nether place for eternity, maybe wracked with guilt for the burglary that stole his soul. A fucking *burglary* for heaven's sake. You didn't even get a life sentence for burglary.

The injustice and unfairness bubbled over me, but as I drew breath to scream my frustration he fingered the glass one more time and gave it a hard yank. His chest bloomed red as the heart attack dropped him to his knees, glass crushed beneath him. He vomited again as he collapsed fully to the floor, twitching, and finally stopped moving. The room was deathly quiet, as though it darkened in every sense.

I knelt down next to his curled up body and checked his pulse at his wrist and his jugular. Nothing.

Leah clattered back into the room. "They're on their w— Oh no, is he dead?"

I straightened him up a little, pushed his head back and blew two hard breaths into his mouth. His lips were smooth, hard stubble around the edges. He felt dead to me. I was kissing a dead guy who was lying in vomit. What the fuck was I doing?

On the top of my lip, something wriggled. I pulled away and looked at his face. Tiny black worms twisted and squirmed their way out of his nose and from the edge of his mouth. They dropped onto the floor one at a time, a writhing puddle of grubs that disappeared underneath him. The tip of a worm poked out of the corner of his eye and as I stared, it grew its length right there, slipping out and down his cheek to join its friends.

I broke my stasis, scooting away from his body and pulled up my knees to my chin. I pushed my own puke back down into my stomach.

"Jesus fucking Christ, Leah, *worms.*"

We stared in horror as the creatures writhed their way down his body and onto the floor.

"Catch one," she urged me, but neither of us made the move to do so. They wriggled away underneath his torso until the last one was out of sight.

My stomach heaved but I kept it down. Just. Caleb's body was still. No creatures. No movement. No life.

"There's nothing left." My diaphragm was so tight I needed to explode and hot tears ran down my face, my belly rocking me with spasms of grief and fear.

The first responder, a medic, arrived ten ghastly, grief-filled minutes later. Leah opened the doors to him and as he came in, he stopped in the doorway, his face impassive.

"What happened?" He stepped in and knelt down by Caleb's side, feeling for a pulse. He looked at his watch for a few seconds, then ran his hand lightly over some of the wounds in Caleb's torso. "Who did this to him?"

"He did," we answered, almost in unison.

"He stabbed himself with mirror pieces?"

I realised I was sobbing quietly, my breathing noisy. He looked at me pointedly as if he thought I was putting it on.

"We heard him smashing the mirror," said Leila, her face aghast at the memory."

I cried harder as I tried to speak. "He was standing there covered in glass like a fucking hedgehog, started pulling the pieces out." My stomach heaved and I jumped to my feet and threw up into the bath. As I lifted my head from the bath I noticed on the floor the jar that had held the urine, empty.

The medic waited for me to finish spewing and handed me a piece of toilet paper. "Did you give him CPR?"

I wiped my mouth and sobbed, "I didn't know how." Then I cried harder. "I didn't want to touch him. I didn't care about him enough. I was more bothered about kneeling in vomit." I didn't mention the worms, had no idea how to explain them.

Leah spoke up urgently. "No you weren't. He was dead. He was already dead."

He was dead from the moment he stole David's key.

She sat next to me on the edge of the bath and put her arm round my shoulder. "It wasn't your fault. You couldn't save him. It's just what my gran said."

She spoke directly to the medic, super polite now. "He's always been crazy, we've known him for years. You never know what he's been on."

The doctor pulled out his mobile phone. "I'll have to call it in to the police, there's nothing more to be done for him here." He left the room.

Leah glowered at me. "He couldn't wait to dump it on someone else."

I bubbled over again, my stomach heaving against my chest, keening against my loss. Caleb had been so real and alive less than half an hour ago and now he was gone forever. Forever. I wailed as grief overcame my senses, awash with everything I'd wanted and never had. Something in me was still connected to him after all this time, no matter how much I told myself I despised him. Where was he now? Lost and frightened, trapped somewhere between the worlds. Pain in my wound brought me back to the present. I took a long, hard, juddering breath and let my middle relax.

Leah grabbed some loo roll and handed it to me. "Cup of tea? I think we both need something."

I nodded glumly and followed her into the kitchenette wiping my streaming eyes.

My wound stung under my shirt but I ignored it and fiddled in the drawer for paracetamol. I couldn't risk the stoned effect from the more effective tramadol.

When the doctor returned he looked at us hard as we huddled over our hot mugs. "The police will be along in due course and I've called the Coroner. Are either of you ladies hurt?"

I was shattered, slumped on the bar stool. But I wasn't dead. My wound twinged to remind me I was alive.

"If you feel anxious or depressed make sure you see your GP for help," he advised.

Leah had regained some composure, her face streaked and shiny with wiped away tears. "Thank you for your help." She at her most polite. Bordering on insincere, her tone was laced with honey. Or cyanide maybe. I guessed she wanted him to leave before the police arrived. She didn't offer him a cup of tea.

Flashing lights outside heralded the arrival of another car. The doorbell rang and the doctor went to let in the police. Male voices echoed round the hallway outside.

Leah looked at me, vexed. "What are we going to tell them?" She tore off a piece of kitchen roll and quietly blew her nose, looking at me all the while.

As the voices entered the flat I could hear a vaguely familiar one amongst them. I thought of Molly after she'd nearly killed David.

"Just tell the truth. I'll tell exactly the same." This time I really would tell the whole truth.

The men entered the bathroom without looking in on us.

Leah's eyes were enormous, filled with panic. "They'll lock us up for being crazy! I don't want ECT!" she hissed.

"You don't have to say you believe it all, just tell them what happened. You helped him."

The men stepped out of the bathroom and with relief I saw at once it was Sergeant O'Brien and another police officer. I burst into tears again, dashing them away ineffectually.

The other officer stared at me. His face reminded me . "Who's this, the grieving widow?"

Tide-like overwhelm rushed over me. I was never his wife. He never wanted me that way. I streamed from my eyes, my nose, my heart. Everything in me flowed past the point of no return. Caleb was gone for good.

"Something we should know?" His tone bordered on belligerent. Through my despair I felt Leah shrink backwards through the doorway into the living room. She sat on the sofa arm around the corner, slightly out of sight.

I wiped my nose and looked directly at him. "What do you want to know?"

"You two don't look like you belong here and he

certainly doesn't."

Riled from his attitude, I smeared snot and tears under my nose. "Just goes to show appearances mean nothing." I gulped and shut up abruptly. Police were not the people to argue with.

"It's the third call out for an ambulance in two weeks to this building." The doctor seemed cockier now the police were here.

The officer opened his mouth again, but O'Brien nodded at me.

"I've met this lady a couple of times already. Why don't you lot get the bathroom checked out properly before the Coroner- arrives and I'll talk to the witnesses." He emphasised the last word gently.

"Want some help with that?" The other officer didn't take hints.

O'Brien pulled the sides of his mouth downwards as if contemplating the possibility. I prayed that he wouldn't go for the suggestion.

"Think I can handle two witnesses by myself."

I thought of the vomit and blood and Caleb's motionless body. The tears ran freely again. Leah cleared her throat very quietly and handed me a tissue.

O'Brien got his notebook out. "We were speaking on the phone when this began, weren't we?"

I nodded.

"Approx seven-twenty PM." He noted it down and turned to the doctor. "Let me have your telephone number and I'll call you if I have any questions. No need to wait, I'm sure you've got live patients to see."

He took down the number and the medic departed. I grabbed a kitchen towel for my tears and busied myself with further tea-making but we could hear more voices in the hallway. Impending dread grew within me, as though this time they would grab me and throw me in a cell while they worked out what really happened.

O'Brien left the room. We could hear him speaking to someone then he and a black-suited man passed the doorway and entered the bathroom. Their voices rumbled but nothing was clear. Leah pulled a don't-know face and O'Brien stepped back into the living room.

He resumed his position at the breakfast bar.

"So what happened this time?"

20. O'Brien Digs Deeper

Leah and I looked at each other across the kitchen worktop. "It's a long story," I mumbled.

"So there was a run up to the bathroom event?"

I nodded. I wanted to tell him everything including the demons and Caleb's brain worms but I didn't know how crazy that would make me. His attitude made me feel safe but I was afraid of the uniform. You couldn't trust police could you? His colleague was an obvious reminder of that.

"Why are you so clammed up all of a sudden?"

His question was too direct and my hand jerked as I passed his mug to him, slopping tea onto the surface below.

I wiped it up with the paper towel. "It's all too weird." I looked up at him, but he didn't look disbelieving, just impassive. His pen was poised to write in his book.

"According to Doctor Merkowic you entered the bathroom to find the gentleman stabbing himself with pieces of broken mirror," he paused, still looking at me.

"Shouldn't you interview us separately?" Leah asked.

"Have you done anything wrong, Miss?" He gestured with his pen for her to fill in the gap.

"Leah Morrison," she said. "No, I haven't done anything wrong."

"I just want the story from both of you." He looked at us both in turn. "We'll take evidence back with me, shards of glass, anything else that can be removed from the scene in a plastic bag and the results will hopefully corroborate your story. If they don't, you'll be hearing from us." He smiled at her. "As long as you tell the truth and you haven't broken the law, you'll be fine."

"Caleb arrived telling me he had worms in his brain," I began. O'Brien's eyebrows shot into his hairline.

"Worms, eh?" He noted that down. "Drug user, was he?"

Leah and I flicked a simultaneous glance at each other.

"Well yeah, he was sometimes," I said sheepishly. "But he swore this wasn't that."

O'Brien looked sceptical. "They always say that."

I shook my head. "He's my ex. I'd have known."

"All kinds of drugs out there nowadays." O'Brien had

already written this off as a drug overdose. "M-cat, spice, you name it. The stuff of gods, until they start to come down."

My head was already shaking by itself. I couldn't hold it in any longer. "It wasn't drugs. He'd have told me if it was. Someone put a hex on him." I risked a glance at him. His eyebrows remained *in situ* but his eyes narrowed.

"A hex," he said slowly. "Like a curse?" He doodled a circle in his notebook. "Not something we hear everyday. So how did we get from worms in his brain to suicide by mirror?"

I retched again. My tea threatened to rise from my gut but I held it down, just.

"He kept asking for help."

"When?"

"In the bathroom."

"You think he didn't want to stab himself with broken glass?"

The question was ridiculous. No-one wanted to be stabbed with broken glass, not even Caleb at his most insane.

"Why do you think he did it?" O'Brien looked at each of us in turn.

We both gave him blank faces. I had to avoid looking like I was fixating on David and I hadn't yet talked to Leah about what she'd said about Caleb not being in control. I noticed the circle in O'Brien's notes had become a pentacle. That struck me as odd.

"It was like someone else had control of his body." Leah supplied the answer, not even looking at me.

"I take it you both put it down to some kind of magic."

Technically that wasn't a lie and his comment—plus the pentacle—felt familiar, as though he knew more than he was letting on too.

Our silence didn't help him so he tried another tack. "Would you say the gentleman was normally mentally unstable?"

I smiled, I couldn't help it. O'Brien noticed, of course.

"He's always had—problems. This wasn't the usual sort of unstable," I explained.

Leah hid a grin behind her hand. O'Brien just waited, no more questions for now. I had to attempt some kind of explanation.

"I thought Caleb had live things in him." I began. "It's a hex spell found in hoodoo magic and maybe some other types. He said he had worms in his brain."

O'Brien glanced at Leah. "Are you into this stuff as well?"

She shook her head emphatically. "No way, I live in the real world."

"So what's your involvement in this, Miss Morrison?"

I butted in. "She turned up at just the right moment."

"A useful skill," he noted. He studied my face for a

moment as I remembered that Molly had 'just turned up', then waved his pen hand at Leah. "So, the right moment. Why was it 'right'?"

"Ask her," Leah retorted. She relented slightly. "My gran's a root worker." She played with her fingers. "Even *she* thought he was beyond help."

"Beyond help," repeated the sergeant. "So you didn't try?"

We looked at each other. "We didn't have time, couldn't get the stuff," said Leah. "Gran gave me an idea."

O'Brien made another note. "To help him?"

"We gave him a jar to piss in," said Leah. She looked awkward. It was weird to say this stuff to a policeman. "Figured if he really believed it would cure him, it would."

"I put some salt in the urine, said a magic prayer and he was supposed to drink it," I told him, bringing his attention back to me.

"Isn't that a con artist thing? Like pulling a snake out of their sleeve and telling them they're cured?"

"No," I disagreed. "All magic's rooted in will and intent. If he drank it and vomited the worms out, it might save him." I glanced across to Leah, but she studiously didn't look at me. Her gran's intention hadn't been clear at all.

O'Brien didn't seem impressed. "So it didn't work."

Leah shot a glance at me now. I looked at the floor but

remembered my vow to tell the truth.

"Actually it did." My voice was small and I wanted to sink below the parquet flooring. "He died anyway, but not because of the worms."

O'Brien raised his eyebrows. "How do you know it worked?"

I buried my chin in my chest. "I saw the worms."

"I see." His pen was still. As I looked up, he pulled his gaze from me and looked at his notebook, still without writing anything down. "So are we going to find worm holes in his brain?"

I shrugged. "He died from the mirror pieces, not the worms."

"Doesn't look like we know anything for sure at this stage." The sergeant laid his pen on the worktop. "I can't report magic caused him to think he had some kind of parasite in his brain. I can state witnesses said he said he'd apparently caught some kind of parasite. A post-mortem will be carried out in due course, so if there is any evidence of a parasite, or something more—standard, like a brain tumour, they'll be able to find it. Of course, if there isn't—"

His statement just hung there.

He cleared his throat. "Otherwise I don't know if there's an explanation for what you saw." He winked at me. "Not one that will be accepted by the system. If he was known to mental health services, that might help clarify his case somewhat, but I take it he isn't."

I didn't know what to think. His scepticism was mild, considering the wild story.

"What state was he in when you got to him in the bathroom?"

We told him the rest of the tale, what Caleb said and what he had done. When I'd spoken to other police officers in the past, their air of suspicion always resulted in me feeling guilty, even if I was the injured party. O'Brien didn't do that. He was focused and interested without coming across like a creep. Probably waiting to see what weirdness came out of my mouth next.

The coroner arrived and O'Brien busied himself showing the man into the bathroom. The coroner and the nasty police officer left with Caleb's body and all the large pieces of mirror. The body bag looked similar to the satchel that held the evidence. The only difference was their size.

I saw O'Brien to the front door and opened it up to the night. The rain was pouring down again and I pulled my cardigan close round my body. He turned, still standing in the porch.

"Just one more question."

I waited.

"Why do you think someone might have wanted to

control Caleb to kill him?"

Above everything, I didn't want to mention David. He would think I was paranoid and ill. And there was the small matter of the stolen ring on my finger. The more I hung on to the secret, the more reasons I came up with not to tell him.

"Who knows why people do this stuff?" I chanced a look at him. He took a step closer.

"You must have some kind of reasoning behind thinking it."

I looked at him hard, could have sworn he knew what he was talking about. "Sometimes I don't know what I believe." I wasn't really hiding anything. It was his job to work things out, not mine. I might be wrong. I might be delusional. I'd wondered sometimes. I pushed that thought away. I wasn't hallucinating.

He gave me a last piercing look and turned abruptly. I felt oddly disappointed, just a little. "Wait!"

He stopped and turned back.

"Indira. Did you find out about Indira? She still hasn't come home."

"I've put a notice out across Manchester and West Yorkshire police. Do you want to report her missing?"

"Should I get hold of her parents first?"

"Got contact details?" He started to fish his pocketbook out of his breast pocket, but stopped when I shook my head. "Greater Manchester Police will have tracked them down by tomorrow. You sit tight."

I watched him get in his car and turn it around. He drove slowly down the drive but when he got to the gate, his brake lights flared red. He reversed all the way back up at speed—the car sounding like a wind-up toy—until he was outside the porch again. He fell out of the car and slammed the door as he ran up the steps to me with a set expression on his face.

"Get inside." He breathlessly pushed me backwards into the hallway and slammed the door closed.

"What? What did you see?"

He held me by both shoulders and looked into my eyes. "What the hell was that outside? Some kind of bat-winged monster out of the movies in my rear view mirror!"

A demon.

"Just one?" Tears welled again like they wouldn't stop today. "Dozens of them outside all the time at night."

"One's enough! Why don't the monsters come in?"

"How do you know they don't?" A sobering thought, one that tripped off my tongue without consideration.

"Are they the reason for everything that's happened to you lately?"

His hands still gripped the top of my arms and I shrugged them off. "I don't know, but I'm still alive."

He looked at me right in the eye. "What do you know, Inayat?"

I shook my head hard. "Nothing for sure."

"Start from the beginning." It was an order.

"I'm not crazy, okay?" It occurred to me that he had seen the demon with his own eyes. If I was crazy, he was too.

"I'm waiting." He wasn't unfriendly, but I was definitely trying his patience. He looked apprehensively towards the door. "Should we go back inside the flat?"

I thought of Leah. She'd had enough to deal with tonight. I gathered my wits. "So I'm into witchy stuff, okay? Pagan, Wicca, that kind of thing." It wasn't quite 'that' kind of thing, but for an explanation it would have to do. "Do you know about any of that stuff?" I was hopeful. It wasn't everyone saw demons.

He didn't even hint at a smile, but something in him changed. "My wife's a Wiccan, if you must know. Saved her life—she's got some mental health problems, but getting into witchcraft seems to have changed her for the good. Gave her a bit of personal power, maybe. I've been to a few esbats with her. Tell me, what's really going on?"

I felt a rush of relief. His disclosure felt genuine, an admission he didn't have to reveal. And his lack of shock when we talked about Caleb's hex, that made more sense now.

I told him about David's visitation and followed it up

quickly with the whole, unmitigated incident in the pub.

"I suppose it was my fault." I looked at my hands and picked the skin on my thumb. "I shouldn't have invited him out again after I finished with him, but I couldn't let him get away with thinking he could just come and get me when he felt like it."

"Like I said before, he doesn't have that right. Hope isn't a defence." His eyes narrowed. "And what about your little friend in the pub?"

"Molly?"

"The same."

"What about her?"

"Where did she really come in?" How he knew that what I'd told him wasn't the whole truth about her, I had no idea.

"After David left the pub, I sat at the bar for a few minutes and Molly sat down next to me, offered me a mojito and told me that man was going to do something bad to me and she had come to get me out." I stopped abruptly. Babbling might get Molly into the shit. I wondered if I was wrong about him after all. "Why aren't you writing anything down?" Probably because it was all batshit again.

He looked hard at me. "The thing you've got to understand is that the police don't solve crimes, Inayat. We're largely here to keep the peace and that means keeping the public in order. Nothing more. When it comes to magic, it's worse. There is no police force. You'd need solid evidence and laws around magic. Even if I know there are people out there screwing up lives like this, the law doesn't recognise it. This isn't Elizabethan England."

I felt silly. I knew all that.

He frowned. "How do you think Molly knew? She wasn't just there in the pub for no reason."

"She's a medium. She said my ancestors told her she had to come and save me and they made her get a taxi to find me."

His eyebrows were back in his hairline. And there was me thinking nothing could surprise him.

"A medium. Like a psychic?"

I looked him straight in the face. "She described a man wearing a turban, carrying a scimitar, with an army of men. My ancestors were Indian, not military at all, but I don't know what the spirit world looks like. She was close enough."

He nodded as though I was describing nothing out of the ordinary. "So you were convinced she was there to help you?"

"All she's done since then has helped me."

"And the rest of the story is like what you told me?"

"Well, yeah." I didn't know where to look now.

He wasn't fooled. "Feels like something's missing. You

think the same guy is responsible for the demonic outside?" His intense stare willed me to say something specific.

I buckled under his dark gaze. "I think so," I blurted. "I'm under siege in this place and now Caleb is gone and Indira's vanished." My voice caught in my throat. "I'm going to call Molly in the morning and see if she knows what I should do." It struck me that 'demonic' was an interesting word to use. Almost as if he knew more about this world than I realised.

He nodded slowly, considering what I'd said. "He came out of hospital and attacked you?"

I hung my head. "Sort of."

"Sort of how?"

I couldn't look at him. But he waited so long I had to look up. He looked concerned and something else indiscernible.

"Caleb took his key and broke into his house and stole some stuff."

"You didn't mention that before." His tone wasn't quite accusing but I was sure he was cross.

"I didn't want to get in trouble."

"Why would *you* be in trouble?"

I closed my eyes and tucked my chin. I didn't want to see his disappointment. "He brought a sack of stuff to me but he didn't tell me where he'd got it from. I figured it out and then took it all back."

"You took it back?"

I spoke into my chest. "I broke into David's house and returned it." I felt like a child relating a misdemeanour to a priest.

"You did *what?*" Now he was angry. "Did you bust the door?"

"I had the key," I whispered. "Caleb gave it back to me."

"If you took it back, why do you think he's after you?"

"Caleb probably took a lot more than the bag. I don't know what else he robbed. I think David knows I was involved and anyway he probably hates me."

"So he came for Caleb in some way and the worms and Caleb's death were a manifestation of that?"

"I think David controlled Caleb somehow. When we saw him in the bathroom, he couldn't speak properly like the words wouldn't form. His mouth was all over the place."

O'Brien's eyes narrowed. "Remote control of his body?"

I nodded grimly. "You know as much as me." Almost. I resisted the urge to glance at the dragon rings but it was tough.

He looked distant for a moment, thinking. "Whatever that was it'll take something specific to send it away. In my professional capacity I can't do anything about it unless he does something in the physical world. But— I may know someone who could help with the overall problem if you want me to put you in touch."

That was a blinder. He knew people who could help. Not necessarily a good thing in my view. I'd had enough trouble. I let the shutters come down and shook my head at him.

"Got some trust issues. I've already had a coven dabble in my problems. Made everything worse. I can't afford for that to happen again."

He pulled out his pocketbook again, wrote down a series of numbers and tore the page out of the book.

"I don't know what's going on in your life in general, Inayat but if you think you need some assistance with magical attack, call me off the record." He proffered the piece of paper. "I'll see what I can do."

He left for the second time and once again I watched him go. This time he drove out of the drive without stopping.

I returned to the flat and tucked his mobile number into my purse. Leah was flicking through the TV channels. As I sat down she gave up and knocked the telly off.

She looked hard at me. "Are you going to be okay if I get on home, babe?"

"Wasn't Jez supposed to come for you hours ago?" Our conversation at the door seemed like months back.

"I texted him after I called Gran."

"I'm fine. Do you want some money for a taxi?"

She shook her head. "I'll walk it to the bus stop."

I sighed from the bottom of my heart. "Please don't do that. Get him to pick you up, there's been too many random attacks lately, don't want to lose you now."

"They found that doctor woman in the canal."

I stared at her. Molly's vision on the phone came back to me, like an echo from inside my head. *Deep water. Dirty water. Metal things.* She'd been looking at David's photo when it came to her.

"They found her?"

"Drowned. Sexually assaulted. Not good."

The feeling of dread began again. "When did they find her?"

"I don't know, do I? The other day. Yesterday."

"Leah, please don't walk to the bus stop. It's so fucking dark out there." I could see everyone I loved being taken from me.

She rolled her eyes at me. "He's gonna screw with me for this. We're nowhere near the canal." She pulled out her phone again and texted him. "He's in town tonight, at least."

She made ready to leave. Her phone lit up and she texted back with a frown. "See what you do to me? Now I'm in trouble with everyone."

"Is he coming for you?"

She nodded. "He's always telling me to stay safe. You'd think he gave a shit."

I knew he did.

"Do you really think Caleb was controlled by someone?" I'd forgotten to ask her. The image of him stood in the bathroom threatened to overcome me again and I gulped the sickening feeling back down again.

She looked at me thoughtfully as she tied the belt around her coat and sat down. "Caleb's fucked up, we know that, but would you stab yourself with pieces of broken mirror?"

"Was."

She blinked.

The lights of the car flashed past the living room windows and she got up to go. "Let me know when your life gets back to normal." She looked me in the eye. "Don't call me before it does." She gave me a hug. "I'm here for you but only when you're not crazy. Take a bath. Do normal. No more crazy!"

Left alone I knew I should go to bed but it felt too early at half-past eleven so I turned off the television and built myself a joint.

As I smoked I considered what had happened and how I was going to get out of the situation alive. The canal thing wasn't good. Molly needed to know about that. My wound stabbed me again. It had been achy but not too bad for the last few hours once I'd stopped doing things. It only needed rest. Tomorrow I would call the surgeon's secretary and get a follow up. And I needed to call Molly. And Indira. I had to find Indira. I wondered if Sergeant O'Brien properly understood what was happening. I didn't know if I even did. Someone—probably David Catcheside—had unleashed the powers of hell on me and there was nothing I could do about it.

But I hadn't had something terrible happen directly to me yet. Maybe he was saving it for me. Panicking wouldn't do me any good. I stubbed out the singed roach and headed to the bathroom for my things. I would use Indira's bathroom, no way could I wash in that room while blood was still on the floor and a clean-up was absolutely out of the question till tomorrow.

Surprisingly, the mess was mainly cleared up although smears of blood and puke and the tidemarks of the various pools were still in evidence. I couldn't just leave it. The thought of all that human gunge being welded on in the morning was too much. I ran a basin of hot water and bleach, hunted down a cleaning rag in the sink cabinet and went to get the rubber gloves.

As I returned through the door the remaining top part of the mirror caught my eye. My heart scudded but I walked up to it to see better. The steam from the basin had misted the mirror with condensation, the words 'COMING FOR YOU NEXT' emblazoned across the fog.

Gutted, I stared at it. He was coming for me. Me. How did he know I would even see this? What if Indira had been—I stopped that line of thought. David knew fine well Indira wasn't here. I looked at the words, stabbed across the mirror in angry lines. He hated me. Hated. Me.

I'd never made someone hate me before. Not even Olivia had really hated me. I grabbed the cloth and wiped the words away, sploshing water on the floor to clean down the horror and fear. Scrubbing at the foul biological remains of Caleb's short and eventful life, I fervently wished that making it clean would get me out of this nightmare. The bleach got into my sinuses and I sneezed repeatedly. I rinsed the rag in the water and let it out, blew my nose on some loo paper and sagged on the toilet lid. At least I didn't have to use this room while Indira was away.

A growly voice spoke in my ear. "He's got plans for you, big plans."

I nearly fell off the toilet.

"What plans?" I asked the question out loud but couldn't tell if the dragon's voice was only in my head or in my ear.

"He's shrouded in an invisibility cloak but he doesn't fool me." His voice seemed cunning, as though he was grinning through his teeth. "He's up to something. Something unpleasant."

"If I was in physical danger would you help me out even if I didn't have time to ask?" He sounded real enough, like he was standing right next to me crouched down to whisper in my ear.

"It's not like I have a choice," he yawned. At least it sounded like he yawned. Warm air brushed softly against my face.

"When does anyone really have a choice?" I asked grumpily. I grabbed my toothbrush and paste and left the bathroom.

Alon's snort was muffled as though shrouded in billowing smoke. "If you truthfully want to know, at least one of the bindings committing me to this ridiculous jewellery compels me to protect the wearer. Obviously it's not one of the pathetic bindings those silly witches tried." His voice was scornful, he'd seen better witches for sure.

"So I can rely on you if I'm attacked." I switched on Indira's bathroom light. I hated both our bathrooms normally because they didn't have windows but tonight it was good to be in a room that was literally at the centre of the house.

"Depends if you need me."

"But if someone tried to physically hurt me."

"You're more capable than you realise." He paused.

"I'm also available for nasty dreams and visitations. No children's parties though." His tone was facetious.

I didn't remember my dreams too easily and I hadn't noticed him when the demons battered at the window. "Why won't he just leave us alone?"

The dragon's laughter was sardonic, unsympathetic at best. "He's not as enlightened as he thinks he is and you're a sitting duck."

"Oh don't take the piss, there's always an actual reason for everything."

"Humphf," Alon huffed. "Power? Failure? His mama didn't love him? Who knows why you creatures do as you do." His disinterested tone was offensive. He didn't care at all. I got it. He didn't want to help me but was enchanted to do so in an emergency. I wondered how bad the emergency had to be before he made that call. But this was no time to be proud or passive-aggressive. I could settle for that. I needed to find someone who could release him. He would lie on my conscience if I ignored his need. Maybe he would be nicer to me if I freed him. In the meantime, he was here for me. I hoped I wouldn't need him.

I brushed my teeth and went to bed, knowing that I was somehow luckier than Caleb and feeling a little safer.

21. Terrible News

All those safe feelings had gone by the morning. I woke to the ringtone of my phone, muffled under my pillow. A Manchester number.

"Inayat?"

I propped myself up on my elbow and gasped from the pain in my stomach. "Indira?"

"Ah, Inayat, always thinking of others, I'm so sorry, love, Indira, has had—" Indira's mum, Munezza, paused with a sniff. "My little girl," her voice was squeaky. I heard some more ladylike sniffs and a nose blow.

I gulped air down noisily. "What happened? Is—Is she okay?"

Munezza openly sobbed. "She had an accident with a truck on the motorway. It drove with her car stuck on the front for miles. The driver didn't see her all that time. Imagine." She blew her nose again. "I'm sorry, love. Are you okay?"

Stunned, I had nothing. No thoughts, the world swirled round me without my involvement. Just an image of a freak accident, the little black car crushed beneath a massive lorry.

"Inayat? Inayat, love, are you okay?"

"Is Indira—alive?" I hated asking, scared of the answer.

"They put her in a coma. She's in Intensive Care but I don't know how long she will hold on."

She was alive. For now. After an impossible accident on the motorway.

I found my tongue. "She's a very stubborn person, Munezza, I'm sure she'll pull through." God knew what shape she would be in.

Munezza blew her nose again. "You are right about her, but she's unconscious, she doesn't know anything."

"Can I visit her?"

"Visiting times are so short. Her father is inconsolable." Munezza's voice was a bit muffled but it came back stronger. "Maybe not just yet, if she starts to get better, what do you think of that?"

I didn't like that. If she died I wouldn't get a chance to say goodbye. "What if she gets worse, Munezza?" The tears welled up from my stomach, a spontaneous spasm of pain. I thought maybe I was being selfish. But she was my friend and as annoying and fun and loveable and loyal as a sister.

Munezza's voice was sympathetic. She understood. "If she gets worse I'll try to call you in time, Inayat. I'm sorry, but I don't think we can cope with other visitors just yet."

She gave me the address of Indira's room so I could send her flowers once she was stable. Afterwards I sat for a full half-hour on the side of my bed, staring into space. I couldn't make myself present, too many images of Indira terrified and hurt in her car, lying in a hospital bed, unmoving.

The torment was too much and I fell asleep on and off for hours. If I dreamed, I didn't remember it. Whenever I awoke I could only think about Indira's plight and I pushed myself back into sleep because all I wanted was numbness.

I wakened fully at ten o'clock and ventured into the kitchen for a coffee, wrapping my robe around myself. In the middle of the living room floor, cold feet on the solid parquet, I felt suddenly exposed—on view—an odd feeling given all the blinds were closed and I had switched on no lights. I moved quickly to the shelter of the kitchenette and viewed the living room perimeter from behind the work surface.

Nothing unusual stood out. My eyes were blurry with

sleep though. I rubbed them and scanned the room again. The window frames on the far wall seemed misty. I squinted at them and noticed a tendril of smoke rising from below the bay window. The more I looked, the more I saw, smoke drifting up from the floor, faintly lining the enormous alcove.

Fire! I dashed two steps around the breakfast bar and skidded to a halt. Something wasn't right. Where was the fire coming from? The cellar?

I sniffed cautiously. No smell of fire. Nothing at first and then I caught it. The smell of Hell itself: rotten eggs. My blood froze. I was inside the belly of the beast.

I turned to the kitchen cabinet, pulling out an almost-full bag of table salt and dashed back to my room. I slammed the door and sat down shakily on the bed, the salt held resolutely in my hands.

I steadied and forced myself to become present. Who knew what I'd just seen. Smelled like brimstone to me, but fear wouldn't help the situation. I concentrated on my lungs and slowed my breathing to encourage my heart rate to calm.

I opened my crown chakra, drew down blue-white light from the universe into my centre and powered it through my right hand into the salt.

"Salt of the earth, cleanse and purify, repel all evil, protect this space! So mote it be!" My voice cracked with the exhortation.

In my mind's eye the salt glowed gently as the light energy flowed. Its iridescence gave me a feeling of determination. I couldn't let them get me. I headed for the most eastern corner of the room—near where my witch bottle was stashed—and began to pour salt along the room's edge in a clockwise direction. Around equipment and boxes, along the skirting boards, under the desk and right around the other side. I did an extra thick line at the doorway.

I sat in the middle of my bedroom and contemplated my situation. The time was ten-twenty-five on a Monday morning. I had to eat. The entities weren't in the flat in a physical sense, unless that smoke was them. But they were right there in a different sense. On a different plane. They could see me clearly, I knew they could. Their gazes felt like so many creepy tickles down my back.

I felt sick and suddenly hungry. Never mind they could see me, they weren't in the house. They were in a different dimension. Demons might still be patrolling the grounds but nothing had broken through the walls of the physical realm. But now I knew they were around in daytime as much as night—I just hadn't seen anything during the day before.

Why didn't they grab me when I walked up to the door? Why hadn't they just come in for me? I hoped they couldn't get me without crossing into this world. Maybe the salt had done better than I expected. I counted my defences. The salt circle, the witch bottle, the LBP—the LBP! I hadn't done that today yet. I was so god-damned weary. My wound ached all the time but stabbed if I moved quickly.

I had to call the surgeon's secretary. That meant I would have to go outside at some point in the next few days. This shit needed sorting out soon. How was I going to do that? I wished there was someone else who could do this stuff for me.

I bowed my head on my knees and bawled. My tears wet my pyjama kneecaps and splashed on my fingers. Caleb was gone, Indira was almost gone. I suddenly felt more alone than ever.

What was the weather like? I lifted my head and peered towards the blinded window. It had rained all night and continued now. I heard a thud from somewhere in the house. And another. And another. They stopped. I breathed silently, ears twitching. Another thud. At least it wasn't a regular beat. I was almost expecting an army of orcs.

I shook myself. They couldn't tear the building down, that was crazy talk. I had to remember where I was at all times. In the real world. No-one else had problems with orcs. Or demons. Well, not many people. I thought of Molly and realised I had to make my appointment before I rang her or she would tell me off.

I grabbed my phone and Googled the number. "Hi, yes, I had an emergency appendectomy under Mrs Sharma and I'm having quite a bit of pain at the moment."

The woman on the other end sounded sympathetic. "If you need to be seen straight away you should go to A&E."

I wasn't ready to leave the building by myself. "I'll probably be okay, but I think she should take a look at it."

"I can fit you in on Thursday afternoon, we've had a cancellation," she said. "Four o'clock okay?"

I agreed, surprised it couldn't be sooner but I knew she'd only make me call an ambulance if I pushed it. As I ended the call, my wound squeezed my midriff as though it knew what I'd done.

As I put the phone down to deal with the pain, it bleeped. Low battery is the scourge of my relationship with mobile phones. I looked for its charger but the plug socket was empty. I'd used it last in the kitchen. The pain subsided a little and I edged to my bedroom door and peered through the glass into the living room. The blind shivered and made scratching noises on the door and my ears twitched in response. I could see right across the room, no sign of any smoke. I opened the door quietly and edged into the bigger room. The exposed feeling washed over me again and I made my way quickly to the breakfast bar. Nothing attacked me. Nothing jumped out but I caught a movement in the corner of my right eye.

I turned to face the smoke behind me, which was now as clear as the daylight shining through the blinds. The glass in my bedroom door had filtered it, hidden it from view.

22. Infernal Enemy

The smoke's density increased and the wall below the window disappeared in a smog-dark cloud billowing thickly. It swelled in size, infernal foam spewing from an invisible crack between the worlds, top heavy and expanding rapidly. I almost expected a mushroom cloud, but the ten-foot-wide space in the 18th-century bay disappeared into a cumulus, wispy around the edges.

Whiffs of sulphur passed by my nose more strongly than before and I realised with a clang of bells in my belly that the smell of the smoke indicated it was in my physical space never mind a different dimension.

Indecision rooted me to the spot. To go to my bedroom would be step nearer to the smoke but otherwise I could hide or run out of the flat. I didn't have anywhere to run to though. I choked on the acrid stench and hid my nose in my sleeve while rotten eggs teased my tongue. A thunderhead morphed from the cloud and formed an anvil shape more perfect than anything I'd ever seen in nature. I almost expected a storm to begin but that reminded me where I was. I'd been dragged into the drama, I had to get out.

I tried to set off for my bedroom but my foot wouldn't lift. My momentum tipped me over and my knees buckled but I stayed upright—just—with a mighty flail of my arms. My feet would only slide as though they were magnetised and the floor was steel.

I slid one foot and then the other, skiing awkwardly, but it felt as though they were moulded into anvils, not just stuck to the floor. Distant thunder began, the wider room now becoming grey and hazy with smoke. I lugged my right leg forward as far as I could step without doing the splits and dragged my left after it, leaning forward for momentum. A huge flash and an ear splitting crash spun me round and I nearly sat to the ground, feet still glued in place, legs twisted around each other.

The cloud swirled around an enormous figure, whose head seemed almost to touch the ceiling. I looked up and up and all I could see through the swirling, angry fog was a monstrous shadow with horns, two tree-like arms. The sound of steel drawn from a scabbard rang out in a minor key and a distant furnace roared.

I backed, still sliding my feet, towards my bedroom door. I didn't know if the salt would hold. I couldn't believe I expected salt to save my life.

Inside the room, my feet released, I threw the phone charger on my bed and straightened up the salt in the doorway. If they wanted to keep trying, I could make it a little bit harder.

It felt like throwing a napkin at a raging inferno, but I stood in the middle of the room facing east and began the Kabbalistic Cross. As I carried on into the rest of the Lesser Banishing Pentagram, I had a sense that someone—something—prowled around the outside of my salt boundary. I looked from side to side, as aware on every level as I could be, feeling the presence slinking around me.

I completed the pentagram and sat down in the middle of the floor again. What the hell else could I do?

I could charge the bloody phone!

I jumped up and scored a shock of pain as I wrenched my wound again. Under my shirt the stitches still held at the top of the tiny wound but the lower one had broken. The gamy edges were a little oozy, dark brown and unpleasant looking and I'd bled a little onto my t-shirt. I didn't know when. Rust-coloured smudges said it had been ages ago. I remembered I'd noticed it bleeding earlier but now had no idea when that had been.

I let go of my shirt and rapidly plugged my phone into the charger. Its bleep was the first relief I'd felt for days.

I wondered where the being in the living room was now and worried how real it was. Presumably it could walk through walls. The reason why it wasn't already tearing my soul from my body evaded me. Looking through the window of the door was pointless as the glass had filtered the magical smoke so I likely couldn't see the demon through it anyway.

I could only attribute being alive to the few protection wards I'd used from the book, but reversal spells that turned back a creature sent by someone else weren't detailed in there. I remembered it said you couldn't protect against something that had already hit you. Sweat sprang from my skin, suddenly unnaturally hot. My wound throbbed. I hoped that didn't mean I had an infection. I had to do something.

I gently took hold of the door handle and squeezed it open. A crack wasn't enough to get a full look at it so I opened it a little wider. I could see some smoke low down near the floor but it wasn't enough of a view. I pulled open the door suddenly and peered around it. And up. And still further.

The entity was mountainous to my flea-like sensibilities, powerful and vile and no longer insubstantial, its terrible physicality swathed in smoke that continued to unfurl across the room. Dozens of snakes hissed from behind its shoulders, darting around its hulking solidity as if they could bite me from there. Flames of red and violet licked around its legs across green flesh muscles churning under immense plates of armour.

With a single mighty arm it brought down an immense broadsword to the ground with a clang but remained standing. It reminded me of a computer game avatar awaiting its controller, swaying slightly but remaining in place. Vicious knives strapped to its arms clattered together with every violent movement. I realised I could see every detail as real as my own hand on the door.

It held aloft arms, sword in one hand and a great orange light shot out of the earth directly below, red and yellow streams twisting together around the monster. The jagged-edged mask and helmet were silhouetted in the fire-like power of the light from below. The demon seemed to grow larger even as I stared.

I dove back in the room and slammed the door.

Lying on the floor I didn't know where to run. Even the space under my bed was stuffed with belongings. The wardrobe wasn't big enough. Something metallic tapped on the glass of my bedroom door. Three taps. Three more. Insistent. Persistent. Creepy as fuck. I stared at the salt line following its path and my stomach heaved. I'd broken the barrier with the door and hadn't put it back. The salt was scattered, not even a ragged line remained, just a dusting.

With a reverberating roar, the wall above the door bulged and caved in, plaster raining down in chunks as the door was felled in one piece. The demon warrior stepped straight through the debris, trampling on broken glass. I scrambled towards the opposite wall but the entity took two strides into the room and picked me up by my arm. My shoulder joint snapped audibly with a sickening crack. He yanked my arm, swivelling me around on my arse and dragged me towards the window. I thought he was going to throw me through it and as I partially regained my feet, pulled back kicking, screaming with pain.

An incessant whirling, rushing feeling grew inside me from my centre, swirling round and round. A huge wind played with me, tossing my body around and upside down, spinning within and around me. Crushing pressure built up inside me and with a final rush I birthed the dragon from my centre.

The demon let go and I fell backwards to the ground, Alon rising solid and real above me, bright copper and orange against the vaulted darkness.

The space jammed up with rapacious shrieks and grunts and screams that tore through my eardrums, left my brain in tatters. I cowered in a crouch, one useless arm trailing on the floor, the other over my head as though it could protect me.

The wind blew wildly like a tornado trapped in my tiny

bedroom. Alon and the demon whirled and flipped around, the dragon's wings enveloping the hellion's torso, his head and lashing tongue craning for a bite of straining green neck tendons.

The demon's hands came around the back of the dragon to grasp its spine, but blue and red blood splattered across the floor and my bed and the monster faltered. Alon seemed to expand, no space left for air. His wings double wrapped the gigantic fiend before it could let go, even as the fire in its eyes overflowed and ran across the pair of them, lava in place of tears. Under the leather of the wings, the devil's hands could no longer reach the dragon's back, but the lava coated everything, turned Alon's wings into lace.

The two of them twisted together became a towering inferno, the flames of hell licking the carpet near my feet. I pressed myself as far under the bed as I could get, but the eggy smell of sulphur filled the room and I lifted my one working hand to cover my airways with my sleeve.

Ruined wings flapped once, splitting the flames and tearing the dragon away. With a final thrust, Alon dove onto the demon and curled his way around its neck, corkscrewed down its torso. He squeezed. A blinding flash blew my eyesight out and all I made out were two writhing bodies still upright and the demon's flailing arms. Then darkness and a heavy thud on the floor next to me.

Silence. I looked around in the nothing, trying to see *something*. All I had was an immense ball of flames imprinted on my retina. As my eyes acclimatised I made out a huge rock in front of the bed. Gingerly, ready to puke at any moment, I reached out with my good arm and touched the rock.

I screamed. I couldn't help it. It wasn't a rock. It was the fucking demon's head. My hand sank into its flesh as though it was insubstantial but a strange, sickly warmth made it real enough. The helmet was tipped forwards over the monster's face, away from me thank god. Why the hell was it still here? Where did the rest of it go? Where was Alon?

Sitting there in the room with a smashed wall and a useless arm, cold and terrified, I didn't know if I was crazy, or experiencing a magical attack.

I tried to take some perspective. If it was real, I wasn't crazy. If I was crazy, it wasn't real. I didn't know which option I preferred. If I was crazy, how come I managed to snap my own arm over my shoulder? I moved my leg to accommodate a new pain in my calf. The crunch of glass reminded me of the door. I looked up at where it had been. The papered plasterboard that sufficed as a wall surrounded a fourteen-by-six-foot hole where the doorway had been.

Crazy was the only way I could explain the damage to the landlord. Nothing less than a sledgehammer would get that effect, a fortune to replace. I leaned back against the bed frame in the silence and the dark and wondered if I was safe yet. I didn't know whether or not to allow myself the relief. Where was Alon?

I realised something. My arm didn't hurt any more. I tried to move it. Nothing. I didn't know if I was being chicken but I didn't try again. I closed my eyes and slept.

When I awoke the evening light had dimmed the room. The decapitated demon's head had sunk into itself like an abandoned leather football, a puddle of esoteric slime on the floor. The helmet had all but worn away, twisted metal undulating and smooth across its surface, the hairy brush on top almost bald. The shadowy shapes of the furniture in the room were solid and still but the gaping hole in the wall changed the feel of the space. Familiarity was gone because everything looked wrong and I no longer felt safe. I checked my phone. I had twenty-five percent battery power. Enough for a call.

"Hi hunny, what's going on?" Molly's chirpy voice had a serious note. I wondered if she knew what had happened.

"Not good news on any front." Tears welled up. "Caleb killed himself, Indira had an accident and is probably going to die, and there's a decomposing demon's head in the middle of my bedroom. What the fuck am I gonna do?" I openly wept.

"Oh God, what? Are you okay?"

No. No I wasn't okay. I cried more. "A demon appeared from nowhere in the living room and the dragon saved my arse." I retched as I looked across at the demon's head. Soft blubs simmered on the surface of the slime.

"Are you injured?"

I tried to move my shoulder. "The demon snapped my shoulder, but it doesn't hurt, I just can't move it."

"You've been in the wars, haven't you? What else has gone on? You said something about Indira?" Her tone softened to sympathy but that only made it harder.

"Some kind of freak accident on the M62, her car got stuck on the front of a lorry." The accident was too freakish. Too weird. "It travelled miles. I don't know if she's going to be okay."

"How do you know about Caleb?"

I tried to squash the tears but my voice came out all squeaky. "He did it in front of me."

"Oh God, that's awful." She paused. "His body was used."

I caught my breath. "What do you mean?"

"He was made to do it, wasn't he?"

"He kept asking for help but still doing it to himself."

"Was there something else going on at the same time?" Her voice sounded weird. Tighter.

I told her about the worms in his brain and she was both impressed and disgusted.

"That David had better not try anything like that with you."

"What else will he do to me?" I felt acutely sick. "You should have seen the size of the fucking demon thing, its head was through the ceiling," I wailed. "My bedroom is in pieces."

"Stop it, just pull yourself together, you know what to do."

"No, I don't."

"Yes you do, stop crying. I can't stand to hear you feeling so sorry for yourself." Her tone changed to a harder sound. "Stop with all this self-pity. You'll need to do a reversal spell. But you know that."

"How do I do one of those? I never did anything like this stuff before." Her attitude surprised me and I was hurt.

"Get a—" Silence.

I looked at my phone. It was dead. "Oh, for fuck's sake!" I stopped myself from throwing the bastard thing at the wall and grabbed the end of the charger. The plug went in smoothly, with a faint click.

The screen remained black. I checked the socket switch. It was on. Still nothing from the phone. I held down the on-switch and waited. Still blank.

The phone was completely dead. Just as she was about

to tell me how to deal with this shit. I sank to the floor and leant my head on the bed, amongst the wreckage of my bedroom wall and let the panic and desperation rise up over my head.

Inayat.

Someone whispered in my ear. I didn't recognise the voice.

23. Drowning in Hatred

Inayat.

It wasn't a nice voice, really.

Inayat, you will come.

It wasn't the dragon, but it was male.

You will come, Inayat. Come.

To my horror, my right arm reached behind me—involuntarily—to the bed and pushed against it to stand me up. My feet took their turn and even though I tried to resist and twist back towards the bed they walked me to the window.

I put my fist through the glass. I couldn't stop my movements. My flesh was obedient to something or someone else's will. I couldn't believe my puny fist smashed the glass.

The remaining sharp edges glinted in the moonlight and to my horror my feet moved and my leg swung me over the jagged frame. Glass dug into my backside but I pushed off with my inside foot and fell onto the ground below, more glass, more sharp cuts on my soft body.

I awkwardly ran across the drive and lurched to the edge of the rockery, not feeling the rhythm of whatever was forcing me to move. The wall loomed, fifteen feet high, but undeterred by that or my damaged arm, I pulled myself into the tree one-handed, straddled a large bough and bunched myself along until the crown of the wall was in reach. It had to be a dream. I only ever ran for the bus. I couldn't even pull myself up a rope when I was a kid.

I swung my leg over the bough and leapt for the top of the wall. By some miracle I grabbed hold of it and dragged my body up until I could sit on the top.

There was no time to ready myself for the leap. As I jumped, I prayed I could fly. Dreams that included superhuman abilities surely had flying, too. I hit the concrete on my toes, bare feet ready for the impact.

No smashed legs, some miracle.

I sprinted, bare footed, across Gledhow Wood Road. I guessed the time at around ten o'clock, possibly even later. Strangely, my mind was my own but my body was disconnected from that. My feet took me down someone's drive, through their garden and over their fence into a back lane.

I vaulted—one-handed—over a smaller fence, through someone's rose bed, down their path and over the wall at the end. My lungs were already out of breath, as much from shock as the running. And still my legs ran, across the cricket field and between two pieces of high security fencing into the school. I tripped and landed full length on the tarmac, legs too tired to pick up my feet. I lay there, desperate for a rest, chasing my breath but already my feet were moving. My hand pushed me up from the ground, unbidden, and I was back on my feet, jogging over the playing fields to an open gate.

Soldier's Field lay ahead of me, Princess Avenue running alongside. I considered screaming for help if I saw a car but nothing approached on the road as I crossed. I passed a shrine to a dead person, flowers taped to a tree and recently lit tea lights in the grass. Princess Avenue was notorious for accidents. As I ran down the hill into the park proper, I could see Waterloo Lake ahead of me. A Georgian man-made reservoir, created by former soldiers just after the Napoleonic wars, it was a pretty walk on a sunny day. Not tonight, Josephine.

I didn't know if it was the gradient of the hill or the unseen force that governed my movements but my legs sped up over the soft turf. I hurtled past the visitor centre and car park, through the trees. The lake was coming up fast. I remembered the grass ended above the path and leapt down the step, but my foot didn't come up fast enough and I stumbled and gashed my face on the sandy hardcore.

My legs still pumped, as though I was having a fit fully conscious and I sprang to my feet for the last time. Again, I stumbled but this time I was pushed, hard, in the small of my back. I heard a scream in the distance. Thought it was my own. My hand grabbed on to nothing in the night air and I hit the water flat side down with an almighty splash.

Struggling in the water my feet couldn't find the bottom. Sixty feet deep. The lake was a quarry, landscaped at the edges to look shallow. Something pushed down on my shoulders and suddenly I knew this was it. Water filled my mouth and ears. I spat it out. My feet weighed like lead, couldn't kick like they should. This was the way he intended me to go. To lose everyone in my life and die a lonely suicide in the lake.

The black hole of pathos threatened to consume me and I sagged under the weight on my shoulders. He bore me down towards a watery grave but I focused my resistance on my bursting lungs as I held my breath. I stopped moving, hung still in the water, no more struggling. Death was preferable to continual attack. I wondered how far the bastard might follow me.

There was peace under the water. If he held me under and I didn't fight it, he'd think I gave in and death would free me.

But I didn't let go of my breath yet. A bright rectangular light flashed behind my eyes. I didn't know if I could damage my brain and still be conscious.

Fuck that, said an angry female voice inside my head. *Pull yourself together. You know what to do.*

What did I need to do?

My breath had no beginning and no end. I neither drew it in nor exhaled. My lungs screamed for air and my heart pounded in my ears as the weight on my shoulders sent me deeper, far below the surface of the lake.

Across my arm and face, I felt the shadowy strokes of all the dead people who had ended their lives in the lake for centuries. Like fronds of seaweed, but in my heart I knew what they were. I was joining them.

What the fuck are you doing? The voice again. My own. Clear and angry.

Anger struck my centre, a lightning strike of red hot fury. All of this—every part—was because he couldn't have me.

My lungs burned. I only had now.

I kicked furiously and shot out my functioning hand, dragging it down past my body. My vision behind my tightly closed eyelids went from black to red and a strong light cut through between my lashes. I writhed and shook my body around, swinging my arm and shrugging my good shoulder.

I was no longer sinking or being pushed further down.

Just an inconstant weight across my head and shoulders, as though he was dislodged. I wriggled my legs hard, unseating the weight on my left shoulder, so I summoned a frenzy of kicks and shakes, twisting in his metaphysical grasp.

I pulled the water away from me above my head and the pressure lessened as my body rose, kicking and swiping my way towards the surface, shaking off invisible hands on my shoulders as I ascended. How fucking dare anyone do something like this, just because he couldn't get what he wanted? Arrogant bastard! I violently wriggled my good shoulder and his hold slipped off me completely, releasing me. With another kick, I burst through the surface of the water, absolutely shattered. No fight left in me.

"Inayat? Inayat!"

A splash choked me and a lifebuoy bobbed towards my head. I grabbed hold of its strings and pulled it close, hugging the ring to me. I was disorientated, unsure what direction to take. The horizon was the same at every angle.

"Come on, girl, kick!" shouted Molly. I floated my body on the surface of the water and tiredly kicked towards the edge of the lake. My limbs were my own again, but my effort was pathetic. I felt like a dead weight, glad for the lifebuoy. The concrete ledge seemed incredibly high, but I knew it was only a couple of feet.

"Here, help her. Get her out, will you?"

A man appeared on the ledge. "Grab my hands," he told me.

"I've only got one arm." The other one was useless.

He reached out and firmly gripped my wrist. "On three," he said. "One, two, three!" With every number he bounced my body in the water using its tension like a trampoline and heaved me out on the third shout.

Molly grabbed my top leg and swung it across the grass, turning me face first into the turf. I lay there for a moment, feeling saved, my leg dangling over the side. The water behind me broke with a splash and something grabbed my foot and tugged.

"Shit!" I shouted. "He's got me!"

The man caught hold of my good arm and hauled me away from the surface, staring at the lake behind. I weakly sat up and looked back. The water churned in a rolling boil, spitting out plumes and steam at intervals. It swelled, mountainous, like an out-of-control water feature and crashed back into the lake. Unnaturally, the surface became calm almost immediately.

The man turned incredulous eyes at me.

"What did I just see? What the hell are you messing with, bombs?" He squinted at us both in turn. "You don't look the fucking type." Molly sighed with a tinge of irritation and he frowned. "I'm calling the police." He fumbled for his phone.

"What are you doing?" Molly's tired tone pulled at a string inside me. She was pissed off. "She's the bloody victim, isn't she? It's not her fault she's in this mess." She stood taller, chin stubborn and he shrank a little.

He muttered, "I don't know what's going on, do I?"

"Try and be a little bit helpful, will you?" snapped Molly. "We'll probably need a lift to the hospital so just wait there." She crouched beside me. "How are you, Inayat? Did you get the help I sent you?" She snapped her head up at the taxi driver. "Put your phone away, we've got this." He stuck his hands in his pockets like a surly schoolboy.

"What help was that?"

She flashed me a smile and spoke in a low voice. "Just say I tossed an energetic grenade in there to clean you up." Her eyes were alight as she winked at me.

"Did it make a bright light?" I remembered the weird flash through my eyelids before I kicked myself away from my watery grave, thought it was just my own body warning me of its peril.

Molly shrugged. "It might have done if you could see it."

"How did you find me?"

She spoke in a normal tone of voice, shooting a glance at the driver. "I couldn't get you off my mind, so I got a cab to your house. But then I had a feeling you were down here so I made the driver come all the way down with me."

The taxi driver shuffled his feet but I didn't look at him. I nursed my wounds for a moment, head hung low and gathered some energy.

"We have to get out of here, you wouldn't believe the dead people right now," Molly whispered.

I thought of the caressing touches deep in the water as they welcomed another of their own.

She nodded over my shoulder. "There's one stood right behind you on top of the water. A kid. Creepy as heck." Now she spoke in a normal voice. "What's up with your shoulder, love?"

My arm hung limply, no life in it at all. I still didn't feel the pain.

"It doesn't hurt. Maybe it'll mend by itself."

"Erm, I don't think so, do you?" She stood up and spoke to the taxi driver. "You'll take us to A&E, won't you?"

Someone had to put me back together.

24. Hospital Again

A&E was busy, so we waited to be called for triage surrounded by parents with sick babies and drunk or ill-looking people. Apprehension permeates the air on bad days like an unpleasant smell. It's why I never wanted to work there. I'd ducked out of a temporary role in that department a couple of years back.

I slopped cold water on my face in the ladies' and straightened up my appearance as best I could. My right eye was swollen, my face, elbow and knees were grazed, I'd pulled muscles in the tops of both my legs. I still couldn't feel my shoulder and when I took a look at my appendectomy wound, it was all washed clean from the lake water. The tiny gash looked less ominous without the dark dried blood, but I thought I'd better mention it to someone. I re-entered the waiting room feeling a little more human and in an unnaturally positive mood considering the circumstances.

Molly brought me a hot chocolate from the machine. "Not exactly BigBean," she said, handing it to me. "But it's a damn sight better than nettle tea." She made a puke gesture and smiled. "How are you feeling?"

"Probably better than some people in here. What am I going to say to the nurse?"

Molly thought about it for a moment. "Just trust in your mouth. Whatever comes out will be right."

I never trusted my mouth, but I was learning. She hadn't been wrong so far. I nodded, watching reception as some drunk people came into the hospital, one man bleeding from a gash in his top lip. Everyone seemed a lot more upset than me. I felt pretty good. I wondered if that was the adrenaline.

"Moll, why you do you think I can't feel my shoulder?" It was a question I didn't want an answer to.

Molly avoided my eyes and looked down at her hot chocolate. "You might want to think about careers you can do with one hand," she said, quietly.

I didn't want to think about that at all. "How did you really know where I was?"

Her stage whisper was strangely comical. "It was your grandfather again. Wouldn't leave me alone." She looked over both shoulders and leaned towards me. "Pestered me all afternoon till I rang the taxi and then popped up in the cab just after we turned off past Tesco. I told the driver there was a damsel in distress and he assumed it was a blind date gone wrong. Never heard the end of it the whole way. 'The Internet's a tool of the New World Order, evil people out there, wouldn't let a woman come out to the lake by herself. Did my head right in." She grinned widely. "He said if you're meeting someone for the first time and they want to meet somewhere really creepy, it's probably not a good sign. He came with me to make sure I was safe. Kept saying he didn't want me on his conscience. I had a job getting him to leave the jemmy in the boot of his car!"

"Do you think this is the last we've heard of David?" I was so hopeful. So fucking hopeful.

She looked into my eyes and shook her head slowly. "We'll have to see, won't we, love? But I'm seeing you home, anyway. Then we'll figure out how the land lies. Got work in the morning, otherwise I'd stop with you."

"Inayat Tate." A woman in a white coat walked into the waiting area with a clipboard. I stood up and walked towards her. Her eyes took in my dead arm. "Follow me."

We walked to an examination room and she closed the door behind us. I sat down in the seat next to the medical desk. She took a seat and clicked a mouse, her attention on the screen.

"You look like you've been in the wars. What happened to you?"

Whatever comes out of my mouth will be right.

I took a deep breath. "My ex-boyfriend tried to kill me, nearly drowned me. Bust my shoulder." It was as close as I could go to the truth without getting myself sectioned.

"Are the police aware you've been assaulted?"

"Me and my friend are going to the police station after you've patched me up." I hoped she would take the hint.

She looked at me directly, her eyes narrowed. "Are you sure you're going to do that? I'll have to report it to the police as an assault anyway."

I nodded. "You should do that. They'll need to know." Would they? I willed her not to call them. She took my details and I took off my shirt and let her look at my shoulder. As she gently manipulated it I realised I might have lost the use of it forever. I felt nothing, physically. I hoped that detachment might help me adjust emotionally. I pushed away the thought of long-term disability and concentrated on what the woman was doing.

"It's strange that you've got no pain," she said thoughtfully. "You've no damage to your back or neck, have you?"

None that I'd noticed. I shrugged my shirt back on and she strapped my arm to my chest. "You'll need this x-rayed, pinned and cast, so head back to the waiting room and stay there till you're called. It shouldn't be too long." She noticed my appendectomy scar as she did up my buttons. "That's seeping, you know. Were you in hospital recently?" She looked at the computer screen and clicked for my history, not waiting for my answer. "A week ago. That wound doesn't look great for a week ago. Should be well on its way by now."

She picked up a swab and diluted some disinfectant in a metal bowl.

"Hold tight," she advised. "This'll probably hurt." She cleaned out the wound with the cotton swab and dabbed the area dry with a piece of cloth. It stung. "Just need a dressing." She ratched in a drawer and pulled out a sterile packet.

Temporarily patched up, she let me back into the corridor. A familiar male voice wafted round the corner. Sergeant O'Brien was here. They must have already called the police. I stood in the middle of the walkway as he rounded the corner, preceded by a handcuffed man.

They walked three steps towards us before he saw me. O'Brien did a noticeable double take. The men proceeded towards me and I stepped out of their way. The sergeant turned his head to me, blue eyes missing nothing even as he passed. "I'll be two minutes."

"We're in the waiting room."

I watched his retreating figure. How did he manage to turn up just at the right time?

The triage doctor nudged my good shoulder. "Do you know the police officer?"

"He's coming back to talk to me. He knows about my

problem." I sighed. "It's been going on for a while, just never got this bad."

Light dawned in the doctor's eyes, perhaps as she recognised the opportunity to do one less task on a busy night. "Wait for someone to call you, it won't be long."

I headed back to Molly.

O'Brien was more serious than I'd seen him yet. I hoped he wasn't angry with me.

He slid into the chair next to mine. "Start from the top, Inayat," he said. "Tell me what happened."

I started from the mist in the living room. When I got to 'demon', he stopped me. "Think for a minute, Inayat. What did he look like, this demon?"

I pictured the creature easily. "About fourteen-foot high, green and armoured. He had a helmet."

O'Brien paused. "So he didn't look anything like the man you believe is causing you a problem?"

If ever there was a pregnant pause, this one was about to drop dozens of baby pausies. I couldn't look at Molly. I didn't even know how to make that decision. How do you press charges against an assailant who wasn't even there? I felt like O'Brien was giving me the opportunity to falsely say it was David.

"I—I have no idea what to say." Once again, tears washed through me. What the hell was I supposed to do? I couldn't claim witchcraft and fight it through the courts with no provision for magic in law. But to make up a story about how he physically dragged me across three miles of parkland and tried to drown me seemed counterproductive. They had no evidence beyond my physical injuries and he would have a nice fat alibi backed up by the fact that it was the truth, so there would be no fighting anything through the courts, except possibly an injunction.

O'Brien nodded seriously. "Just give me the truth as you see it. As you know, the law doesn't allow for demons or MK Ultra-style mind control, but it does allow for coercion and abuse. Someone with mental health problems and occasional psychosis would be considered very vulnerable in the face of gaslighting and suggestion." He sat back in his chair. "My reports—so far—have taken an 'as seen for myself' viewpoint, so no mention of the—less conventional information you've provided. I'm pretty sure my initial instincts were correct, so I'm going to recommend we go to court over his initial attempted assault." He leaned closer and spoke quietly. "But CPS won't go for more than that unless we've got evidence for your claims and I'm still not convinced they'll pick it up anyway. If you were having a mental health crisis stimulated by an abusive relationship, we might have something. Magical demons, not so much."

Molly spoke. "Can't prove what isn't there."

I stared across the waiting room at a sleeping baby in his mother's arms. Proof. The only proof would be enough to land me in a psychiatric hospital. I had no demon head. All trace would be gone when I got home. I had no proof that the lake had risen up and tried to drown me. No proof of some invisible force that compelled my legs and arm to have huge strength and agility for a few wretched miles. The police wouldn't do anything about it, whether it was magic or a mental health crisis. They wouldn't protect me against his magic, even if he was put away for a made-up abusive relationship. There wasn't any point in going to court over it and I definitely didn't want a mental health assessment—God knew what they might find—I didn't even want to prosecute David for the first assault, or 'attempted' assault, as O'Brien now put it. I just wanted the bastard to stop.

I looked back at O'Brien. "So we pretend this didn't happen and hope we get him on the first assault anyway?" I stuck to my own words.

O'Brien nodded. "Everything gets recorded, but it can be extremely brief, especially if no arrests come of it." He cocked his head on one side, flickered a look towards Molly and back to me. "Tell me more about the demon. What shape was its helmet?"

I frowned. "It had hair coming out the top, like a horse's tail and the sides framed his face, jagged edges, left the front open from the mouth downwards."

"Like a Roman helmet?"

"A fancy one, like a centurion, with a brush on the top but more like a horse's tail."

He nodded and flipped his pocketbook to the back to

write it down. Molly looked at him suspiciously. "You know what that was, Sergeant?"

He glanced at us both in turn and held my gaze longest. I couldn't tell what he was thinking but the lengthy eye contact hastened my heartbeat.

He sighed. "Off the record of course." We both nodded, Molly with the tension of a bridge cable. "Sounds like a General class demon. Something powerful, with a lot of personality and a demon horde under his command. Not too pleasant." He gave a half smile. "At least that tells us a bit more about how he's attacking you."

I stared at him. He'd said it was his wife who was Wiccan, but he knew way more about the demon than either of us. Probably more than the average Wiccan, too.

"You haven't heard the rest." Molly's scepticism was dismissive, but he prevailed.

"Let me guess. He's got a piece of jewellery with a demon entity bound to it." He caught my sudden glance at Molly and looked sterner. "You don't dabble in that stuff, do you ladies?"

I shook my head. "He made them into vessels. It was his magic."

O'Brien gave a slight frown. "Catcheside made it?"

I cleared my throat. "I had one of his pieces. Not a demon. A dragon. It told me who had bound it." We really were in cloud cuckoo territory now. I could feel reality bearing down on him.

He stared at me. "Not something to do with the jewellery items you said you gave him back?"

I hung my head and tried to look sorry. I couldn't feel the chagrin I should, because Alon had come in useful when he did.

"I wouldn't be alive if it wasn't for the dragon." My voice was very small. "He came out of me and bit the demon's head off, but they both vanished and I haven't seen him since."

Silence crashed onto the waiting room chairs.

Molly frowned and leaned forwards. She picked up my hand that had held the rings. "Gone."

I hadn't realised. Not at all. My fingers were knobbly, still dirty with muck under the nails and totally bereft of jewellery.

"So then what happened, Inayat?" O'Brien prompted me. I risked a glance at him and saw no judgement on his face. Strange feeling.

As I described the experience of having my body taken over, the similarities with Caleb's behaviour hit me. He hadn't been in control of his own body either.

I completed my story with the scene at the lakeside and Molly butted in. "I got told by her ancestor again, woken up in the middle of the night and pestered until I called a taxi. He guided me to the lake and that's where I found her. Taxi driver got her out of the water and brought us to A&E."

O'Brien was quiet for a while, jotting down notes in an indecipherable scrawl that could have been shorthand for all I saw.

I remembered what Leah had said about the woman in the canal and Molly's vision again. I hadn't remembered to tell her before.

"Did you find the doctor in the canal, sergeant?"

His head snapped up. "That was a physical attack. She'd been assaulted prior to being drowned."

Molly's face dropped, her eyes wide. "It was the doctor in the water? I thought it was Inayat." She was genuinely shocked.

"What?"

Molly and I looked at each other. She looked panicky, as though she was in trouble.

"I saw a vision," she said, embarrassedly.

"What kind of vision?" His gruff question made me feel as though I was in some sort of alternate reality where the police took information from psychics and magic was real to everyone.

"Just..." Her voice trailed off. "Probably nothing."

"Tell me anyway," he encouraged, though I sensed he was tired of the whole thing. Psychic visions were hardly admissible in court.

Molly faced him, her chin lifted up a little, almost defiant. "I saw a photograph of this David character. Had a vision of drowning in deep water. I thought it was about Inayat, but the water was murky, bicycles and metal objects in it."

"Unlikely to be the lake?" he asked.

She shrugged. "I'd put it down to that tonight, but I didn't know the doctor had drowned in the canal."

"And that—vision, that was stimulated by seeing his picture?"

She nodded silently.

He wrote some more notes across the bottom of the page of his pocketbook.

My attention wandered and my eyes followed the tiny hand of the baby in its mother's hold as it flapped its arm. A man in a blue shirt with a name badge walked into the by now almost empty A&E.

"Inayat Tate?"

The baby's head twisted round unnaturally, from front to back, its mouth wide open in a grotesque mask of a child. A forked tongue flicked out as it looked at me with evil, longing eyes.

25. Reversal Spell

Molly and I piled into yet another taxi and headed for Gledhow Hall. I would need to get a loan out for all the taxi rides in the past couple of weeks. I'd narrowly avoided a hospital stay—they would attempt to reconnect my nerves and pin my shoulder but NHS resources were low at five-thirty a.m., so I was booked in to return for an appointment on Thursday. The same day I was supposed to see my other surgeon. What a mess I was. Lucky it was all at the same hospital or I was bound to miss one.

I leant against my headrest, hopeful that everything was over. I didn't even know where to begin to sort out my life. I couldn't do my typing work with one hand! The doctors were baffled by the lack of pain. With every tendon and ligament pulled in the joint and the joint itself dislocated, nothing could be done about the use of it until they'd joined everything up. They fitted me a temporary brace and fixed my arm to my body. I was uneasy about my employment prospects.

We rounded the corner onto Gledhow Wood Court and glided into the drive. I saw no sign of the demon hordes as we pulled up at the porch. Molly paid the money to the cab driver and we made our way to the door. The early morning air was cold and crisp and I could smell dead leaves, a fresh, mouldy aroma that danced on the breeze. I was alive.

As we reached the door I realised I didn't have my handbag or my keys. "I left through the window." I slumped. God only knew what mess the place was in. I wanted to be at home. So close but still so far.

Molly shook her head. "Is there anyone else in the building?"

Maggie had been taken to hospital. No-one was left in our wing.

"We'll have to go back through the window, then." She smiled. "I'll do it."

We walked round the balustrade and up to the smashed-up window. Molly cleared away a few pieces of glass still in the frame and passed me her handbag.

She winked. "I don't know if I can get my leg over that."

I groaned at her joke as she clambered in and watched

her walk through the bedroom. Everything was a tip. I limped round to the front door again and met her there. She was holding the keys. "You left them in the door of the flat."

I walked into the hallway and staggered slightly as the floor seemed to falter beneath me. Molly grabbed me. "Come on, chick, you're home now."

As I walked into the flat I remembered everything that had happened in snatches, like a dream I actually recalled for once. I tottered up to the massive hole in the wall in my bedroom doorway. We viewed it for a shocked moment.

"He was a big one," said Molly, looking at the devastation. She didn't seem worried, but I didn't know where she got her assurance from.

I stepped forwards through the crater into the bedroom. The wind breezed round the room from the smashed and cleared window. Everything was as I remembered it, my bed clothes bunched up in a heap in the corner, a chunk taken out of the wardrobe. The broken window from the other side and just a dark patch on the floor where the demon's head had fallen. Still no dragon. I supposed, now the rings were gone, I'd never see him again.

Molly walked up to the window over the broken glass. "That's going to be draughty. Have you got an old box we can flatten and tape over here?"

I shrugged with my unbroken shoulder. "No way am I

sleeping in here tonight." She nodded. Indira's bed was free. I fervently hoped that was only for now.

"Come on," she said. "Let's have some tea." She left the room and I heard her put the kettle on. I looked out of the window into the early morning dullness. The sky was more blue than black, the dawn pushing its way to the other side of the house.

"You know what you need to do, don't you?" She called out. I wandered through, dejectedly. I didn't feel so chipper any more. The adrenaline must be wearing off. I wondered again why I didn't feel my shoulder.

Molly pottered around with mugs and teabags so I sat on the barstool. "I don't know anything any more."

"You can sleep in a few minutes, but get a pen and paper. You'll need to remember this stuff."

I grabbed some notepaper and a pen straight away.

When she left I turned back into the flat and felt outwards from my centre. Despite the devastation, the whole space was an arena of tranquillity, the witch bottle's green aura strong and unbroken. Nothing there but me.

I slept for twelve hours. In Indira's bed.

I awoke to the cheerful sound of my mobile ringtone. As I scrabbled in the dark under a pile of clothes on the floor, it stopped abruptly. I found it and lay back down. A moment later, a message bleeped.

I closed my eyes and grounded, reaching mentally into the room. Although the room was quiet and filled with nothing, I pushed outwards from the house feeling upwards into the sky. A grim, ominous presence filled the stratosphere. It hung there like a nuclear rain cloud, a dark-green oppression weighting everything down. No happiness could be found. No lightness.

I flicked open my eyelids and dialled the answering machine number for my saved message.

It was my work agency 'business associate', Gwen. They called all their employees 'associates', to make them feel like they were important to the agency. Actual agency workers like me didn't get fancy titles. We were expendable.

Her message was direct and to the point. "Hi Inayat, we were wondering when you're thinking of coming back to work. You can get statutory sick pay, you know, so give me a call when you get this and we'll talk about the terms."

Gwen wouldn't want to pay me sickness when she realised I wouldn't be able to come back to work. Then I twigged. She only knew about my appendix. I Googled statutory sick pay. Eighty-eight quid a week was better than a kick in the teeth. She didn't need to know about my arm until the money ran out or I figured out a new life. I suddenly felt very alone without Indira.

I'd lived on my own before, but it would have been comforting to share this nightmare with someone else. Poor Indira. She hadn't deserved what happened to her. Neither had Caleb, come to think of it. My misery and regret swept over me and I wept again. I felt so useless. I was being useless.

I sat up on the side of the bed and stretched out for the bedside lamp. It illuminated Indira's Middle-Eastern-style boudoir beautifully, highlighting rich silks and the lustre of the soft cushions on the bed.

I didn't know where to start to replace an interior wall, a doorway and a window, but it would all have to wait for tomorrow. I wasn't useless, though.

I had a reversal spell to deploy.

I stood in the centre of the living room on Indira's expansive fluffy wool rug. Candles blinked around the edges of the room, lighting it in a mysterious glory. Shadows flickered on the high ceiling and walls and I saw a candle flame reflected in Indira's photo.

I was doing this for Indira and Caleb. I had to send everything back to where it had come from, with love. See, love is an energy frequency. Hit the right note with your own internal twang and you access its vibration.

I held myself still, even the skirt of my black dress hung in drapes, unmoved. I focused on the moment. This shit was going back. With love—I kept having to remind myself of that. David's behaviour wasn't 'normal' on any level. If he was doing nothing and we were totally wrong about him, a reversal spell wouldn't cause him any problem. If we were right, then presumably he was suffering in some way too, which meant my response shouldn't be too powerful.

I smiled. Prancing around in my living room didn't feel particularly powerful, but magic worked and I knew the bigger the show, the more effective it would be.

Getting everything ready with one hand had been tedious. Over an hour just to change my clothes and despite the dress, there was nothing dignified about the process. I would have to come up with some strategies. Being more organised seemed the only solution—not something that came naturally.

I faced east and readied myself, stilled my mind and became consciously aware. I sank deep into my ground, sensing rivulets of my grounding threads growing millions of tributaries into the earth. I drew down divine light above my head. I pointed my right hand at the light and drew the golden ray through my forefinger like a laser beam. "*Atah!*" I yelled, as I touched my forehead. My hand moved to my breastbone, my heart chakra. "*Malkuth!*" The light pierced my centre and shot down between my feet into the ground.

"*Ve-Geburah.*" I pointed outwards to my right and invited the light into my heart again. As it pierced my chakra, I bellowed "*Ve-Gedulah!*" I willed my left arm to lift, imagined it was there, let the ray of light streak through its fingers though it lay uselessly at my side. "*Le Olahm.*" Golden light continued to flow through my heart chakra, from crown to ground and right through left.

I brought my right hand to my sternum for half the sign of supplication and bowed my head. "*Amen.*"

Strength ran through me as though I had tapped into an energy line. I was more powerful and intentional. I completed the LBP, the pentacles electric blue in my mind. All the imagery was creative visualisation, but the presence of the archangels was the strongest I'd ever felt. They towered above me, twenty feet high, in front, behind and to each side. They held an impression in negative space as clearly as if they were solid and in my mind's eye, they glimmered with colour—purple and yellow, blue and white, red with green and green with red. I finished on a respectful '*Amen*' and stepped back to face east.

With my forefinger, I traced a circle on the back of my head to unscrew my crown chakra. I twiddled it out until the cap was in my hand and threw it into the air, through the roof, far above the rafters of the old building. A gentle pressure gripped my head, steadily holding me still, and I dropped my attention to my centre. Two golden rods of energy shot through my root chakra to the deep earth below.

As I inhaled, I brought energy from the ground into my feet, sparking up my legs, lightning connections patterning my lower half and filling my centre with a hotspot. I pushed down again, as though sinking a syringe plunger into the earth, and drew it back up, higher each time, wrapping my body in electrical power. And again, a third time, to finally bring it all to my centre, the brightest light I'd ever imagined, so dazzling I could see it without thinking.

It was time to complete my safety net.

I felt outwards through my crown chakra, into the firmament, seeking rapturous joy and love, engagement with the universe and its sacred energy. First gentle, then pulsing at a frequency that boosted my heart rate, glorious euphoria with every throb. I channelled it into my crown carefully, joyfully, feeling as though I stood on the pinnacle of the earth, an antenna for divine force. It took on clear violet light as it passed through the chakra, pouring into my body, a torrent through every chakra into my centre.

The energy surged with a flash from my centre through my body to the outside, surrounding me in a protective shield. It took my breath away, but I gathered myself. The room darkened around me like the lights had gone out in the corners, but my own light shimmered and glowed.

I'd planned to stay inside, rather than risk bumping into anyone. But then I realised. I was the only person in the wing with Maggie gone, too and no-one from the other side of the house would be around. I looked hard through the window. No demons. I sensed they were gone. The world outside felt empty, somehow.

I replenished the dragonsblood incense on the charcoal, checked that all the candles were safe and took the smoking burner into the corridor with me. I stopped for a moment and felt outwards into the space and beyond into the rest of the wing. The place felt still, calm. I pulled the door firmly but it stuck at the catch, so I yanked it closed with a slam and padded to the front door. Looking out from the top step the drive stretched on vaguely lit by a street light on the other side of the wall, a pale orange. The moon hung low in the sky, lighting up the clouds to the east.

I listened. The breeze rustled leaves in the crook of the wall and swirled the incense smoke, snatching it away with the next puff. I shivered. At least there were no demons.

As I stood in front of the house, I raised my one arm to the heavens in a half-goddess position. Even if that's not a real thing, hell, I tried. If you're going to work energy, don't be half-arsed about it. Magic works a lot more conclusively if your actions show how determined you are.

I visualised the nasty grey esoteric slime that slathed the roof and sides of the mansion. It dripped from the gutters like long strings of snot, smearing paintwork and window glass alike. A moment of insecurity. Perhaps I should burn it off with the violet light, instead of doing what Molly told me. Destroying the nasty and despatching its remains into the light seemed to have a much smaller karmic price. Turning a bad person's magic on themselves might be just, but who was I to behave like judge and jury?

I pulled myself back to the present. Each remedy would produce different results and there had to be a reason Molly had come up with this. Her accuracy so far had been uncanny. She hadn't been wrong up to now, so whatever reason would be a good one. I didn't feel qualified to change the plan.

I gathered myself and raised my arm again. As present as I could be, I visualised the slime coming off the roof and sliding down the house walls in huge gloopy clots. It crawled across the flagstones into a central point in front of my broken bedroom window and more came from round the side of the house. The ground itself melted unctuously and slid towards the pulsing pile of phlegm. Esoteric snot.

I brushed myself down, dragged the sticky substance from my hair and face and nose, even out of my throat. My grasping hand scraped globules off my body and pulled it out of my vagina as though this stretchy string of negative mucus were a sickening rope. I rubbed my hand on the ground and watched the slime slick its way towards the creepy pile. I had to send this away with love. No anger allowed, just love. I concentrated on feeling love, sending love to David.

Not the kind of love David thought he desired—deserved, even. A universal love of peace and calm and gentle understanding. A warm glow inside me, contemplative emotion. Still, to be on the safe side, I emphasised it with a bright pink velvet bow wrapped around the massive snot clot. The bow was the love. I changed the pink to a softer pastel. It was ready to go.

I spoke aloud. "Corvidae come." I waited a breath. "Corvidae. With love, come." I pictured myself as a beacon of light calling to crows and ravens across the city, vibrating love towards them. I raised my voice slightly. "Corvidae, come." Another pause, then louder yet. "Corvidae, come to your kin, your kind, come." I listened. Nothing. No sound of footsteps or human voices.

"Corvidae come to your kin, your kind, and return this energy to the man who wrought it for me. Lay it down there for him to find, corvidae come to your kin, your kind." I pictured a flock of crows overhead, the vanguard landing in the drive and on the wall behind me.

Louder, I chanted. "Corvidae come to your kin, your

kind, and return this energy to the man who wrought it for me. Lay it down there for him to find, corvidae come to your kin, your kind." The rhythm laid into me now. "Corvidae come to your kin, your kind, and return this energy to the man who wrought it for me. Lay it down there for him to find, corvidae come to your kin, your kind." I stamped my foot in beat to the pulse of my words, a physical emphasis for the command.

The early landers moved in past me, inspecting the lump of slime. In my mind's eye, the air was thick with wings. I noticed, with a lurch, a shadow move in the corner of my vision but when I looked, all was normal. Another shadow flipped, higher up in the reflection of the upper unbroken window pane. Bats. It had to be bats. Fitting for a witch.

A real raven cawed behind me and I literally jumped into the air.

26. "He's here."

My heart pounding, I turned around. Tens of corvids stood in feathery rows—there could have been two hundred. Ravens, crows, rooks—even smaller jackdaws. They wheeled above the troops, banking to land. Not quite military, but the effect was the same. The black mass of feathers and heads and beaks of different yet similar birds marched forward, strutting and skipping past me, many wings to surround the giant slime ball.

I shouted at full volume, pointing at the heavens with my one arm.

"Corvidae come to your kin, your kind, and return this energy to the man who wrought it for me. Lay it down there for him to find, corvidae come to your kin, your kind."

They lifted off, synchronised for one more moment,

then the first one dove and grabbed the ribbon of the bow.

The entire band dove on to the surface of the slime and grabbed it with their feet, flapping, snatching, squawking—a chaos of crows, never mind a murder. Slowly, awkwardly, they lifted off, wings flapping with a rush of wind, only the base of the slime in sight, the top half covered in pulsing, urgent black wings.

As they disappeared over the wall, I imagined their flight over the suburbs, David's home in the distance, getting nearer. They flew at the house directly, dropped the slime over the porch and shot upwards together into the sky as it exploded. The black cloud of birds vanished into the night, scattering as they went and the slime splattered across David's porch steps, silvery lines and blobs glistening in the moonlight.

I opened my eyes in the dark, brought myself back. I stepped forward to pick up the brass dish with the incense burner and held it to the sky. Lava-like bubbles in the melted dragonsblood resin released little puffs of smoke. I caught the smell in my nostrils and focused on it, clamped my gaze on the smoke nearest the burner and filled my lungs with air.

"Mighty one, Morrigan, hear my shout and restore my sovereignty here and now. Sustain my power and strengthen my goals. Empower me to defend my soul."

As I yelled my request, a pinprick of red light pierced

the smoke, no more pronounced than distant Mars on a winter's morning, though it swelled quickly. I quelled rising excitement and focused on the red abyss as it grew in size and dimmed its brightness, spreading out at the edges like an endless puzzle. A translucent haze of blood red mist swept slowly over me and I placed the dish in the middle of the drive.

I stood tall, my head held slightly back, and breathed in the power of the goddess as she stood behind me, feathery cloak outstretched like wings encompassing me and my world. Her dark light passed through me and for one unmistakeable moment I was nowhere in time or space. My third eye pounded in the centre of my forehead and I dropped to a squat and laid the palm of my hand on the ground. I pushed my awareness deep into the earth, felt its solid, stable surrounds and knew I was safe. I quietly asked for the ground to soak up any magical residue. The sweet puffs of dragonsblood tantalised my nose buds and the breeze brushed past my face.

"With all my love, for the best will and the good of all, so mote it be."

I looked upwards, hoping to catch true sight of my crown chakra returning. Nothing. I still wasn't clairvoyant, no matter what I thought I'd experienced. I visualised it plummeting miraculously to my position, grabbed it out of the air and screwed it back into my head.

I focused on the violet light that still burned within my

centre even as it shielded me from outside my skin. As though my attention poured oxygen on its flame, it intensified, brighter and bigger than ever. I added glittering diamonds to its colour, their hard sharp edges sparkling white, extending its power. With a final push of will and intent, I swept etheric violet light over me, burning off the residue of the nasty negative slime I had worn for so many weeks.

Wisps of black smoke emanated from a few remaining sites of negativity and were snatched away by a mysterious breeze. The light tugged at the skin on my face, pulled at the muscles around my diaphragm and legs, spent time on my shoulder and across my bruised ribs. I let my load lighten for a while, breathing in and out steadily.

I held myself still in the night air and drew down soft turquoise light, bathed myself in its heavenly glow and let peace fill me. Completeness wrapped around me.

A noise on the porch snapped my eyes open. A silhouetted figure watched me from the open door. My breath caught in my chest and I stepped closer, blinking. Indira herself walked forwards to the top of the steps—and then I saw. She was no more than a willow-the-wisp, a flickery light with my friend's features. My gut twisted. She was dead. Indira glided down the steps, her cobweb veil flowing behind her. She stopped just a metre away.

If I didn't look directly I could see her worried

expression more clearly. "He's here, babe," she said, her signature hard stare boring into my eyes. She faded a little, drifted on the breeze and was gone, a few ripples of light in the darkness.

Overcome by grief, my stomach retching, I abandoned the incense burner and stumbled into the house. I leaned against the closed heavy door for a moment, searching for some kind of calm inside the panic. What did she mean 'he's here?'

Was David actually in the building? The place was literally a fortress, there was no way he should have been able to sneak in. I wondered, creepily, if he had come as a dreamwalker again. I hardened my heart and trod down the fear. He had killed Indira. There must be a way to make him pay.

I took another two steps towards the flat door and noticed the door latch. I stopped with a thump of adrenaline in my gut. The catch was against the frame, keeping the door ajar. But I'd closed it. I knew I'd closed it.

I tiptoed to the front door and snuck down the steps and around the edge of the stone balustrade. I edged along the wall, past my broken bedroom window and leaned up to the glass to peer between the slats of the blind. I saw no-one in the living room and the lights were all off. The flat was filled with shadows, not a stalker waiting for me. I was being paranoid.

Indira a snatch of imagination borne of fear, nothing more.

I turned to walk back to the door, but anxious butterflies fluttered around my centre. Listening to my intuition was a lesson I should have learned by now.

A large glint on the ground amongst the sparkly broken glass caught my eye. I bent and picked up the solid silver dragon ring. I looked around it, searching. The garnet lay under the windowsill. Who knew if they still held a link to Alon, I needed every bit of help I could get. I slipped the rings onto my left hand, the one attached to my dead arm.

I re-entered the porch and closed the big door carefully. For the first time since I acquired the injury, my shoulder emitted a horrific throb. The pain grew from the joint and spread across my torso as though something had taken a bite out of me. My traitorous stomach swelled with nausea and I grabbed the door handle to steady myself.

The agony was so encompassing, it took the breath from my lungs even as I gasped it inwards. I doubled over, couldn't even feel the still aching appendix wound. Through torturous mists, I understood the only thing that had changed was the reversal spell. The painlessness must have been a magical result of David's casting. I wasn't ready for this level of sensory stupor. The arm was still useless, but now there was no escaping the one thing that had baffled everyone by its absence. My whole body shuddered and I keened against the paroxysm as it radiated across my torso.

Panic rose. I couldn't cope with this without help. The tramadol was in the top kitchen drawer, all I had to do was go in there and swallow the pills.

I edged forwards, one slow step at a time. Without touching the door, I felt outwards from my centre, through the throbbing and into the space in the flat beyond. Grim dread filled me, the level rising fast.

I backed away and sat on the stairs. As the physical punishment pulsed across my body again, my stomach rose close to the back of my throat. I needed a better plan. I became aware of my phone in my pocket, didn't even remember putting it there. I drew it out, slowly and lit the screen. 99-percent battery and four bars of signal. Almost unheard of.

I could barely see the screen, but typed as well as I could, hoping the words made sense.

> *I think Dacid's in my gflat. I'm*
> *outisde. I need pain killeers. What*
> *shuld I do?*

I waited.

And waited.

Seconds ticked past.

My body sagged in the rise of the rising tide of yet more agony.

I couldn't wait.

27. Confront the Devil

I burst into the flat noisily, as if I didn't know anyone was there. Hell, maybe no-one was there and I was just paranoid as fuck. I pretended I was taking my coat off, focusing on staying present, as though a super-focus away from the agonising pulsations across my shoulders could save me. If I was attacked in the hallway there was a chance I could get away, even in this mess, but no-one appeared in the doorway to the living room.

I stopped and listened hard for a few seconds. Nothing physical hinted to me of a living room occupation, but I'd be a fool to ignore the sense of dread. It had served me well already. My head pounded in response to the onslaught of hurt.

I reached out for the door handle to the living room.

Its cold, hard metal feel grounded me briefly and I swung open the glass panelled door with a flourish. My gaze took in the empty space and relief soared through my chest—

—and collapsed as he turned around. David stood in the bay window, next to the floor length velvet curtains that we never used. His long black coat helped him merge into the background and it was only his pasty-faced head turn that gave him away. He said nothing.

My legs nearly gave out and my shoulder throbbed harder in response. I needed the tramadol. Fuck him. I headed for the kitchenette and rummaged in the drawer. A box emerged and I plucked three tablets from the pack and swung open the fridge. I was now out of view of the silent intruder.

Was he actually there, or was it some kind of projection?

I downed a glass of milk with the pills and said a prayer for my liver. He still hadn't spoken. What the fuck was I supposed to do? As anger briefly overwhelmed the pain, I considered the immediate situation in its context of hell we'd just been through.

We hadn't asked for this shit. No-one had, none of it was proportional to any of the crimes we were supposed to have committed. Poor Indira. She hadn't asked to be killed. Caleb didn't kill himself willingly and didn't deserve to die for stealing—no-one did. This bastard had ruined people's lives forever, for nothing. Even if my shoulder would never work again, at least I was alive—for now. And all for what? Because he had wanted to rape me?

A scuff on the living room floor made me look up. He was nearer than I expected, glaring at me from the other side of the breakfast bar. I felt hunted, like quarry but I didn't want to show him how helpless he'd made me. I wasn't helpless.

"What have you done, David? What were you thinking?" I looked at him in tears and fired a hurt look straight between his eyes in hope it would reveal a final vestige of human decency.

He shot daggers in return and responded in a mocking tone, "What am I supposed to have done, Inayat?"

"I know it was you. I know what you've done. You're a—murderer."

He paused, then his face split into an almost sunny smile. "I don't know what you're talking about."

He'd known something. I stood square onto him across the counter and gripped the surface edge. "If you know nothing about anything, what are you doing in my flat?" I couldn't let the tension out, afraid to reveal my terror. My voice was freezer cool and monotone. I pushed the pain away, my focused mind determined to stay on topic.

He chuckled, a cold, unpleasant sound. "I know why I'm here. Why don't you guess again." He looked at me meaningfully and chuckled in a slow, sarcastic way.

I didn't know what he meant. I wasn't guessing. I couldn't think of anything else it could be. I delved deep into my ground for calm and steady peace. "The thing is, David," I said in a harsh whisper, "It doesn't matter how I look at it, I can't see how being turned down for a date would get this sort of reaction. It's not—proportionate, is it?"

He whispered back, sarcastically. "The thing is, Inayat, I'm not here for you. I'm here for something you stole from me."

The floor plummeted from beneath my feet. I didn't even know how I was still upright. With everything that had happened, I'd almost forgotten that Caleb had given the fucker a justification for his shitty behaviour.

Panic shocked me into denial. "I didn't steal anything from you."

"Some would say all the—problems—you've had were nothing but rightful retribution," he offered glibly, watching me beneath his eyelashes.

"'Some' can fuck off. I didn't steal from you. If you're as powerful a magician as you're making out, I don't know why you don't know that."

His tone was that of someone whose patience was worn thin. "Inayat, you're wearing a ring that belongs to me." He was tired of my shit now.

I glanced at my hands, as if I'd forgotten about it.

"I don't honestly care if you technically robbed me, or if that no-good boyfriend you found was the perpetrator. I know you were in my house."

I flinched, but held his eye contact as though he couldn't affect me.

"The fact is you have something of mine that I'd like you to return."

My eyes were so wide they felt dry. My brain went blank.

I finally blinked and looked wildly around the flat. Couldn't argue with the logic. I was the one who had been victimised, whose friends had been killed, but because of my idiocy around the dragon ring, it was my fault. I was nothing more than a common thief. No better than Caleb. I glanced up at David, but found his face full of cruel amusement and that hooked me back to reality.

My phone vibrated in my back pocket, a token of reality in an unreal situation.

My head cleared slightly and I realised the pain had dimmed a little. I was wrong. I wasn't a thief. It wasn't my fault he'd attacked us. He chose to do that. I'd tried to return the ring but everything had been against it. The dragon had saved my life. I couldn't regret that and I didn't think he wanted to go back to the magician who had captured him.

I tried to bring the situation down a notch, change the track with a reasonable tone of voice. "What made you like this, David?" I couldn't help using his name. Anything to nudge his humanity if he had any left.

He looked at me with cold, dark eyes. "Just nasty thieving rats, really." He had a conversational tone, just playing me, matching my efforts. "It's like a violent allergic reaction."

I persisted, shook my head. "All the magic. Why? Where's the need?" My eyes searched his, an almost personal moment that sickened me. He looked hurt but it passed.

"Magic saved me," he said simply. We stood silently looking at each other, a moment too long but not long enough to see what was really going on. His eyes were dark, dead pools. They reminded me of shark eyes.

I wondered where the dragon was. Prayed he knew I needed him. Begged the universe to bring him back in, even though he was no longer attached to the rings. Now he had the choice, I needed him to respond. Not that I'd given him any reason to help me. The agony across my shoulders blurred a little more and the nausea abated too. My mind was a little more free even yet. There had to be a way I could get him out of the flat without anything more happening.

I knew how magic could save a person. It provides avenues you wouldn't otherwise have. Desperate people are common users of magic, but outside of the right conditions it can have—interesting—consequences. Tragedy is always waiting around the corner, because magic pulls the very threads of the fabric of the universe. It changes so many things in a chain reaction.

"Are you okay, David?" I asked gently, but my heart pounded so hard that my voice wobbled.

He stared back, eyes hardening. "No, Inayat, I'm not okay." His face became a thin-lipped mask, muscles so taut, he barely moved his mouth as he spoke. "I've never been 'okay'. From the first moment a woman laid her hands on me, I was lost. And even though I saved myself from the thing that gave birth to me, built myself, made myself whole, yet again, a duplicitous woman has come into my life and fucked with me. Every time I think 'maybe this time will be different' and every time it isn't."

He would kill me. Panic rose and I pushed the thought away.

He sneered, his mouth turned downwards, chin jutting forwards, like some kind of evil frog on cocaine.

"I've never had a date with a woman who really wanted me. Can you even imagine that, Inayat? I tried—just to see—the internet sites. The bitch didn't bother to show."

"At least you got three dates with me as a result," I retorted and immediately regretted it.

His scorn was clear. "Three dates for what? A bang on the head, a hospital visit and countless magical tools and artefacts stolen. Did I miss anything?" He shook his head in mock tiredness. "Fucking women."

The bastard thought he was justified. I went hot, flushed, my face skin sweating, then cold and clammy in the blink of an eye. He wasn't justified. He was a twat, a narcissist who thought he should have anything he wanted just because. My skin tingled and a boom of adrenaline exploded in my centre.

"The bang on the head was because you assaulted me," I raged. "That was after you'd attempted to assault me in my dreams." I slapped my hand down on the work surface for emphasis. It twanged my tendons up my arm and infuriated me more. "It doesn't matter what you say your intentions were, your actions show that you wanted to cause me harm."

He grabbed my wrist and held it against the counter top. "You don't get to come in my house and take things." I tried to rip my arm away, but his grip fixed me in place, so I leaned towards him aggressively, faced him angrily, even as he pressed his weight onto the back of my good hand.

"If you hadn't come intending to attack me you wouldn't have left your wallet and keys. It fucking well serves you right." I spat in his face with every hard consonant. "I didn't know the key had been stolen till the bag of jewellery showed up and I brought that back, didn't I?" I twisted my wrist with difficulty out of his grasp. "I didn't intend to keep the ring, I just kept finding I still fucking had it. Believe me, I'd give anything to get you out of my life."

His lips curled at one side and now I could see the broken teeth from when Molly had bashed him face first onto the flag stones. He was a caricature of an evil nemesis, just needed a bit more face paint.

"You're doing a great impression of someone who wants me and mine with them for the rest of eternity."

I drew myself up to my full height. "I hope you're going to stay a bit longer, but I think you'll want to leave." I sounded like a restaurant manager. "I already called the police." Even if he didn't believe it, I could plant the seeds.

He laughed. "When did you call the police? On your magic invisible mobile phone just now?" He replaced the grin with a scowl. "Give me the ring, Inayat."

I shrugged. "Doesn't matter what you want, you're on your way to prison. Cup of tea?" I knew I looked like a defiant teenager, but that didn't matter. My head was starting to swim, but I forced myself to concentrate on his face. The bridge of his nose, between his eyes, so I didn't have to look directly in them.

"You didn't even know I was here. You're a shite witch, didn't notice when I passed you doing your little spell casting outside just now." His grin was smug—as though he thought he was smarter than me—and it stung.

He shuffled his feet a little and I panicked. "The longer you hang around here, the more likely you're going to be taken away."

"You just want me to leave." He walked around the end of the breakfast bar and stood directly in my escape route. "You've caused me a lot more bother than you're worth, little lady. I don't like losses."

"Not missing a—" I tried to remember what O'Brien had said. "—Chaos demon general and a small demonic army by any chance?" I almost laughed, it sounded so ridiculous.

He spat onto the floor in answer. "You have no fucking idea how much trouble you've caused."

"You didn't have to attack me."

He took another step into my space. "You humiliated and stole from me."

"You'd already attacked me while I was sleeping. Thank God, I woke up!" I was so tired now. Sick of the endless drama. How could he just come here and harangue me without some kind of payback?

"You turned me down but you didn't know the half of me, you didn't even want to get to know me. You didn't give us a chance." His eyes were staring and intense, as though he truly believed what he was saying. He was too close, a couple of arm lengths away.

"Us? There was no *us!* I wasn't attracted to you. I didn't want to sleep with you. I didn't want a relationship with you. Why would you force yourself on me? Who the fuck would want a relationship with someone so god-damned fucking creepy? No means no, but you *still* pushed yourself on me, in my fucking *sleep* for fuck's sake."

He smirked. "Everyone loves a sexy dream."

"No-one loves rape except creepy weirdos who need locking up permanently. Why are you even here right now?"

"All women love rape, Inayat. That's why they drive us to it." He pulled something long and dark out of his messenger bag. A Maglite torch, heavy and over a foot long. Things were looking bleak right now. "So where's the dragon?"

I sneered. "He's never far away, don't you worry." I knew nothing. Alon had seemingly vanished and I was running out of time. I could tell my words were beginning to slur. The tramadol was way too strong for my body and three pills were technically an overdose. I dragged back my focus from the fear and pushed it into my centre for stability.

"Give me the dragon back and I'll leave you alone." Tiny blobs of foamy spit had formed at the edges of his mouth and on his bottom lip. He didn't give a fuck. And now I let the anger take over with an unexpected cool detachment as I regarded him.

"You'll leave me alone when I've removed my last vestige of protection? Right. Because you're great at leaving people alone. You do it all the time." I spat in his direction clumsily. "Piss off. You just spent a month terrorising me and people I know!"

I stopped short of the real point. He was powerful enough to menace me magically from a prison cell with no apparatus at all. He wouldn't stop just because someone told him not to. He would only stop because he was stopped.

He shook his head slowly. "You don't get it yet do you?" From the inside of his coat, he pulled out a glass vial with a cork stopper. The bottle was covered in wavy rust-brown lines. "What kind of jewellery do you like the best, Inayat?"

His face was stiff, mocking and pale, a parody of manhood, and in the dim light of the living room, looked like a badly drawn cartoon. I blinked. What did jewellery have to do with it?

He took the stopper off and stood both items on the breakfast bar.

"You can't have it both ways. If you want to keep the dragon, that's fine. I'm a reasonable man. But you don't get to keep the dragon and tell me to fuck off. You'll have to give me something comparable in return." He stroked the bottle with a soft finger and smiled, a sinister smirk that sent me a shudder. "Something comparable, Inayat."

He wanted my spirit for his jewellery. Devastating waves of panic punched me in the gut. A comparable return for his loss of the dragon. An eternity on his finger or in a box in his room of magic tricks. No body of my own. No choice but to follow what he commanded of me. No company other than the vestiges of creatures and demons and beings that he'd collected from his travels.

He took another step in a slow, smooth motion and suddenly he was less than an arm's reach away and I was already up against the sink with no room to step back. He raised the massive flash light and brought it down towards my head. Everything slowed. I closed my eyes and ducked to a crouch, but all the winds of the world tore through me and tossed me across the kitchen floor as if he was no longer there. The clatter of the torch as it hit the ground opened my eyes. Alon rose high and gigantic into the rafters of the living room like a striking snake, long neck in a graceful s-bend, eyes mesmerising his prey.

David picked himself up off the floor. He was now between me and the sink.

"And so it is unsurprising, really, that we meet again." The dragon's tone was deep and not unfriendly. He reared over us both, controlled and yet a little wavy round the edges. "I'd ask you now to kindly remove the binds you placed on me, but—"

David squinted his eyes. "I see nothing. There are no binds. You're free."

"Oh, am I?" The dragon seemed to inspect his claws for a long, drawn-out moment. Then he swooped.

"No!" I screamed into the tornado. He would kill him. "Wait!" The wind twisted around them in a dust-grey cone whipping up photographs from the wall and ornaments on the mantelpiece. A chair lifted up and all Indira's cushions. My hair swept over my head in the same direction and I gripped hard on the edge of the breakfast bar, praying its fixings would hold. Through the debris Alon's orange form snaked around a dark core. The winds slowed and the clouds thinned. Alon remained aloft, David's struggling body held a few metres above the floor with one elegant scaly foot, a claw embedded in his side.

"Wait? For what?" asked the dragon in a surprised tone.

I gathered what focus I could find within my soul and plunged my cords into the ground with a long exhalation. As I breathed back in, I sucked energy from the earth and as it reached my centre, focused on Alon himself. Buffeted by the wind energy that surrounded his mighty shape, I reached out instinctively towards him and drew another breath. His warmth hit the palm of my hand and I inhaled fire and air, power that I had never known before, bringing it into my body and deep into my heart, gathering it together. Light, fire, air, earth, everything that I was, all the pain and suffering of David's victims. And there had been so many. I heard screams of rage and fear, caught glimpses of terrible, beautiful faces, distorted by terror that could never end for them. I opened my mind to them and shut down the physical responses of my beaten body. With their energies I could inhale forever, for as long as it took to draw in the energy I needed. The wretched spirits of his previous conquests pressed in around me, as though they held me up, pushed me to perform what needed to be done.

As I exhaled the same impossible breath, head down, I directed the energy through my body, shooting mercurial light from my outstretched arm, through my forefinger directly at David himself. Around him I poured a mirror-like shield, the opposite of the slime I had painstakingly removed from our lives a short time before. As I opened my palm upwards and raised it towards the ceiling, a pool of shining reflective matter rose up spinning, a whirling tower, a curtain of energy around him. I turned the vortex inside out, bright energy on the inside, transparent on its outer limits, giving a clear sight of the captive within. Witih strengthened resolve I saw now the shadow that stood around David, immense and black, white teeth like curved needles around its gaping maw and eyes of fire that swirled and shifted, the tiny man an inconsequential living part.

With a howl of fury, David formed a triangular shape with his hands and a deep purple light zigzagged towards me and another and another, laser beams of the darkest power I had ever sensed. As they hit the side of the inverted mirror shield, the beams bounced haphazardly around its interior. They sliced the shadow into multiple sections and smacked David repeatedly in the side of his head. The creature that possessed him roared furiously, the edges of its shape becoming ragged and wispy. It faded from sight and David's body snapped forwards, bent double, saved from the floor only by the dragon's hold.

Alon let go.

28. The Truth Will Out

"Police!" In ran O'Brien, a lone figure in black and neon. A sudden change of pressure in the room made a loud sucking noise as the dragon disappeared and the room atmosphere cleared instantaneously. The sergeant skidded to a halt just through the doorway.

David was crumpled in the middle of the floor, one arm at an unnatural angle, his legs curled around so that his feet were level with the small of his back. A shining pendant around his neck hung skewed around his neck, the long chain pooled on the floor before him.

"Do we need an ambulance?" O'Brien eyed him warily. As he stepped towards the body, David flinched, and twisted himself straight. He rolled onto his side and dragged himself to his feet, resisting the police officer's assistance.

He muttered something unintelligible.

"Say what?" O'Brien didn't make a move towards him.

"Am I under arrest?"

O'Brien stared at him. He leaned forwards to peer at the pendant still plainly visible against the magician's black shirt.

"Distinctive pendant there, I think we both know where you got it from."

David stared at him and took a step back. I tried to see the pendant. It was like a misshapen 'O', but I couldn't tell any detail from that distance.

"David Catcheside, you are under arrest on suspicion of rape and murder. You do not have to say anything, but it may harm your defence if you do not mention when questioned something which you later rely on in court. Anything you do say may be given in evidence." He got his handcuffs out of their pouch and reached for David's nearest arm. He shook him off, but I could see that his other arm was loose by his side.

O'Brien shook his head and grabbed his arm. "Better give yourself up. You're not in any fit state for fighting."

I watched open mouthed. How could he arrest him for Caleb's murder? Who did he rape? My drug-fugged mind wouldn't process what was happening.

O'Brien dragged his other hand and brought it around

the front to meet the handcuffs and David grunted in pain. "Get the fuck off, that arm's injured."

"Need an ambulance again? We'll get you assessed at the station this time."

O'Brien pulled what looked like a mobile phone from his uniform and pressed just a couple of numbers.

"Request backup at Gledhow Hall, need a patrol car to bring someone into the station."

He listened for a moment. "Just the one. Think we may have our doctor killer, but I don't think he's in much state to do a runner."

My ears prickled with static anticipation. The doctor in the canal.

My own pain had almost subsided, just a dull ache where excruciating agony had been. I drew in a shuddering, wondering breath as I realised the tramadol had more than carried out its job. The room dimmed.

"Are you all right, Inayat?" O'Brien's voice rose with concern. "Inayat, are you okay?"

The world swirled and the pattern on the floor slid into itself, black lines marbling the varnished oak. Blue lights flashed across the walls and windows and I concentrated on staying upright. I forgot about David and O'Brien. Forgot they were there. I couldn't close my eyes but neither could I see through the pervasive darkness that came from the edges and across my vision. A strong arm under my shoulder hefted me to the sofa. Nausea rose and I thought I was going to be sick but I pushed it back down, gulped it back and breathed deeply.

Someone lay me down on the sofa, supporting my head. Another someone took my temperature and spoke to me. She asked me my name but I couldn't move my lips. I sank into blackness, emerging a few minutes later as I was transferred from the sofa to a gurney.

A welcome and familiar voice came loudly down the corridor and my newly pinned shoulder twinged as I twisted around from texting Leah. Molly burst into the ward, arms full of flowers and a bulging Cath Kidston shopper. She looked around the room till she found me and her face broke into a delighted smile.

"I hope this is the last time I have to come see you in hospital." She sat on the end of the bed and plonked everything on my legs. She looked at me for a long moment and ruefully shook her head. "Life's never dull with you around, is it?" She got out a bottle of posh lemonade from the top of the shopper. "Lemonade?"

I took the glass and sipped it slowly. I could see the staff nurse looking but I didn't think she would bother Molly. "What's going on, Moll? Owt or nowt?"

"Depends what you've got in mind for the next few weeks." She pulled out some brochures. "You'll be getting a nice little payout, won't you? Compensation or something?"

I grinned. "I don't know how! David wasn't even arrested because of anything to do with me!"

"Maybe it'll happen, you never know. What was he arrested for?"

"Rape and murder," I remembered. "Something to do with that missing doctor. Do you really think I'm going to get some money from somewhere?" I didn't know what I was going to do if something didn't come.

She looked innocently in her shopper and pulled out a box of mini quiches. "You never know. Goat cheese tart?"

"Thanks for the picnic, this is amazing." I sank my teeth into salty, soft goat cheese and caramelised onions.

She shoved the rest of the box towards me without taking one. "Can't stand them myself, but I know what you think of hospital food." She pushed the brochures nearer. "Take a look at them. Think we can go on one of these? I think we need it."

I picked up the nearest two and opened the first. A meditation retreat above the wild Yorkshire moors. The second was in Shropshire. Three-hundred-and-fifty pounds per person per week.

"Have a look at the courses they're offering. There's a

full-on Wiccan crash course and a bunch of psychic development workshops that might be good for you but I thought this one just outside of Halifax would be perfect for both of us."

"How long is it away?"

"Three weeks. At least that'll give you a chance to get your head clear. There'll be all kinds of cleansing things going on, apparently. It's like some kind of spa, but with spiritual workshops and energy manipulation instead of hot tubs. Can we afford it?"

I laughed. "When do I ever have the money for something like that?"

She smiled and looked right in my eyes. "You'll be able to afford it. I'll put the deposit down." She was dead serious.

"When does it happen?"

"It's a once-a-year event, been going on for years."

"You're sure there's no 'special' reason to go I should know about?"

Molly looked confused. "That depends what you mean by 'special'." She flashed me a grin, got out an orange and a knife, and expertly sliced the fruit into segments in her hand. I lined three up on my lap.

I knew the exact moment the staff nurse's nostrils detected the smell of the orange. Her head snapped up with a gimlet stare in our direction and she knocked her cup of tea over. God forbid a patient might have some food with nutritional value. As I sucked my orange quarter, I watched her mop up the mess, wiping down individual pages of dripping patient notes.

I couldn't shake the feeling that something was up. "Why are we really going to the retreat, Molly?"

She looked at me for a long moment. "Think we both need a few lessons in controlling our talents. You need to dial it up a bit and I've got to keep my head on."

I must have looked dubious. I still couldn't work up the enthusiasm.

She lowered her voice. "We've all got our soul contracts to fulfil, Inayat. You've got yours and I've got mine. You already know it isn't all about light and love. Sometimes you've got to go over to the dark side to help people." She wiggled her eyebrows. "The bloke is supposed to be amazing but you never know unless you try it yourself. It might work great for me but not suit you, you just don't know."

I didn't fancy being exposed to yet another powerful magician so soon. "How will we know he's okay?"

She nodded. "I've heard of him before. He's got a good rep as far as I know. But you can never really tell with these people."

I thought of Geraldine. She had seemed perfectly nice to begin with. Sort of.

"The best thing is, if he likes us we could easily attend his regular group, it's in Oakwood of all places." She stared at me, almost defiantly as if she thought I might not agree to it.

Oakwood was only the next suburb over from Gledhow. Joining forces with other people hadn't been top of my list for obvious reasons and certainly not with someone who was only around the corner from where I lived. I definitely didn't have the luck and I knew that even before David, Geraldine and Caleb's interfering.

"Don't worry, love, this lot will be all peace and love and light, you know the crowd, none of this magician crap. They'll be the same sort of people you get at all these things, spiritualists, yoga types, the odd green witchy type. Usual stuff."

That sounded a bit more positive. "It's okay, I'm up for it in theory. But I'll decide how I feel about the bloke while I'm there." I'm a pretty good judge of character, usually. Says she who had suffered a prolonged magical attack from someone whom she had only dated because she felt sorry for him.

Molly smiled again, a beaming grin. "You'll get the money, don't you stress about that. Make sure you put some of it away. You're going to need it. How long is your arm going to take to heal?"

"It might not get better at all." The doctors had been sensitive but the information wasn't what I wanted to hear.

"They reckon we'll just have to see how it all knits together. Something about the nerves not talking to each other." I bubbled up with unexpected tears, tried unsuccessfully to push them back.

"What, and that's it?"

I sniffed noisily and she passed me a napkin to use as a hankie. "I honestly don't know what to do. I can't type like this, can I?"

"Don't worry about it. You'll find something to tide you over. Trust me." I always felt like she knew something I didn't. Even more than you'd expect from a medium.

"I'm supposed to be coming out today." I felt glum. I wasn't sure they were letting me out today because normally they pack you out in the morning to sit in Pharmacy, so all I could do was hope.

"You can come and stay with me for a couple of weeks. Your room's ready. We can get a taxi back to yours to pick up your clothes and then you can head over to mine. You're in Bex's old bedroom."

I had no argument to that. Going back to the devastated flat alone was not high on my list.

The door to the ward swung open again and another familiar figure walked in. Sergeant O'Brien. Ridiculousness washed over me. The nurses had made it clear that I was needlessly taking up a hospital bed and now I felt like a celebrity.

O'Brien waved at the staff nurse and strolled over.

"So, ladies, good to catch you both here."

I just stared at him.

"How are you doing, Inayat? Feeling any better?"

I dropped my eyes sheepishly. "It was a tramadol overdose, I took three in one go."

"You said you were in pain in your text."

I remembered the text I'd sent him before I entered the flat. "I couldn't even see properly when I sent that."

"I could tell," he smiled. "Are they letting you out today?"

I nodded. "They've done what they can with my shoulder, so that's that."

"You going to get the use of it back?"

I shook my head. "I need a new career. And some money. A miracle would be good."

He beamed at me. "That's what I came to tell you. Dr. Meriweather's parents offered a reward for anyone with information leading to the arrest of her murderer. You're going to be set up for a while."

Dr. Meriweather. I said her name under my breath.

"How did you know it was David?"

O'Brien pulled up a chair and sat closely to us both.

"You ladies gave me the initial information with your

vision," he nodded at Molly. "But it wasn't until I saw the pendant he was wearing after his fight with you. Then I knew."

"What was it?"

"The pendant? A miniature pelvic bone."

I frowned. "How—"

"A gift from her father. Micro-engraved with a laser, so identifiable."

I screwed up my face. "How is that evidence he did it? Couldn't he just have found it?"

O'Brien shook his head. "We got him on a couple more things than that." He leaned forwards more closely. "He bit his victim during the attack. Left a perfect set of prints on her skin. A bit blown out by the time we retrieved her body, but there was a nice anomaly in his mouth. They matched it with his dental records and he's pled guilty. No escape from justice in the end."

"And the other thing?" Molly was fascinated.

"He attacked another woman in the park. Different set of charges coming for that. She caught sight of a tattoo on his groin."

The light dawned for me again. "The woman in the *Evening Post*. She drew a picture of it."

He nodded. "A Solomon's Seal. Everything we needed, all on one man."

I frowned. "So no need for my stupid story in court?"

He nodded, watching me like a hawk. "I rather thought you'd prefer that?"

I did. I preferred that like nothing else. I didn't want to be picked apart, found lacking, a crazy, stupid white woman with no idea of how to handle herself with men, living in a fantasy world usually reserved for children in books.

A thought occurred to me. "Why did he hate his mother so much?"

O'Brien frowned. "When did he say that?"

"He called her the thing that gave birth to him."

He sat back in his chair, thinking. "Maybe some kind of abuse. His mother left his father when David was a kid."

So much hatred, I mused. And for what? A few weeks of feeling like a god. Some people took drugs for that. Others raped and killed women.

I lay back in my bed. "Why am I getting the reward money?"

"Inayat." He looked hard at me, as though his blue eyes would pierce my brain. "You cast a reversal spell, didn't you?"

How did he know things? I stared at him for a long moment. "Only about ten minutes before I texted you."

"Did you do something else too? He'd had an invisibility cloak wrapped around him."

Molly's jaw nearly hit the ground. A long silence ensued. I looked up to find him staring straight at me, waiting for an answer.

I dropped my gaze. "I bound him in a mirror shield." I felt ridiculous, saying something like that to a policeman. "Something wicked had taken him over."

"A mirror shield. Interesting choice. Why that?"

I shrugged. "He could still come for me even if he was in prison. I needed him to be locked up tighter than that."

O'Brien nodded wisely. "A strong choice." He looked towards the goats cheese tart and I offered him one automatically. As he ate, he continued. "You couldn't see it, no-one could, but he'd magically made himself invisible to the authorities for a long time. Your shield lifted the mists. When I interviewed him the first time, I had no idea he was a serial offender. Just seemed a bit harmless to me." He swallowed. "I don't normally miss things like this." He took another bite. "The mirror wiped the slate clean, left him open to external realisations that would otherwise have passed him over." He grinned. "He was so shocked when I arrested him."

"How did you know he had an invisibility cloak if you couldn't see it at any time?" Molly's practicality jarred my brain.

O'Brien looked coy. "Let's just say I know a thing or two, okay?" He smiled. "I see things no-one else does. I can safely say I've never made a false arrest. I knew you two were good people, didn't I?"

Molly and I looked at each other. A police officer who believed in magic, knew what a general class demon looked like, knew a reversal spell had been cast, understood mirror shields and recognised when an invisibility cloak had been removed. She shook her head almost imperceptibly. I said nothing more. We'd probably never know.

More things in heaven and earth.

Three Weeks Later

I dragged my bursting holdall into the hallway and put on my coat. I turned and felt backwards into the flat. All was calm and serene.

I looked at myself one last time in the mirror and slung my handbag across my body. My hair was neater, recently trimmed and my eye make up was just the right level of sultry. I looked good, despite the dodgy arm. I flipped the coat collar out from under the strap, when I heard the house front door opened. A banging and clattering entered the building and a high-pitched woman's voice echoed around the tiled hallway outside the flat door.

A key scraped in the lock and Indira walked in.

"Aw babe, you picked now to come back, I'm just leaving." I couldn't believe her timing.

"Oh no, I thought you'd just got back from that. I don't want to be by myself!" Typical Indira and timing.

We hugged, a long moment between us, then she stepped back and Munezza came through the door with some plastic bags.

"Inayat, darling, so glad to see you. Everything's happened so fast." She hugged me too. I stood back a little to view Indira as a whole. She moved in a stiff way but was far better than I'd imagined.

"We said in three weeks' time. That was only Friday!" I scolded them.

"She was too desperate to come away. We'll stay the night and see how she goes," said her mum. "Might go straight home tomorrow and come back in three weeks." She gave Indira a meaningful stare, from which I took she hadn't known the original arrangement.

Indira rolled her eyes dramatically. "I forgot, obviously." She fluttered her eyelashes at me and took on a pensive mood. "Do you have to go right now?"

She loved her parents, I knew that, but the chat we'd had on the phone had been urgent sounding. She needed space to be herself. And she hated spending time by herself, so that was how bad it must have been.

I nodded. "I'm so sorry, I've got to go, I paid for it, but I'll tell you all about it when I come back." I offered her another hug and she took it. "Stay the night, there's wine in the cupboard if you're stopping."

She pulled away. "I will be staying, but I don't drink any more, babe," she whispered. "Near death experience gives you something to think about."

I nodded. There wasn't time to get the details, but I knew she was as strong and stubborn as ever and that meant she was well within herself.

"There's stuff in the fridge, but I've been mostly eating from the freezer. Only got one working arm." I pointed to my left shoulder. Three weeks was a long time with one hand and I hadn't really pulled myself together with any useful strategies. Molly had given me so much help, I'd started to lazily rely on her and now I was back in the flat, simple things were driving me to tears. Getting ready today had pretty much taken all day. Normally if I managed to get my pants on the right way around, I was happy.

She stared at me—hadn't noticed my injury inside my coat although she knew about it—and grinned. "Life's never dull when you're around, babe. Hopefully it's going to be in a good way from now on." She stuck her tongue out at me.

We hugged again and I left.

Inayat will return...

An otherworldly Yorkshire castle, out-of-body experiences, spiritual healing techniques, evil incarnate and a possible love interest for Inayat to screw up.

Keep an eye on ABagfulofDragon.com for updates!